The New Moon's Arms

also by Nalo Hopkinson

The Salt Roads

Brown Girl in the Ring

Midnight Robber

Skin Folk (short stories)

edited by Nalo Hopkinson

Mojo: Conjure Stories

available from Warner Books

The New Moon's Arms

NALO HOPKINSON

WARNER BOOKS

NEW YORK   BOSTON

Original poetry on pages 1, 217, and 316 are from "Uncle Time" by Dennis Scott copyright © 1973.
Warner Books
Hachette Book Group USA
1271 Avenue of the Americas
New York, NY 10020

Visit our Web site at www.HachetteBookGroupUSA.com
Book design by Fearn de Vicq
Printed in the United States of America

FIRST EDITION: FEBRUARY 2007
10 9 8 7 6 5 4 3 2 1

Library of Congress Cataloging-in-Publication Data

Hopkinson, Nalo.
    The new moon's arms / Nalo Hopkinson.—1st ed.
        p. cm.
    Summary: "A mainstream magical realism novel set in the Caribbean on the fictional island of Dolorosse. It tells the story of a 50-something grandmother whose mother disappeared when she was a teenager and whose father has just passed away as she begins menopause. With this physical change of life comes a return of a special power for finding lost things, something she hasn't been able to do since childhood"—Provided by publisher.
    ISBN-13: 978-0-446-57691-8
    ISBN-10: 0-446-57691-3
    1. Grandmothers—Fiction.   2. Caribbean area—Fiction.   I. Title.
    PR9199.3.H5927N48 2007
    813'.54—dc22   2006020985

Acknowledgments

I worked almost three years on this novel. In that time, it changed quite significantly, more than once. My deepest thanks to everyone who helped me with my research, read endless drafts and excerpts and gave their feedback, listened when I got whiny, fed me when I got hungry, lent or gave me money when I was broke, and generally provided an utterly humbling base of support. The list below is as complete as my memory and my notes can make it.

Daniel Archambault, Sarah Banani, Tobias Buckell, Rich Bynum, Grandma Ermine Campbell, Carol Camper, Carol Cooper, Steven Dang, Esther Figueroa, David Findlay, Mici Gold, Jeanne Gomoll, Kathy Goonan, Peter Halasz, Liz Henry, Patricia Hodgell, Keita Hopkinson, Matt Hughes, Juba Kalamka, Paul Klaehn, Ellen Klages, Dave Laderoute, Jaime Levine, Don Maass, Freda Manning, Farah Mendlesohn, Nnedimma Okorafor-Mbachu, Victor Raymond, Kate Schaefer, Dennis Scott, Joy Scott, Susanna Sturgis, Peter Watts, Pat York, Fem-SF, the miracle that is the Interwebs, Green College (University of British Columbia), my blog readers, the Writing Squad

ACKNOWLEDGMENTS

(Hiromi Goto, Larissa Lai, Martin Mordecai, Pamela Mordecai, Jennifer Stevenson).

And, for those who don't know, a *lime*, when it's not a fruit, is a party.

The New Moon's Arms

Uncle Time is a ole, ole man . . .
All year long 'im wash 'im foot in the sea
Long, lazy years on the wet san'
An' shake the coconut tree-dem quiet-like with 'im sea wind laughter,
Scraping away the lan' . . .
                              —Dennis Scott, "Uncle Time"

1

A CROWD HAD GATHERED AROUND MRS. WINTER. The commotion at the graveside vibrated with suppressed hilarity. Me, I wasn't able to keep properly solemn. When my shoulders had started shaking with silent laughter, I'd ducked behind the plain pine coffin still on its stand outside the grave.

I bit my lips to keep the giggles in, and peeked around the coffin to watch the goings-on.

Mrs. Winter had given up the attempt to discreetly pull her bloomers back up. Through the milling legs of the mourners, I could see her trying desperately instead to kick off the pale pink nylon that had slithered down from her haunches and snagged around her ankles.

Her kick sent a tiny flash of gold skittering across the cemetery lawn to land near me. I glanced down. I picked up the small tangle of gold-coloured wire and put it in my jacket pocket for later. Right now, I had some high drama to watch.

Pastor Paul, ever helpful, bent to the ground at Mrs. Winter's feet and reached for his parishioner's panties. Lord help me Jesus, he was really going to pick them up! But he drew his fingers back. He looked mortified. Maybe he was thinking how the panties had recently been snugged up to Mrs. Winter's naked flesh. I thought my belly was going to bust, I was trying so hard not to laugh aloud. I bet you Dadda would have laughed with me, if he wasn't in that coffin right now.

Mrs. Winter got the tip of one of her pumps caught in the froth of pink nylon. She cheeped in dismay and fell heavily to the ground. Lawdamercy! I bent right over, shaking with laughter, trying to not pee myself from it.

Pastor Paul and Mrs. Winter's son Leroy were pulling on her arms now, trying to get her off the ground. "Oh, Dadda, oh," I whispered through my giggles. "Wherever you are, I hope you seeing this." I held my belly and wept tears of mirth. Serve the old bat right for insulting me like that. Not a day went by at work that she didn't find some sly way to sink in the knife. She had to do the same thing at my father's funeral, too?

Mrs. Winter was halfway up. She had one arm hooked around Leroy's neck, and Pastor Paul was pushing her from behind. A few of the mourners asked her if she was all right. "Oh, migod," was all she said; "oh, migod." My laughter was edging up on hysteria. Too much; death and mirth all at once. I rested my hands on my knees and took little panting breaths to calm myself. I couldn't hide behind the coffin forever.

At least the tingling in my hand had stopped. A few minutes

earlier, standing at the open grave, I'd suddenly felt too warm, and my hand had gotten pins and needles.

I took the scrap of wire out of my pocket. It had been crushed flat. I pulled on the loops of wire until something of its original shape began to emerge. I had a good look at it, and gasped.

I held the pin up against the sunlight. It caught a spark of light, threw blades of sunshine at my eyes. It had gotten warped over the years, forced into service to hold up Mrs. Winter's loose drawers. It used to be a decorative pin for wearing on a blouse, its gold wire looped in the shape of an ornate C, T, and L: *Chastity Theresa Lambkin*. My girlhood name. Mumma'd given me that pin for my eighth birthday. Years ago, after they'd declared Mumma dead and we'd had the memorial service for her, little Chastity-girl me had noticed it missing. And missing it had stayed; no time to look for it in all the commotion of the hearing, of moving to my aunt and uncle's, and the children at school whispering to each other whenever they saw me.

Where in blazes Mrs. Winter had found my pin?

"Mum? What's going on?"

Ife was standing there, holding young Stanley's hand. Ife's black dress hung off her shoulders, its hem crooked.

Stanley gave me a shy little wave.

Ife had gotten the best bits of me and her father combined: the glow of his perfect dark brown skin; his lips, the way they peaked in the middle when he smiled. My dimples, my well-shaped legs. She was plump, like all the women in our family, but that never stopped a West Indian man yet. Not a real man, anyway. If I could just get her to wear clothes that suited her!

Not my Ife. She covered up her charms with baggy, ankle-length dresses in unhelpful colours, slouched around in rubber flipflops or those horrible wide-toed cork sandals from abroad. Been so long since I'd seen her legs, she might as well not have any.

Nothing could hide that smile, though. She turned it on me now, and even though it was an uncertain smile today, it made my world a little bit brighter.

But I firmly squashed the joy at seeing her sweet face, made mine sour. I tucked the warped pin back into my pocket and turned to my daughter Ifeoma, to whom I wasn't speaking. Well, not really speaking. I mean, I would say 'morning and so, you know, but nothing more until she took back that awful thing she'd called me.

"Mrs. Winter tripped," I told her as I hugged her. "And you know I wish you wouldn't call me 'Mum' like that." Using the hug for cover, I stroked her back. No bra again. That child had no respect for the dead. And no fashion sense either; that dress! My seventies throwback hippie girl child. At least she wasn't wearing sandals and socks today, but proper high heels.

"You're my mother," Ife murmured into our hug. "It's not respectful for me to call you 'Calamity,' like . . . like . . ."

I pulled back and glared at Ifeoma. "Like what? You'd best mind yourself with me. You know I'm vex with you already, after last night."

Ife pressed her lips together. She used to do that as a little girl when she didn't want to eat her greens. ". . . like you're my sister," she said quietly.

And just so, she squashed my heart like you crush a piece of paper into a ball you're going to throw in the trash. I turned my face from her.

Stanley stood at the lip of the open grave, peering in. He pulled at his collar. This might be the first time in his nine years that he was wearing a suit.

"You're my mother," Ife said. "Why I can't just call you 'Mummy'?"

Last night, she'd called me a "matriarch." Like I was some wrinkled, prune-faced dowager wearing a hairnet and clothes thirty years out of fashion.

Mrs. Winter was standing all the way up now. She was favouring one ankle. She still had one arm wrapped around Leroy's neck. The other was around Pastor Paul's. Mrs. Saranta was fanning her face with a prayer book. One of the ushers, a long, skinny young man with big eyes and hands like shovels, had picked Mrs. Winter's tiger-print handbag up off the grass and was collecting all the things that had spilled out of it.

We used to be as close as sisters, Ife and I. The night I took her out to celebrate her twenty-first birthday with her first legal drink, the bartender had asked us both if we were of drinking age. And we'd laughed, and flirted with him the whole evening. I didn't tell him she was my daughter until after I took him home that night and made him call out for God in my bed.

But now I wasn't just old; I was fully an orphan, too, instead of the half of one I had been for so many decades. And finally, the tears came. "He's gone, Ife. Dadda's gone."

Ife took me into her arms again. "Ssh, it's all right." If she'd been irritated with me before, there was no sign of it now. For all I'd tried to teach her, she'd never learned how to hold a grudge good and hard, like a shield.

I let myself sob into her neck for a while. My breath rushed and halted.

Mrs. Winter said, quite firmly, "I want to go home." Good. Interfering woman was probably too shamed to stay after half the town had seen her smalls fall off. Why she had to come today? Bad enough I had to endure her at work. Mrs. Winter thought it was her job to supervise me into an early grave.

Pastor Paul offered to have one of the ushers help Leroy walk her to her car. But no, she wanted the pastor. He gazed around until he spotted me. He gave an apologetic shrug, held up five fingers, and mouthed, *Five minutes?* I nodded. The three of them hobbled off towards the parking lot. Now our funeral party could recover some of its dignity. *What a pity you all alone in this time of trial, child.* Chuh. Never mind *her*; I'd rather fuck the horse she rode in on.

But that was no proper way to be thinking at my father's funeral.

"You feeling better now, Mum?"

"Right as rain. But I wish you'd worn something a little more tailored, you know?"

Ife smiled at me, tentatively. "This is my best black dress," she said. "It's the one I wear when I want to impress. Stanley, come away from there. You might fall in."

"I won't fall," Stanley replied.

"Come over here, I said."

He did. I wouldn't let Ife change the subject, though. I knew her tricks better than she knew them herself. "That dress is black crushed gauze, my darling. You look like a big turkey buzzard flapping through the air."

Ife's smile hardened like ice. "So we're going to talk about my looks again?"

I took her face in both my hands. "Your looks are fine. Why you always so worried about looks? You only need to pretty yourself up a little bit." I don't know where Ife got her meek nature from. Not from me. "I keep telling you, Ife; you should have more self-confidence. Shorten the skirts a bit, wear some prettier colours. And show a little bosom. We Lambkin women have more than enough to display."

Ife glared. "Clifton likes me this way. You're so old-fashioned, Mummy."

God, "Mummy" was even worse than "Mum." And since when was I "old-fashioned"? In high school, the other girls used to call my fashion sense scandalous, and I'd loved scandalizing them.

I could see Pastor Paul hurrying back from the parking lot. I took Stanley's hand. "Come and say goodbye to Dadda," I told him. The three of us moved closer to the rest of the funeral party. A trim, dark man, maybe sixtyish, made room for us. Peggy Bruce, who had arrived late, nodded a greeting. Even when we were in school, Peggy had always been late. "We going to start again soon," I said to the mourners. "Pastor Paul on his way back."

"Did Michael come?" Ife asked in a whisper.

"Who?" I whispered back.

Now Ife's eyes had the glint of obsidian. "Michael," she said, a little louder. "My *father*." John Antoni peered at us, hungry for gossip.

"Hush," I said under my breath.

A kiskedee bird zipped by overhead, laughing its high, piping chuckle at me before flying into the branches of one of the frangipani trees in the cemetery.

Ife said, "I thought you were taking care of the invitations! How could you just not tell him that his own father-in-law was dead?"

I lifted my chin. "Dadda was never Michael's father-in-law." Tears that had been on the verge of brimming tipped back into the bowls of my eyes again. The eye water was cold.

"Gran?" said Stanley. "I mean, Calamity?"

Lovely boy. I hunkered down to his eye level, balancing on

the spikes of my black stiletto pumps. Huh. *"Matriarch."* Could a matriarch do that? "And what can I do for you, my handsome boy?"

Stanley ran into my arms. He was all woodknuckle knees and awkwardness, his hair trimmed short, with a W pattern buzzed into the back and sides. His father Clifton had told me it had something to do with American wrestling on the tv. Stanley and I could chat for hours, about school and comics and food. His mind was like a new country; always something fascinating around the next bend. I didn't see him as often as I liked. Seemed he always had homework to do on the weekend, or soccer practice. Ife and Clifton kept him busy.

"Does Great-Grandpa look scary?" Stanley asked.

"You can't even see him," said Ifeoma, butting in. "The casket is closed. Isn't it, Mum?"

I inhaled the child's pre-adolescent smell of spit and sweat. "Yes, my love," I said to him. "It's closed."

Stanley sighed. He looked disappointed. "But I wanted to see," he said. "Godfrey Mordecai at school said that Great-Grandpa would be a skellington, and he would be scary, and I would be frightened. I wouldn't be frightened. I want to see, Gran. I want to see a real live skellington."

" 'Skeleton,' dear." I felt a smile blooming on my lips. A live skeleton. Stanley was a little unclear on the concept. "Stanley, you have a curious mind. This is how I know you're my blood." I rose, smoothed my skirt down, and took his hand. Pastor Paul was scurrying our way. I told Stanley, "Let's see if we can get the lid on the casket raised for you." He grinned up at me, and we went to meet the pastor halfway. I took care to mind my ankles in the wobbly stilettos. They weren't made to walk on grass.

Ife caught up with us. "Mum? Don't do anything to frighten Stanley, please? He might have nightmares. Mum?"

What a way she overprotected that child!

"Mistress Lambkin," said Pastor Paul. He was puffing from the exertion. "So sorry for the interruption. Shall we, ahm, continue with the proceedings now?"

He was another one who would never call me "Calamity," no matter how much I asked him to. But he'd picked the wrong day to cross me. I nodded at him, all meekness. "Yes, thank you, *Egbert,*" I said in a clear, carrying voice.

Stanley giggled. A man standing close to us hid his smile behind a cough. Egbert glanced around. Oh, yes; plenty of people had heard me. If he hated his bloody name so much, why he didn't just change it? I had changed mine.

Ifeoma snickered, flicked me an amused glance. Now, *that* was my girl; the one I'd raised. It was the same grin she'd given me that day in the grocery store, all those years ago.

I had just started working at the library. My first paycheque wouldn't come for another month. I'd been feeding myself and little Ife on macaroni and cheese, and we'd run out of cheese. How old would she have been then? About seven, I think. We were in the cold foods aisle. I was trying to choose between eggs and a block of cheese. I could get only one of them. I was trying not to look at the packets of chicken, of stewing beef, of goat meat. I couldn't tell how long it had been since we'd had meat. Ifeoma loved roasted chicken legs. Suddenly my crazy girl child took it into her head to start singing "Little Sally Water" at the top of her considerable lungs, complete with the moves. I was about to scold her when I realised that people were looking at her, not me.

"Rise, Sally, RISE!" Ifeoma had yelled, leaping up from the ground, "and dry your weeping eyes . . ."

Quickly, while she was turning to the east, the west, and to the one she loved the best, I'd slipped two packets of chicken legs and one of stewing goat into the big pockets of my dirndl skirt.

With all the gathered material in that skirt, nobody would notice the lumps. Only then did I order Ife to stop making so much commotion. And damned if the child didn't straighten up immediately, smooth her dress down, and come and pat one of my pockets! And such a conspiring grin on her face! The little devil had been providing distraction so I could feed us both. I missed that Ife. The sober, responsible one standing beside me at the cemetery now was no fun at all.

Egbert took a solemn few steps back to the graveside. "Everyone, please gather round," he said.

Ife, Stanley, and I moved to stand beside him. I bent and whispered to Stanley, "Don't worry, I didn't forget. We just have to finish this part first."

He gave an eager nod. Ifeoma said nothing, but she made a sour face. I composed myself for the rest of the funeral.

"Dearly beloved," said Pastor Paul, "James Allan Lambkin has come to the end of his life on this earth, and the beginning of his life with you. We therefore commit his body to the ground."

When I was nine, Dadda had shown me how to fish. But for months he wouldn't let me bait the hook myself. He did it for me, because he was afraid I would jook my fingers.

"Earth to earth," said Pastor Paul.

When I was twelve and woke up one morning to blood-stained sheets and my first period, Dadda ran to the store and brought back a big shopping bag with pads in all different shapes and sizes. He stood outside the closed bathroom door and called out instructions to me for how to put them on.

Ifeoma sniffed and wiped her eyes. Stanley's bottom lip was trembling. Damn, now I was tearing up, too.

"Ashes to ashes, dust to dust."

When I was thirteen and had passed my entrance exams to

get into high school, Dadda took me to the big island to celebrate. We went to a fancy restaurant. He bought me ice cream and cake, and drank a toast to me with his glass of sorrel drink.

"In the sure and certain hope of the Resurrection to eternal life."

When I was fifteen, I told Dadda that I was four months pregnant. He raged through the house for two hours, calling me nasty names and demanding to know who'd done it. I wouldn't tell him. He stopped talking to me. He wouldn't eat when I cooked. On the third day he ransacked my room and threw away all my makeup and nice clothes. On the fourth day I packed a small bag and moved out. Went to the big island and knocked on the door of Dadda's sister Aunt Pearl and her husband Edward. Auntie Pearl let me know that I had shamed the whole family, but she and Uncle Edward gave me a roof and fed me, and they didn't lecture me too often. I got a part-time job as a page in the library. Until my belly got too big for it, I worked all the hours they would give me, saved my money. It was Auntie who was with me the day I had Ifeoma. Auntie, and Michael.

I dashed my eyes dry. Old brute. He'd had his ways, but if he thought I was going to get sentimental about him now that he was dead, he was sorely mistaken.

"Amen."

"Amen," responded everyone at the grave site.

Pastor Paul turned to me and Ifeoma. "Now we're going to lower the coffin into the grave," he said. The word "grave" applied to my father was a shock. I felt it, like a blow over my heart. Dadda was in that box, and now they were going to cover him with dirt. I opened my mouth, but I couldn't make words come out.

"That's fine," said Ifeoma to the pastor. "Let's just do that."

Stanley was tugging urgently at my wrist. I patted his hand to let him know I understood. "We have a request first, Egbert," I said to the pastor.

"Yes, Miss Lambki . . . Calamity?"

Good. He'd managed to force it out. "Pastor *Paul*," I said as his reward—when the puppy obeys, you give it a treat—"can we open the coffin, please? I want to see Dadda's face." My voice broke on the last word.

"Of course, Mistress . . . Calamity; of course."

"Oh, dear," murmured Ifeoma. She pulled Stanley to her, wiped his face with the corner of her dress. He squirmed. She rummaged around in her handbag; one of those handwoven things made of jute or hay or something ecological of the sort. I gave Stanley a shaky wink. He looked scared and excited all at once.

"Let me give you your asthma medicine first," said Ife.

"I don't want it!" he replied, trying to wrench himself out of her hands. "It tastes like ass!"

I snorted, pretended I was blowing my nose.

"Stanley!" said Ife. She gave Stanley's shoulder a little shake. "You have some respect for the dead!"

Fine thing for her to say, Ms. Braless. Stanley scowled at her, then looked down at the ground. I whispered to Ifeoma, "It tastes like—"

"Not so loud!" she muttered. "He hears these things on American television."

I chuckled.

Pastor Paul called over the usher with the big hands, whispered to him. The usher nodded and got one of the others to help him slide back one corner of the coffin lid a little.

"Are you sure this is a good idea?" Ife asked.

"Yes, darling. Stanley, are you ready?"

Stanley started to shake his head no. Turned it into an uncertain nod.

"Good boy. Never back down, you hear me? No matter what people say to you, always hold your spine straight and look them square in their eye. You understand me?"

"Yes," he said in a small voice. He was staring at the casket.

I hoisted him up onto my hip and walked to the head of the coffin. Together, we looked inside.

It took a while to make out Dadda's wizened face in the darkness of the coffin.

"What you think, Stanley?"

"He's all skinny."

"It's true. Smoking isn't good for you."

"And he's wrinkly."

"Yes. He didn't have a whole lot of flesh left on him. But he was still your great-grandpa."

"And he's not a skellington," the boy said in a rush, "and Grandma?"

God, I hated when he called me that. "Yes, dear?"

"Why does he got makeup on his cheeks?"

Ifeoma answered, "They did that at the funeral home, to make him look more natural. Don't you think he looks natural, Stan-Stan?"

"No," said the precious boy. Oh, babes and sucklings. "I wanted to see a skellington. He just looks *funny*."

"Stanley!" said Ife. "Manners!"

"Never mind, Stanley," I said. "I agree with you. He just looks funny. You want to get down now?"

"Yes, Grandm—"

"Calamity."

"Yes, Calamity."

I sighed as I put Stanley to stand beside me. *Ca-lam-i-ty*. Easy to say. Just four small syllables, and not even so different from my childhood name. Just more truthful.

I nodded at the ushers. They put the lid back and commenced to lowering the coffin. It was slung into some kind of fantastic contraption, a scaffolding of metal and straps, by which they winched it down. Two years I'd been the one supporting Dadda's dying weight. Now that he had turned to earth, he was too heavy for me. This metal cradle would have to do it.

We watched the coffin sink smoothly into the grave. People started throwing in wreaths and flowers. The man who had been standing close by turned to me. "I'm Gene Meeks," he said.

"Pleased to meet you." He wasn't bad-looking, in a "gruff black actor who always plays the honourable old-school army officer" kind of way. A little too lean on the bone for my liking.

"You know your father used to tutor me, yes?" he said. "You were just a girl then. Maybe fourteen."

I stared into his face, trying to subtract the years from it. "Yes, you look familiar."

"Mr. Lambkin was the only reason I got into college. My science subjects, you know? I graduated secondary school with high honours because of him. He was like a second father to me."

"That must have been nice." After I left home, Dadda never once asked after me, not even when Auntie told him that I had had the baby. He didn't meet Ifeoma until she was four years old.

The ushers escorted us to the funeral home's reception parlour. Pastor Paul installed me in the only armchair; everyone else had to make do with the flimsy stacking chairs. Ife gave Stanley her car keys so that he could get his precious glider and play with it outside.

The food that people had brought to share was already on the tables. The covers and lids came off, the mourners began to help themselves, and I spent the next hour enduring the slow, polite torture of the receiving line. Over by the decrepit piano, two cousins of Dadda's I didn't recognise—now, *those* were old women—belted out hymns while endless people shook my hand, told me how well they'd known my father, how much he'd done for them, how much they'd loved him. I recognised some of the ones who'd come to visit Dadda while I was looking after him. The rest were a blur. I smiled and said thank you until my teeth ached. Gene and Ife brought me some refreshment: a slice of the black cake I'd made, and in a little plastic cup, some fluorescent pink punch I hadn't. I sipped it. My left eye spasmed against the sour-sweet chemical taste. "Jesus," I said. "Who bring this?"

"Me," answered Gene. "You don't like it?"

He looked like somebody had kicked his puppy. I resigned myself and took a big gulp of the drink. I swallowed hard. "It's wonderful," I told him. "Just what I needed."

He beamed and patted my hand. I found myself gripping his hand back like a lifeline. I squeezed my eyes shut to blink back the sudden tears. Opened them again. With a sad smile, Gene nodded, gave my hand a firm squeeze. We stayed like that for a second or two. "You want me bring you some more?" he asked.

I released my hold. "Of the drink? Oh, no. That was quite enough."

Mrs. Soledad stepped between us, neatly eclipsing Gene. For a little old woman, she knew how to take up space. She hugged me. "He on the next leg of the journey now," she said. "One day you and he will catch up."

I murmured a thank you. I didn't know how else to respond. She cotched herself on the padded arm of my chair. "Don't worry," she said, seeing me get up to offer her my chair. "This suit me better."

Mrs. Soledad had been Dadda's neighbour. Her family had been salt farmers on Dolorosse since way back. She wouldn't tell anyone her age. Her standard answer was "Somewhere between sixty and 'oh God.'" She used to sit with Dadda when I was at work.

"I guess I won't be coming by the house so much any more."

"I guess so."

"You know what you going to do yet?"

I shook my head.

Mrs. Soledad went to the big island only when she absolutely had to. She had a quarter-acre salt pond on her property where she still farmed solar salt, the way she and her husband and their families used to do. No way they could compete with the Gilmor Saline factory, but Mrs. Soledad sent her specialty salts to big island on the workers' co-op boat every few weeks, to be sold in the Cayaba tourist market. She and Mr. Soledad had sent their son to university on salt—first one in both their families to get a degree—and she wasn't going stop now. For food, she phoned her order in to Boulton's grocery on the big island and paid on her credit card. The grocery delivered the food in boxes to the waterbus. She would put on some of her dead husband's working clothes, meet the waterbus at the Dolorosse docks, pile everything into a wheelbarrow, and haul it up to her house. If you offered to help her with it, she would blister your ears for you with some choice swear words. Dadda once joked that if her bark was this bad, he never wanted to feel her bite. And she was hale. Hiked from one end of Blessée to the other every day, for exercise.

But right now, she simply sat beside me, in silence. The most settling silence I'd had all day. This was a side of her I hadn't seen before. Hell, I'd never seen her in a *dress* before. In a little bit, my shoulders eased down from around my ears. I took a deep breath. "Nice hat," I said. "Impressive."

Mrs. Soledad preened. Today's confection was a smart little black pillbox with a huge peacock feather thrust through it and curling around the nape of her neck. The feather started off black at its base, and prismed to iridescent greens and purples at its tip. A scrunched half-veil in black netting completed the look. "You like it?" she asked.

"It suits you." I hoped she wouldn't notice that I wasn't exactly answering her question. Where was Gene? I tried not to make it too obvious I was looking around for him.

Mrs. Soledad never went without a hat. "Protecting my head from the cancers," she would say, pointing at the sun. I'd never seen her wear the same hat twice, and she liked them old-fashioned, gaudy, and extravagant. As far as Mrs. Soledad was concerned, every day was an Easter parade. She was Hindu, but that was just a minor detail.

"Well," she said, easing her feet down to the floor again, "I just see somebody bring out the white rum. I going over there. It's not a funeral if you don't knock back a dram or two. To honour the dead, you know?" Off she went, before I could thank her for everything she had done for Dadda and me.

Gene came by. He had a plastic cup in either hand. He held one out to me.

"I don't want any more," I said.

He nodded. "I finally tasted it; the punch, I mean. I didn't taste it when I made it. It was nasty! I just poured the rest of it down the drain."

That got a little laugh from me. "Then what is this?" I took the cup, looked inside. Water? I sniffed it, and gasped as the fumes went up my nose.

"High wine," Gene replied. Overproof rum. He poured a little of his on the floor in libation. "Spirits for the spirits."

I copied him, then we each knocked back the remaining rum in our cups.

I coughed. "Thank you," I rasped.

"Your father was my hero," he said.

"Mmm."

"I never believed the people who said it's he who did it. Not Mr. Lambkin. He wasn't like that."

Suddenly I felt ill. Feverish. The world started to recede. I grabbed for the arm of the chair. Damn. Not this again.

There was a crash of breaking crockery. It startled me back into myself. I opened my eyes. At my feet lay the remains of a blue and white plate. Somebody must have dropped one of the dishes they'd brought to the potluck. Pastor Paul shooed people away from the shards. He shouted, "Whose plate is this?" No one answered. One of the singing cousins scurried to find a broom.

"Hello, Mother." My son-in-law Clifton leaned over and gave me a peck on the cheek. "Sorry to take so long. My plane was delayed." He peered into my face. "You all right?"

"I think I going to be sick."

Clifton leapt right into action. He helped me up out of the armchair, put an arm around my shoulders. I was tottery on my stilettos. "She had a hard day," he said to Gene. "She need to rest."

"Of course, of course." He backed away.

In two-twos, Clifton had made apologies to Pastor Paul for me, collected Ife and Stanley, and had gotten us out the door.

I stopped when we were outside the building. The afternoon

sun beat down on my shoulders, but it didn't stifle me like inside the funeral home. I took a deep breath of air that wasn't buzzing with whispered condolences.

"How you feeling?" asked Ifeoma. She looked worried. Stanley too.

"Never better. I just needed to get out of there."

"Gene was trying to sweet-talk her," Clifton told Ife. "At Mr. Lambkin's funeral!"

"It wasn't like that." I made a mental note to check in with the doctor about those bloody spells. That was the fifth or sixth one. "I'm okay to walk on my own now. Let's just go."

Clifton took his supporting arm from around me, and we all headed for the parking lot. Stanley was concentrating on the controls of his glider, making it fly on ahead of us. He tripped, but Clifton caught him by the back of his suit jacket before he fell. "Bring that thing down and stop playing with it," he ordered. "Ife, how you could let him bring a toy to a funeral?"

"It's not a toy!" said Stanley.

"He didn't have it during the funeral," Ife responded mildly. "I sent him outside to play during the reception. He would have died of boredom in there."

I had it. "Willow Tree."

Ife looked confused. "What?"

"That plate that dropped and broke. It was the Willow Tree china pattern. I used to have one like it."

"Let us take you home, nuh?" Clifton said. "Ife could drive your car. Me and Stanley will follow in ours."

"No, no. Don't go to all that trouble. I'm fine. Fresh as a daisy in spring!" I threaded my way through the cars in the lot. The tarmac was softening in the heat. If I ruined my stilettos, I was going to blister Egbert Paul's ears for him.

"You sure you don't want us to drive you?" Ife asked again.

"I don't need minding. The matriarch don't need a full-time nurse yet." I was smiling, but the words came out harsher than I meant them.

"Mummy, please stop it. You know I didn't mean it that way. I just meant that you were a grandmother. In some cultures, grandmothers are honoured."

"And in all cultures, grandmothers are *old*," I snapped. Damn. Temper again. We were at Victoria, my red rattletrap of an Austin Mini car. I hugged Ife by way of apology. "Really. I'm okay."

Nobody would do me a favour and steal that car. The left back window was brown paper covered with plastic wrap and held on with masking tape. A crack in the front windshield had long since walked its way from the bottom to the top of the glass. I wasn't even going to ask the mechanic how much it would cost to replace the windshield. I still hadn't finished paying him for when he'd fixed my brakes last year.

Clifton was frowning at Victoria. "You should get that muffler fixed, you know, Mother. It hanging a little low."

Hanging low? Rusting away and falling off was more like it. I got my keys out of my purse, opened the car door so it could cool inside a bit before I put my behind on that hot seat. I rubbed my itchy hand.

"Your hand hurting?" asked Stanley.

I realised I had been rubbing that hand since we left the funeral home. "No," I answered. "Allergy, maybe. Probably Gene's punch."

Stanley made a "yuck" face.

I laughed. "I see you tried it, too." I did that little dance you had to do to get into a car wearing a pencil skirt: sit sideways on the seat first, with your legs outside the car; then knees and toes together, lift the feet into the car, swivel till you're facing the steering wheel. Clifton closed the door after me. Such a gentleman.

I rolled down the window. It only stuck once. "I going straight home. Promise."

"You have to work on Monday?" Ife asked.

"Yeah. Shit."

"Grandma said 'shit'!" burbled Stanley.

"Stanley, you will not use such language," his mother told him.

"They gave me a week's bereavement leave," I said. "I wish it was a year."

"Maybe Mrs. Winter will have to be off work till her ankle get better," said Ife.

I rolled my eyes to the sky. "Please God."

"Grandma can say 'shit,'" muttered Stanley. He crossed his arms, pushed his lips out in a sulk.

"Grandma's a big old woman," Clifton told him. "She can say what she wants."

"I am *not* old!" I started the car over his apologies. Old. I called out the car window, "Men your age still soo-sooing me in the street." I tried to remember the last time anyone had wolf-whistled me. Chuh. Probably wasn't so long ago.

The engine switched over to idle. "All right," I said to them. "The old witch—excuse me, the old *matriarch*—is returning to her cottage in the woods now. She's going to talk to her mongoose familiar and brew up some spells."

"Spells?" Stanley looked delighted.

"Oh, yes," I said. "Snips and snails and puppy dogs' tails—covered in *chocolate*."

His mouth fell open.

I put the car in gear. As they walked away, I saw Ifeoma put one arm around Clifton. Stanley took her free hand.

Damned punch was bitter in the back of my throat.

I was at the exit to the parking lot when I heard a car horn blowing at me. I stopped. A beige sedan pulled up alongside me.

Gene got out and came to my window. "I think I upset you in there just now," he said. "I'm sorry."

"Don't fret," I replied. "Wasn't you. It's just the strain of . . . everything." Like waking up four mornings ago to find that Dadda had died in the night. The arrangements. Putting on a good face. I was tired like dog, the little bit of arthritis in my left knee aching. I couldn't wait to get home to the peace and quiet. No more Dadda and his secrets. Just me in the empty, lonely house.

"You could do me a favour, though," I said to Gene.

"Anything."

"I'm feeling little bit shaky. You could shadow me in your car? Just until the ferry dock? I want to be sure I get to the waterbus all right."

He nodded. "I'm right behind you."

Alexander tremaine unlocked the door that would take him to the Zooquarium's outdoor exhibits. *Not this morning,* he prayed silently. *I just want a normal day.* Alexander hated filling out Incident Reports. Since taking this job as manager of the outdoor exhibits six months ago, it's like he had one every few weeks. They had to be in triplicate, and Mrs. Thomas smirked whenever he handed one in. *Again, Mr. Tremaine? You sure?*

If Mrs. Thomas ever set foot outside the administration office, she'd see for herself what he meant. But she was very proud of the fact that she had been through the zoo only once: on the obligatory tour they'd given her on her first day at the job. Mrs. Thomas hated animals.

Alexander stepped out onto the cement path that snaked around the outdoor exhibits. Look like Dennis had already washed the path down with the hose this morning; the cement was dark with damp, though it hadn't rained. Alexander checked in on the turtle rehab, the first stop. Mountain Girl was going to be okay. She was recovering from her encounter with a speedboat. She was eating well. On his way to the spoonbills, Alexander murmured a good morning at Dennis, who was using a big yard broom to sweep leaves and fallen almonds off the path. The spoonbills were happily trolling in their man-made mangrove swamp. Their colour was a little faded. Alexander made a note to ask Dennis to put some more pellets in their feed. Visitors didn't want to see roseate spoonbills that weren't rosy.

Only six-thirty in the morning, but the sun was beating down already. Management was in no hurry to install shade roofing for the walkway. If the heat kept visitors moving quickly through the exhibits, the Zooquarium could funnel more of them through in a day, plus fill up the Zooquarium cafeteria with people looking to sit down and have a cool drink or some soursop ice cream after the hike through the exhibits.

The seals were next. Alexander could smell the heavy piss scent of seal urine. He slowed down. He took his handkerchief out of his back pocket and mopped his face.

He couldn't put it off any longer. He left the path, walked up the grass-covered incline that led to the seals' enclosure. He reached the waist-high cement wall and looked down into the enclosure. Monk seals were nocturnal, and asleep or sluggish during the day when the visitors came through. Disappointed children would stand at the seal pen and whine that this was boring. Not a month went by that some visitor didn't complain that the seals weren't moving and Something Should Be Done.

Every year, Management talked about closing down the seal exhibit and putting in a dolphin show instead. But the Zooquarium was funded by the Ministry of the Environment, which had a mandate to educate the public about the protected seals, so they stayed.

There was Henny, dozing on the bottom of the pool. Well out of Henny's territory was Penny. She'd hauled out onto one of the "dunes" and was snoring blissfully as she basked. Crab Cake and Hippo were sleeping on the rocks, too. Vampire (he bit) was in one of the sheltered caves, only his rear end sticking out.

One, two, three, four, five, Alexander counted. Six. Seven.

But the Zooquarium owned only five seals.

Alexander sighed. It was going to be an Incident Report morning.

THERE WERE PARKING SPACES topside on the waterbus. I wedged my car between a beat-up old VW and a flashy new RV that was scarlet as an arac apple. Somebody was showing off that they had the money to import an expensive car from "foreign." Dadda called cars like that "penis extensions."

Used to call.

Gene had found a space for his car a few rows over. What was I doing, accepting his offer to see me all the way home? I didn't even know him, not really. Ife and Clifton would have come home with me.

I got a flash of Dadda's coffin in the grave, the dull thumps of earth falling on it from the backhoe. I hugged myself to hold in the sobs threatening to shudder up from my belly.

We were underway. A few people got out of their cars and went to the railing of the waterbus to look out. Gene was one of them. He looked around for my car. I looked away, pretended not to see him.

Damn Gene. I had been trying to put my doubts about Dadda away. But with one sentence, he had them welling up inside me again.

I couldn't keep still in the car. I got out of Victoria the Rust-bucket and picked my way to the back of the boat, where Gene couldn't see me.

Saturday evening. Peace on the water. No cargo ships taking equipment to the new salt plant. No speedboats, sport fishing boats, or glass-bottomed boats, either. Most of the pleasure boats had docked for the night. The dining rooms of the big hotels would be filling up with tourists. Later, the clubs would be filling up with locals and visitors. So long I hadn't been out dancing.

I stood beneath the setting sun and watched the evening exodus of bats streaming out of the towers of the harbour buildings, flitting erratically, catching insects. They looked happy, like bat school was out and now it was time to play. A few of them dipped to the surface of the water, came away with small silver fish in their claws. The waterbus started making its stops: Tingle Island, Vieille Virgèn, Creek Island. The cars thinned out as people drove off at their stops.

"Nice evening," came a raspy voice from behind me. I turned.

"Oh, it's you, Mr. Mckinley."

He jerked his chin at the water. "Not really evening till the little ones come out." He was from Cayaba, made his living as a fisherman. More a white man than any other colour, from the look of him; but after a lifetime in boats in the sun, his skin was brick-ruddy, and wrinkled as a dirt road in dry season.

"Little ones?" I asked. "The bats?"

He leaned with his back against the railing, put his foot up on the big yellow tackle box he always had with him. "Yes. Some nights I like to go out in the rowboat, so it's quiet. Bring a flashlight to draw them to the boat."

In blackness, surrounded by warm velvet skins, flapping, touching your face . . . I shuddered. "Don't sound to me like a good lime."

"I like to hear them singing all around me in the dark."

"The bats sing?"

"Well, kind of a chirp, you know? Like birds."

"You right! Now I remember! Used to have clouds of them in the sky come nighttime, out around Blessée. You don't see so many any more."

He shook his head. "No. They used to roost on Tamany Heights. Fill up the whole cliff wall."

"Mm." Tamany Heights was now the Grand Tamany Hotel. "You going to bring me some red snapper next week?" Every Saturday morning, Mr. Mckinley or one of his sons came by with the morning's catch. "So long now you haven't had red snapper."

He frowned. "Saline plant been messing up the water from since. Only few little snappers in the nets nowadays. Going to be worse now we have two plants."

"Or some shark. Shark would be nice."

"If we catch any, I bring it for you."

"When I was small and I would tell Dadda that the bats were chirping, he never used to believe me."

"Mr. Lambkin? How he doing?"

My heart lurched. "He passed. Tuesday. I just now coming from his funeral."

"Awoah," said Mr. Mckinley softly. "I see. So sorry to hear that."

"Thank you."

"Chastity? Everything all right?" It was Gene.

"Calamity."

"Yes. Sorry."

Mr. Mckinley reached out and shook Gene's hand. "I was just telling Mistress Lambkin how sorry I am to hear about her daddy. So many years now I know Mr. Lambkin. From before Blessée went down." You know how some working men get tongue-tied around people who had high schooling? Not Mr. Mckinley.

"Mr. Mckinley, I'm so sorry. If I knew you and Dadda were friends, I would have told you about the funeral."

He smiled. "Don't fret yourself. Knowing somebody is one thing. Friends is something else."

Gene pulled a flask of white rum out of his back pocket and unscrewed the top. "I liberated it from the funeral parlour," he said. "A drink to Mr. Lambkin?"

"Thanks." I took the bottle, knocked back a swig of it. "To Dadda."

I passed the bottle to Mr. Mckinley. He looked surprised, but he took it, drank, made his toast: "Jimmy, walk good, you hear?" To us he said, "I make the mistake one day and tell him if his wife get bored with him, she could always come to me. He never speak to me after that again."

"Dadda was always jealous for the women in his life."

"Mm-hmm. So I find out."

Gene made his own toast.

Mr. Mckinley nodded to me and Gene. "Thank you for sharing your flask with me. Some people wouldn't want to drink from the same bottle as a working class man." He picked up his tackle box. "Well, Jimmy had a hard row to hoe. But every man will put his past mistakes behind him, one way or another. Good evening to you."

When he was gone, Gene said to me, "He and all?"

"He and all what?"

"He was talking about your mother disappearing." He sighed. "This blasted island. Everybody always up in everybody else's business. And nobody will forgive, nobody will forget." We passed the bottle back and forth in silence for a bit. Then he glared at me, red-eyed. "You think Mr. Lambkin did it, too? Killed your mother?"

"Gene, he was my father. Two years I looked after him."

He turned his face away from me. He knuckled at one eye. "Beg pardon. I just feeling guilty that I lost touch with him. Years now. Shouldn't be putting that guilt on you."

The revving of the waterbus's engines slowed. We were nearly at Dolorosse. "We stopping soon," I told him. "When I drive down the ramp, just follow me."

"All right. I sorry, eh?"

"I know."

We went back to our cars. Lots more cars getting off at Dolorosse nowadays; families moving to work at the new saline plant. There were some familiar faces, too. But I knew scarcely any of them by name. I hadn't moved to Dolorosse to socialize.

Dolorosse Island was the last stop on the waterbus's run. Blessée used to be the last; the last liveable island on the arm of the Cayaba archipelago. I'd lived on Blessée for the first fifteen years of my life before moving to the big island. When I was twenty-

seven, a hurricane had hit Blessée. We weren't ready for it—
Blessée was outside the hurricane zone, and we hadn't had one
in over fifty years.

The 1987 storm pulverized Blessée in a matter of days. The
survivors had been evacuated. Mr. Kite on Dolorosse had taken
Dadda in, and Dadda had remained in that house till now.

Did I think that Dadda had killed Mumma? I hadn't answered
Gene's question. Couldn't give him an answer I didn't have.

The cars drove down the waterbus ramp onto the island. The
sun had taken its nightly dive headlong into the sea. In the dark,
the little cement ferry house had its one yellow light on. From
behind the station house window, Mr. Lee waved the incoming
cars through. I flashed my ferry pass at him and took the gravel
turnoff to get to Dadda's house. Gene followed.

I got my cell phone out of my handbag. Speed-dialled. "Stanley? Let me talk to Ife, nuh?"

People were yelling in Ife's house: Clifton's voice, and Ife's. I
thought Stanley had sounded upset.

"Hello?"

"Ife, what you did to make Clifton so angry?"

"What *I* did? That is what you call me to say to me?"

"Lord, what a way you harsh! I thought you wanted to know
if I get home safe."

A sigh from the other end. "Yes. I'm sorry, Mummy. So you
home now?"

"Nearly there. I'm on Dolorosse. But tell me, nuh; why you
and Clifton fighting?"

"Our anniversary is next week. I bought us tickets to attend
that speech on labour reform by Caroline Sookdeo-Grant."

"Not what you would call romantic."

"I have to see somebody to know if to trust them, you know?

See if they look down and to the left when they lying—'cause you know a politician going to tell you lies—or up and to the right. My NLP teacher says—"

I burst out laughing. "Ife, is what kind of stupidness that? You going to decide who to vote for by some kind of obeah?"

"It's called Neurolinguistic Programming. I'm taking a four-week course: 'Instant Rapport Through Rapid Eye Movements.'"

"Instant rapport with who?"

"I was hoping with Clifton. We not getting along so good right now."

"Ife, don't mess things up with that man, you know. You will suck salt before you find another one like him."

Silence. A sigh. Then: "Yes, Mummy. You rest good tonight, you hear?"

And she was gone. I listened to the phone static for a second, playing the conversation back in my head, hearing where I had made it go wrong. Again.

I kissed my teeth and snapped the phone shut. I threw it back into my handbag on the passenger seat, next to the yam I'd bought from a roadside vendor before we took the waterbus to Dolorosse. I led Gene the rest of the way home and parked in front of my house. When I started to think of Dadda's home as mine?

Gene pulled up behind me on the gravel road. We got out of our cars. He came towards me. Poor man; he looked a little shaky too from the funeral. "You're home safe now," he said. "So I will just go back and wait for the next waterb—"

I felt a sudden panic. "No, don't be silly." I gave a little laugh. "The waterbus not coming for another forty-five minutes. At least come inside and have a cool drink."

He frowned. "But—"

"No, I won't hear any objections. I hauled you out all this way. It's the least I can do."

"All right," he said doubtfully. "If you're sure."

"I'm certain." I wasn't, but I led him up the five steps to the porch.

He pointed to the green wicker lounge chair and armchair that sat beside each other. "I'll just wait out here," he said.

When I first moved back to Dolorosse, Dadda would sometimes let me help him out to the porch of an evening. I would lower him into the lounge chair, put his legs up so he could lie back. I would put a blanket around him and we would sit and watch the stars. Months now he hadn't been able to do that. I started to ask Gene whether he liked grapefruit juice.

Instead, I began to bawl.

Gene leapt to his feet. "Mih lord," he said. "You should sit down. You want me to bring you some water?"

I tried to say, *It's all right*, but words wouldn't come out. The sobbing just got worse. It went bone deep, racking me to the core. Pretty soon I was wailing out my anguish, keening loud and harsh, like I was labouring.

"Come," said Gene. "Sit over here." He tried to guide me to the chair, but my knees failed me. So he tried to bear me up, but I'm no fine-boned bird of a woman. I collapsed onto the floor. Best he could do was take some of my weight so I didn't land *braps* like the soil on Dadda's coffin lid.

This wasn't me. I wasn't the type to faint away. I didn't cry in front of strangers. But all I could do was pull my knees to me and rock, rock. And weep. A word came this time; pulled out of me with my breath: "Daddaa!" It spiralled up into the evening sky like a fleck of ash from a fire. It thinned out till I couldn't hear it no more. The crying let up little bit.

Gene got a good grip under my arms and tried again to lift me. This time he got me up and sitting on the edge of the lounge chair. He sat beside me. I hugged my arms around myself and rocked and wept. My muscles were rigid, like stone. They had to be. They had to hold me together, or I was just going to fly apart.

Gene propped one elbow up on his knee, lowered his head into his hand. From the jerking of his shoulders, I knew that he weeping, too. So quietly. My rocking stopped. Slowly, giving him time to stop me if he wanted to, I put my arms around him. He choked out a sob; just one. He was making the soft, mewling sounds of someone trying to cry without noise. I shushed and rocked him like any baby.

"I can't believe he's gone," Gene gasped. "When I heard, it was like somebody punch me in the belly."

That got me crying again. I pressed my head into Gene's shoulder. We held on to each other. Our tears wound down. "I wanted to sit with you on the floor," he said. Through my face on his shoulder, I could feel his voice vibrating against my skin. "But the old hip have arthritis, you know?"

I laughed tears. "Thank you."

He raised his woeful face. I leaned forward. And then we were kissing, wiping the eye water and nose running from each other's faces with such tenderness. We managed to stand up together. In the back of my mind I was thinking this was wrong, this was disrespectful. I had just covered my father with cold earth. But all my body knew was that it had touched death, and it needed the antidote. I reached my hands inside Gene's suit jacket, pulled out the tails of his shirt. I laid my hands against the warmth of living skin, flushed with blood from a beating heart.

Gene was running the back of one hand gently down one side of my throat, then the other. We couldn't seem to break eye contact. He whispered, "This is all right?"

All I said was "Come inside." I took him to my little bedroom. There, with tears running ignored down our faces, we helped each other remove the black grieving clothes, and took comfort in each other's frail, living flesh.

She had come out of that cave on Blessée. Chastity wasn't supposed to go into that cave. But she saw the little girl step out of it, squint into the sun, and look confused. Maybe the little girl's parents let her play in the cave! Chastity felt jealous one time. But a little bit curious, and happy, too, to see another little girl like her. Except for school break times, Chastity didn't have too many people to play with. Her school friends' parents didn't make the trip to the out islands often.

"Hello," said Chastity.

The little girl shaded her eyes and frowned. She didn't say anything. Her hair was tall for so; all the way down to her bumsie. And it was all knotted up, and the little girl wasn't wearing her bath suit.

"What's your name?" Chastity asked her. The girl just stood and looked at her. In the silence, Chastity could hear the waves whooshing in and out of the cave behind the little girl. "Did you lose your bath suit?" Chastity said "lose," because that was what she always told Mumma and Dadda;

that she'd lost her bath suits. But really, she just didn't like wearing them. She'd taken the last one off in the sea. Walked in up to her chest, rolled the suit down her body, stepped out of it, and watched the waves take it away. The water had felt so nice, flowing over her. That time, she'd told Mumma that a dolphin had stolen her suit. Mumma just shook her head and rolled her eyes.

Something was wrong with the little girl's skin. It was mostly a normal colour; sort of light yellow-brown, like Melody's at school. But it was sort of blue-ish brown, too, like Chastity's hands would get when she rooted around in the freezer for her favourite flavour of Frutee Freezer Pops. She liked the blue ones. Once she'd asked Dadda what kind of fruit made that bright acid blue. He'd told her it was sky juice. Next day she'd asked Mumma how they got the juice down out of the sky to make blue Frutee Pops, and Mumma had laughed her belly laugh that Chastity liked. The one with the little snort at the end of it.

The little girl still didn't speak.

"Are you dumb?" Chastity asked. There was a little boy at school who didn't speak too good. When he said words, they sounded all gargly. Jane Labonté who wore pretty red ribbons in her hair to school every day said that Walter was deafanddumb and her daddy said he should be in a home. But Miss said that Walter was fine, he was just deaf, and couldn't hear how his speech sounded, and they mustn't call him deafanddumb. He was taking special classes to learn to speak better. Chastity liked Walter. He would trade his orange juice with her at lunch time for cashew juice. Chastity liked the way the word "dumb" sounded. She would sometimes sing it over and over to *herself when no-one was around to hear: dumb, dumb, dumb, dumb.*

The girl took a hobbling step forward; another. She walked funny. She kept squinting at the sun and covering her eyes. She waddled over to Chastity, who laughed at the way the girl walked. But then Chastity remembered how Dadda had told her not to make fun of people. "I'm sorry," she said to the girl. "How you hurt your feet? They going to get better?"

The little girl just made a gargling noise, reached out her hand, and stroked the fabric of Chastity's sundress.

"Where are your clothes?" Chastity asked her. "Your mumma and dadda are going to be mad at you for losing them. They're going to say, 'We're not made of money, you know? You should be more careful.' Then your mumma and dadda will fight, and your mumma will go away and stay on the big island with relatives until she isn't mad any more."

The little girl tugged at the shoulder strap of Chastity's sundress.

"No," Chastity told her. "You can't have mine."

The girl didn't seem to mind. With a look of amazement, she slid her hand under the strap. She pulled at the neck of the sundress and stared down the front of it. She laughed, a wet, snorting sound. Water came out of her nose. She grabbed at the hem of the dress, yanked it up in the air, looked at Chastity's bare legs, and laughed some more.

Chastity pulled her hem back down. "You don't have to laugh after me," she said to the girl. "I don't like clothes either."

And to prove it, she shucked the dress over her head and threw it up on the rock. Her panties followed, and her sandals. She could climb and run better without them anyway.

The little girl watched solemnly until Chastity was as naked as she was. She gurgled some more, and smiled.

"Come," said Chastity. "Let's go swimming." She started off towards the beach, even though she knew she wasn't supposed to go there if she didn't have a grown-up with her. They wouldn't go in very far.

But the little girl wasn't following her. Chastity stopped. The girl was still standing by the entrance to the cave, looking puzzled.

Maybe she hadn't heard what Chastity had said. Walter from school had to look at you to know what you wanted. "Come," said Chastity again, motioning with her hand. The girl seemed to understand that. She ran a few steps, then put her hands on the ground and ran on her feet and hands, with her bumsie in the air. It looked like fun. Chastity tried it, but she couldn't go as fast as the girl could. So she ran on just her feet. The little blue-brown girl loped along beside her like a mongoose. No, not blue. She didn't have that funny blue-y colour to her any more; just pale yellow-brown skin.

Chastity could smell the briny sea before she saw it. Then she could hear it. They rounded the last corner on the path: past twisty scrub grass and big rockstones stuck in the white sand; past the line of sea grape bushes with their shiny round leaves that stretched out along the beach as far as they could see. They were on the sandy beach now. The leaping water gleamed blue before them in the sun. Chastity knew why they called them "waves"; because they waved at you, beckoning you to come in and play. "It's like sky juice, right?" Chastity said. "Only salty."

Laughing, they raced each other to the forbidden water.

Gene was spooned behind me, half-dozing. His chest hairs were damp against my naked back.

The booming of the sea sounded muffled. Light fog had rolled in. *Sea or advection fog.* So many years since Dadda would make me quote my lessons back to him, but I still remembered. *Occurs when a body of warm moist air moves over a cooler sea surface and is cooled to dew point, which is the temperature at which condensation takes place.* Cayaba had another name for it, though: jumbie breath. Was under cover of a night like this that Potoo Nelson and eighty-two other slaves climbed up the mountain and threw themselves off the cliffs into the sea at Rocky Bottom and drowned. In jumbie breath weather, people said the dead slaves came up out of the water and walked, looking for the man who had led them to their doom.

I could hear the branches of the coconut trees thrashing. The breeze had picked up little bit. The fog drifting past my window was tattered and shredding now.

Gene put his arm around my middle. My waist had gotten thicker these past two years. Even had a little overhang. Embarrassed, I pulled his arm higher, to under my breasts. He cupped one breast. We lay in that empty, floating bliss that comes after good sex. For the first time in days, my nerves didn't feel stripped raw.

The clock radio on my bedside table clicked on. "Chuh," I said. "I keep forgetting to unset that alarm."

I felt Gene roll onto his back to look at it. "An alarm for nine o'clock at night?"

"Mm-hmm. Time for Dadda's last medicine of the day."

He grunted. We listened to the newswoman, her Cayaba accent clipped to near-BBC diction. Apparently Caroline Sookdeo-Grant had visited Holy Name Girls' Secondary School yesterday. She had told them that women were half of Cayaba and the country needed their strength.

"You think she could win?" I asked Gene. Election day was in a few weeks. The campaigning was hotting up.

His grin was languid. "Over Johnson? You know he not going to lose any election he could buy."

"Mm. I don't pay much mind to politricks. Never met a politician who wouldn't try to convince you that salt was sugar." I rolled onto my stomach, propped myself up on my elbows.

The radio announcer continued: *"The government of Cayaba has been in negotiations with the American institution the FFWD, the Fiscal Foundation for Worldwide Development. Today, Cayaba Public Radio learned that completion of these critical negotiations over Cayaba's debt repayment difficulties has been delayed for a month. Samuel Tanner, economic advisor to prime minister Garth Johnson, said the delay means that Cayaba will be tardy for its deadline to reach an accord on an economic management strategy with the FFWD. The interest alone on loans from the FFWD currently exceeds $750 million. Without concessions from the American foundation, the country faces falling further behind in its repayments."*

"Chuh," I said. "Don't need to be hearing that nonsense right now." I reached over Gene and turned the radio off, enjoying the feeling of his chest hair tickling my breasts. Lazily, he stroked my arm.

I was feeling a little warm. No, I was very warm. Then way too fucking hot. "Woi." The heat rushed up through me like when you know you're going to puke. My cheeks were stinging, sweat popping out on my forehead. I sat and fanned myself with my hands. So I was looking right out the window when it happened. I saw it happen. My breath stopped in my throat. "Holy shit! You see that?"

"See what?"

I didn't answer; couldn't. I shoved myself off the bed and over to the window. Only wisps of fog left, and the crescent moon glowing down to help me see. I knew the distant silhouette in the window; knew it in my bones. "That wasn't there before," I said. My lips trembled as I spoke.

"What?" Gene was up out of the bed now. He joined me at the window.

I could only point. My extended hand shook. Rooted on the cliff as though it had always been there was the almond tree from my childhood. "That tree."

"That tree?" Gene echoed.

"It just appeared out of nowhere."

"It just appeared?"

Pique was better than terror. "What, like you turn Polly parrot?" I said, trying to sound teasing instead of scared no rass. "Yes, the tree. It just came there now. Wasn't no tree there before." I grabbed the window ledge to hide my shaking hands. I'd spent the morning up in that tree the day that Mumma was really gone for good. Now I was cold and shivering, damn it all to hell. I stepped into the lee of Gene's body for some of his warmth.

Gene stared out the window, frowning. His face was creased with sleep and puffy with weeping. He looked like an old man. How I come to find myself knocking boots with a senior citizen?

"I don't quite follow you," Gene said. "That tree. You never see it before?"

I nodded, my mouth open. "I saw it," I whispered. "It wasn't there, and then it was. Is from Blessée. Went down when the island went down."

Gene stepped completely away from me; turned and began gathering his clothes off the floor. "You need to get some rest," he said.

"You think I imagined it!" I fought to keep my teeth from chattering. I was shuddering with the chill.

Gene stepped into his underwear, pulled up his pants. "You will feel different after a good night's sleep. Grief make a person see and do strange things." He zipped up.

I made myself turn my back to the window. "You mean like bringing some strange man home and screwing him in my father's house?" I meant it to sound like a challenge, but the words came out trembly, half shame, half plea.

Gene stopped buttoning his shirt. He shook his head. "No, that's normal." His voice sounded so ordinary, the way you might say that of course it rains after the rain flies come out.

I glanced back out the window. Tree still there. "*Normal?* How you can say that what we just did was normal?"

"Funeral sex."

"What?"

He came over to me, took my two hands in his. "I said, funeral sex. Never happen to you before?"

"No. People don't drop dead on me regularly."

He gave a wry smile and let me have my hands back. "You must be younger than me, then. Two strangers at the same funeral find themselves in bed right after. Don't feel bad. It's a thing grief does. I see it before." I hated the compassion in his voice. "It just never happen to me before," he said sadly.

I asked him, "You know what else never happen before?"

"What?"

"That tree, damn it! It wasn't there before!"

"I know that's what you believe." He went and flicked on the light. I squinted in the sudden, painful brightness.

"*I know that's what you believe,*" I mocked him. "You *don't* know. Don't you dare patronise me in that mealy-mouthed kind of way!" I found a nightie in my dresser, pulled it over my head. "You sound like Ifeoma. I didn't see that tree before because it wasn't there before!"

A hardness came over his face. "Calamity, you're hallucinating."

I strode over to the bedroom door, yanked it open. "And you are leaving."

"Damned right." He brushed past me. From the hallway he said, "Drink a lot of water and try to get a good night's sleep."

I leaned out the door and snapped, "Don't you tell me what to do!"

He glared at me. Stomped out into the living room. I stood in my bedroom. Every time I looked towards the window, I got the shakes. Gene came back into the bedroom.

"I told you you could come back in here?"

He made a face, squared up his shoulders. "Sorry for trying to give you orders," he said. "Bad habit."

Just like that.

"You're a strong woman. I can see that. Looking after Mr. Lambkin all those years. But who looking after Calamity?"

He wasn't going to get around me by being nicey-nicey. "Calamity looking after Calamity. She one."

He set his mouth hard. "So I see. Calamity don't need nobody. You going to come and lock the front door behind me?"

I looked away from him. I didn't reply.

"All right, then."

I listened to the sound of his feet walking down the hallway and through the living room. I heard him open the front door, close it back with a deliberate gentleness. Little more time, I heard his car start up.

"That's right," I muttered. "Take your skinny behind away from my front yard." I went and locked the front door. Returned to the bedroom and threw myself onto the bed. In the lighted room, the window was just a square of black. The blindness was worse than being able to see it. I leapt up again and outed the light. There was the tree, looming in the dark. "You don't scare me," I said to it. I lay back down. My pillow was damp and it smelled of sweat. I clutched a corner of it tightly. The rumpled top sheet was on the floor where we had kicked it. My funeral clothes were all over the floor, too. Fucking hell. That had been beyond the pale, even for me. Bury the father, come straight back to his house with a man, and . . . "I'm sorry, Dadda," I whispered.

Oh, shit. The yam. It would rotten in the closed-up car. I sucked my teeth and got up again. I went out to the car. From the passenger side seat I picked up the piece of yellow yam. It was nearly as big as my head, its dark brown, rooty skin rough against my palms. I took it inside, to the kitchen. I put it on the kitchen counter.

Truth to tell, I wasn't sleepy. By the clock set into the stove, it wasn't even ten o'clock yet. And I didn't want to go back to my bed to stare at the almond tree and try to figure out if I was finally going stark, staring mad.

I wasn't in the mood for tv. I opened the freezer and took out the two books I had in there, knotted into separate plastic bags. I squinted in the low light from the open fridge, trying to make out their titles. Oh, yes: *Buxton Spice* and *The Life and Loves of a She-Devil*. The books had been in my freezerversity nearly three months now; more than enough time to kill a full life cycle of bookworm. Hadn't read much in Dadda's last few weeks. In the evenings after I'd fed him and got him to take his medicine, my mind had been too fretful for book learning.

I put one book on the kitchen table. Took the other one out of its plastic and cracked it open. But I wasn't really seeing the words. I put it down, looked around the kitchen. My eye lighted on the piece of yam. I grinned. Night picnic on the beach. Like old times.

I found matches, lit a hurricane lamp and took it into the pantry. Its yellow-brown light set shadows to flickering on the pantry walls. My shadow did a devil-girl dance in the light.

On a shelf in the pantry stood two lonely bottles of store-bought cashew liqueur. Our pantry in Blessée used to have shelves full of cashew wine and liqueur; gallon bottles. Dadda had managed to save a few when Blessée blew away. He used them to bribe the Coast Guard rescuers to let him off at Dolorosse instead of taking him to a shelter on the big island like everybody else. They'd probably thought he was crazy to take the chance. They had probably been right. He had camped out right there on the beach for a day in the wind and the rain with the few possessions he had left. The Coast Guard was coming to remove him forcibly when Mr. Kite had taken him in. Mr. Kite was a weird old white guy from Germany. Came to Cayaba and went native.

I hooked two fingers through the handle of one of the liqueur bottles. Took it out to the kitchen table. Back in my room I stood off to one side so I couldn't see out the window. I peeled out of my nightie and tossed it on the bed. No need to dirty more clothes; I just put on back the underwear and the skirt and blouse I had thrown on the floor before jumping into bed with Gene. Nobody to see how they were wrinkled. The panty hose were crumpled up and lying beside the bed. The translucent fabric looked like shed skin. One leg was laddered. I tossed them into the waste basket.

Back in the kitchen, one of the big cloth shopping bags hanging under the sink held the yam, the salt and pepper, and a stick of butter from the fridge. I slung the bag handles over my arm and hooked the liqueur bottle by its handle again. The hurricane lamp went into the other hand, to light my way. Barefoot, bare-legged, I went down the front steps and took the road to the beach.

The rockstones and the sticks on the path jooked my feet. So long I hadn't walked on hard ground with no shoes. When I got so big and grown up, wearing shoes all the time?

The sea smelled salty and meaty tonight, like dinner. Once I reached the first stretch of beach sand with its scrub grass, the warm sand was soothing under my feet. The waves slushed at me in rhythm, like an old person puffing as she dozed.

In the dark, the hurricane lamp threw a protective circle of light around me. Grandmother Sea was snoring in her sleep, and I was feeling better already.

I set down the shopping bag and searched the beach until I'd found enough driftwood. I buried the yam in the sand. Over it, I piled the sticks, used flame from the lamp to get a fire going. I dug a shallow hole nearby, waited for it to fill from the bottom with sea water. The butter went into that, so it wouldn't melt in the warm air. I stood the bottle in the sand, close to the fire. The heat would warm the liqueur a little.

Fuck. What I was going to sit on? I had forgotten about that. Walk all the way back to the house? If I went, I probably wouldn't come out again tonight.

I had a naughty idea. I checked the beach up and down.

Nobody. I pulled off my skirt and laid it on the sand. I felt so wicked, with the sea breeze blowing through my legs! But now I had a picnic blanket. I sat on my skirt and stared into the fire. It chuckled as it burned. I reached for the bottle of cashew liqueur, put the bottle of warm, sweet alcohol to my lips, and drank. With no dinner in my belly yet, I began to feel the booze one time. So I had more. The sea made its warm whooshing noise. I crooned to it, "The moonlight, the music, and you . . . ," and took another gulp. I tucked the bottle into the cradle made by my knees and thighs. The cool glass felt good against my skin. Up in the sky the new moon swung, yellow and sickled as a banana. A round shadow sat inside its horns. "Old moon sitting in the new moon's arms," I whispered to it; a phrase I'd learned from my freezerversity. I picked up the bottle, took three long pulls at it. I tucked its smooth roundness back against my pubic bone.

I was pleasantly woozy. The tingling spread out from the centre of me to my legs, torso, head, arms. My toes and the soles of my feet were warm. My fingertips prickled. I rubbed my hands together, so that friction increased the lovely heat.

"How my yam doing?" I asked of the fire. It made cheerful popping sounds back at me. The smell of smoke and burning wood was glorious. To just sit here, not a care for the clock, no need to go and check if Dadda was all right, if he needed anything. This is what I should have done in the first place, instead of taking Gene home. Ife would be so scandalized when I told her! Oh. But I wasn't talking to her. Not really.

I drank a toast to Dadda, and one to Mumma. They were back together now. Maybe.

"Dadda, you ever wonder what happened to Mumma that night?"
"No."

"Why not, Dadda?"

"I know what happened; she went away and left us."

Just like she used to threaten to, any time she and Dadda argued, any time I had been bad. "I going to go far away and never come back," she would say, trying to keep the smile from her lips. "Then allyou going to be sorry."

We were.

I never pressed Dadda for the whole story. I was afraid of what words might come out to break the silence. And now I would never get to ask him.

I lurched to my feet. Whoops; a little unsteady. With my bottle and hurricane lamp, I went walking along the beach, looking for a good strong stick. Tiny red crabs scurried out of the light into their holes.

The wind was stronger, the waves tossing more. The night air was freshening, so Grandmother Sea was restless. I faced her and bowed to her. "Old woman," I greeted her. "But still wet and juicy, eh?" I laughed. The wind swallowed the sound.

I pulled a handful of big, platter-shaped sea grape leaves off their stems, found a stick, and hurried back to the heat of the fire. With the stick, I poked in the sand underneath the fire until I unearthed the yam. The tip of the stick went into it easily. Perfect. I hooked the yam out of the fire and onto the sea grape leaves I'd spread as a plate. My fingers were still thrumming from the alcohol. Made me feel tingly all over. I took another drink so that the feeling wouldn't end too soon. With my stick, I broke the piece of roasted yam in two. A delicious smell rose in the steam from it. My belly rumbled. I fished the butter out of its cool water, unwrapped it, dug my fingers in, got a good handful of it, and spread the butter into the crumbly yellow of the roasted yam. Then salt and pepper. I crouched over my dinner, pulling and eating pieces of buttered yellow yam out of its burned skin as soon as they cooled enough to handle. In between, I took swigs from the bottle. Should have brought fresh water with me. But I would be back at the house in a little bit.

Damn. That was more than sea spray misting my shoulders. There was the occasional warm drop of rain. I stared blearily into the darkness, but I couldn't see beyond the fire. In the yellow-lit circle, splashes of darker beige were appearing here and there in the sand. Raindrops. They were spattering my head and shoulders now. I needed to finish the yam, fast. Its hot flesh burned my fingertips, but I kept plucking at it and popping the buttery-salt pieces into my mouth.

The sea had woken up. It roared and rushed the shore. A spear of lightning lit up angry, cresting waves. Thunder boomed back at the fuming sea. "Grandma Sea and Grandpa Sky," I said, "why all you fighting?" I chuckled. "*Poopa* Sky, like your wife getting the Change, or what?" I snickered at my joke.

Three flashes of lightning, quick upon each other. Thunder shouted and the sea roared back. Just a passing shower. The water felt good on my skin.

I was full. I stood up in the spit-warm rain and flung my scraps into the water for the fish, almost throwing myself off balance. I drank the liqueur, watched the sea, and rubbed my burned and itchy fingertips against my thigh.

A rush of cloud water put out the lantern. It doused most of the fire, too. Gradually, my eyes adjusted to the darkness. The firelight had been hiding the beach from my view.

The sky pelted down raindrops and the sea flung spume back

up. The clouds threw javelins of lightning. "Don't fight with her!" I yelled at the sky. "She's your wife! You must love her!"

The wind blew my words away. "Don't hurt her," I whispered.

Taking my drink, I wove my way along the sand. Small crabs scuttled sideways out of my way, running on claw-tips into their holes. I sipped from the bottle.

In a few minutes I reached the low, flat rock. It was about waist height on me. I stood the bottle on it. Some evenings I would come out here and sit on it to watch the sunset, feel my bottom toasty on the sun-warmed surface.

This rock signalled the end of the beach; a few yards farther along, an exposed escarpment of the coral that underpinned Dolorosse jutted way out into the water. Trying to clamber over that was a good way to cut your feet to shreds.

I wiped rain water out of my eyes and heaved myself up onto the rock, beside the bottle. The movement set my head spinning. I sat as still as I could and waited for the dizziness to pass. The dance of lightning from the sky was magnificent. Bloated waves reached high, high, trying to push away the stabbing lightning. "That's right!" I shouted to Mumma Sea. "Protect yourself!"

I shuddered in the rain. My burned fingertips buzzed. Vertigo spun the world around again. I groaned and lay down on the rock. Better. Its surface wasn't warm tonight, but lying down felt so good. I pulled my feet up onto the rock and rolled over onto my back. I opened my mouth to catch raindrops. For a little while I made a game of that, giggling at the feel of rain splashing my skin. Suddenly, my skin was burning with fever. I sat up and reached for the bottle. The rock spun, and me with it. I threw myself down on it and clung, just trying not to fall off. A spectacular jag of lightning split the sky open. The boom of thunder made my ears buzz. I whimpered and shivered for a time. Then there was nothing.

∽

The little girl got all excited as they hit the waves. She sucked in deep breaths of air. She waddled the first few yards, then a wave struck her in the face and rushed on to shore. The little girl laughed and shook water out of her eyes. She stood and did her awkward walk a bit further, leaving Chastity behind. Mumma and Dadda never let Chastity go out this far by herself. She hesitated. Took small steps backwards.

The water was chest high on the little girl now. She looked back at Chastity. She was smiling. She looked so happy! The little girl called out something that Chastity couldn't hear over the sound of the sea, then turned and leapt into an oncoming wave that was as tall as she was. "Wait!" Chastity yelled, but the little girl was gone. What would the little girl's parents say? Chastity began to feel worried.

The little girl surfaced, floating in a trough between the waves. She waved at Chastity.

She looked like she was having fun. "I'm coming!" Chastity shouted. She lowered her body into the water and started to dog-paddle towards her friend. The next wave lifted her up, then down, making her tummy flip-flop in a delicious way. The girl dove, came back up again, grinning. The next wave slapped Chastity full in the face. She got a noseful of water. It stung. She started to cough, dog-paddling the whole time. She got more water in her mouth. She was coughing too hard to see now, and another wave hit her. She was below the water. She couldn't breathe. Frightened, she closed her eyes, her arms striking out for where she thought the surface was.

A hand grabbed her and pulled her up. Her face was in the air again. She took a big whooping breath, spat out water. The little girl was holding Chastity by her upper arm. She helped Chastity rise and fall with the next wave, and the next. She kept pulling them out deeper. "Whee!" Chastity said. "Go out more!" She helped by dog-paddling with her legs and her free arm. The little girl gurgled and grinned at her, and swam strongly. Pretty soon they were out really deep. The shore was far away. There weren't even any waves out here. That meant that Chastity could swim without getting water in her eyes. "Let me go," she said to the little girl, who was all blue-y again; a deeper blue this time. The little girl wouldn't understand her, so Chastity pried the helping fingers off her arm. The little girl let go, and Chastity paddled around her in a big circle. "See what I can do?" she asked the little girl. "I'm a good swimmer. Mumma says so."

The little girl did a roll in the water, holding her ankles. And another one without stopping, and even another 'nother one. She brought her head back up, laughing. She shook her long, matted hair. The dark knots sent water flying.

"How you do that?" Chastity asked. "Show me." She tried to reach for her own ankles, got more sea water in her nose for her troubles. She sputtered it out. The little girl floated upright in the water, brought her knees up to her chest. She babbled again. Chastity looked down. She could see the little girl reaching to clutch her own ankles.

"Oh," Chastity said. "Let me try."

She could do that part, but she couldn't roll without getting water up her nose. And she was tired, breathing hard. She reached for the little girl's shoulder. The little girl seemed to understand. She curled her arm around Chastity's body, under her armpits. Together they swam in the direction of the big rock that stuck up out of the water. Chastity had always wanted to go there, but Dadda said it was too dangerous. Now she was going to see what the big rock was like! She liked the yellow girl.

As they went, Chastity looked down. There was a lobster below them, a big one, all shiny-brown and yellow and spiny. Chastity thought of its pincers reaching for her exposed toes. She curled her feet under her and kicked them, trying to help herself and the little girl go faster.

They swam through a school of tiny fish, nearly colourless, each tiny as the first joint of Chastity's pointing finger. They tickled when they passed over her body. Chastity giggled, until she saw what the little girl was doing. She had her head under the water while she was swimming, and her mouth open. She brought her head up, chewing and smacking her lips happily. "Nasty!" Chastity said to her. "You eating raw fish!" The little girl grinned a fishy grin.

They were through the school now. The girl just kept swimming. The rock was right in front of them. The sea was making waves as it crashed against the rock. Just small ones, but the power of the water was driving them towards the rock. Chastity was afraid they would be smashed against it.

Suddenly the little girl dove, taking Chastity under. She spluttered, tried to cough, breathed in more salty water. Then they were up again, in the air, touching the rock. The little girl was holding on to a part of it that stuck out. Choking, Chastity reached for it too. For a while, all she could do was hold on and cough. The waves tried to suck her into the water and bang her against the rock, but she held on.

The little girl looked concerned. She peered closely at Chastity, making question sounds in her throat. She rubbed Chastity's back. "I'm okay," Chastity reassured her. "Just . . . Can we climb right up on the rock?" Chastity didn't wait for an answer. She braced her legs on the rock and started climbing up. When she got stuck, the little girl pushed her from beneath, then scrambled up onto the rock herself.

The rock was dark brown and full of lots of little holes with sharp edges. It hurt to stand up on it. Gingerly, Chastity moved around until she found a smoother place, right at the very top. It was warm from the sun up there. Almost too warm, but the water running off her body was cooling a part of the rock. Chastity sat on the cooler, wet part. She was glad of the sun's warmth, because coming out of the water had chilled her body. The little girl came and lay beside her, chattering away in her liquid tongue.

"I like you," Chastity said to her. "You want to be best friends?"

The little girl looked up at her, squinting into the sun. She put one long-fingered hand to her forehead to block out the glare. Her eyes did something funny. She smiled at Chastity. Chastity guessed that meant yes, they were now best friends. She smiled back.

The little girl squoonched herself down into a ball. With a crazy, yodelling scream, she sprang off the rock and cannonballed into the sea below. She popped up again, like the yellow almond fruit that floated when they fell into the sea. She gurgled at Chastity.

Chastity stood. Just before she made the jump, she thought she saw a bunch of rounds lumps rising from the water, like heads. It startled her, threw her off her stride. She jumped anyway; just not as strongly as she'd planned. "Yaaahhhh!" she yelled. She flew through the air, then plunged down, down, down towards the blue, knowing that it would be all right, that she would rise up again, and her friend would make sure she was safe.

What she hit was not water, but an outcropping of rock that was hidden just below the surface of the sea. The impact was brutal. Her whole body electrified with the shock of it; a jangling that made thought, even breath, impossible. Chastity didn't know what happened from that moment until she awoke high up on the shore, well out of the way of the tide, in the lee of the sea grape bushes. Mumma was touching her shoulder and calling out her name. Mumma was crying softly. Chastity tried to lift her head, but the thrashing pain behind her eyes made her lay it back down onto the sand.

"Oh, God, God," her mother moaned. "She wake up. Chastity, you all right? What happened to you?"

"Where's the little girl?" Chastity whispered. She turned her head despite the pain.

"We have to get you to hospital," Mumma said. She bent and picked Chastity up.

Weakly, Chastity held on around her mother's neck. "Where's the little girl?" she asked again. "The little blue girl."

Her mother was hurrying towards the house. "Where your clothes, child? What you were doing?"

"I fell," Chastity told her. Better not to say that she'd jumped. "Off that big rock." She pointed at one of the large climbing rocks that were all over the beach.

"After I told you not to come and play down by the water by yourself!"

But she hadn't been by herself. The little girl had been with her.

"I only turned my back for two-twos!"

Chastity whispered, "My head hurts." She looked over her mother's shoulder. There were footprints in the sand. They disappeared at the water line.

There was something on her head. Chastity put her hand up to her forehead and pulled at the thing she found there. Her head hurt so much! Through half-closed eyes, she looked at what was in her hand: seaweed, loosely braided into a bandage. Its shiny brown leaves were bloody. It had been tied around her head, covering the big gash she could feel above her ear. Chastity probed the gash with her fingers, which came away sticky with her own blood. That was when she finally felt frightened, and clung to her mother, and started to cry.

At the hospital, they said she had a mild concussion. They wouldn't let her sleep all that night. Every time she was descending into blessed rest, a nurse or Dadda or Mumma would shake her awake. Her memories of that night were mostly of exhaustion, and crying, begging to be allowed to sleep. Towards morning, delirious with fatigue, she began to talk about the yellow girl with blue-y skin, and about the lobster that had wanted to eat her toes. She remembered

Dadda, haggard from lack of sleep himself, whispering to her mother, "Hallucinations. Poor thing." The hospital let her parents take her home that day, and she slept and slept until sunrise next morning. Her parents grounded her from the beach for a week, and forbade her to ever take her clothes off when she was outside in the open.

She never saw the yellow-blue brown girl again.

2

T HE SUN DROVE BRIGHT SPLINTERS OF LIGHT THROUGH my half-open lids. "Ow! Shit." I snapped my eyes shut again. Blind, I took stock. From the feel of rough stone under me, I was lying on the rock on the beach. Don't tell me I passed out there drunk last night. How I could do something so stupid? Suppose the tide had come up and swept me away?

It was certainly no longer night. The sun's heat was searing my thighs and the side of my face. My mouth tasted like I'd been eating carrion. Hot *buttered* carrion. A kettle-drum orchestra was playing in my head. Off-key. My belly served me notice that it was disgusted with my behaviour, and that it was about to violently register its protest. I rolled onto my stomach just in time to puke over the side of the rock. The taste and smell were awful. Everything was awful. On my stomach, I rested my head back down on the too-hot rock. I was parched and woozy. The sweaty smell of the ocean was making me queasy. The coconut trees shook and rustled their laughter.

"Oh, God, beg you, do," I muttered, "please let death come and take me this minute. I think is the only thing that will remove this taste from out my mouth."

I'd glimpsed something when I leaned over the side of the rock. What?

Gingerly, I lifted my head and looked again.

You know what? People really do go cold with fright. There was a thing washed up on the sand, not too far from my rock. It was completely covered in seaweed, except for a brown hand poking through. I was down off the rock and moving in that direction before I knew it.

I stubbed my toe against something. I gave a yip of fear and leapt back. But it was no torn-off limb. It was my bottle, half-buried in the sand.

It could stay right there. Would be a cold day in hell before I could stand the smell of alcohol again.

The hand sticking out of the bladderwrack shroud was a child's. My gut twisted again. I dropped to my knees and vomited into the sand.

I had another look. The still-wet seaweed glistened. I reached out a finger. My skin crawled. I couldn't bring myself to touch the body. There was a piece of sea grape root sticking out of the sand not far away. I crawled over, wrenched it free, brought it back. I took a deep, shuddering breath and extended the stick. The tip of it trembled so wildly that it took a second before I could aim it. I made the tip of the stick touch one end of the seaweed lump. The opposite of where I figured its head was, if it still had a . . . no. I wasn't going to think about that. My stomach agreed that it was a subject best left unexplored.

All I could feel was springy seaweed. Maybe I hadn't pressed hard enough with the stick. I breathed again—a gasp, really—and poked a little deeper this time.

The body moved. This time, I jumped back about eight feet. My bladder gave a little squirt.

Now a small groan came from inside the seaweed. How badly had the sea broken the person inside?

The child moved slowly, pushed a second arm and a leg through the seaweed. At least those were working. That got me past fear. I rushed to the child's side, started pulling the seaweed off it. "Are you hurt?" I said. "You all right?"

It was a boy, a little brown boy. He looked about two, maybe three years old. His clothing had been torn off by the sea, and his hair was a mess: shells and sand matted in it. And it was long so like a girl's.

He started a thin, hiccoughing sob. I dragged the rest of the seaweed off him. He was cut and bruised all over. His ankle was puffy and discoloured. I touched it, and he screamed with pain. He looked at me with liquid eyes, his small brown face a mask of misery. He reached for his injured leg, and moaned when his own touch hurt.

He needed a hospital. And damn it all to hell, I didn't have my cell phone. Nobody else around to help me. People didn't come out to this beach plenty; too rocky, and the sand brown with mud from the mangroves.

There was an emergency phone installed near the middle of the beach. I couldn't leave him here, alone and scared, while I went for help. Maybe I could move him? But suppose he had a broken rib and I made it worse by picking him up? I cursed myself for not bringing my cell phone. He was crying, his open mouth downturned and the sides of his tongue curling up, like babies' tongues do.

"Help!" I scanned the beach, the bushes. Still nobody.

I would have to move him. "I going to pick you up, okay? I'll be real careful."

"Hello, hie!" someone shouted. "You need help?" A man was clambering out of the water.

"Yes, please! This child—he's hurt!"

"I coming!" He was big. Had a kind of mixed look to him; black and Indian, maybe. He was wearing a garish red and black wetsuit and carrying a snorkel and fins. His thick middle jounced a little as he ran. He stopped in front of us, panting.

"You have a cell phone?" I asked him. Lots of tourists carried their valuables in waterproof pouches when they dove. "We have to call Emergency."

He shook his head. "Sorry, no." He knelt in the sand, reached for the groaning child.

"Careful," I told him. "I think his ankle break. I don't want to move him. You will stay and watch him while I go to the emergency phone? It's just over there."

"Yes. But we have to move him anyway. He too close to the water line."

"Shit."

"It's all right. We will take care of his spine. We could brace him on this." He held out one of his fins, turned it over to its flat back. Yes, it was almost as long as the little boy. I got down as low as I could—blasted knee!—and helped the man slide the fin underneath the child's back. "You take his head," he said. Together we picked the boy up. He screamed.

"Sorry, baby," I said. "We only trying to help." We carried him out of the way of the water and set him back down in the sand.

"Go and phone," the man said. As I was running away, he shouted, "I'm Hector! Goonan!"

God, yes. Should have asked him for his name. Like I couldn't do anything right today.

The emergency phone was protected in its own small shelter safely away from the tide line. Seemed to take forever to get there. My lungs started to burn. It was like breathing glass. I kept going. I was nearly weeping by the time I reached the phone. I picked up the receiver and waited the few seconds of forever until the call rang through.

"Coast Guard. What is your emergency?"

I started to babble, gasping for air: child, storm, hurt, please.

"Slow down, ma'am. Is the child breathing?"

"Yes. I think his leg break."

"Is he conscious?"

"Yes. He's bawling. And he have cuts all over his body."

"Stay on the line, please, ma'am. You going to hear me talking to someone else. I'm dispatching them to come and get you."

"All right." Fuck, what was the name of this beach? How was I going to direct them?

I heard the dispatcher talking, and the crackly voice of a man responding via some kind of machine. She told them which phone my call had come from. Of course! They could trace us that way. I breathed a little easier. *Crackle-crackle*, said the other voice.

"Ma'am?" The dispatcher was back on the line.

"I'm here."

"The Dolorosse paramedics are on their way."

"Yes, I know them." It's them had answered my call when I found Dadda on Thursday.

"Is the child with you?"

"No, he's where I found him, over near the end of the beach. Somebody's with him."

"Which end of the beach, ma'am? Northeast or southwest?"

My mind went blank. "I can't . . . I don't . . ."

"Ma'am, take a deep breath. They know the island good. They will find him. Any landmarks where he is?"

"Ahm . . . yes. A big, flat rock. About waist height. Wide enough for somebody to fall aslee . . . the mangroves!" Only one end of the beach had mangroves.

"He's near the end where the mangroves are? By a big, flat rock about waist high?"

"Yes." At least part of my brain was working.

"All right. I will tell the paramedics that. Hold again, please." I heard her talking to the paramedics. Then, from the road I couldn't see because of the wall of sea grapes, came the *wahwah* of the ambulance going by, and the popcorn sound of tyres on gravel. They were going the right way.

The dispatcher came back on the line. "They going to reach in another minute," she said.

"Okay. Thank you—"

"No, don't hang up!"

"But I have to go back to him!"

"Please stay in telephone contact with me until Jerry and Pamela tell me they find him."

"You right. That make sense."

"You doing good." Her voice had gentled. "That little boy is lucky you found him."

"Heh. I guess sometimes when you find Calamity, it's a good thing."

"Beg pardon?"

"Never mind. They reach yet?"

"Not quite . . ." The crackle of the radio call interrupted her. I wished I could understand what they were saying.

"They have located the patient, ma'am. They want me to tell you that from the racket he's making, his lungs are probably fine."

I managed to laugh a little. Now that I knew the child was getting help, reaction was setting in. My whole body shook. My sunburned face and leg were screaming at me.

"There's a Coast Guard speedboat waiting at the dock to take him to hospital."

"Already?"

"Two minutes three seconds from Cayaba to Dolorosse," she said proudly. "You could go back now."

"Thank you. Thank you." I hung up the phone and began the walk back. The drums inside my head had changed to a chorus of gongs. Two minutes, three seconds. Took almost half hour by waterbus. I stopped to wait for a bout of the spins to pass, then kept walking.

When I reached back to the little boy, the two paramedics were kneeling beside him in the sand. They had put some kind of contraption under him; like a slotted spoon with no handle. He had a hard plastic collar around his neck. The man who had helped us—Hector?—was holding the boy's head in his two hands, keeping it still. Everybody was wearing blue rubber gloves. The boy looked so frightened! "It's all right, small one," said Mr. Goonan. "Everything going to be all right." He had long black hair pulled back into a ponytail. Why a perfectly good-looking man would go and do that kind of stupidness?

Jerry looked up and saw me. "Hey, Miz L."

"He hurt bad?" I asked. "His neck?"

"The collar, you mean? Just a precaution. Pam, hand me the stethoscope there, nuh?"

The child, sobbing, said something. I didn't recognise the language.

Pamela got the stethoscope out of the black doctor bag sitting on the sand and handed it to Jerry. She looked *off*. Stone-faced, like jumbie walking on her grave. Pam was a strapping red woman with light brown skin. Not this morning, though. Her face was yellow, bloodless.

Jerry listened to the boy's chest, handed the stethoscope back to Pamela. "You check his pulse yet?" he asked her.

"Sorry." With two fingers, she touched the boy's wrist like she was touching a whip snake. "You want me to check his pupils, too?"

"No. Nothing wrong with them. Small and reactive. Miz L., you the one who found him, right?"

I told him what had happened. As I talked to him, he put his hands around the child's hips, pressed his thumbs towards each other. He started working his way down the child's good leg. "Hector, you okay there?" he asked.

"Doing fine."

Pamela said, "Pulse is regular and full at 115, BP 94/80, resps 24, SpO_2 100 percent. You want the monitor on?"

"Nah. We can do that later. Either of you know this boy? You ever see him around the island?"

I said no. Hector told them he wasn't from Dolorosse. Pamela asked, "Either of you recognise what language he speaking?"

Jerry sighed, gave her a hard look. "I recognise it. I don't understand it, but I hear it before. He don't have aphasia."

Pamela pressed her lips together. She didn't reply. Jerry was feeling the thigh of the boy's damaged leg now. "You say he was unconscious when you found him?" he asked me. "When he woke up, he vomited?"

"No, but I di . . . I don't think so. I can't remember. I'm sorry."

Jerry was close to the boy's knee. The child got agitated. He was complaining, saying the same words over and over. Jerry said, "Hector, most likely I'll hurt him when I touch his lower leg. Make sure you don't let his head move."

"All right."

"I going to work as fast as I can. Miz L., I need you to hold his torso for me."

"You sure you don't want Pamela to do it?"

"No. You the one who found him. He might remember that. And the two of you keep talking to him, all right? Look in his eyes and reassure him. Say anything you want; look like he can't understand you anyway. But keep your tone of voice calm and soothing."

"All right." I moved in to brace the child's torso. I smiled at him. He stared at me, took a shivering breath. His eyes flickered. I said sweetly, "You having a rassclaat of a morning, nuh true? Poor babbins."

Hector's startled eyes met mine. I shrugged one shoulder. He smiled.

Suddenly the boy screamed, tried to arch his back. I held him.

"I nearly finish," Jerry told us. "Allyou doing good."

The child screamed again, then burst into tears. "Look at me," I said. "Look." He did, his eyes wild and clouded. I sang,

Jane and Louisa will soon come home,
Soon come home, soon come home.

Hector joined in with me:

Jane and Louisa will soon come home,
Into this beautiful garden.

The boy's sobbing trailed into whimpering. Hector went right into

Mosquito one, mosquito two,
Mosquito jump in a hot callaloo.

I made a kissy face at the child. "Old Hector's so silly, nuh true?" I cooed. "Everbody know it's *'mosquito jump in the old man's shoe.'* "

Hector snorted.

"All right, I finish," Jerry told us. "Keep holding him, though. That will help him stay calm. Pam, look like a tib fracture. He got good sensation in the toes, good cap refill. You want to do the splint?"

Silence.

"Pam?"

"Okay." She sounded like she was agreeing to have her teeth pulled without anaesthetic. Why they let somebody so flighty work as a paramedic? But she was gentle, and quick. The child never screamed once. When I got up a little bit later, he had some kind of bright blue plastic sheath around his lower leg, keeping it from moving.

Pamela and Jerry put straps around his body and the stretcher to keep him still. Hector let go, shook his hands out. I said to him, "You have a gorgeous singing voice."

He smiled bashfully. "Men's choir. When I was in grad school."

"I'm Calamity."

His smile became a grin. He shook my hand. "Interesting name. Must have a story behind it."

Pam and Jerry picked up the stretcher. There were trails of tears on the boy's face. He must have been exhausted from battling the sea. How long he had been out there? And then strangers tie him down and take him away. "We taking him to the waterbus dock," Jerry said. "Coast Guard will take him to hospital. To Cayaba Mercy."

"I'm coming with you."

"No. I'm sorry. Regulations. You could go and visit him after. Besides, a Coast Guard officer going to want to talk to the both of you, since you were first on the scene."

"I'm right here," said a familiar voice. I turned.

It was Gene. "I decided to walk," he told Jerry. "See what I could see." His face completely neutral, he held out a piece of sandy black cloth to me.

My skirt.

"ABOUT WHAT O'CLOCK you think you found the boy?" asked Gene.

I finished wriggling into my skirt. I zipped it up. "What time it is now?" I couldn't make myself look him in the eyes, not after what he and me did last night.

"Ten of eight, ma'am."

Ma'am. Thank heaven. He wasn't going to make people know that he knew me. "I found him probably about six-thirty, quarter to seven." I swallowed. Now that some of the excitement was over, my belly was starting to turn again.

Hector nodded. "Yes, it's about that time that I heard you shouting for help."

Gene examined Hector a little longer than was necessary. He scribbled in his notebook, then said, "You went for a sea bath? You still have some sand on your skirt there. Left hip."

"Thanks." I brushed the sand away. What had him so vexed? Never mind. Stand tall. Look him in the eye. "Yes. I went for a sea bath."

"And your relationship to this gentleman?"

My headache made itself known again. "No relations—I mean, no relation. I never saw this man before this morning."

"I see." Gene made another note in his book. His face was a little less grim now. "So, you came down to the beach, at about what o'clock, you would say?"

"Maybe six-twenty?" I lied.

"And where you were when you discovered the child?"

"On that rock over there." I needed water. My head was spinning.

"So, you were lying on top of a big, flat rock with Mr.—?"

"Goonan," said Hector. "But I wasn't—"

Shit. "No, he wasn't—"

"I wasn't with her. I was snorkeling. Didn't see her until later. I was just heading back to my boat when I heard her calling for help."

"And what condition was he in when you found him?"

"He was under a pile of seaweed."

"You know what kind of seaweed?"

"Bladderwrack, I think. It's still over there. I could show you."

"In a bit, ma'am. Any jellyfish were around the area?"

I couldn't remember. My head was spinning. "No, I don't think so." I felt queasy. "Anybody have drinking water?"

"Here." Hector held out a water bottle wrapped in a screaming-red neoprene sleeve. He had unclipped it from the waist of his suit. The sleeve matched the suit perfectly. "I been drinking from it," he said. "Sorry."

"I not fussy."

"Evidently," Gene grumbled. Fuck him. I grabbed the water bottle and sucked in huge mouthfuls. The water was warm and stale, but to me, it tasted wonderful. My stomach began to settle.

"He was conscious when you found him?" Gene asked me. "Or not?"

"I . . . I not sure. All I saw was a lump of seaweed, you know? He was under it. When I poked it, he moved."

Gene nodded, turned to Mr. Goonan. "That tallies with your memory of the events?"

"I wasn't there when she found him."

Gene pressed his lips together. Scribble, scribble. Bastard! He been trying to see if he could catch Hector in a lie! "And you are?" asked Gene.

"Hector Goonan. I lecture at you-wee Mona. I'm visiting Cayaba."

Mona campus, University of the West Indies. Yes, I had marked the Jamaican accent.

"And you lecture in what, Mr. Goonan?"

"Marine biology."

I took another swig of water. The sudden movement of my head brought on another wave of nausea. "Excuse me," I managed to choke out. I ran behind the rock and puked.

"You all right?" It was Hector. Gene was with him.

"I'm fine. Something I dra . . . I ate." I washed my mouth out with more of Goonan's water. Spat. I stuck out a hand.

"Somebody help me up?" They both leapt forward, almost crashing into each other in the process. Gene made it to my hand first. He helped me to my feet.

"You sure you're fine?" asked Gene.

"Yes. You were right. A drink of water can work wonders."

His face went frozen. "Then will you show me exactly where you found the child, please?"

Oh, my overquick mouth. "Over here," I said.

The headache had faded to a sullen, low gonging. The smell of the sea wasn't making me so queasy any more. The storm had washed up the usual detritus; plastic drink bottles, shivered timbers, a shredded shirt embedded in the sand. The scrap of cloth was bright pink, with a pattern of hibiscuses and dancing girls. Just looking at it made my head want to start pounding again. Give thanks, no one would be wearing that monstrosity any more. One less piece of tasteless tourist attire gaudying up Cayaba. We came upon my bottle sticking up out of the sand. Gene pulled it free, sniffed at the neck of the bottle. I pretended I didn't recognise it. When we reached the seaweed, Gene knelt and prodded at it. Hector and I stood out of his way.

I drank again from the water bottle in its garish sleeve. Plain water to give me plain courage. For it was time to be honest with myself. To survive all the shame this world will throw at you, you have to hold yourself tall, look your accuser straight in the eye. Even if it's your own face looking back at you.

You know the story about Old Joe, the slave who helped dig all those people out way back then after the big hurricane? 1831, I think. For four sleepless days, Old Joe worked with the rescue team. He just seemed to know where there were people buried in the rubble. Since then, Cayabans talk about people who are "finders."

You must understand; finders probably rank right up there with Bigfoot and the Loch Ness Monster. But still; sometimes, not often, little Chastity used to find. Seemed so, anyway. I found little things: dropped paper clips, lost keys, the change that slid down behind the sofa. Made sense for a little girl to find little things, nuh true? Once in a while I would get a prickling in the fingers of my left hand; the last two fingers that were fused together at the lowest joint. Sometimes when that happened, I could just put my hand on something that had gone missing. Not every time. But often enough that Dadda used to joke about his little finder girl. Often enough that my school friends would beg me to help them look for things they had lost.

I grew up. Eventually you stop hoping that Atlantis was real. The finding itch stopped, even though I was sad to see it go. I hadn't felt it for decades now.

But yesterday, my fingers had begun to tingle again. All these years willing it to work again. And when it did come back, I didn't take it seriously. Maybe it's not this morning I'd found that child. Maybe it was last night. Maybe my itchy hand had been telling me he was out in the water, in need. But I had been too busy throwing myself a pity party.

You can't find your very large ass with two hands, said my rational mind. *No such thing as finders. What you would have done if you knew he was out there? Charged into that rough water? Drowned yourself trying to help?*

But logic didn't make a difference. The part of me that didn't pay no mind to reason sobbed, *My fault. Mine.*

"*By the pricking of my thumbs,*" I whispered to myself.

"Pardon?" Hector said.

"Nothing. Nothing." I might have found the boy before

he broke his leg, before he lost his family, before he nearly drowned.

"Calamity, you saw anything else when you came down to the beach this morning?" asked Gene. "Maybe pieces of a broken boat, anything like that?"

"Not a thing." He'd slipped, used my name. I hoped Hector hadn't noticed.

Gene frowned. "And no reports of any capsized boats in the storm," he said almost to himself. "I wonder where his parents are?"

I wondered where my skirt had been. And why the rass my so-helpful fingers hadn't led me to it before Gene had found it.

In my head, something was surfacing.

The daylight was hurting my eyes. I shaded my face from the sun. I blinked in the glare.

My breath stopped in my throat. The sun went still in the sky for an eye-blink, and the waves hovered mid-curl. *A membrane had flickered across the boy's eyes whenever the sun got in his eyes. He didn't seem to understand clothing. He had a bluish tinge to his skin.*

Memories sideswiped me: of a bluish-yellow brown body bobbing and swimming as though the sea were its home, gurgling at young Chastity in an alien tongue.

Dadda and Mumma had told Chastity that she'd imagined the little girl! Would the little boy waddle when he walked upright? Did he play at swimming through schools of tiny fish, his mouth open to catch them?

Gene stood and looked out to sea as though he were hoping a boat would show up with the boy's parents in it. Maybe that would never happen. Maybe the child's sire and dam didn't need boats to travel the waves.

And maybe pigs would fly out my ass and dance the lambada.

Gene was right: grief turning my brains to shit. Imagining mermaids behind every tree; imagining the trees and all.

But just suppose . . .

"You need me here any longer?" I asked Gene.

"No, I suppose not." What a grumpy voice!

"Good. Then I'm going to the hospital. Mr. Goonan—"

"Hector, please. After what we just been through together. I could give you my number?"

Oh, nice. "Certainly," I said.

His face like thunder, Gene tore a page out of his notebook so Hector and I could exchange numbers. "I work nights," said Hector, "and I have to get some sleep now, or I'm going to drop right here. But please call me tonight and tell me how the little boy doing?"

"No problem. Or you can call me." Then I hurried away. I wanted to take a good look at the little boy's eyes. Wait till Ife heard this! Not now, though. Maybe she wouldn't be up this early on a Sunday morning. Didn't want to disturb her. Not after the way I'd messed up with her last night.

GENE WAS ALREADY IN THE HOSPITAL waiting room when I got there. The grim face went back on the moment he saw me. Probably mine didn't look too welcoming, either. "What you doing here?" I asked.

"My job. Trying to help that child."

There were about twelve chairs against the walls of the waiting room. White enamelled metal with padded vinyl seats. Probably standard hospital issue. Another man was sitting on the other side of the room, leafing through a magazine he wasn't really looking at. I sat in a chair next to Gene. Under my breath I muttered, "Coast Guard, enh? You didn't tell me."

"Wasn't any need. Besides, you didn't tell me about Hector."

"Hector? I met him this morning. Minutes before you did." What the ass was this? One sympathy fuck and now he owned me?

"Hello, hello," said a woman in a doctor's lab coat as she bustled into the waiting room. Her features looked Chinese. "Who's here for the little boy who doesn't speak English?"

"I am." Gene stood up and flashed his badge. "I'm Officer Eugene Meeks, with the Coast Guard."

She shook his hand. "I'm Dr. Chow. So pleased to meet you."

The name. That stuck-up voice and manner. The face. "Evelyn?" I said.

"Yes?" She turned towards me, chin high. She still had the same hauteur. Her mouth still formed perfect, pinched syllables.

I stood up. "Evelyn, it's me. Calamit . . . Chastity. Chastity Lambkin."

Evelyn slid her glasses from the top of her head onto her nose and squinted at me. Her face cleared. "My God," she said, "it's Charity Girl!"

I discovered that I still hated her. I wished we'd never studied that bloody novel in school. Evelyn's nickname for me had followed me until I left. "It's Calamity now," I told her.

"Of course it's a calamity! That poor child!"

"No, Evelyn. My name. It's Calamity now."

"Calamity?" said Evelyn. "That's your *name*?"

Thank heaven I'd put on some decent clothes to come to the hospital: good pants, the fitted cream blouse with the cap sleeves, a bit of lipstick. At least I looked respectable to face Miss Priss Evelyn Chow. I turned up the corners of my mouth in a fake smile.

"How is the boy, Doctor?" asked Gene. "Mistress Lambkin probably wants to know, too; she's the one who rescued him."

"Me and Hector. You know; who I just met today?"

Evelyn boggled. "*You* rescued him?" She still looked like a hungry baby bird when she let her mouth gape open like that.

"Well, I found him . . ."

"But my dear! How wonderful of you!" She beamed at me and patted my hand like I was five years old and had managed to recite my ABC's in mostly the correct order. "Lucky little boy. What a good thing you had your wits about you."

Well, eventually I had, anyway. "He will be all right?" I asked. I pulled my fingers out of her too-warm grasp.

"We think so. No apparent head injury." She turned to Gene. "He blew overboard a boat in the storm last night, I think your people said?"

"We don't know for sure," Gene told her. "No sign of his parents. His leg is broken?"

"Yes. A greenstick fracture. Common for children. Their bones are so flexible that they often don't break all the way through, just bend and splinter. Like when you try to break a green twig."

I winced. Ifeoma had broken her leg when she was young. I still remembered the horrible dull crack when she had jumped off the roof of my car and landed wrong.

"I've got him in a cast. He has some bruises, but other than that and the fractured ankle, he seems all right. Physically, anyway. Can't really tell, for nobody here can understand him. But he's had no adverse reactions to any of his treatment so far. We'll monitor him over the next few days, just to make sure." Evelyn frowned. "There are other things about him that are disturbing me, though."

"Like what, Doctor?" asked Gene.

"For one thing, his chest is overbroad for a child his age. I wish I could understand what he says!"

"Maybe it's German?" Gene suggested.

"No, I speak German. It's not German."

Of course she spoke German. And French, I remembered. Had been top of our class in school. And she was still as graceful as a hummingbird. Bitch.

"His eyes are strange, too," she said. "He seems to have some sort of haw."

"Of what?" I asked.

"A transparent third eyelid," she said.

My heart jumped a beat.

"Sometimes a reptile is born with haws," continued Evelyn; "a throwback, you know? And cats and dogs have vestigial ones. Humans too. Not usually fully developed, though. And he has rough skin on his inner knees."

"Like callous?" asked Gene. "Could somebody have been keeping him bound up?"

Evelyn looked horrified. "Oh, God; you really think so?"

He shrugged. "It's possible."

"I didn't notice any ligature marks, though."

"Can I see him?" I asked. Maybe if I looked at him closer, I could convince myself he was just a little boy. Bigfoot wasn't real, either. Or happy endings.

"You know," Evelyn said to Gene, "you might be right. That big chest, the eyelids, the webbed fingers and toes . . ."

Webbed? Oh God. He really was like my mermaid girl. "I want to see him," I told them, a little louder.

"Even the webbing is odd," she said.

"How you mean?" I asked.

"Some humans are born with fingers and toes fused together."

"Like you forget?" I held up my left hand, the two last spread to show the membrane of skin that didn't quite come up to the lowest joint. "Partial syndactyly."

"I *did* forget." She flushed. "Yours is pretty common; only between two fingers, and so slight it doesn't impair your ability to function. His is like that, too; tiny. Not like some people where it's so pronounced that it pulls the longer fingers down to match the shorter ones, and the whole hand curls up. His not worth putting him through the trauma of surgery. They will be something for him to impress his school friends with." She smiled.

"So what's strange?" Gene asked.

"To have them between all four fingers."

He nodded. "With all those deformities," he said, "maybe his parents are embarrassed about him. They keep the child locked up, sometimes restrained. They don't teach him language or social skills."

"What a horrible thing!" said Evelyn. "And no sign at all of his parents?"

I felt a wave of anxious heat. "I need to see him," I whispered. I rubbed my sweaty, tickling hands against my thighs. The rush passed through me.

Then a high wail came from down one of the corridors. "That's him!" Dr. Chow gasped. She took off at a run. Gene followed, me at his heels.

The little boy was standing on the floor of his room, feet wide apart, holding on to the leg of the crib for balance. There was a nurse bent over him, shaking a finger at him. "Bad! You mustn't get out of bed, understand? You're sick!" The nurse turned as we came rushing into the room. "I'm sorry he disturbed you, Doctor," he said.

"It's all right."

There was a thick plaster cast on the boy's leg. They'd diapered him. With his plump body, the diaper gave him the appearance of a tiny sumo wrestler. He'd been crying. Would he let me pick him up?

"Evelyn, it's okay for him to be putting weight on that leg so soon?"

"Yes, if it's not hurting him. It will help him put down new bone tissue."

All I needed to hear. "Come to Auntie Calamity," I whispered. I reached my arms out to him. He stretched his out to me, his palms wide. Yes, he did have webbed fingers. Then he dropped down onto his hands and tried to walk to me, bumsie in the air. Like the blue girl had. Must have hurt his leg to do that, for he lifted it in the air and started crying again. I rushed to him and picked him up, ignored the twinge in my lower back. I cradled his frightened little body to me. He immediately put a thumb in his mouth. With the other hand, he grabbed my ear.

"Ow!" I tried to pull his hand away, but he wouldn't let go. He had reached for comfort, hard, with both hands. If my heart had been melting for him before, it was like butter in the hot sun now.

"Look how easy he went to you! You got to be his mummy!" said the nurse.

"No." He didn't belong to me. *Yes,* said my heart. *Mine.*

"Odd, that crawl," Evelyn said.

"Maybe they kept him somewhere where he couldn't stand all the way up," Gene told her.

"Please don't tell me that. I don't even want to imagine it."

"He's had a long day," I said. I pulled myself tall and officious. Maybe they would go for it if I brazened it through. "He's coming home with me, right?" Child needed someone to mother him, not a hospital bed in a lonely room.

Gene said, "No, I . . ."

Evelyn frowned. "To your home? No, my dear. That's not how we do things."

Chuh, I thought. *Go 'way with your stoosh big island self.* And what was this "my dear, my dear," like she was my bloody mother? After me and she were the same age.

"He has to go into custody till his parents are found. Isn't that right, Mr. Meeks?"

"Yes. Quite right. We're looking for them. Going to want to talk to them about this boy's injuries."

Damn. "But I can visit with him today?"

"If you really want to," replied Evelyn.

That would have to do. Gene glared a "good day" at me, and Evelyn left to finish up her work. I sat on the chair beside the bed. The boy had fallen asleep in my arms. "I'm sorry," I whispered to him. I tried to see the insides of his knees, but he stirred. I couldn't bear to wake him. Besides, he felt good in my arms. Not like I had anywhere to go.

By the time the little boy woke up mid-afternoon, everybody at the nurses' station knew my name, where I worked, how old I was; hell, probably my bra size and all.

The child lay on his back and looked around him. He had a puzzled frown, and tear-tracks down his face. I went to his crib. They'd put the slats up to keep him from falling out. "Think I'll remember how these blasted things work?"

He stuck his thumb in his mouth and stared at me. When

small children look at you like that, it's like they're seeing right into your deepest heart.

Took me some fiddling, but I finally was able to lower the slats at one side of the crib. He'd raised himself up on his elbows to look at me. His legs were spraddled, so it was plain to see the marks on his inner knees and on the ankle without the cast. Gently, I sat beside him on the bed. I licked my thumb and used it to wipe away his dried tears. And still, he just *looked*.

I reached to touch the marks on his knees, but an orderly bustled in, wheeling a food cart. I pulled my hand away. "Lunch time!" she chirped. She parked the cart, checked the boy's chart at the foot of his bed. "Ohmigod," she said. "He the boy who nearly drowned last night. Nuh true?"

"Yes. This is him."

"God bless. God bless." She hauled out a wheeled table from behind the door, and put his lunch tray on it. "The nurses could feed him," she told me.

I pulled the tray towards me. "No. I will do it." *Mine.*

She nodded. With a final "God bless," she pushed her cart out of the room.

The child informed me of something or other. "You think so?" I replied, improvising. I took his hands, spread the fingers to see the membranes again. So strange! But not unheard-of, Evelyn had said. I peered into his eyes. They just looked like eyes to me. He pulled his head away and spoke again, sounding frustrated this time. I felt foolish, inspecting a lost and injured child, looking for what? Gills? Scales? Jesus. Had to stop fooling myself. The sea didn't have people living in it. Somebody would know what language he spoke. Somebody would find his parents, or the remnants of them.

I took the lids off the containers on his tray. I picked up one of the dishes and a spoon. "Well," I said to him, "look like you and me can't palaver. So let me introduce you to the joys of grape Jell-O."

The spoon seemed to be a complete mystery to him. He opened his mouth wide for it, all right, but then he clamped his corn-kernel baby teeth down on it, hard, and refused to let go. Either his parents had made him eat with his hands, or his brain was abnormal, like his body.

Gently, I tried to tug the spoon free, but he kept it in his teeth and tossed his head back and forth like a puppy's. Surprised a laugh out of me.

And then he did something precious. He giggled; a liquid, happy noise. My heart lifted to see that he could feel joy. The parents hadn't quite broken him, then.

The Jell-O was not a success. After that first, accidental mouthful, he wouldn't swallow any more. He just screwed up his face and spat it out. Next try, he wouldn't even do that; he pulled away from the spoon I'd put to his lips and twisted his head from side to side. "If Ifeoma had been this fussy when she was small," I said to him, "she would be bony like one stray dog now."

I had better luck with the applesauce. Got a little of it into him. But the real hit was the porridge. He swallowed the first spoonful and immediately opened his mouth for more. And the minute I looked away, distracted by a nurse who'd come to check on us, he had the bowl up and overturned on his head. The long tangles of his hair were slimy with porridge.

They gave me a basin of water so I could wash the mess out. Ignorant of his cast, he tried to climb entirely into the basin. God knows what kind of deprivation they had been keeping him in. He was new to everything. It was like having a baby again and discovering the world again with him. He drew me in like a sponge draws water. I swear a current flowed between us, warm and fluid.

I towelled his head dry; as dry as that mess of dreadlocks would get. Some of the trash in it had been *tied* there; pieces of shells, mostly. How anybody could do that to their child's hair?

His gurgling chuckle sounded like "agway, agway." He gazed up into my face like I had all the lovely secrets of the world written there. He whimpered if I tried to go from the room. I didn't mind. I stayed.

As far as he was concerned, his bedsheet was a toy. He clambered around in it and twisted and turned until he was practically mummified.

"No, Agway," I said, unwinding him. Looked too much like the seaweed he'd been wrapped in on the beach.

He kept pulling his diapers off. Didn't bother him to piss and shit right where he was. "Someone going to have to toilet-train you," I told him, "before it's too late for you to learn." And milord, that hair. I was itching to wash it. Fine if his parents wanted to be Rastas and smoke ganja and make their hair grow wild like any rats' nest, but it wasn't right to drag a child into it.

Little more time, he began to reach for his injured leg and wince. I rang for a nurse. She had a look at him, then brought him some liquid painkiller in a dropper.

"Not baby aspirin?" I asked her.

"No. Could kill them."

"You lie! That's what I used to give my daughter when she was little."

"Me, too. Nobody told us different."

"She liked the taste of it too bad."

"Yes. You have to keep those things away from them."

Agway got the hang of the dropper pretty quickly. I guess it was sort of like a nipple. He startled at the taste of the first drops of the medicine. The look on his face was priceless.

The nurse pulled the dropper away. Playing stern, she shook her finger at him. "Don't spit it out, now," she said. We made encouraging faces at him, mimed taking medicine from the dropper, pretended it tasted good. He screwed up his face, but he finally took it all. "That's a good boy," crooned the nurse. She patted him on his damp head and left. He whimpered again. His leg was still bothering him.

"Never mind, babbins. The pain will stop soon." I gathered him up, took him to the armchair over by the window. I sat in it and rocked him. "The pill bottle was on my bed," I told him. "Rita and Sharmini and me used to work in that gift store down by Post Road. I can't remember the name of it now. Selling all kind of stupidness to the white people, you know the way; dried coconuts carved into monkey heads, shit like that. Anyway, Rita and Sharmini came over to my apartment the Friday night for dinner. They had a case of Banks beer with them. By the time we finished eating our buljol and I put Ife to bed, we were three sheets to the wind. I found a radio station playing tumpa. We turned it up loud. Pretty soon we were dancing around the room, laughing and carrying on. Ife just slept. She was used to my carousing."

Agway made a little sobbing sound. He laid his head against my chest.

"Next morning," I said, "I had one motherass hangover, you see? And all I could find in the apartment was a half-empty bottle of baby aspirin. I took about six. Went to the kitchen for some water to wash them down. Found a Banks beer left in the fridge, so I opened that and drank it instead."

Agway put his thumb in his mouth and stared up at me.

"Don't look at me like that!" I said. "I was only nineteen! I just turned my back for a *minute!*"

I rocked him. "When I got back into the room, she was sitting on the bed, eating down the aspirin. No safety tops in those days. Such a big grin she had on her face, so proud of herself. She offered me the bottle with three tablets left in it. She wanted to share the pretty sweeties with me. Child always had more heart than sense."

Agway sighed. He tangled his free hand in his own hair. What was this obsession with grabbing onto hair?

"I called the doctor. He told me to stick my finger down her throat to make her throw up, and if that didn't work, to go to Emergency quick. It worked, though. She heaved up a little orange ball of baby aspirin."

Agway's thumb fell out of his mouth. He took a long, shuddering breath, held it forever, then let it out. Poor thing was deep asleep.

And it was now evening. Time to leave him. I wanted my dinner. My stomach was so empty, my belly button was trying to kiss my backbone.

I took him over to the crib and laid him down in it. He never woke. I pulled the thin cotton sheet up around him and kissed his cheek. I put up the railing. My hands remembered how to work it now. I'd slipped right back into the groove, like three decades hadn't gone by since Ife had been this small. "I going come back tomorrow, babby." I reached in and patted his good leg. My hand touched the calloused knee. I jerked my fingers away. Then, curious, I touched the rough spot again. He didn't wake. The spot was rough and scraped my fingers till I ran them the other way. Then it was smooth. What callous felt like that?

I tiptoed out of the room. Fry bake for dinner. Yes. With butter. And saltfish. Telling Agway that story had put a taste for saltfish in my mouth. And maybe some callaloo for Dadda. His mouth was too soft nowadays for fry bake.

I stopped where I was in the hallway. Rewound my mental tape. Deleted the thought about callaloo. Love them or hate them, people get hooks into you. When they leave, you have to take the hooks out, one by one.

I went to the nurses' station. The nurse who'd brought Agway's painkiller smiled at me. "Heading home?" she asked.

"Yes. I going to come back tomorrow."

The nurse consulted her clipboard. "No, Children's Services is transferring him tomorrow."

"So soon? To where?"

She gave me a sympathetic look. "The home where they send orphans. On Gracie Street, by the old post office."

Oh, great. A baby detention centre. "How long they going to keep him there?"

"Couldn't tell you, you know. Probably till they find his parents or a foster home for him."

"I can foster him," I heard myself saying. Crap. What the behind was wrong with my brain? I didn't want to foster nobody.

"They have official foster parents. You can't just volunteer to take a child so."

"That's all right, that's just fine," I said. "Sure he's in excellent hands. So good night, enh?"

"Good night."

I made a relieved escape towards the car park. No way I wanted to mind a three-year-old at this stage of my life.

*   *   *

Aɴᴅ ᴡʜᴀᴛ ᴀ ᴘɪᴇᴄᴇ ᴏꜰ ᴄᴏᴍᴍᴏᴛɪᴏɴ when the waterbus reached Dolorosse! Coast Guard and police cars lining the strip of grass around the ferry dock. Light from must be a dozen flashlights dancing over by the low cliff beside the waterbus dock. Men's voices shouting from over there. Yellow police tape blocking off the edge of the cliff. What in blue blazes . . . ? I drove down the ramp, pulled up beside the little covered plaza where pedestrians could wait for the waterbus.

Mr. Lee was *outside* his booth, pacing up and down *on* the plaza! I almost didn't recognise him; I only ever saw his head and his chest. He came towards the car.

"Evening, Mr. Lee." I held up my waterbus pass for him to see.

"Evening." He held my car door open for me. He wasn't paying any mind to whether I had my pass or not. He kept glancing over his shoulder to what was going on at the cliff.

"What happening? Like somebody get hurt?"

"Somebody get dead."

"What?" I peered around him. Over by the cliff, a man was preparing to climb down a rope lowered over the side. It's a wetsuit he was wearing? I couldn't see for sure. "Somebody fell over the side? Who?"

"Don't know yet. They still trying to get whoever it is out of the water."

"Lawdamercy." I made it almost to the yellow tape, Mr. Lee jittering along behind me, before a policewoman stopped us.

"Step back, please."

"But who it is?" I asked. I craned my neck. An inflatable dinghy was bobbing in the water. Three people in wetsuits inside it. The Coast Guard logo shone from its side.

"Just step back, please, madam."

Blasted woman wouldn't let us get any closer. Me and Mr. Lee fell back a few feet to where an empty ambulance was parked. He had his arms clasped around his narrow upper body. He looked a little shivery. "You all right?" I asked him.

"I don't like to be near the dead," he said. "You ever been to those little islands over there?" He pointed out over the sea.

What that had to do with the dead? "You mean like Dutchie and St. Cyprian's? They off limits." Except for the official boat tours. Those islands were monk seal mating grounds, and the seals were Cayaba's cash cows.

Mr. Lee smiled. "You ever know 'off limits' to stop young boys? They didn't used to guard them so well when I was small. Me and my friends had a way to row over to Dutchie after school. Collect booby eggs, roast them over a fire."

"Awoah. Nowadays they fine your rass if they catch you with a booby egg."

"And if Johnson get back in power, he going to turn it to a jail sentence. Anyway, the boys and me stopped going after a while. Shallow water out there, rocks jooking up. Those rocks tear up a slave ship once."

"Yeah, yeah, and the ghosts of drowned slaves haunt the islands to this day, blah, blah. I read the brochure."

He hugged himself more tightly. "All right then," he said. "I won't tell you what me and Tommy Naya saw out Dutchie way that day. But I don't like to be near the dead. They don't stay peaceful."

My skin pimpled. I was never going to hang out with Mr. Lee again. "You don't have to stay, you know. You must be done work for the night."

He gave me a sheepish grin. "I want to see what going to happen."

So we kept each other company.

Who knew rescue work was so boring? I found out about Mr. Lee's bad back, his cousin in the Philippines who was a lawyer, and the best way to cook bitter melon. He knew I had a daughter. He even knew her name. "Yeah, man," he said. "After she been visiting you here for so long now? Sometimes while she waiting for the waterbus, she will get out the car and come talk to me. How she going with her Neurolinguistics course?"

"All right," I said. So Ife and Mr. Lee were friends. Me, I only knew his name because Dadda had told me it.

There was a hollow shout from down at the base of the cliff. A couple of the policemen ran to look over the edge. "Like something happening," said Mr. Lee.

Our Cerberus was still guarding the way, but she was more interested in what was happening behind her at the cliffside. She had her head cranked over her shoulder to see better, so she didn't notice when we snuck around in front of her and went to the other side of the cordoned-off area. It was darker over there; maybe we'd be able to get closer.

"Come under the tape with me, nuh?" I said to Mr. Lee.

"You better not," came a low voice from the darkness at our feet. Mr. Lee gave a little yip of fear, bit it off quickly.

Jamdown accent. "Hector?" I said, peering into the shadows.

"Yes." Hector stood up from the ground to his full height. Mr. Lee grabbed my arm. Hector stepped out where we could see him better. This time, the wetsuit had bright blue panels contrasting the black ones.

I patted Mr. Lee's hand. "Don't fret. I know him."

Mr. Lee blew out a hard breath. "Jeezam. Nearly make me jump out my soul case and gone. You nearly kill me, man."

"Sorry," said Hector. His voice was flat. He looked to where the police were now yanking on a couple of ropes, pulling something heavy up the cliff face. The flashlights were dancing double time, and the shouted advice coming faster. The policewoman was over there now, shouting along with the others.

"They tell me I have to go down to the station and give a report," Hector said. "It's me who found them. The bodies."

Mr. Lee squeaked, "More than one?"

"Yeah. A woman and a man. I don't think they were dead long. Not enough decomposition. But the waves mash them up against the rocks."

I swallowed. "They fell in?"

His face was grey. He looked desolate. "You know how it feel to touch an arm when all the bones in it break?"

"Fuck."

"Jeezam."

I asked him, "How you come to find them?"

"I was swimming."

"At night?"

"That's when the seals are awake."

"The seals?" Who watched seals at night?

Over by the cliff side, the policemen pulled up a body bag, heavy with its contents. Then a second one. Hector's gaze was grim.

"Jeezam," said Mr. Lee.

Hector said, "I think it's the little boy's parents."

"Don't joke," I whispered.

"No joke."

A knot of people moved away from the cliff side, bearing the two body bags. "Oh! They taking them over to the ambulance!" I said. "Come quick!"

We got there as they were opening the back doors of the ambulance. Three policemen and a paramedic helped the others to load the bodies in. A Coast Guard man, looking around, called out, "Mr. Goonan?" It was Gene.

Hector shouldered his way under the yellow tape. "Right here," he said. "We going now?"

Gene turned and spotted me and Mr. Lee at the same time that the policewoman did. Gene started forward. The policewoman barrelled towards us, shouting, "I told the two of allyou to remove yourself from the premises!"

Hector said, "They were keeping me company."

"Madge," said Gene, "I think they could stay." Madge glared at us but didn't say anything.

"Watch it!" yelled one of the men packing the bodies. Too late. The body they were carrying slipped out of the open front of the bag like a guinepe slipping out its skin. It thudded to the ground.

"Ohmigod," groaned Mr. Lee. Hector put his hand to his mouth.

"Put him back in the bag!" Gene barked. "Now!"

Everybody knew that the Cayaba Police Force and the Coast Guard had a steady rivalry going between them, but right now, nobody bothered to tell Gene that he was out of order for giving orders to policemen. They just started stuffing the man back into the bag.

But I had already seen. A black man, maybe mid-twenties, skin torn and bruised all over. Not a stitch on him; naked as a johncrow scalp. He had a dark patch of callous on the inside of the knee I could see. Agway's father?

The men were having trouble getting him bagged. His tubby body was loose like a sack of flour, his limbs snaky as noodles. Even with the tangle of dreads, I could see that his skull had a strange dent in it. All the bones broken, Hector had told us. I must have sobbed. Mr. Lee had tears in his eyes.

"Please come away," said Madge, gently this time.

Mr. Lee nodded and began heading back to the plaza. "I going," I told Madge. But I couldn't make myself move off just yet.

The men got the body into the ambulance. As they were closing the double doors, one of the man's arms flopped out of the bag. In the glow from the flashlights, I could see the webbing between his fingers, like a duck's. I gasped, loudly enough that Gene heard me.

"Fucking hell," muttered the paramedic. He rushed between the two policemen, shoved the arm in, slammed the doors closed. I glanced at Hector. He had his head down, a hand covering his eyes. He hadn't seen.

I said, "Gene, is he . . . ?" Like his son? What were the chances that exactly the same abnormalities would breed true?

Gene caught my gaze. Held it. Shook his head slightly. So I didn't finish the sentence. What? Don't make like I know Gene? Or don't ask the question I had been about to ask?

"Mr. Goonan," said one of the policemen. "Come with us, please."

"Yes. Of course." Hector followed him, got into the back of a police car. Gene was still looking hard at me. He pressed his forefinger against his lips: *sshh.* My mind was in turmoil, my heart pounding. But I nodded. Whichever one he was asking me to keep quiet about, I wouldn't say anything.

I turned and stumbled back to the plaza. The two adults and Agway, in their boat. Got caught in the storm. Blown off course. That must be what happened. The boat, caught in the Shark's Teeth, just like Captain Carter's slave ship. Agway's fat beach ball body buoyed up. Swept to shore. But the adults didn't make it.

When I reached the plaza, Mr. Lee's car was pulling out. He stopped and stuck his head out his window. "You're a drinking woman?" he asked me.

I nodded. "Oh, yes."

"Then take a dram or two tonight," he advised me. "I know that's what I'm going to do." He waved me goodbye and went his ways.

I was shaking. I leaned against the hood of my car for support. Maybe Gene had only been telling me not to make a fuss, not to upset Hector even more. Hector, swimming through the ink of the sea at night, and bumping into a body whose every bone had been smashed to shards . . .

The ambulance rolled over to the waterbus dock, followed by the police cars and the one Coast Guard car. Gene wouldn't let his two eyes make four with mine. I looked for the car that Hector was in. There. He waved at me from the back seat, but before I could go over there, I heard the thrum behind me of a waterbus pulling up to the dock. A waterbus so soon? But they never came on time, much less *early*. Oh. This would be a special run.

I watched until they were all loaded onto the Coast Guard ferry and on their way. I got into my car, but my hand was trembling too much to turn the key in the ignition. So I sat. My breath shuddered in and out of my lungs.

In the quiet, the only thing left to hear was the boom of the waves below as they crashed into the overhang they had worn into the cliff, century by century.

I usually loved to fall asleep to the booming sound.

Those waves could wear down rock, and pulverize bone.

I wouldn't be getting any sleep tonight.

Ife! I hadn't called her about any of this! I tried a few times, longing to hear her voice, but the reception to Cayaba was bad tonight. I couldn't wait until Gilmor Saline boosted the cell phone signal on Dolorosse.

When I got home, the house felt so lonely and strange. I didn't have an appetite any more. Didn't want to call anybody. Didn't want to go down the dark hallway to the darker bedroom. Thought about a drink, but this morning's hangover was still strong in my mind. Eventually I just sat on the settee, reading *Buxton Spice*.

A wash of hot air came and went in the living room, like somebody had opened the front door. Mrs. Soledad still had a key; and the Lessings from over the way. "Hello?" I called out.

No answer. I took off my reading glasses and went and peered down the hallway. The front door was closed.

I heard a little *thump* from over by the settee. A toy car lying on top of my open book tipped over onto its side. The fuck? Where that came from?

I'd gotten chilled, sitting so still for so long. I turned the ceiling fan off. Rubbing my arms to bring some warmth back to them, I went to investigate the toy car. But it wasn't a car. I picked the toy up. Dumpy! Chastity's old dump truck! Dadda must have saved him from the sea somehow. Just like the bastard not to tell me.

Dumpy was smaller than I remembered him. His yellow and blue body was dinged and half his red trim had peeled off, but my fingers still knew the scratchy feel of him, and the right back wheel with the nick in it that made him wobble as he rolled. There were even some sparkly grains of sand still in his hopper. Decades-old sand.

How he came to be on the settee, though? I couldn't see

anything to give me a clue. I knelt down and looked under the settee, which reminded me to take today's aspirin for my arthritis. Didn't look like anything was under there.

As I got back up, I braced myself on the settee cushion with one hand. The weight compressed the cushion till I could feel the springs of the settee frame beneath. Awoah. I took the two cushions up and found a ballpoint pen with the nib missing, two ten-dollar coins, and an afro pick. So long I hadn't seen one of those. Bet you Dumpy had rolled down to the back of the settee years ago.

Someone banged on the front door. I leapt about a foot in the air, my heart pounding back a response. Who the rass . . . ?

A muffled voice called, "Mistress Lambkin? Calamity?"

The hands on the clock said almost midnight. The banging went on. I stomped to the door. Somebody was going to get their ass handed back to them on a platter.

I yanked the door open. It was Gene. Again. This was getting creepy. And he was Coast Guard, too. Just what I needed; a stalker *cop*. "Officer Meeks," I said, keeping it formal.

"I want to talk to you. I could come inside?"

Not a bit of it. I stepped onto the porch. At least he wouldn't trap me in the house. "Well, it's kind of late and I had a long day. I'd be happy to talk to you tomorrow."

With a look of surprise, he checked his watch. "Jeezam. It late in truth. I didn't wake you?"

I shook my head and edged towards the steps.

"I came to say thanks," he said.

"For what? Oh." For keeping my mouth shut back at the cliff.

"And I came to apologise. I had no business acting possessive on the beach this morning."

"Huh. No, you didn't. And what about at the hospital?"

A look of embarrassment came over his face. "At the hospital, too. And I had no right getting into an argument with you last night. I know better than to tell somebody under that much stress that she delusional."

"Damned right. I didn't imagine the blue girl, neither."

He looked confused.

"Never mind," I said. "Something that happened long ago."

He gestured towards the wicker lounge chair. "I could sit down? Before I fall down?" His uniform was rumpled and his eyes were red with fatigue.

"All right," I said warily. If he was reclining, that would slow him down if he tried to grab me or something.

"Thank you." He sighed and plumped himself down in the wicker lounge chair. And it's like all the starch went out of him. He looked up at me. "Beg pardon, Calamity. I didn't want to disturb you. Been a long day for me, too."

"Say what you have to say," I told him.

"All right." But for a little while, he just pursed his lips and looked doubtful. "It's difficult to talk about, you know?"

"I don't know."

"True that. I mean the dead man tonight."

"Something you want to tell me about him."

He nodded.

"Something you don't want to talk where other people can hear."

"You're a very wise woman," he said.

"Wise women are *old*."

He looked amused. "Sometimes they're just wise. And I saw you inspecting that little boy's hands."

"Checking to see if they were bruised."

He said, "Maybe. But I think you know what I want to tell you about his daddy. Rare for them to come so close to where people live."

I risked a step or two closer to him. "Say the words," I demanded.

"Which words?"

"Say what he was."

"What you think he was?" he asked. He was playing cautious. Me, too.

I sat in the chair beside his. "I can't say it. Only crazy people would believe a thing like that. Crazy people and Ifeoma."

He frowned. "Who?"

"Ifeoma not crazy, that's not what I'm saying. Sometimes I think she saner than me. But all the shit she do: if you spill salt, throw some over your left shoulder to keep the jumbies away; don't step on a crack or you put your grandmother in traction; never wear white shoes after Labour Day."

He smiled. It suited him.

"It's like she think . . ." I reached for the words. ". . . she think that the marvellous things in this world, the wondrous things, we can find a *trick* to them, you know? And if we work the trick just right, well then, we can control them." I kissed my teeth. "Why you want to control a miracle? Then it won't be a miracle no more!"

He leaned forward, closer to me. "So you frighten that if we believe in mermaids, they going to disappear?"

"No, I frighten that hope will disappear when we find out they don't . . ." I stopped and stared at him. I knew my eyes had gone wide. "Mermaids?"

His grin got even broader. "That what you call them?"

"You said the word first. Don't play with me, Gene." Because

I wanted a world with mermaid boys in it, not one where parents kept their children tied up and locked away.

He frowned, sighed. "We scarcely talk this out loud. Even those of us that know they're there, we don't really palaver about it. Because you can't tell who to trust; if you open your mouth to somebody, they might go and talk to your boss or your wife, and next thing you know, you're in a room in the psych ward, getting Prozac every few hours and eating peach Jell-O with a plastic spoon."

I sat back and crossed my arms. "Don't expect sympathy from me," I said. "You know what they say: the best prevention is abstention."

"Come again?"

"If you really wanted to keep your big secret safe from me, you wouldn't be here talking to me in the first place."

His laugh sent a little lizard on the wall scurrying behind the light fixture. "You're a hell of a woman, you know that?"

"No, no, no!" I shook my finger at him. "Don't try to sweet-talk me, neither. I too old for that." I stood up. "Time up, Gene. Say all you have to say and say it plain, or please to come off my property at this late hour in the evening." I tried to look stern, but I was having fun in a way.

He leaned back in the lounge chair. Gave me a measuring look. "They don't have fish tails," he said. My mouth went dry. "But you know that already. And they don't breathe water. Like you saw tonight, they can drown. So they not mermaids in that sense. But anybody who work near the sea around Cayaba will buck up one eventually. Fishermen, Coast Guard, Emergency Services. Not the doctors, for the most part. They scarcely do outcalls. Even the police know about this. We all know it. We just don't talk it. But they real. The sea people? They real."

I just stood there, blinking.

"Calamity?"

"You . . ." I tried to swallow, but my mouth was too dry. "You not making a joke on me?" My voice came out squeaky.

"What happened this morning when Pamela and Jerry saw the little boy?"

"The two paramedics?"

"Yes."

"Pamela's hands were shaking, and her voice, but nerves could do that. She looked at the little boy like it's jumbie she was seeing. The man—Jerry?—I think he wanted to shake her. He kept trying to keep her mind on what she was doing."

"Pamela is a trainee. She been kinda suspecting, but this is the first time she ever see one of them up close." He shook his head, chuckled. "She did better than me. The first time I saw the body of a sea person . . ."

His eyes flashed up and to the right.

"You're telling the truth." I sat down hard in the wicker chair. "They're real."

"Yeah."

"Or maybe you're *hallucinating*," I said evilly. "You know, the stress, the fatigue . . . You been drinking enough water? Maybe you just need a good night's sleep."

"I guess I deserve that. But I've touched other sea people corpses before. Examined them."

My familiar world left me with the breath I let out. When I breathed back in, it was the air of a foreign land. "Shit. Agway."

"Who?"

"The little boy. That was his family! They were real, and now they're . . ."

"Dead is still real. Just gone."

"You were just stringing Evelyn along with that story about child abuse."

He shrugged. "The sad thing is, it was a plausible story."

"What going to happen to him? You will send him back?"

He shook his head. "He on the books now. If he disappear, there will have to be an investigation."

"But you could manage it somehow, couldn't you? Say that he wandered away and got lost; something!"

"Maybe. But think about it. They won't let us get close to them. I think they can smell us coming. If we put the little boy out there and leave him, anything could happen before his people find him. High tide. Tiger shark."

He saw my face.

"Sorry. Don't think about it. We just have to hope he will find a home on land." He stood. "I'm saying goodnight, Calamity. Past time for my day to end." He stopped at the top of the steps. "Maybe somebody will adopt him."

I didn't reply. I had had two years of not being my own person, of changing diapers and feeding someone pap from a spoon. Plus I had raised a girl child, on my own. I had done my share. Time for some freedom now. So I would keep my mouth shut. And hate myself for it.

The dada-hair lady didn't know what to do. She'd been scared when they'd snatched her as she was drawing water from the well outside her village. They'd gagged her when she

screamed. And they had been rough; pushing and chivvying her until they reached the long forced march of people, all chained by the neck. They'd added her to the end of the line. There was never enough water to drink by the time the ladle reached her.

The dada-haired lady had tried to tell herself that even bound and forced to walk was better than being at home, taking orders from Chiefo's first wife.

In her village, she had kept her ability hidden as well as she could. Bad things happened to women accused of being witches. But word did get out. Some of the women knew. They would come, furtively, asking for help for every problem under the sun. She had to explain that she could only tell them where the things they'd lost were, and only during her blood time.

When they'd reached Calabar, the big ship anchored offshore had been a wonder she'd never seen before; the papa to the small canoes she knew well. Chineke! How something so large, large as a village, could bob like cork on the water and not sink! She'd wondered what was inside.

She'd gone wild with panic when the strange men forced them onto the ship.

The sailors had taken the men to another part of the hold. The women and children they forced to clamber into a dark space in the belly of the ship. They had been packed in so tightly that everyone's back was jammed against the belly of the person behind them. They were chained together in threes. You couldn't stand. You had to crab-walk when you needed to get to the necessary, treading on other people and dragging your two other shipmates grumbling along with you.

With a creaking of timbers the ship had started on its

journey. Many of them had never been on the sea before. The nausea soon had them retching. Often you couldn't reach the necessary in time. Within hours, the heat and the stench in the hold were unbearable, and there wasn't enough air. Women and children moaned and cried out, and eventually stopped. In the first weeks, one small child, unable to keep any food nor water down for more than a few minutes, had died from sea-sickness.

Back in the village, the dada-hair lady had told Chiefo's newest wife Ngoli that she could not make the child in her womb come out a boy. That made Ngoli angry; angrier still when she gave birth to a girl. Two days after that, the dada-hair lady had been kidnapped. So no use wishing for rescue by her family. She had a pretty good idea who had sold her to the white men.

The dada-hair lady would have rejoiced at giving birth to any child, girl or boy.

3

I THOUGHT IT WOULD BE LIKE RIDING A BICYCLE; YOU know they say you never forget how? But I was beginning to have my doubts.

There I hung where I'd found myself. No, where I'd *put* myself; halfway up the trunk of the almond tree on the cliff, my arms and legs wrapped round it in a grip so intimate it was practically lewd. And I was stuck. Shit. I weighed almost three times what I had at ten years old, and I now had arthritis in one knee.

I managed to turn my head and look down. It was a good seven-foot drop to the ground. Little Chastity would have leapt the distance like a tree frog and barely noticed the effort, but when I even thought of jumping down from that height, I could practically hear my kneecaps warning me of the consequences. They would pop right off, they promised. They would roll down the hill and over the cliff, and nobody would ever find them again, and I'd be lying under the tree, kneecapless and sorry.

I tightened my all-fours grip on the tree trunk. The first crotch of branches was fanned out just above my head. All I had to do was reach up with one hand and grab that nice, sturdy branch right there, lever myself up into the tree by it. I tried to extend my arm. But that caused a quaking in my other limbs. I wrapped my arm back around the trunk.

My left foot began to slip on the smooth almond bark. I was going to slide all the way down the trunk! I tried not to imagine what that would do to my inner thighs.

My toes touched a hard knob of living wood. The Knot! That was how I used to get up into my tree. This tree had a knot just like it. Just like it.

I used to put the toes of my left foot on the Knot, just like they were now. That would give me just enough purchase so that I could reach up around the torso of the tree with my left hand, like so . . . yes, there was the stub of a torn-off branch; the Handle. I hoped it would bear my weight. I grabbed onto it, stretched my other hand up and got hold of a good solid branch that forked out from the tree's crotch. I wrapped both my arms around it.

What did I used to do next? I stayed there for a while, catching my breath and trying to remember. Oh, yes. Oh, shit. Was I still that flexible? I looked down again at the drop to the ground. I'd better be.

It took five tries, but I finally managed to lever my right leg up over the branch I was holding on to. By then my arms were trembling like coconut jelly and my fingers were beginning to let go.

But I knew that my legs wouldn't let me down. "Thunder Thighs," Mumma used to call Chastity proudly. I hooked one leg around the branch and flexed. I shifted a little. I squeezed harder, used my arms to twist my body. The motion pulled me up into the crook of the tree. I heard the inner seam of my clam-diggers giving away from the stress and the friction, but I'd done it! I had gotten back up in my almond tree, after all these years!

Not as skillfully as I'd imagined. I was lying in the crook of the tree, curled around its trunk. My inner thigh muscles were burning, and I'd probably skinned a few of my fingertips. And I was too exhausted to move. A nasty big greenwhip snake could come down out of the tree after me right now and I wouldn't budge, not a rass.

But thinking about a greenwhip slipping through the branches towards me, I found that I could move after all. In fact, I was al-ready sitting up and somehow edging my bottom over to that branch over there that looked sturdy enough for me. Careful, girl, careful.

And there I was, wedged into a V of branches like the one that used to be my childhood seat. It didn't fit my fifty-three-year-old behind very well, but jammed in like that, at least I wasn't going to fall. My problem would be getting unstuck.

Chuh. Worry about that later. I braced my feet on another branch, leaned against the trunk of the tree and got as comfort-able as I could. Now for my book. A lazy morning reading a trashy mystery.

I'd put my book down to have my hands free to climb. There it was, lying at the foot of the tree, at the wrong end of gravity. "Fuck!" I screamed, scaring a kiskedee bird out of a sea grape bush.

A movement out on the beach far below me caught my eye.

A man, strolling. He'd better be a resident. There was a kind of tourist that didn't give two two's about private property. I wrapped my arm around a branch above me and tried to pull myself free. If that was an intruder, I was going to give him a good West Indian style cussing; burn his ears right off for him and send him on his way.

I pulled on the branch. My ass stayed wedged. I pulled again. Nothing. I pushed down on the arms of the branches entrapping my behind. That worked, though it tore the seams of my clam-diggers open a little more. But I was on a mission now. Full of the fire of righteousness, I swung myself down towards the trunk. It would have worked, too, except that my already exhausted hands wouldn't hold me. My fingers opened and I crashed to the ground, flat on my back.

"Oww! Damn it all to hell, man!" My body was thrumming like a quattro string. For a few seconds, I just lay where I was, taking stock. Head felt okay, though rattled. Back holding up. Elbow—ouch. My elbow had banged a rockstone when I landed. Hurt like blazes, but didn't seem broken. Legs? Yes, I could move them. Toes too.

Slowly, I rolled to one side, then up onto my knees. The arthritic one yelled at me.

I was shaking. The muscles in my arms could scarcely bear my weight. But I made it to my feet, started brushing the dirt off my behind.

What was lumpy in my pocket? I put my hand in, and came away with the bread and butter I'd brought for my breakfast, squashed to a third of its former width. It was oozing butter onto my hands. I threw the wretched thing into the sea grape bush and wiped my hand on the almond tree bark.

Oh, that man on the beach was really going to get it now!

I grabbed up my book and stomped down the path on shaky legs, working up a good head of steam. People wandering all over other people's homes, looking for "local colour," always going where they weren't supposed to go.

By some miracle I made it to the shore without tripping. I approached the man.

It was Hector. I couldn't tell for certain at first. He had his back to me. Sure looked like his kind of outfit; bright green wetsuit with purple inserts. I wasn't sure about his colour sense, but I couldn't hate a suit that showed off his assets like that.

He turned and caught me staring at his butt. Oops. "Oh, hi, Hector," I said with a silly little wave.

He smiled as though someone had just brought him a surprise present. "Calamity!"

I hadn't had a chance before to look at him good. He was a nice-looking man—the kind of solid, easy-to-smile face you could imagine waking up to see every morning. "I just wanted to find out . . . Well, these are people's homes on Dolorosse. You know that, right?" Oh, damn. I was babbling.

"Well, I—"

"Every year we get tourists bothering us." I have a thing for beefy shoulders. "Sneaking out here, getting drunk . . ." And that wetsuit was so tight I could make out his nipples.

"But I have—"

"Playing their music loud enough to wake the dead, taking their clothes off . . ." Whoops. Wrong thing to put my mind on. I tried hard to keep my eyes above the belly button. I almost succeeded.

"Next thing you know, some white woman with more rum in her belly than sense in her head going to mistake a seal for a mermaid . . ." *Or see a real one.* ". . . and half-drown herself trying to swim after it . . ." I stuttered to a halt. Damn. Get me bothered and I get snippy. And garrulous. Not a good combination.

"I have permission to be here," Hector said.

"Yeah?" If I stuck to monosyllables, maybe I wouldn't make a total ass of myself.

Now he looked mildly amused. "Yeah. From the government of Cayaba. Research permit."

"Oh. That's all right, then." Then I *giggled*! I don't *giggle*. Damned man was making me simper.

"I could bring it and show you, if you like."

"No, that won't be necessary. I believe you." Thank heaven for skin dark enough to hide that I was blushing.

"I promise I won't bring any drunken tourist women to cavort naked on this beach."

Sheepish silence while we grinned foolishly at each other. Sheepish on my side, anyway. "I saw you from the almond tree on the cliff," I blurted. That would get us off the topic of nakedness. "I was up in it."

He looked to where I had pointed. "Wow. Not too many people our age climb trees."

"Our age? How old would your age be, exactly?"

"Forty-three."

"Well, I'm one or two years older than that, but I made it up into that tree today. Yesterday, it didn't even exis . . ."

Yes, it *had*. It had been there all the time.

But the Knot, and the Handle . . . ?

"Can I show you something?" he asked. He took me to the edge of the surf and pointed to some slabs of rock jutting out of the water.

There were three adult monk seals and two babies, sunning themselves. They usually preferred the small, uninhabited islands.

"Aren't they marvellous?" He said. "People hunted them nearly to extinction, but they're hanging on. By rights monk seals shouldn't even exist, you know. They're phocids, for Christ's sake. In the tropics! They're balanced on an evolutionary knife edge."

"You mean because they're almost extinct?"

"Not just that. You know what the biggest problem is for a seal?"

"How to catch fish without any hands."

A puzzled frown.

"It's a joke," I said.

"Oh." Derailed, he seemed at a loss for words for a second. Then: "Their biggest problem is heat."

"Well, they solved that. Plenty of heat here in the tropics."

"But you see, water has twenty times the conductivity of air."

"Beg pardon?" I had no idea what he was talking about.

"Water will chill your body down twenty times faster than air. Even warm water will do that."

"All right," I said, "so seals need to stay warm. That's why they're so fat, right?"

"Yeah. Works fine in the water. But they haul out onto land every so often, to sleep, to breed, to moult . . . And they don't have sweat glands. So in this part of the world, they start to overheat in about ninety minutes."

He glanced at me. "Sorry," he said. "If you start me up on this subject, I sometimes forget to stop. And these seals," he continued, forgetting to stop, "the Cayaba seals; they have a big mystery to them."

"How you mean?"

"They're not Caribbean monk seals."

"Why not? They're in the Caribbean."

He shook his head. "Don't matter. They're *Monarchus monar-*

chus, not *Monarchus tropicalis*. *Mediterranean* monk seals. I'm trying to figure out how they got here in the first place. That's what I'm studying. But first, I need to get an idea what the real size of the population is: study their movement patterns and return rates, tag any newborn babies, conduct a census of them every few days." He frowned. "I have to work on that. I keep getting the numbers wrong."

"The Cayaba government don't do that research?"

"The Zooquarium does, yes. But they haven't gotten around yet to figuring out how a colony of *monachus* ended up way over here."

I was boiling. When the sun got so hot?

". . . most primitive living pinnipeds," said Hector.

God, the heat was getting worse.

". . . derelict fishing nets . . . danger . . ."

Hector didn't even seem to notice it. Me, my whole body was burning. I could feel the tips of my ears getting red, my cheeks flushing.

". . . *Brucella* . . . Calamity? You all right?"

"I don't know. Too much sun." I wiped some perspiration from my brow. My hand came away wet.

"You sweating like you just run a marathon."

"A lady doesn't sweat." Dried sweat was irritating my hand. I rubbed it against the fabric of my pants. "Jesus, it so hot!"

Hector looked worried. "That tree over there will give you some shade. Come."

But before we could take a step, something soft and light grazed my head from above, then landed at Hector's feet. "The hell is that?" he cried out. He bent to pick it up.

"It didn't hurt me. I'm okay." Much better, in fact. The heat was passing off rapidly. I was even chilly.

Hector straightened up. "Where this came from?" He looked up at the sky. I followed his gaze. Nothing but blue. Not even the cloud that must have just covered the sun and made me shiver.

I looked down from the sky, blinked the glare away. Hector showed me the thing he was holding.

I grabbed her out of his hand. Bare Bear. Chastity's Bare Bear. Held so tightly and loved so hard that her little stuffed rump was threadbare, her little gingham dress long gone. "Where this came from?"

"Look like it just fell out of the sky."

"No, man; don't joke. It must have washed up with the tide."

"And landed on your head?"

"I don't know; maybe this was on the sand already, and something else fell on my head." Bare Bear winked her one glass eye at me. So long I hadn't seen her. "A leaf from out a sea grape tree, something like that. Right, Bare Bear?" I hugged Lucky Bare Bear to my chest. I grinned at Hector. "She get small over the years. Or I get big." She still fit in her old place, up against my breastbone.

"You feeling sick?" he asked. "You didn't look too good just now."

"I feel wonderful," I answered. "Don't fret. Tell me more about your seals."

He frowned a little, but he didn't say anything. Just turned and started pointing out the seals again. "The babies not weaned yet."

"How you know?"

"Their coats still black."

A baby seal was humping its way over to one of the adults.

"He's fat. Like Agway."

"Agway?"

"The little boy on the beach yesterday morning."

Whose dead family Hector had found. He looked stricken.

"Sorry." My damned mouth. "I didn't mean to make you think about them."

"It's all right."

The baby reached the adult, butted its head against her belly. She rolled so that it could get at one of her teats. She propped herself up and looked at the baby as it latched on and began to nurse. She lay flat again, to continue her basking. I watched the baby pull, and my own nipples ached in response.

"I have to go," I told Hector.

"So quick?"

"So quick. Visiting a new friend. But maybe you would like to come by the house some day? I could cook you a meal."

His face brightened. "Sounds nice."

"All right. Call me when you're free."

Then I rushed home to change out of the torn-up pants and grab my purse. I had time to catch the next waterbus. Maybe I could see Agway one more time before they moved him out.

On the Saturday that Mumma didn't come home, I woke up early. Couldn't hear Mumma or Dadda moving around yet. I went to my dresser and found a t-shirt and my favourite climbing shorts, the red denim ones with the shiny gold buttons on them like pirate doubloons. The back left pocket was half torn away, and Mumma had told me not to wear them again until she'd mended them, but Mumma hated

mending, and Chastity loved those shorts. I was very quiet.
Mumma was probably still mad at me after the day before, so
I didn't want to give her any reason to notice me.

I tucked my new book under my arm. Three-Finger
Jack, it was called. Deliciously scary. About a robber man
from long time ago, over in Jamaica. I tiptoed out of the
house and went down to the shore. I picked sea grapes from
the bushes and stuffed myself till my tummy rumbled and
my fingertips were purple. I walked barefoot on the wet
sand, feeling it scrunchy and cool between my toes, and
watched the little crabs skitter into their holes. I felt a small,
guilty glee that Mumma hadn't called me yet to breakfast
and do chores. She would probably give me extra to do
today, as punishment. I would have to face the music soon,
but not yet. On borrowed time, I hiked back up the rise and
around the bend to my special almond tree—the one on the
cliff that overlooked the beach. I wasn't supposed to go past
the almond tree to the edge, but nobody had said I couldn't
climb the almond tree. I had slipped my book into the back
waistband of my shorts and climbed up the tree to that
comfortable spot where three joined branches held me up
like a hand. I settled in and stayed there the whole morning,
watching the sea breathe, reading my book. All that time, I
felt nothing. No finger tingle. I didn't notice that Mumma's
dinghy wasn't pulled up on the beach. I felt nothing but the
joy of a solitary Saturday, left to my own devices. You can't
find something if you don't know you've lost it.

When it got to be late morning and still no Dadda or
Mumma, I began to wonder. Plus I was hungry, for a real
breakfast or an early lunch. I went back to the house. In the
kitchen was a grumpy Dadda, washing dishes. He usually

did them at night. Dadda snapped at me to go and plait my hair and wash my face and come back for lunch.

The fried breadfruit slices were burnt and the eggs were hard. Dadda barely touched his. He kept glancing out the window that looked towards the beach. When I couldn't stand it any longer, I asked him if I should go and do my Saturday chore of picking up the fallen cashew apples, juicing the flesh, and putting the nuts out to dry. He said yes. He didn't seem to be paying attention to me. By now I was wondering where Mumma was. I asked him. He said, "Gone. Out." I didn't dare ask him the question that was worming away at my gut: Mumma mad at me? Is that why she's staying out so long? If he didn't know what I'd done to make her mad, I didn't want to tell him.

Later, I brought in the bucket of cashew juice and another one of pressed cashew apple flesh. Dadda was on the settee in the living room, glowering at the tv. I put the buckets in the kitchen. Chores done, I took the phone to a corner of the living room and sat on the floor. I spent the rest of the afternoon chatting with Evelyn. Three-Finger Jack was on my knee, and I read in the spaces between our words.

Then it was dark. And Dadda was calling me to supper, and smiling a determined, too-frequent smile, and telling me that Mumma had said she might spend the night in town if she missed the last waterbus. That made sense. Mumma would come back in the morning, and we would all be friends again. I ignored the little knot of uneasy I always felt under my breastbone when Mumma stayed away. Tomorrow I would ask her if we could have a picnic on the beach, just her and me.

What book was I reading, Dadda asked. I chattered

away happily to him about Three-Finger Jack. *He took
advantage of the book's setting in Cockpit Country to
quiz me on my geography, but I was ready for him: karst
topography, limestone dissolves, which creates underground
caverns. We played Snap, and I won two games and he won
two games. True, he was a little preoccupied, but he always
was when Mumma was gone like this. Then a bit more tv,
then I went to bed.*

*Mumma's dinghy drifted back to shore the next day,
empty.*

*A week later, Dadda was in jail under suspicion of
murder. That same day, I was taken from our house to go and
live with Auntie Pearl and Uncle Edward.*

Three weeks after that, Evelyn stopped speaking to me.

*I knew something that poor Agway was finding out: being
an orphan sucks ass.*

Evelyn lifted her stethoscope off Agway's chest. She took the
earpieces out of her ears and hooked them around her neck.
"Apart from the bruises and the fracture, he's actually pretty
healthy," she said. Agway was sitting naked on the examination
table in front of her. She tapped the bowl of the stethoscope
against her chin and smiled at him. "He has worms, but we can
fix that."

"Worms?" I shuddered. Dadda used to give me a dose of
cashew bark tea twice a year, just in case I had worms.

"Intestinal parasites, really."

"How he got those?" All our parents did it: senna pod tea, castor oil . . . A day's worth of diarrhoea twice a year, just as a precaution.

Agway reached for the stethoscope. She took it off and gave it to him.

"Well, that's the odd thing. Normally you would get those parasites from eating undercooked fish."

Agway pulled on the rubber tubing of the stethoscope. He stretched it a good foot longer than its natural length. Gently, Evelyn took it from him.

Dadda would try to hide the taste of the cashew bark tea by mixing it with cream soda. I still couldn't smell cream soda without gagging. "Hang on, undercooked fish?"

She made a face. "Yes. Or raw."

Well, that made sense.

"God, what horrible people," she said. "They wouldn't even cook the food they gave him. I don't say I wish anybody harm, but maybe it's for the best that his parents, well."

Agway pissed, completely unconcerned. The urine made a beautiful yellow arc in the morning light, heading straight for Evelyn's smock. She danced away, grinned and shook her finger at him. From the blank look in his eyes, he didn't connect her gesture with what he'd done. She patted his chest.

I took a fresh diaper off the folded stack of them that Evelyn kept in her office. Evelyn watched me diaper him. "You really want to foster him?" she asked

I nodded. "Thinking of it, yes." I tried wrestling him back into the t-shirt they'd given him. He wasn't interested. Blasted boy been practising wriggling with the eels.

"Children's Services prefers them to go to whole families, you know."

"I'm not broken, Evelyn." Agway had managed to get his head and one arm jammed through the neck of the t-shirt.

She looked embarrassed. "Of course not. But they like families that come with a mummy and a daddy and two well-behaved children, preferably one girl and one boy."

"Ifeoma was as well behaved as any normal child her age," I told her.

"Who?"

"My daughter. The reason I left Holy Name."

The tips of Evelyn's ears went pink. "Right. Some of the girls told me why you didn't finish out your final year."

"I raised her well. All by myself."

She gave me that nod, the wobbly "yes" nod that really means no.

I gave up on the t-shirt; pulled it off and hoisted Agway onto my hip. He immediately stretched up and tried to grab my hair, and threw a tantrum when I wouldn't let him. I sat him back on the examination table to calm down. He stormed and slapped his hands on the table. "What a fuss and a fret!" I said to him. "Evelyn, I can look after one little boy."

"I'm sure you'd be wonderful." She broke my gaze, looked off to the right as though there was something to see there. Was it up and to the right for lying, or down and centre? She said, "There's a proper procedure for doing these things, you know."

I wasn't going to beg Evelyn Chow to do me favours. In my mind's eye I saw her at fourteen, dewy-perfect, looking up from her desk as I walked into class late, still sweaty from rowing the dinghy from Blessée to Cayaba and walking the two miles to school because I didn't have bus fare. In my mind's eye, she was flinging a swathe of beautifully groomed, glossy black hair behind one ear, giving me a breezy smile, and saying loudly enough for the whole class to hear, "Oh, *there* you are, Charity Girl! Been rowing around Cayaba in your old boat again?"

I tickled Agway's tummy. He chortled and kicked. Evelyn said, "He's so happy when you're here."

"Did you ever have children?" I asked her, curious. "Did you want any?" I didn't ask her if she'd gotten married. That was a tender subject with me.

She didn't answer immediately. "He's not having a good time here, poor soul," she said. "We're only trying to look after him, but he doesn't know that. We poke him with needles to draw blood, and it makes him so frightened. The X-rays, the ultrasounds; they terrify him."

I nodded. "And he doesn't understand about knives and forks, or many kinds of food."

"Samuel—that's my husband—is lovely. And no, we don't have children. I look after children here at work every day, and Samuel has a whole side of nephews and nieces. That's enough for us."

"Oh." She'd been a perfect girl, was now a perfect wife, and had a perfect life with no encumbrances.

"My job in a case like this is to consider the best interests of the child."

And I was a broke, aging single woman living on an isolated island. "I understand."

"When you're with him, he isn't so frightened."

I looked at her. A ribbon of hope uncurled in my belly.

"So I just want you to know that I've told Children's Services you can visit him as often as you want," she said. "Until we find him a permanent home. Okay?"

And that was it. She would let me visit him to gentle him, but she would not let me take him. "Yes," I answered. "Okay." She was going to throw me only one dry bone. And, damn me, I accepted it. Calamity.

～

"You and your boys hanging out weekend coming?" teenaged Chastity asked Michael. It was only Thursday, but I was already feeling sorry for myself.

"Yeah, I guess so." His newly breaking voice squeaked on the last word.

Michael and I had been tight for four years now. He knew when I'd first had my period. I knew when he'd had his first wet dream. But it was when his voice broke that something in me changed. I began to see him differently, to notice things I hadn't before: how large his hands were, and how graceful; how his arms and shoulders were filling out his shirts. The smell of his sweat when he came to hang out with me in the stands after his class's weekly soccer game made the secret parts of me twitch.

The jangle of lunchtime voices in the school caf screeched, bellowed, and roared all around us. Two stray dogs, rib-thin, slunk through the open-air caf, hoping for crumbs. Most of the students just ignored them.

I looked in my lunch bag. Dadda had put in some of the dumplings from last night's dinner, and the stewed fish, spiced with pimiento berries and browned onions. Cashew juice, of course, in a little plastic bottle. And the yam left over from dinner, too. I didn't feel for yam that day. I forked it onto Michael's plate. He didn't look up. He called the dogs over. They came, suspiciously, fearfully. At the table in front of us, Neil kicked out at one of the dogs as it passed. He got it squarely on the flank, but it made no noise, just staggered a little and kept going. The two hid under an empty table a little distance away, looking hopefully at Michael. I glared at Neil, who grinned at me, that broad, I'm-so-sexy grin that had all the girls writing him notes during class. I shook my head and rolled my eyes at him.

"What allyou going to do?" I asked Michael. He was scraping the ground meat out of his patty onto the floor for the dogs. He was on a vegetarian kick recently. "You see that new karate movie at the drive-in yet?" I could hear the edge of envy in my voice. My Friday night would consist of a waterbus ride back to Blessée with Dadda, then a few hours of homework. Afterwards maybe a solitary walk to the cliff in the dark of evening to smell the sea. And to watch it respire in the darkness, and to hope something marvellous would happen soon and save me from dying of boredom.

Lately, I'd been examining Michael's every gesture, every expression, for a clue whether he was seeing me differently now, too. That pensive look: was he thinking about touching me? When he called me early on a Saturday morning, was it because he'd spent the night in a lather, thinking about me?

"Ey. Dreamboat," I said. "You don't hear I'm talking to you?" I managed to keep my tone light and teasing, like it used to be before Michael's voice broke.

Michael still hadn't said anything, or looked up. He was only chasing the yam round and round on his plate. "What wrong with you?" I asked him. He'd moved his feet away from the patty innards on the floor. The dogs were jostling for the scant two mouthfuls of meat.

Michael wouldn't meet my eye. "Carlton."

"You and he fighting again? You know it will blow over. Come tomorrow, you two going to be thick as thieves again. You and Carlton and Delroy and Ashok like the four legs on that dog, always running everywhere together." There. That sounded like the old Chastity, nuh true?

There was a shriek from over by one of the big tables. Consuela and Gillian were having a food fight, using it as a way of drawing attention to themselves. They were like twins, both with high chests and taut thighs. "Fucking hell," I said to Michael. "If Gillian's skirt was any shorter, you'd be able to see what she had for dinner last night."

Michael grimaced. "Chastity, I think I like Carlton." Finally he met my eyes. The doubt, the fear on his face made my throat catch. "Like I supposed to like girls, I mean. Oh, God, what I going to do?"

I stared at him and didn't let my face change. Not one bit. Inside, I was wailing.

Michael's top lip trembled. "You can't tell anyone. Not one soul."

"I won't." My mind was stewing. I didn't know whether I was embarrassed for him, or embarrassed at myself.

"Please, Chastity."

"For true! I won't." In Civics class just before lunch, I'd been trying on names, writing them in my notebook: Chastity Theresa Jasper. Chastity Jasper-Lambkin. Mr. and Mrs. Michael Jasper. Shame curdled the food in my belly and chilled my skin.

"Thanks." Michael tried to mash the yam with one of the plastic forks from the cafeteria. The fork broke off in his hand. He cussed and threw the broken handle down on his plate. Stood up.

I touched his arm. "Michael."

"What."

"You know for sure?" My voice trembled. If he said yes, I was going to die right there, I knew it.

He frowned. Frisbeed his paper plate of food into the open garbage can a few tables away, alarming the dogs, who ran out of the caf. He got a shrieking round of overenthusiastic applause from Gillian and Consuela, who were both hot for him. He scowled at them, shook his head. "Don't talk so loud. No, I don't know."

A chance, then. A tiny chance. "Why you don't test it and see?" I asked him.

He shot me a look of pure panic. "What? You mad? Carlton would kill me. Then he would tell everybody."

I didn't point out that once he was dead, he wouldn't give two shits who Carlton told. "No, not with him." Carlton was a pimple-faced idiot who could only talk about cricket and girls. No way Michael could like him over me. Right?

I touched Michael's hand. He jumped. "Test it with me," I said.

"It's menopause," said Dr. Nichols. "You're having night sweats, hot flashes." He smiled. "Though it might help a bit to think of them as 'power surges.'"

I sat across from him in his office, trying to understand what all those words had to do with me.

"So what I can do about it?" I asked him after a pause. I had some vague notions; stuff I'd heard on the radio and television but hadn't paid much attention to. "Eat lots of tofu, get eight hours' sleep every night, shit like that? This hot flash stupidness has to stop so I can get on with my life."

Dr. Nichols blinked at me. He examined the perfectly manicured nails of his left hand—something he always did when he was stalling for time. He'd been my G.P. for thirteen years now. I could read him like a friend, almost. Mind you, is how long I hadn't been to see him? Two years? Three? "The hot flashes will stop eventually," he said. "My wife Miriam—"

"Cedric, how many years you been reminding me that you have a wife and her name is Miriam?"

He blinked at me some more, a hurt expression on his face. So many years gone by, and he still hiding behind Miriam's skirts. And all I did that one time was bring the man some chocolate! And a card, and a new pen, for his old one had been skipping. And a houseplant for his office, to brighten it up a little. From then on, I couldn't stop hearing about blasted Miriam. My blouse hadn't been *that* low-cut that day. The ones I used to wear to the club would probably have made him faint.

I relented. "Beg pardon," I said. "This business have me short-tempered."

Cedric nodded. "You can expect irritability over the next little while."

"Bet you nobody will notice any difference in me. So what Miriam have to say on the subject of menopause?"

"It made her irritable, too. She says she used to get so mad at the slightest little thing, it would feel like her head was exploding. And some people get actual headaches. And maybe bouts of rapid heartbeat. And flatulence. You might notice you're getting some hairs on your chin, but the hair will be thinner on your head and . . . everywhere else. Weight gain, loss of libido, dry vagina."

"I see. And depression is a symptom, too?"

"Well, yes . . ."

My shoulders slumped. "Lord, just strike me dead now and done, nuh?"

"Oh; and you might have irregular periods."

"How you mean, 'irregular'?"

"Some months it won't come at all, some months it'll come twice, and you might have breakthrough bleeding in between."

"Hence the irritability," I muttered.

"Pardon?"

"Never mind." Cedric wasn't too quick to get a joke. I wouldn't have enjoyed being his girlfriend anyway. "So what I must take to stop it?"

Cedric was scribbling on his little doctor pad. "To stop what?" he asked me.

"I know both of we getting old, but like you the one going doltish," I grumbled at him. "What I must take to make all this nonsense stop?"

He frowned at me. "Nothing will make it stop until it's ready to stop. You just have to wait it out. I can give you estrogen and progesterone to ease some of the symptoms, but other than that, you just have to give it time. Is a normal—"

"Yes, I know. 'Normal,' 'maturity,' all that shit. How long I going to be waking up drowning in my own sweat?"

"In some women, it lasts more than a decade."

"To rass."

"You make sure you take care of yourself for the next little while. Get enough sleep. Eat properly."

"And eat plenty tofu. I know. Thanks."

He wrote me a prescription for estrogen patches and gave me a glossy pamphlet. As I was heading out the door, he said, "Oatmeal compress."

I stopped in his doorway. "And which one of my senescent body parts you want me to apply that to?"

"Miriam say it used to help her plenty. For the itching in her extremities."

"Thank you, Cedric. Say hello to Miriam for me."

So. Looked like I wasn't finding again after all. Menopause explained the itchy fingers. And forgetting that the almond tree had always been there.

And Dumpy had been stuck down inside the couch, so he didn't even count.

But what about Bare Bear landing on me from out of the sky?

Even when I had been convinced I was a finder, things didn't used to come to me; I went to them.

Goose was walking on my grave. *Symptoms of menopause: clammy feeling.* I went into the mall to get a hot drink. But at the counter, I changed my mind. Not coffee; a mango smoothie. "With soy milk, please," I said. Might as well get started on eating right.

While I waited in the line, I had a good look at Cedric's pamphlet, *The Best Years of Your Life.* It pictured a slim, smiling white woman in a tasteful navy one-piece bath suit. She was climbing up a ladder out of a pool. She was about thirty-five years old, her hair in a perky grey bob that was obviously a wig; I guess to fool us menopause-addled women into believing that she was in her sixties, and that if we only used their fine product, we could look like that, too. An equally trim and dignified man waited for her on the pool deck. He was leaning back in one of two matched lounge chairs. He had a little touch of grey hair at each temple. A full head of hair, too; no male-pattern baldness for this fellow.

He wore modest and nondescript swim trunks. I guess he was handsome, in a 1950s martini ad kind of a way. In fact, there were two martinis—his with a green paper umbrella, hers with a pink one—on the little table that sat between the two lounge chairs. It was all so perfect I could gag. Jesus. Death by connubial bliss. Apparently, if I took Cedric's pills, I'd turn into a Stepford wife and get married to a Ken doll.

Though at least I'd have a man.

I wondered what Gene was doing right now. *Bouts of rapid heartbeat.* He hadn't called. And fool that I was, I hadn't asked for his number. *Disturbing memory lapses.*

The pamphlet had sections with titles like: "Life's Next Big Step," and "A Healthy Attitude." I got my mango soy smoothie. I spied a free seat in the food court and headed towards it. A young man's body glanced me, nearly knocking the smoothie out of my hand. He didn't notice. He just kept walking, chatting with his friend.

Next I got mobbed by a tittering of young women, all tight jeans, short skirts, and straightened hair. They flowed around me, chattering. One of them dropped her change purse. "You lost something," I said to her. She turned, searched her friends' faces to see who had spoken. I waved the hand with the pamphlet in it. "Over here." I swear she looked at everybody else before her eyes settled on me, not five feet away from her. I pointed to the ground. "You dropped your change purse."

"Oh," she said. "Thank you." She picked it up and moved off with her friends.

I sat in the free seat, played both incidents over in my mind. No, she hadn't looked at everybody else before she looked at me. She had looked at all the *young* people. I wasn't quite real for her, or for the guy who'd bumped me. I kissed my teeth and sucked a big glob of the smoothie up through the wide straw. It tasted like ass. I crumpled the pamphlet up, stood, tossed it and the drink into the nearest garbage can. Then I dropped into the pharmacy. Turned out I didn't have enough money to pay for the prescription. Liquor store for me; what money I had would stretch far enough for a flask of Cayaba's good red rum. *Dizziness, light-headedness, episodes of loss of balance.*

My poor old red Mini Moke sat in the parking lot in her crumbling paint, looking nothing like the queen after which I'd named her.

And wait; was she listing a little to one side, or were my glasses dirty again? I peered through the specs, trying to find the right place on the tri-focals that would let me focus at that distance. See why I scarcely wore the damned things.

Motherass. Victoria was leaning, yes. The right back tyre had a flat. Shit.

How the hell I was going to get home? Maybe I could call Ife. Then I remembered that the bus stop was just on the other side of the parking lot. And there was the bus, only half a block away from the stop. I started to run. What had possessed me to wear heels today? But I'd been walking, running, dancing in high heels since God was a boy. I moved faster.

The bus was nearly to the stop. *God,* I thought, *please don't make me miss it.* I threw myself into an all-out run in my stilettos. A sleek Mercedes had to slam on the brakes to avoid me. I landed hard on one foot, and felt the heel of my stiletto give. Shit. My best pair of shoes. The driver glared at me and smoothed back her perfectly pressed hair. She wore her sunglasses on her head, so fucking fashionable.

The bus was at the stop. I shouted, "Wait, please, driver!" and continued the fifty-yard dash. Thank the heavens for short slit skirts. The legs might be fifty-three years old, but they were good legs. Running was showing them off real nice, so long as I made sure not to wobble on my broken shoe. The bus driver stayed put to watch my thighs in action, and that gave me time to run up the stairs. "Thank you," I said to him, trying to look fetchingly windblown, when what I really felt was good and winded. He put the bus in gear and drove off. Victoria's one good headlight eye looked at me mournfully as I pulled away.

"I just going to catch my breath," I said to the driver. He gave my legs one more look and nodded. I found a seat and rummaged around in my purse for the fare.

Only a few coppers in there. I'd paid for the smoothie with the last of my money. Shit, shit, shit. When I left the mall, my plan had been to drive to the cambio to withdraw some cash to pay for the waterbus home. I still had a few dollars in there until payday. When Dadda began to sink, I'd started working part-time at the library so I could be with him more. Money was tight.

Maybe the driver would forget me. I scrunched down small in my seat and tried to disappear. The bus rocked and belched on its way into town. I would just sneak off at the nearest cambio, get some cash, go home.

The bus stopped, in between stops. The driver leaned out of his seat and turned around to look at me. "Lady, like you forget you have to pay to ride this bus?" he said, loudly enough for everyone to hear. An old man in one of the side seats stared at me, his eyes avid, waiting to see what I was going to do. A little girl in a St. Rose's school uniform snickered.

I thought I was going to dead from shame right there. "I just . . ." I said, stalling for time. I got up to go and talk to him so he wouldn't have an excuse to shout any more of my business right down through the whole bus. Maybe I could persuade him to carry me as far as a cambio and wait till I got some money out. If I had any money in there. I even owed Mr. Mckinley for the grunts I had bought from him two weeks ago.

"Chastity!" called a voice from the back of the bus. "Calamity!"

Lord on a bicycle; it was Dr. Evelyn Chow, witnessing how badly I managed my affairs. I sighed as any chance I'd had to take Agway home with me evaporated. I must be was born bad-lucky.

Evelyn bustled up to the front, waving her purse at me. "Renny," she said to the bus driver, "it look like you catch my friend here without any change for the bus?"

"She have to pay, Doctor," he said.

"Don't worry, my dear," she said to me. "I always have extra tokens." She fished in the change purse and dropped one into the fare box. Renny nodded and drove on.

"Thank you," I whispered to her.

"Not at all, not at all. Come and sit with me then, nuh?"

"Yes. All right." She'd paid the piper, she got to call the dance. I would bloody well have to sit with her. I fell in behind her as she made her way back to her seat. The St. Rose's school girl was still laughing behind her hand. I lifted one side of my lip at her, doglike, to show her my teeth. She gasped and stopped her stupid giggling. Good. She reminded me of Jane Labonté from my school days. Jane could make me feel bad just by looking at me. Make me feel like the common class poor relation. In high school, she and Evelyn had paired up to make my life a hell.

"Let's sit here," said Evelyn. She pointed to two empty seats side by each. I slid in beside her.

"I'll pay you back," I whispered.

"Don't worry about it. How come you're on this bus? The waterbus is the other way."

"Yes. I was going back home, but my car broke down," I said. "I was just trying to get to a bank machine, and forgot I didn't have bus fare on me."

"Well, that's an inconvenience! Where's your car?"

"In the parking lot of the medical centre."

"Oh, there's a lovely restaurant in the mall there! Really good Mediterranean cuisine. Have you ever been?"

"No, can't say I have."

"Expensive to eat there, though. My husband likes to go there of a Sunday evening, but my dear, I have to say I prefer a beer and a fish and chips at Mrs. Smalley's Chicken Boutique any day."

"You do?" My lord. I had a sudden vision of the proper Evelyn Chow in her white lab coat, sitting at one of Mrs. Smalley's brukdown tables with a Red Stripe beer at her left hand and a heaping plate of the house's fresh fried grunt fish in front of her, sucking the flesh from the bones.

"How was the little boy when you left him?" she asked.

"Fine. Sleeping."

She looked at me. "You're worried about him. Don't fret; we'll find someone qualified to take care of him."

"I'm qualified. I've raised a child of my own."

She patted my hand. "I'm sorry, Chastity. I just think it would be too much for you to take on."

"But—"

"You and I not getting any younger, you know." She smiled. "Time to slow down now."

"Arawak Court!" yelled the bus driver. The St. Rose's school girl got off. She stood on the pavement and watched the bus pull away. As she came level with me, she stuck her tongue out at me. I flashed a silent snarl. Of course she'd waited until she was safe. Little spring chicken with her high bust and her tight thighs.

"Friend of yours?" asked Evelyn.

"Something like that." The bus was following the coast road. I stared at the blue strip of water. Agway's home.

"You're quiet," said Evelyn.

" *'Quiet here on this rock; sitting still and thinking,'* " I quoted. Bad bookworm habit of mine.

" 'The Cayaba Fairmaid.' "

"You know that story?" Evelyn had surprised me for the second time in five minutes.

"We did learn it in school," she reminded me.

"Yes, I know. But most people seem to forget about it afterwards."

"You know the one about the blue child?" she asked me.

"I kinda remember it, yeah." Now she was a folklorist, too? She seemed more the ballet and art cinema type. "Old lady finds a blue devil baby in a hole, the baby tries to force her to do something, I forget what. Old lady throws the baby into the sea, thinking that will drown it."

Evelyn nodded. "When the blue baby hits the water, it grows huge, turns into the devil woman of the sea who drags ships down. That's what the baby had wanted the whole time; to reach the sea."

Huh. That story had quite a different cast to it since my experiences of the past few days. Now I would be willing to bet that it was a fictionalized story of somebody else bucking up with a sea person.

"When I was young," said Evelyn, "I used to wish that the oldtime stories were true."

"You did? You never told me."

"You would have laughed after me."

"No, I wouldn't have."

"Yes. You would have. Your mouth hot now, and it was hot then."

I decided to make nice. "All right. Maybe I would have." I was busting to talk to somebody about the sea people, and I hadn't heard from Gene. I had been like that from since; when I learned something new, I had to tell somebody, anybody. But I had to lead Evelyn to this gently. "It's interesting, you don't find, that we have all these stories about devils living in the sea?"

She shrugged. "Sea kill plenty people in the history of Cayaba. It make sense the devil would live in the sea."

Shit, how to get her to think this through? "You know the legend about Captain Carter?"

Her face brightened. "Yes. Such a beautiful love story."

"I guess. Except the lovers throw themselves into the water and die."

She kissed her teeth. "You have to have a litte romance, man. The story says they transformed."

"They adapted to living in the sea."

"I suppose you could think of it that way." She looked out the window, checked her watch. I was losing her.

"When I was a girl," I said, "I used to try to figure out how I could go and live with the dolphins."

"Oh. Well, that's different. If you were going to remain an oxygen breather, the rest is pretty easy." She sat up straight, started counting off on her fingers: "Extra body fat like whales and seals have, to protect the organs from the cold."

Check. Agway was fat as mud, just like his daddy, and the little blue girl. "What else?" I asked her.

She thought a little bit. "They would need broad ribcages."

Check. "Why, though?"

"To make room for lungs with a lot of surface area; they'll be going under the water for long periods, so they'd need to be able to hold extra oxygen in their lungs. And their lats and delts—these muscles here, in your upper back—would be hyperdeveloped, to help with swimming."

"So their arms would change, too?" I couldn't help coaching her just.

"They wouldn't have to. But it would be nice if their limbs were relatively short. More streamlined for swimming. Oh! I just thought of another one!"

She was practically jigging in her seat. We used to compete in school for who could answer Teacher's questions first.

She said, "This one would be really cool, okay? You know that webbing between the fingers and toes? Like Agway has? All humans have that in the womb. If our mermaid people never lost it, it would help them swim better."

"Uh-huh . . ."

"Eyes! Really big eyes. It's dark down there. Nictitating membranes would be *so* cool! Imagine being able to have your eyes closed *and* open at the same time! I don't know what function those patches on the inner thighs would have, though . . ."

Her eyes opened wide. She put her hands to her mouth. "Oh, my God!" she blurted through her fingers.

"Courtice Plaza!" announced the bus driver. The bus clattered to a halt.

"This is my stop," I said. "I pay you back the bus fare tomorrow, all right?" I stood up and headed for the door, my heart going *pow-powpow*. Please. Please.

She grabbed her purse and ran to catch up. "I'm getting off

with you," she said. "You can't just ups and leave me with this idea you put into my head."

"What idea?" I chirruped at her over my shoulder. I stepped down off the bus stairs and right onto the broken shoe heel. Miracle I didn't twist my ankle.

"Good night, ladies," Renny called out.

A soft evening breeze was blowing. There was the overpowering ice cream smell of frangipani blossoms from somewhere, and the sky had that look of evening turning into night; like someone had poured black ink into blueing and was stirring it.

Courtice Plaza was in front of us; a small, three-storey shopping centre built around a courtyard. The designer said he'd had the Hanging Gardens of Babylon in mind when he constructed it. Looked more like one of those Escher drawings, with staircases leading every which way. Confused the eye. I could never remember which level the cambio was on, and which set of stairs would lead me to it. I hobbled up to the plaza. A woman with matted hair and tattered clothing sat on the grass verge. She was barefoot. The bottoms of her feet were black horns of callous. She spied us.

"Please, lady, do," she said to me. "Beg you little money. I ain't eat from morning."

"I'm sorry. I don't have any." It was the God's truth. I didn't have one red cent.

"Please, lady," she said again.

"Here." Evelyn gave the woman a bill.

"Thank you, lady. Bless you."

We went on. I stopped and dithered around a bit, looking from one entrance to the other. Evelyn dithered right alongside me.

"That little boy," she said. "It would be incredible."

"What would?"

"It's just possible; an isolated archipelago like this. An evolutionary branch . . ."

This sort of looked like the entrance I wanted. I began up the stairs. Evelyn followed.

"It worked for Darwin," she said. "The finches, you know?"

"The library archives are full of reported sightings of mermaids off Cayaba," I said. "Newspaper clippings, people's diaries from long ago."

We passed a fancy women's clothing store. It was lit in screaming pink and yellow neon. The skirt on the mannequin in the window was so short that even though she was plastic, I felt embarrassed for her.

Time was, I could have gotten away with a skirt like that.

We rounded the corner, and there was the food court, and the cambio. I made for it. Evelyn stood beside me while I punched in the numbers. She was almost vibrating, she was so excited. "You knew this whole time, didn't you?" she said. "About the child, I mean."

"I don't know, I just suspect. Could be wishful thinking." Nothing in the chequing account. "But I think I bucked up another one like him when I was a little girl."

"You lie!" Wide-eyed, she grabbed my arm. "When? Where? Did you talk to it? How come you never said?"

I stopped and looked at her. "At school, you mean? To whom?"

"To your friends," she replied. Then, "Oh."

I didn't have to tell her that she and I hadn't yet met when it had happened. All is fair in war. "Anyway. I was there last night when they brought his parents out of the water. I saw the daddy. He had the same adaptations as Agway." I tried a cash advance on my credit card. It laughed in my face. I didn't even bother to check my savings account. It had always been a joke. Savings accounts were for people with something left over to save. I took a deep breath. "Evelyn?"

"Yes?"

"Can you possibly lend me the money to take the waterbus back home, please?" The words hurt coming out of my mouth, like spitting out glass.

"Oh! Yes. Of course." She dug in her purse and I looked away, ashamed.

"Wait a minute," said Evelyn. Her hand was still in her purse. "Where you said your car was?"

I sighed. "At the mall by the medical centre."

"So how you plan to get to your house when you reach Dolorosse?"

"Walk." In my high heels, one of them broken. Over the rocky ground.

"And how long that will take, Chas . . . Calamity?"

I shrugged. "An hour, maybe." More like two, and massive blisters on my feet, shoes on or off.

"No, that won't do." She snapped her purse shut, linked her arm through mine. "Come along." She began walking me back through the mall.

"What? Come where?"

"Why are you walking like that?"

"I broke my shoe. Evelyn, I have to get home."

"And I will take you home. Let me just see if Samuel's finished work yet." She pulled a phone out of her purse, hit speed dial.

"Samuel? Hello, my love. Surprised you're at home at all. No, I'm at Courtice Plaza. I'm with a friend. No, I . . ." She giggled. "After you know I don't have eyes for anyone but you. Listen; you can come and get us? Me and my old school friend Calamity. We have to take her home to Dolorosse."

I knew that tone so well. Had heard it a million times in the school cafeteria as Evelyn organized her posse to do just what she wanted them to. I pulled my arm out of hers. "You don't have to take me anywhere. Just lend me the waterbus fare. I'll pay you back tomorrow." I had no idea how I was going to do that, but never mind.

"What?" Evelyn asked me. Into the phone, she said, "Hold on a minute, nuh?" She took the phone away from her mouth. "Calamity, we're going to take you. All right? End of story."

Anger was like a red mist in front of my eyes. She started to talk to Samuel again. I turned on my heel and walked away from her. Maybe a passer-by would lend me waterbus fare.

"Calamity!"

I ignored the sound of shoes tap-tapping behind me. I headed for one of the exits.

"Calamity!" She caught up to me, put her hand on my elbow. I yanked it out of her reach.

"No, Evelyn. You can't order me about. You're not queen of the schoolyard any more. You can't always have your way. Go home to your beloved Samuel and leave me alone!" I could feel my eyes springing water. Somehow, the blurriness made the garish micro minis on the mannequins in the clothing store look even more shameful, if that were possible. I was to the steps, making my way down with that careful, crabways movement that old women in heels adopt. When had I become an old woman?

"Calamity. I'm sorry."

I stopped. She was standing at the top of the stairs, cell phone dangling from one hand.

"Sorry for what?"

"I'm sorry I was so awful to you."

Good thing I was holding on to the bannister, or surprise would have pitched me down those stairs one time. "When?" I asked, milking it.

"Just now. I should have asked you if you wanted a lift. But Samuel says he's willing to take you, and we—"

Her words were music. I wanted more. "When else?"

She drew herself up. "How you mean? I said I was sorry."

"Not sorry enough." I kept clanking down the stairs.

I heard her give a deep, shuddery breath. "Calamity, come back here! You stubborn as any mule, you know?"

I spat the words at her over my shoulder. "That's a change. You used to say I was as *ugly* as a mule."

"Stop it, stop it, stop it!" she screamed, her voice weepy.

I kept going.

"All right, then! Jesus. In school."

I stood still a moment, puffing. It was work to walk *down* stairs nowadays. I used to run up stairs like I was ascending to heaven. And Cedric had just told me it was only going to get worse. "In school what?" I said.

"I was horrible to you in school, all right? I been thinking about it ever since I saw you the other night. And I'm sorry. I'm sorry. I'm sorry I said all those awful things. I'm sorry I egged my friends on to make fun of you. I'm sorry I super-glued your locker shut." She snuffled.

"I don't know where your necklace went, Evelyn."

She crossed her arms and looked away. "Huh. Well, I don't know about that."

"It was only a game we used to play, anyway! Sometimes I got lucky."

"You told Mr. Baldwin where to find his calculator. You found Ahmed's maths book behind the tennis court. You found Ulric's tobacco pipe. But the one time your best friend asked you for help, you wouldn't. I still don't understand why. That was my favourite, my birthday necklace, with the moonstones."

"You lost your necklace a few weeks after Mumma disappeared."

"So what?"

I sucked my teeth. "Think, nuh? My mother got lost at sea. What you suppose happened to her?"

"That she probably fell out of her boat somehow and, you know, drowned."

If she'd even gone out to sea that night. "And what you think her body would have looked like if it had been found?"

"Bloating, necrosis, morbidity." The doctor's training had kicked in. "Extremities nibbled away by . . . oh."

"Exactly. You think I wanted to find my mother's body in that condition?" Or chopped to pieces? I thought. "So I stopped the finding game. Completely. And it went away. Even if it was only luck why I found things, I turned it *off*. I'm a blasted luck repellent, let me tell you."

She was crying, the tears glowing neon, reflecting the stores' lights. She had always been able to turn those tears on and off at will. She sniffed. "I was jealous of you, you know," she said.

"What?" I took two steps back up the stairs.

"I was. So envious I hated you sometimes."

"What the fuck did you have to be jealous of me for?"

"They let you climb trees. They bought you toy *trucks*. You know how bad I wanted a Johnny Lightning Plymouth Duster?"

She saw my blank look.

"Hot Wheels! The Plymouth Duster was acid green."

"Ah."

"And you could swear!"

"Not in front of Dadda. Mumma didn't mind. She thought
it was funny."

"Both my parents minded. Ever had your mouth washed out
with soap?"

I screwed up my face. "No."

"Daddy only did that to me once. He never had to do it again.
To this day, I can't stand the smell of Pears soap."

"So you got your mouth washed out with soap. My mother
died, Evelyn. Ran away from me and Dadda and got her damned
self drowned. You made my life in school hell for five *years* because your parents wouldn't buy you a toy car?"

"When you wouldn't help me look for my necklace, I thought
you'd stopped liking me."

"Not then, no. But you sure made certain I hated you afterwards."

"I'm sorry." She was sobbing outright now.

"Oh, stop it. It's not your fault Mumma disappeared. But it is
your fault that you were being a jealous, selfish brat who couldn't
look beyond her own spoiled self long enough to see how I was
grieving."

"Oh, God, I'm sorry."

My feet hurt. I sat on the stairs, sideways so I could still
see Evelyn. Her tears slowed a little. She watched me cau-
tiously. She looked bloody pitiful. "So," I said, "you were jealous of me because I could get away with saying 'fuck' every
so often?"

She sat too, at the top of the stairs. "And because you lived in
such a cool place, and your parents let you climb trees, and you
got to row to the mainland in your own boat."

"Whenever I had to do that, it felt like my arms were coming out of their sockets by the time I reached the mainland."

"Yes, but you got to do it. Mummy drove me everywhere, made me sit properly in the car in my proper little dresses with my knees properly together. Proper little China girl."

"Oh, poor you."

"You don't give a damn, do you?" She hit the word "damn" shyly, like someone unused to saying it.

"No, I don't. I don't because of you putting mud in my hair, because of you getting everyone else to call me 'Charity Girl,' because of watching you get everything: all the nice clothes; all the nice lunches; all the nice friends."

"Yes, if you think of it that way, I guess I wouldn't care about me either." She shuddered.

"Lots of people cared about you. You had all those friends. The teachers loved you. Your parents loved you."

"And I never once climbed a tree, or rowed a boat to one of the out islands."

"You never rowed a boat because you never had to. Poor little rich girl."

"Rich little poor girl."

"Well, that was original! What the rass you would know about being poor?"

"Nothing. And what you would know about having to be perfect all the time, to be good in Home Ec *and* Maths? Nothing."

"They expected me to be good in all of them. And they were both right in the same school with me. They knew everything I did. So don't give me that shit."

"Huh." It was part rueful laugh, part sob. "You right, you know? No wonder we were friends."

"*Used* to be friends."

"I'm sorry."

"Stop it. You wearing it out."

She sniffed again, wiped her nose with the back of her hand. "God, that's unhygienic," she said. "If the nurses saw me, they would be horrified. Calamity, you don't have a tissue or something I could use?"

I sighed and trudged back up the few steps towards her. "Here." I pulled out the pack of tissues I carried in my bag and handed it to her.

"Thank you." I sat on the step below while she cleaned up.

"Whatever happened to your father?"

"Dadda? Dead. A few weeks ago."

"I'm sorry."

My belly grumbled. I hadn't eaten since lunch. Food was at home.

"What was it?" she asked. "Your father, I mean."

"Lung cancer."

She handed me back the packet with its remaining tissues. "That's a hard way to go."

"It's why I've been living on Dolorosse. I was looking after him for the two years before he died."

"Just you?"

"He only had me."

"They never found—"

"Mumma? No."

Silence.

"Well," she said, "can I?"

"Can you what?"

"Call Samuel. Take you home."

Silence. I looked down at my toes in their pinching, cracked-heel shoes. Those shoes had cost me half a month's salary.

"Goddamned baby Jesus on a tricycle in frilly fucking pantaloons."

"That means yes?" She tried a tentative smile.

I met her eyes. I did not smile back. Hers faded. "Let's go, then," I said.

She nodded and got her cell phone out again.

⌒

Michael sat on my single bed, his whole body tense as a spring. I stood on the floor near him. I sucked in my lower lip, then remembered Dadda saying he could always tell when I was nervous, 'cause I tried to suck my bottom lip right off. Michael glanced at me, gave a shame-faced giggle. "Look at the two of we," he said.

I smiled at that, though it felt like a school of tiny fish was making sport in my belly. "Yes, look," I replied. I sat on the bed beside him. "Dadda still in town. Going to a fancy restaurant with that woman from the post office. They tell me they 'on a date.'"

"That's sweet," whispered Michael. In his lap, his hands were shaking.

"It's revolting. Dadda have no business dating."

Michael pulled back and looked at me. "What, you want him to stay alone forever? Five years now your mother's gone."

I didn't want to think about it. "He not coming home till late tonight," I said. I reached to touch Michael's shoulder, but overwhelmed by a sudden terror that he might think I was starting anything, I smoothed a section of the bedsheet instead. Michael and I had always been easy physically with each other, hugging and holding hands. But this was different. Staring at the faded paisley pattern on my childhood bedsheets, I said, "I don't know what to do now."

Michael barked with laughter. "God, you're asking me? Ain't this was your idea?"

I sighed. It came out trembly. "I know. But—"

"You're a girl, Chas! I always thought I would do this with a man first."

"You did? Always?"

"Yes."

"But you never told me." I always hoped I would do it with you.

"I never told anybody."

Even-steven, then. I never told you my secret, either. My throat was constricting. I swallowed around the obstruction. "You want to not do it, then?" Please, I thought. But I didn't know which: please yes or please no. I didn't dare look at Michael's face, so I concentrated on a point below his chin. There was a vein jumping in his long neck. My eyes grazed over his body. I could see a bit of his chest where his white school shirt was open a bit at the collar. He was propped up on his elbow, one hand lightly covering the other. His hands were wide and strong, the nails buffed. Even in his tailored school greys, it was obvious that his legs were hard and shapely. He was a calypso of muscle, style, and grace, and he was beautiful. Too beautiful for me.

"Let's—" I blurted out, intending to call the whole project off.

"I want to do it," he stammered at the same time.

Well, that was that, then. I pulled my eyes up to make four with Michael's. He was looking at me gravely, his face ashen. "Like you frightened, too?" I asked him.

A rueful smile. "What you think, girl?"

I reached for his shoulder, instead found my hand settling in the warm hollow high on his collarbone, between his shoulder and his neck. He shuddered. He sat up with a jerk, his face rushing in towards mine too quickly. His lips were pursed for a kiss. It looked silly, and terrifying.

My brain shut down. I closed my eyes, made to kiss him back. Our foreheads met with a clunk.

"Ai!" yipped Michael. "Ow, man!" He held his head and laughed, looking sidewise at me. I put my palm to my own aching forehead and laughed along with him. The release of tension only made me even more shaky than I'd already been, but laughter; that was familiar. That we could do together. We giggled, then chuckled, then roared till we were both helplessly weak. Our arms tightened around each other. We were lying in each other's embrace. How had that happened?

I gulped. I looked up at Michael. "Lewwe try that again, nuh?" I said. I didn't pay any mind to how my voice croaked out the words.

"What, the head-bumping part?" he asked with a broad smile, which vanished when he followed it up with "or the kiss part?" His voice broke on the word "kiss."

"The kiss," I whispered. I put a hand on the back of his neck. It was warm and slightly oily, the way flesh gets after a day in the tropical sun. His neckbones pressed into the flesh of my hand. Skinny Michael. I pulled his head slowly towards mine. He moved with the touch, leaned in close, stared at me with a look of wonder. So close I could count all his pores. No. I wasn't going to burst out laughing again. This was too important.

His lips and mine touched. Warmth of lips, my eyes

crossing as I tried to keep them in focus. A giggle threatened to erupt from my throat. I closed my eyes. That was more romantic anyway, wasn't it? Why didn't all the blasted sex books tell you the important details?

I was so busy trying to deal with each new sensation that I nearly missed it when Michael's tongue came fluttering nervously against my closed mouth. Startled, I opened my lips a little way, let him in. His tongue tasted warm. That was the only way to describe it. Warm and friendly and muscular and basically harmless. I touched it with my own.

His breath was coming faster. A small moan vibrated up from his throat, entered mine. I was getting damp inside my panties, I could feel it. Was that okay? Would it disgust him? Frozen, I kept kissing him, not knowing what to do next. He smelt faintly of sweat, a good smell. His face filled my field of vision. I fumbled with one hand until I found the buttons of his shirt, started to undo them. My hand descended until it touched his belt. That meant I was close to . . . I jerked the hand away.

Michael sighed, took his mouth from mine. He wouldn't meet my eyes. With a determined look on his face, he put his hands to my waist. He undid the belt that cinched my school uniform. I thought my heart would explode, it was beating so quickly. "You want me to take the uniform off?" I asked him. He nodded, still not looking me in the face. I stood, pulled the pinafore over my head, let it fall to the floor. Even in the warm air, my legs pimpled from the chill of being uncovered. My fat legs. Some men liked them that way; I knew that from the comments I got when I walked through the streets of Cayaba. But some didn't like it. I sat quickly back on the bed, so that the tails of my white blouse gave me some coverage.

Michael sat up and yanked his shirt open. But he hadn't undone the very last button, the one below the level of his belt. It popped off and flew across the bed. He tried to smile at that, his face a rictus. I just looked. I couldn't stop myself. Michael and I had been swimming together many times. I'd seen his chest before. This time, the sight of it made my mouth dry. Before I could think about what I was doing, I unbuttoned my own shirt and drew it off. At the bottom edges of my vision I could see the white flashes that were my cotton panties and bra. I was a little, raw girl, trying to do something big.

Michael wouldn't look at me! He snapped his own belt open, undid his fly faster than I could see. He lay back on the bed, lifted his hips and pulled the pants down to his ankles. He was wearing snug briefs, bright blue. The contrast with his brown skin was lovely. Legs akimbo, he struggled to get the pants off his feet. "I'm sorry," he muttered.

"It's all right," I whispered. "I guess this gets easier with practice." He threw me a stricken look, and I remembered that we might never do this again. But surely we would with other people? Now I felt too awkward to try to explain what I'd meant.

Michael finally had the pants off and deposited in a bundle on the floor. He sat on the bed beside me.

"Michael."

"Mm?"

"Take your socks off too."

When we were done with our experiment that afternoon, Michael lay beside me, still shivering. He looked up into the ceiling, stared at the empty white space as though there were something there to see. He'd drawn my thin blue cotton *sheet over his middle. There was barely space on my narrow single bed for the two of us. I tried to lie beside him, wanting his warmth, but taking care not to let my body touch his. He didn't respond. I curled around my own belly, feeling my skin cool. I tried to take in the unfamiliar feelings of having been entered by another person (my private explorations with an empty, conveniently shaped deodorant bottle had felt more under my control), of having felt my internal spaces shift to make room for a new presence. Of the stickiness on my thigh, fast drying to a powdery glaze. Tried to decide whether I'd liked it. "Michael?"*

"Shit!" He sat up suddenly, nearly tumbling me off the little piece of the bed I was cotched on. I reached a hand to the floor to steady myself.

"When your father coming home?" he asked.

"Late, I told you."

"He might change his mind. I have to go." He was on his feet, already had his briefs on, his shirt. He was stepping into his pants as he talked.

"But—"

"And I have homework to do, girl." He perched on a corner of the bed, far away from me, started putting his socks on. He flashed me a brief, bright grin that went no further than his teeth. "Trig, you know? Blasted Mr. Pape. He's going to take up the assignment in class tomorrow."

I sat up, reached for my dress. "Let me walk you to the dock, then."

"No, no, no. It's all right. Don't fret yourself."

"But . . ."

He was out the door before I knew it, still buttoning up his shirt. I watched him run along the rocky road, his book bag tucked under his arm. He held it tighter than he had held me.

I stared at the fleeing flag of his white shirt until the dark swallowed it up. "You Make Me Feel Brand New" was playing on the asinine pink radio Dadda had given me two years before. When the song got to the lyrics "Precious friend, with you I'll always have a friend," I yanked the plug out of the wall. I sat on the bed and blinked until my eyes were no longer brimming. I got up and pulled on a smock top and my favourite jeans—wide-legged elephant pants in a soft brushed cotton. Then I went and made myself a quick supper. I had homework to do, too.

Next day when I went into the caf for lunch, Michael was already sitting at a table with his guy friends, talking and laughing. He saw me, but I looked away. I found an empty seat at the other end of the cafeteria.

Evelyn's husband Samuel picked us up in a Beamer, tastefully grey, that did not so much drive as it floated silently through the streets of Cayaba. I was used to bumping and grinding along in my rattletrap old Victoria. Samuel's car glided as though there were no gravity. The ride was so smooth, I could barely tell up from sideways. I felt a bit queasy.

Samuel was a quietly handsome light-skinned black man, his features vaguely familiar. His temples were a distinguished grey, and he reeked of money. I wondered if *he* gave a smooth ride too. I gulped down my queasiness.

"So," he said, looking at me through the rear view mirror, "you're a librarian?"

"No, a library supervisor."

"Chuh," said Evelyn. "Probably no difference. Chastity was always so modest."

"I get paid many thousands of dollars less a year than a librarian," I told them. "Was too busy looking after Ifeoma to get the Master's degree. Couldn't have afforded it, anyway. I would have had to go abroad to study."

The conversation went dead. I seemed to be good at making that happen. But pretty soon we were at the waterbus docks. Dealing with the business of paying our fare and navigating the car onto the waterbus kept Samuel busy. Evelyn looked out the window and drummed the fingers of one hand on the dash. Once the waterbus was underway, I said, "Samuel, thanks so much for rescuing me, eh?"

"It's all right, man. Don't mention it."

Perfect gentleman. "I'm just going to stand by the front." Never mind I wouldn't be able to see anything in the dark. But it was a relief to ease myself out of that silent car and step into the night air and the sea breeze. Evelyn's gaze after me was wistful, but she didn't say anything. When I pushed the car door closed, it snicked shut with a quiet, solid thump. You had to slam Victoria's doors to get them to close properly. The sound she made was like dropping a tyre iron, and was usually accompanied by flakes of rust snowing down onto the ground.

I moved around the other cars parked on the waterbus. Not too many at this late hour. The wind slid cool, delicious fingers along my scalp. I made my way to the front of the boat and stood there. The boat's running lights threw a widening, disappearing triangle of yellow onto the water. Outside of that, there was nothing to see, only endless dark. The prow of the boat pitched and jumped over the waves, occasionally spraying a fine mist of water over me. I looked down, tried to imagine sea people stroking through the water. I shivered. I hated night swimming.

Off in the distance was one of the Gilmor Saline barges, heading for the other side of Dolorosse. These past few weeks, the amount of dust blowing around Dolorosse from the construction was a lot less. The plant would be officially open for business soon, the week before the election. Don't tell me that Johnson hadn't planned it that way to make himself look good.

We were coming up on Dolorosse. As I got back into the car, Samuel turned to look at me. "When we get there, you have to direct me to your house, all right?"

He had a really warm, friendly smile. It was hard to keep hating him just on principle. I smiled back. "All right."

We drove down the gangway onto Dolorosse. The car took the gravel lanes of Dolorosse with the same mute grace with which it had handled the streets of Cayaba. "Left here," I told Samuel, directing him between the two silk cotton trees which arced towards each other on either side of the road.

"They look like people holding hands," he said. "The trees, I mean." So he had imagination, too. Another point for Samuel.

Evelyn was craning her neck all around, seeing what she could of Dolorosse in the dark. "You know," she said, "I've never been here. And after the hurricane, I just didn't have the taste for making the trip."

"Dadda told me that a lot of Cayabans stopped coming out to the islands after that hurricane."

"Good thing, too," Samuel said. "Gave the seal population time to get their numbers up."

"Now you sound like Hector," I told him.

"And who's Hector?" Evelyn had a sly, knowing kind of tone to her voice.

"Strange man from the university."

"A handsome strange man?" she asked playfully.

"If you like that type." I did, but I wasn't going to tell her that. "No, he's a biologist. Marine biologist. He's studying the seals. Lives in a little launch on the water all day and night, watching them through a scope and making notes."

"That sounds romantic," said Evelyn.

"Seals are all he can talk about."

"Oh." She looked back out the window again. Shame on me, bad-mouthing poor Hector. But I didn't want Evelyn getting too nosy.

"Why he studying the seals?" Samuel asked over his shoulder.

"You asking me? We don't talk much about that."

Evelyn couldn't resist. "What you talk about, then?"

Stuffy in here. I needed some fresh Dolorosse air on my face. "Samuel, how you roll down the windows in this fancy car of yours?"

"The little green arrows in the door," he told me. "Up is up and down is down."

"And never the twain shall meet?"

Evelyn giggled at me. I pushed the "down" button, inhaled the cool, salty breeze. You would think someone with enough money to run a car like this could keep the air conditioning going.

Ant crawling up my bare arm, I could feel it. I slapped it off, only to feel another one on the outside of my right thigh. *Inside my panty hose?* I rubbed my hand over the spot to squash it. But then there were more, crawling up my shins, down inside my

THE NEW MOON'S ARMS

blouse, the back of my neck; more than I could sweep off with my hands. "Shit!"

Evelyn looked over her shoulder. "What happen?"

By now I was doing a strange dance, trying to rub the ants off me from everywhere I felt them crawling. "I think you have ants in your car, Samuel."

"What? Evelyn, you left a raisin bun in the glove compartment again?"

"No. That was only the one time."

The tickling was driving me mad. "Stop the car, please. I need to get out and brush them off."

Samuel pulled the car over and stopped. I hopped out. But all I rubbed my skin, slapped at the tickling places, the sensation wouldn't stop. "Jesus!"

Evelyn opened her door. "Can you see them?"

"The ants? In this dark? No."

Now Samuel was leaning over into the back seat, searching for ants by the light of his cell phone. "I don't see anything here," he said.

The little feet had stopped crawling all over me. I waited a second, then said, "It's all right, Samuel. I think I got them all." He and I checked the back seat before I got back in, but not a thing we could find. "Let's just go," I said to him.

He got back in the driver's side. "I'm so sorry, Calamity."

"But you don't have to apologise. There's nothing in the car. I wonder where they came from?"

"Maybe you picked them up from the waterbus?" Evelyn asked me.

"Maybe." I slipped my shoes off. After all day in the sweaty panty hose, my feet were itching.

"Make a right here, Samuel."

Now my hands were itching, too. I scraped at one hand with the nails of the other, switched. Christ on a crutch—don't tell me I was allergic to ants now. "Just follow this bend around to the right," I told Samuel.

My heart was pounding, my body feeling trembly inside. "Evelyn?"

"Ah?"

"You carry anything like Benadryl on you?"

"No. Why?"

"Nothing much. The ant bites just making me a little itchy. A left, Samuel." The itching promptly got so bad I had to fight not to claw at my hands and feet. "A right here, Samuel."

Thank heaven, the itching was easing up. It was almost gone now. Looked like I'd be all right.

The air in the car was thick and close. Heat blossomed in my chest and swept upwards to my head. Sweat broke out on my face. I panted for air, trying to do it quietly so Evelyn and Samuel wouldn't hear. I leaned over and turned down the other window. Evelyn glanced briefly back at me. "Samuel," she said, "turn off the air conditioning. I think Calamity prefers the night air."

The air had been on all this time? "You sure the air conditioning is working?" I asked them. "Make another right, Samuel." I fanned my face with my hands, parted my knees to let some air get to my thighs. "Woi," I said. "Hot night, you don't find?"

"Oh!" said Evelyn. "How about we keep the air on *and* the windows open? Believe me, I know how the Change of Life can be."

The Change. Knowledge landed on me like a sack of bricks. "Shit. You're right."

"Pardon?" said Samuel.

Bare Bear; Dumpy; the almond tree; every time something had shown up, I'd been perishing for heat and scratching those two fingers.

"Calamity?"

"It's menopause. That's what's doing it."

"Well, don't be ashamed, my love. It's nothing Samuel hasn't heard from me, plenty times."

"Samuel," I said, "it's the next left." What had manifested now? And where? Must have been something big, to be putting me through all this.

We passed Mrs. Chin's place, and Mr. Robinson's little store where he sold candles, eggs, and so: basic items for people who didn't want to make the trip to the big island just to get one or two little things. I was still gasping a bit. I stuck my head out the window, sucked in air, pulled at my damp clothing. What I saw up ahead brought on chills. "Samuel, you're going to make a right at that . . . thing there in front of us."

He peered at it. "What that? Some kind of sculpture or something?"

"It's stones. Big, flat rockstones piled on each other. The island children made it."

"How sweet," Evelyn murmured.

In fact, only one island child had made it, because there'd been only one child in those days. Me. That sculpture came from Blessée. I'd built it over the days of one long summer to mark the border of our property. I'd pretended the yellow-blue brown girl from the sea was helping me, hauling rocks alongside me, and urging me to come and swim when we got too hot.

It was me. Every time I had a power surge. I shuddered, not burning up any longer. Chilled.

We were coming up to the corner; around the bend was Dadda's house. Behind my ribcage, my heart was splashing like a drowning man in the sea.

"Chastity?" said Evelyn. I didn't correct her. I was back in small-girl days. Chastity was the right name. "You didn't tell me your father had started up the cashew farm again."

He hadn't. My skin pimpled at what I saw out the car window. Our cashew grove. From Blessée. Resurrected.

"I didn't think to tell you," I murmured as we passed the fence, the mass of trees that had once been neat rows, but which Dadda had neglected until the seeds they'd dropped had spawned a cashew jungle, battling with their parents for light and air. Casuarina pines ringed the orchard as they had when I was younger, to protect the cashew trees from the wind. The spiny casuarina leaves rattled in the slight breeze, like the coco broom Mumma used to use to sweep any dead leaves away from the orchard, so we could better collect the fallen fruit. There it all was in front of me. I thought I was going to be sick.

"You cool enough now?" Samuel asked. I saw his concerned face in the rear view mirror.

"Never better," I told him, trying not to let my teeth chatter.

There was the house in front of us. The Dolorosse house, thank God, not the drowned one. I let out a shivery breath, then another. "That's it," I told them. "There's no real driveway. Park anywhere, except over there." I pointed. "I have some tomato bushes coming up."

The car drifted silently to a place in front of the house, off to one side. Samuel turned it off. It was scarcely any quieter than when it had been running. We sat in the dark as the engine ticked down. A thought unfurled in me like ice water poured into my veins. *Dadda.* Mr. Lee said the dead don't stay quiet.

"Calamity?" came Samuel's cultured voice. "You want us to see you to the door?"

"Don't you be so polite," Evelyn chided him. "I want her to invite us in." She turned to me. "Just for a little while, please? I know it's late. But you and I still have to talk about children from the sea."

"Isn't that a brand of tinned tuna?" Samuel said with a chuckle. Evelyn play-swatted him over the head.

If Dadda was back, *what* was back, exactly? What shape was he in? I didn't want to move out of the car.

"Calamity?" Evelyn was facing me in her seat, kneeling in it like an eager young girl. "Please? Only if you say yes. Otherwise we will just see you to the door and leave you alone. You and I can talk tomorrow."

Leave me *alone*? With a jumbie walking somewhere thereabout? Not a rass. I leapt out of the car, yanked Evelyn's door open. "No, no; come on in. Sit and have a drink with me. Please."

I led them to the front door, my skin prickling the whole way. The cashew trees shushed the night. Mumma used to tell me that the sound they made was their way of reminding bad little girls to go to sleep when night come. So many nights of falling to sleep with the crash of the sea coming in one window and the whispering of the cashew grove from the other.

I unlocked the door and threw it open wide. It banged against the wall and rebounded. Samuel stopped it with his hand before it hit me in the face. I reached inside, swiped my hand over the light switch and pulled it back outside before anything unknown could touch me. The hallway light was dim when it came on. I kept meaning to change that bulb. Its dusty yellow light revealed the narrow space, cluttered with two and a half pairs of my tennis shoes, a towel from the last time I'd had a sea bath, and a stack of books I kept meaning to return to the library. Good thing I didn't have to pay overdue fines. "Come on in," I said to Samuel and Evelyn. I picked up the towel as I stepped in ahead of them. If Dadda's jumbie came at us from the darkened house, I could throw the towel round his head, or something. Did a jumbie need to be able to see to grab you? I went on into the house, my protective towel wrapped around my hand and held before me.

"Everything okay?" Samuel asked.

"Oh, yes. Never better!" My voice was so bright, it was blinding. I reached around the entrance to the living room with the towel-wadded hand and flicked the light on. I stood bravely in the entrance, barring Evelyn and Samuel from going in until I checked it out. I looked around. Unless he was hiding behind the sofa, Dadda wasn't in there. And by the end, he hadn't been agile enough to crouch down anyway. But the skin on my arms was still horripilating. I took a surprised Evelyn by the hand and marched her into the living room with me, Samuel following. Nothing leapt out at us, smelling of the crypt. "There," I said to them. "That's all right, then. Cashew liqueur, anyone?"

They looked at me a little uncertainly. "Yes," said Samuel. "That would be nice. Just a small one for me. Driving, you know." Gingerly, they both made to sit on the settee. I managed to retrieve a dirty bowl with three half-exploded popcorn kernels in it before Samuel sat in it.

"I'll get you your drinks," I told them. I turned towards the kitchen. Its darkened doorway hunkered at the other end of the living room. The light switch for the kitchen was well inside the doorway, by the fridge. "Evelyn," I said companionably, "you want to come in the kitchen with me? To powder our noses, or something?"

She stood up. "Don't you powder your nose in the bathroom?"

"You, maybe. I like the light better in the kitchen. Natural. Kinder to our aging features, you know."

"But it's nighttime," she told me. "It's natural dark, not natural light."

I didn't reply. With my be-towelled hand, I gently pushed her on ahead of me. She stumbled into the dark kitchen. Lord forgive me, I waited about half a second. When I heard no screams of terror, I found the light and switched it on. "Samuel?" I called out. "You still okay out there?"

"Of course," he called back. "Mind if I look at your books?"

"No, man. Go ahead."

I opened the doors of the cupboard where I kept the glasses, looking for the crystal ware. "Evelyn, you think you could get the liqueur out from the pantry for me? It's that door over there." I couldn't face another dark room just now. "Look for a big green glass bottle on the shelf just in front of you when you go in."

"Sure, man." She let herself in. "Where the light switch?"

"You see the pull chain hanging down? Should be right in front of you."

She exclaimed. I was at her side before I thought about it. "What, what?" I asked.

She was standing safely in the doorway, staring amazed at row upon row of jugs, jars, and bottles filling almost every shelf in the ten-foot-high pantry space. Holy. Fuck.

"Calamity, what is all this?"

"Well," I said slowly, "if I remember, the jars have in cashew fruit jelly. The bottles have in cashew liqueur. The jugs is cashew wine."

"Your father made all this, or you?"

"Me? No. Was Dadda."

"He kept doing it even while he was sick?"

"Uh-uh," I said, staring at the bottles, "the cashew farm went down with Blessée." Too late, I remembered that the cashew farm had reappeared outside the door. "I mean," I said, "he was too sick to do plenty. All this is remaining from when he left Blessée. They almost wouldn't take him with everything he wanted to carry."

She smiled. "Remember how nice those roast cashews used to taste? Your father would bring them to school in those little rolled-up cones of newspaper. They used to sell them in the cafeteria."

"And is who you think roasted all those cashews with Dadda and rolled them up? That was what I did come the weekend. That and homework. Helped to stretch the paycheque."

"Oh. I'm sorr—"

"Stop it." I took the bottle of liqueur from her, poured some of it into each of three glasses. I gave her one glass. She followed me as I took the remaining two into the living room.

Samuel turned from the bookshelf, a book in his hands. "*Peter Pan?*" he said.

"Where?"

He grinned. "The Change really making you forgetful, I see." He held the book up. "From your own bookshelf."

The torn dust jacket—Chastity never could keep those undamaged. It was mine, all right. I gave Samuel his liqueur, took the book from him, handed him my glass as well.

Old possessions have a life to them. That book felt so much like *itself* in my hands, so much Chastity's copy of *Peter Pan and Wendy* and nobody else's that I nearly wept. I inspected the bookshelves. "I have *The Borrowers* too," I said, "and *Return from Last Man Peak*." At least I did now. Or again, or something. More of my rediscovered treasures, come sailing back to me on the seas of a night sweat.

"Children's books?" asked Evelyn. Her curious eyes took in Dumpy in his place of pride on the coffee table, and Bare Bear sitting in a corner of the settee. "Oh! Look, Samuel!" Evelyn plumped down onto her knees. From under the coffee table she pulled out an ancient Magic Slate. The grey sheet of plastic was creased and rumpled. Great. Now she thought I was in my second childhood. "So long I haven't seen one of these! Calamity, where you find these things?"

"Oh, you know. You'd be surprised where things turn up." I took my glass from Samuel. "To you and yours," I toasted them. Then I knocked back my drink in two burning swallows. Evelyn and Samuel sipped theirs.

"This liqueur is nice," Samuel told me. He and Evelyn sat on the settee.

"Yes, Dadda was good at making it. You want some more?"

He raised one eyebrow, but only replied, "I'm still working on mine for the moment, thank you."

Evelyn peered down the corridors leading to the rest of the house. "How long it takes you to get to work from here?"

"Forty-five minutes in rush hour; an hour if the waterbus late again."

"I see you have running water—"

"Jesus, Evelyn. It's not the Dark Ages out here, you know." But I couldn't be boasty like that. "Cell phone service not too good sometimes. And the electricity could be sometime-ish."

"But the land line works?"

"Yeah, man. Why?"

"And how many bedrooms you have?"

"Ev!" Samuel said. "Why you fasting up yourself in Calamity's business?"

"Three," I replied. What was she after? I wanted to play the game out. "Mine, Dadda's old room, and the guest bedroom."

"You have plenty activities outside of work? You come home late in the evenings?"

"No, I'm home a lot. Couldn't take on anything much while Dadda was dying. Cut back to part time at the library."

She nodded, took another sip of her drink, then swallowed the rest of it almost as briskly as I'd done. She stood up. "Samuel, you ready to go?"

He gave her a surprised look. But he put his mostly full glass down and stood.

"Dolorosse has a day care?" Evelyn asked.

Oh, fuck me sideways. Was this cruel Evelyn, or repentant Evelyn? "No," I said, "but Mrs. Soledad from over the way used to stay with Dadda for me when I was at work."

"She know how to look after children? You trust her?"

"She and her husband ran an artisan salt farm and raised three boys and a girl, and none of them in jail, and none on the street. She cared for Dadda like he was her own. Why?"

"Come into the hospital tomorrow and apply to be a foster parent. I'll give my recommendation for the little boy to come and stay with you in the mean time."

"You will?"

"Provisionally, you understand. If it doesn't work out, they might still find him another home."

I was stunned. "How come you changed your mind? This isn't more of your guilt, is it?"

"Not a bit of it. Not where a child is concerned." She

looked around. "You have the time, and the experience, and the space. You have toys and books for him to play with. He trusts you. And I have a feeling he might like to be close to the sea."

All I could do was gape at her. She smiled. "And this way, I can come and visit him and you both. Make sure you getting on okay." She grinned at the look on my face. "Maybe talk about fairy tales coming true," she said.

Samuel looked baffled. "I don't know what going on with the two of you, Calamity, but I've learned never to come between Evelyn and her schemes. I'd advise you not to even try." He took her hand. "Come on, darling. Let me take you home from a long day of playing the rescuing angel. Calamity, my dear, thank you for your hospitality."

"You're welcome."

As I walked them to their car, Evelyn said, "Tomorrow I'll send Martin around from the mechanic's to the hotel to get your car and fix that flat tyre."

"But I—"

"You're going to need a functioning car now that you have a child to look after all the way out here. If you can't pay for it now, I'll tell Martin to run you a tab. There's a stipend that comes with being a foster parent, you know?"

"There is?"

"You can pay Martin out of your first government cheque. I'll vouch for you."

I was too dazed to even wave as they drove away. The Beamer disappeared down the path, leaving me in the whispering dark with the cashew grove.

And the jumbies. It took me a while to get up the courage to go back inside.

"Keep your part of the bargain now," said the devil girl. "Pull me up out of this hole."

So Granny did that. The devil girl was slippery. Her skin was a deep blue, like the water in Blue Pit, the bottomless lagoon. And she was heavy for so! Granny managed, though. But before Granny could stop her, the devil girl shimmied up onto Granny's shoulders, wrapped her legs around Granny's neck, and tangled her long blue nails in Granny's hair. "Carry me to where you living, Granny; beg you do," said the devil girl.

And she squeezed her legs tighter around Granny's neck.

4

IN THE BRIGHT SUNSHINE OF THE NEXT MORNING, fears of Dadda's jumbie coming back to haunt me faded. There was something bigger to deal with; something real, waiting just outside my front door.

I put it off a little longer by scrambling eggs for my breakfast. Through the window, I watched Sir Grandad, the resident mongoose, slinking through my tomato plants. He'd better not damage a one. I turned my eggs onto a plate and took them to the kitchen table. I wasn't good at putting off the inevitable. I wolfed down breakfast and left the dirty dishes right there so, hoping that Sir Grandad wouldn't smell them and break into the kitchen while I was gone.

In the hallway, I scuffed my feet into my tennis shoes and took a deep breath. What Ife used to call a "calming breath" when she was in her yoga phase. After she sprained her back tying her body up into knots, I didn't hear anything more about chakras and kundalini energy again. She'd taken up t'ai chi after that, and then food combining. For two months, she would have only fruit and three pints of water for breakfast, then spend the next two hours running to pee every twenty minutes.

I went out onto the porch.

Cashew fruit. Family: Anacardiaceae. *Genus:* Anacardium. *Species:* humile. *Variety: Precocious Dwarf. Other Names: Cashew, Cashew Apple. Part Used: False Fruit.*

The dwarf-cashew grove was still out there, solid, real, and in full riot. The trees stretched their branches up, making alleluia to the first taste they'd had of the sun in over three decades. Something else must have been nourishing them down beneath the waters. The leaves were healthy and green, and each tree was bowed down with the red and yellow weight of cashew fruit. Overripe cashew apples had already started dropping to the ground.

I found myself at the gate of the fence to the grove. Then I was undoing the latch, my fingers remembering how the tooth of it always caught and you had to give it a little extra push for it to open with a click-crunch sound that only one thing on this broad Earth made: the gate to Dadda's cashew grove. I pushed. It opened. I glanced at the latch; no rust. Mumma used to be forever oiling it.

I stepped inside. The ground was dry, not soaked with brine. There was the same little patch of scrub before you hit the scrum of trees. Little after Mumma was gone, Dadda ceased to care them. The fallen apples had sprouted trees which had grown to fill the rows in.

I stopped at the first line of trees. They were bowed down with red and yellow pear-shaped fruit, each with a shiny grey shell hanging below it. A few of the branches dipped so low that they touched the ground. I'd have to prune those back; they could root and sprout whole new trees that would compete with the others for soil and light. But watch at me! Thinking like I was going to take this straggly copse of cashews seriously.

I went a little way in amongst the trees. It was dark in there, spotted in places with shifting sunlight.

The smell. I had forgotten it; the cloying sweet smell of hundreds of fallen cashew apples. The reason I hated cashew juice, though I could drink distilled cashew liquor; the smell of the alcohol was quite different than the smell of the fruit. And now I was mashing overripe cashews beneath my feet with every step, releasing that overpowering odour into the air.

I squeezed through a few more trees, pulled a cashew apple off a low branch, remembered how the smooth, shiny scarletness used to feel in my hands.

A shadow moved at the corner of my vision. When I looked, nothing was there. I went still, held my breath to hear better. Was that a rustling noise? I threw the cashew apple I was holding in the direction of the sound I thought I'd heard. The apple flicked leaves and twigs in its trajectory, landed with a thump. There was another small rustle. The sound of feet moving out of the way?

"Hello?" I said. My voice broke. It was fucking *dark* in here. Maybe jumbies didn't need nighttime; maybe they only needed *darkness*. I was surrounded by trees, their branches interlaced like fingers. My scalp prickled. I took a step backwards. Right into someone's arms. I yelled. He wrapped them tighter around me. I pulled his thumb up to my face and bit into it. The arms released me one time, and I spun around to fight.

I once pulled Ife out of the way of a car before my brain had time to understand that my eyes were seeing a red Volvo bearing down on her. Same way so it was now: I was already cocking my elbow to drive into the man's belly when it began to dawn on me that he had been speaking. And that the words had been: "Ow! Calamity, it's Gene! Don't—"

Momentum. Hell of a thing. Was a good 189 pounds of Calamity moving at speed behind that elbow. The blow was already in progress, and I couldn't stop it.

Gene took a little step backwards and pushed on my arm. Not quite quickly enough; I gave him a glancing strike across his body. The air whuffed out of him as he fell. My elbow caught air. I overbalanced, and went right down beside Gene onto my bad knee. The pain made me shout. Gene was on his back, gasping a little for air, one hand on his solar plexus. He was sucking the bitten thumb of the other hand, watching me warily.

"What the fuck you doing in here?" I asked.

He scowled. "Getting my hand bit off by a crazy woman. Every second word with you have to be a swear word?"

"You didn't have no right sneaking up on me like that!" I pushed myself up to my feet. My knee made a popping sound. "Ow."

Groaning, Gene rolled to his knees. I offered him a hand up. He ignored it. I shrugged. "Fine by me," I told him.

I held onto a tree trunk, shook my leg out to straighten it. The pulp of a cashew apple I'd landed on came detached from my knee and plopped to the ground.

Gene managed to stand up. Grimacing, he slowly straight-ened his back, one fist pressing against the small of it.

"I hurt your thumb bad?" I asked him.

"Jesus Christ, woman! You know how much bite force a human being can produce?"

"About sixty-eight pounds of pressure per square inch, on the back teeth?"

"No, that's only for regular chewing. If you bite down delib-erately, it can be up to twelve hundred pou . . . How you know that?"

"You're fast on your feet," I said. "Didn't know you could move like that." But actually, I'd experienced how agile he could be. "Come to think of it, I shouldn't be surprised." My face flushed.

He twisted his torso, making joints in his back pop. "I getting too long in the tooth for this kinda fighting, though. Going to pay for it tomorrow."

"And your hand's bleeding. Come into the house. I'll throw some white rum on that cut."

He grumbled, then said, "All right. But bring that thing with you." He pointed with his chin.

In the dark, it took me a little while to see what he was talking about. It was a rusty cutlass, lying at the foot of one of the trees. I picked it up. "You . . . came with this? To see me?"

He kissed his teeth. "Don't flatter yourself." He stomped out of the grove, headed for the house. I followed him.

"You coming to put that alcohol on?" said Gene from my front door. "I don't want to catch anything from you, you know."

"It's like they say." My knee crunched and ached up all five steps. "Don't trouble trouble or trouble will trouble you."

* * *

"Where you left the cutlass?"

Where had I put it? "I think it's out on the porch. It had mud caked all over it." Menopause memory loss, I guess. I smoothed the Band-Aid onto Gene's thumb. "So, you want to tell me why you were sneaking around in my cashews? Help yourself to some paw-paw." I indicated the orange slices of paw-paw I'd put on the kitchen table.

"Thank you." He reached to pull a chair out from under the table, then stopped. "May I?"

"Awoah. *Now* you asking permission. All right, sit down." He did. I sat in one of the other chairs, got myself a slice of paw-paw. The faint, soapy smell always made me want to blow bubbles.

"I just wanted to make sure you were all right," Gene said. "The last few days must have put you through some changes."

That surprised the laugh out of me. "If you only knew. Fuck."

He grimaced at the word. Too bad if he didn't like my potty mouth. He helped himself to a slice of paw-paw, cupped his hand under his chin so he wouldn't get its orange juice on his uniform. Then, uncertainly, he said, "Those trees. Where they came . . . I mean, I didn't see them the last two times I was here."

"You didn't? Why, Officer, you must be under some serious stress. Trees don't just appear out of nowhere like that."

"All right. All right."

"You think maybe you should have a glass of water? Maybe you're dehydrated."

"All *right*. I'm sorry, okay?"

"Maybe okay. I'm not sure." I was wearing my tough broad face, but inside I was giddy. *He came to see if I was all right.*

"How you knew about the biting force thing?" he asked me. Strips of orangey-green paw-paw skin were accumulating on the kitchen table.

"How I knew what?"

He frowned. "You just said it back in the trees. Humans? Bite force?"

"Oh! That. Chuh. Can't remember what I said twenty minutes ago, but the project I did on sharks in Fourth Form is still crystal clear in my head."

He nodded. "I know the way. You get to be a certain age, you start to find the past make more sense than the present."

"Excuse me," I said half-jokingly, "I don't think I'm quite at that age yet. And if things in my past didn't make any sense then, I don't think they going to start now."

"Maybe not." He glanced at his watch. "I have to catch the next ferry, or I'm going to be late for work." He stood up. "You have a plastic shopping bag you could give me?"

"Yeah, man." I got him one from the basket under the sink.

As we walked through the living room to the front door, he asked me, "How you learned to fight like that?"

"Michael taught me. When we were young."

"A boyfriend?"

"Michael was *never* my boyfriend." *But* you *came to see if I was okay,* I thought. Gene was starting to look more my type after all.

We went out onto the porch. Most of the mud on the cutlass had dried to a clay-pale colour. Gene picked it up carefully. Bits of dried mud sloughed off in clumps. He wrapped them and the cutlass in the plastic bag.

"Why you carrying around an old piece of something like that?" I asked him.

"Found it, just lying around." He gestured vaguely out over the island. "Somebody could get hurt. I'll dispose of it."

Sweet guy. I waved till his car was out of sight. Went in

and took a quick shower, changed into clothes that didn't have cashew apple smeared on them. Time to get Agway yet? My belly was all butterflies from happy nerves. I looked at my watch. Good. Plenty of time to be on the next waterbus. I grabbed up my handbag and headed out.

On my way out, I glanced over at the trees. Now that I was watching them from out in the sun again, they looked only un-kempt, only goofily short. Last week in the mall I'd spied a woman with a Chihuahua in her handbag. Her handbag, imagine! Sup-pose it had pissed in there, or shat? So shrunk up, it had looked like a rat. Any self-respecting member of its canine cousins could have had it for dessert. The dog had looked at me and I swear it'd trembled, mortified at what it had been bred to be. The trees looked like that Chihuahua. They were trembling too in the cool morning breeze. Just fermenting fruit on truncated trees. Maybe Agway would like cashews.

I HEAVED AGWAY UP ONTO MY HIP. I was really getting to take him home! He murmured at me and started playing with my necklace, a string of bright red-and-black jumbie beads. "Don't let him put those in his mouth," Evelyn said. "They're—"

"Poisonous. I know. Went through that already with Ife. These are fake." Still, I pulled the beads away from Agway's hands.

"Let me walk you to the car." She held the door to her office open to let me and Agway out.

"Chastity? Chastity Lambkin?"

It was Mrs. Winter, limping painfully towards me. Her ankle was wrapped. She was leaning on a cane on her left side, and on the arm of her son Leroy on the other. She eyed Agway in my arms.

"What happened to you?" I asked.

She stopped, puffing hard. "You remember, dear. That unfortunate accident. Your poor father's funeral. I sprained my ankle when I fell. And I bruised my tailbone."

"I'm so sorry," I told her.

"Yes, well," said Mrs. Winter. "If people are going to have outdoor events, dear, they really should secure the premises first. Make sure there are no hazards for others to trip on. Your father would have done that."

Agway was staring curiously at Mrs. Winter. She frowned at him. "Your grandson?" she asked.

I wasn't going to answer that. "I'm sorry you got hurt, Mrs. Winter."

She peered at me little harder, and her nosehole flared. Her eyes widened. She looked like a marabunta wasp had stung her.

"That's my pin!" she said. "You're wearing my pin!"

Her pin? I had straightened out my gold pin that she'd been using to hike her drawers up, and I was wearing it on my blouse. "No, it's mine."

"Yours?"

"Yes, I found it the day of the funeral. I'm so glad to have recovered it. I lost it when I was just a little girl." Holy crap. At the funeral—the pin! That had been the first magical power surge!

Mrs. Winter straightened up, gave me her best patronising smile. "No, Chastity. I lost it at your father's funeral. I've had it all these years. I was using it to . . . I was wearing it that day."

She'd been wearing my pin at her panty waist, to hold it together. I tried to keep my lips from twitching. "See what the letters spell, Mrs. Winter?"

She looked at the pin again. Agway reached to touch it. Gently, I pulled his little hand away. It had a sharp point, that pin. "Those aren't letters," spluttered Mrs. Winter. "They're—how you call it—rococo."

Evelyn leaned over and looked at the pin. "C, T, L," she spelled out. "Chastity Theresa Lambkin. Oh, and I recognise it, too! Isn't that the gold pin your mother gave you for your birthday? The eighth or the ninth, wasn't it? I remember you bringing it to school and showing it off!"

Huh. I owed her for that one. Owed her for a lot, right now. Never mind.

"Yes," I replied. "It's mine." I turned to Mrs. Winter. "I'm so glad you found it and kept it safe for me. All these years. What a generous thing to do."

Mrs. Winter's face was a picture.

"Well, you know Mummy," said Leroy, amused. "Too kind-hearted for her own good."

Agway burbled at me. He was getting restless.

"I have to go," I said. "Time to give Agway his lunch."

"Agway?" asked Mrs. Winter.

"Yes," answered Evelyn. "Calamity is doing a wonderful charity for us; this poor boy's family drowned at sea, and she's fostering him."

"*She's* fostering him?"

"So good to see you, Mrs. Winter," I burbled, heading for the doors to the outside. "See you at work next week?"

"That woman is a witch," declared Evelyn once we were outside.

"True that." Oh, this next thing was going to hurt. "I need to

thank you," I said, "for helping me just now with Mrs. Winter."
I managed not to choke on the words. "And for letting me look
after Agway, too." I sighed. "And for the car."

"You're welcome."

We walked in delicate silence the rest of the way to my car.
The mechanic hadn't patched the flat tyre; instead, he'd re-
placed all four and the windshield. Evelyn had paid for it. Victoria perched on her spanking new wheels like a dowager in shiny
patent pumps.

I opened the passenger side. A fiery belch came from inside;
the car had been sitting in the sun for an hour. So I opened the
driver's side, too, to let some air flow through. Agway stared curiously at Victoria, and at the others in the parking lot. He pointed
at it and asked me a question.

"I'm sorry, babby," I said. "I don't understand you."

He looked frustrated, repeated himself, this time more irrita-
bly. He pointed at the car again.

"It's a car," said Evelyn. She tapped on the roof of the car.
"Car. Can you say that?"

He just frowned at her.

"Calamity!" came a voice from behind me.

I turned. Leroy was running up to us.

"Yes?"

He stopped, panting a little. "I just want to ask you . . .
Mummy's too shamed to ask you herself, but I know she wants
to know."

"What?"

"Don't laugh when you hear this, all right? Or I won't be able
to keep my face straight when I go back to her."

"What she want?"

I didn't have to do a thing. He was chuckling the moment he

began to say the words. "She never found her bloomers that she lost that day at the funeral. She been thinking maybe somebody find it and been keeping it for her."

Evelyn flashed me a look of mock-horror. I mouthed, *I tell you later.* "No," I said. "Nobody did. At least, Parson never told me about anyone finding it." I'd materialised the plate, too! The one that had dropped in the funeral parlour! Chastity used to have a favourite blue-and-white plate.

Leroy nodded, got his face under control. "All right. Thank you." He left in the direction of where he must have parked his car. I had left that plate in Dadda's house when I moved in with Auntie Pearl and Uncle Edward.

"What *that* was all about?" Evelyn asked.

"Mrs. Winter is my supervisor at work. Her panties fell off at the graveside during Dadda's funeral."

Evelyn cackled. "You lie! Right in front of everybody?"

I nodded. "Ee-hee." *I had had a hot flash in the funeral parlour, and my favourite plate had dropped out of the sky and broken.* "She tried to kick the panties away so nobody wouldn't see, but they tangled up her foot, and she fell. That's why her ankle sprain." *Found, and then lost again.*

Evelyn chuckled. "Man, I wish if I had been there."

"You don't hear the best part yet; it's my pin she was using to hold the panties up. It was all warped out of shape when I found it on the grass."

"Lord Jesus."

That was the same look of devilment on young Evelyn's face the day we were drawing pictures in school of what everyone would look like naked, and passing the pictures back and forth during Biology class. I wanted to tell her: *Ev, I'm finding again.* She would understand. But I didn't say anything. Still too much rawness between her and me.

The car was cool enough now. I deposited Agway into the passenger seat and went round to the driver's side. "Later, then," I said to Evelyn.

She nodded, staring at Agway. "Such an incredible theory you have. About sea people, I mean."

"Mm." Theory, my big black behind.

"I want to drop in and see him from time to time. Just look him over, you know? Write up some notes for myself."

I stiffened. "So, this is how I'm to repay you? By letting you treat him like a research subject?"

Her face went hard. "Calamity, why you have to be so harsh all the time?"

"I had good teachers."

She sighed. "Well, most likely it's nothing. These things usually are. I have to tell you, though; for Social Services to let you keep him, I have to confirm that he's doing well with you."

I glared at her, but she had the power to take Agway. Maybe he had, I didn't know what—sea aunties, or cousins, or something. Fuck, if only he and I could talk! "All right," I said to Evelyn. "When you want to come and see him?"

I had forgotten that gloating smile of hers when she got her way. "How about Sunday coming?"

"Six o'clock do you?"

"Six is perfect!" she chirruped. "See you then." She waved, made an infuriatingly dainty Evelyn twirl, and went her ways. I kissed my teeth and got into the car.

WELL, if clothing was difficult to make Agway get used to, the car's seatbelt was impossible. It was like trying to chain an eel. When we were both exhausted and he was weeping with frustration and anger, I finally gave up. I drove very carefully to the waterbus docks, just praying he wouldn't try to climb into my lap. I kept all the windows but mine rolled up. Luckily, with a newly broken leg and a heavy cast, he didn't seem inclined to move around much. He just gaped through the window glass and pointed, babbling away happily at the wonders he saw out there. From time to time he knotted one fist in his own matted-up hair with the shells in it. He even sucked at the shells.

If I never found his family, he would have to stay on land, go to school.

Oh, look; it's Charity Girl!

Nobody was going to make this child a laughingstock. Not while I was around to draw breath. "First thing you need, my boy, is a haircut."

When we got to the dock, Agway got excited. His first glimpse of the sea in two days. He tried to climb out his window, but only clunked his forehead against the glass. I ran my window up. He complained at me, clearly telling me that he wanted the stupid force field to go away. When that didn't work, he tried pushing at the glass with his hands, grizzling the whole time. From grizzling he progressed to whining; from whining to something that sounded a lot like cussing; from cussing to a full-blown toddler tantrum of shrieking, bawling, kicking, lashing out. I had to slip the waterbus fare out with one hand through a chink in the top of my window. With the other one, I was trying to keep Agway quiet in his seat.

The ticket-taker peered into the car to see what all the commotion was about. "That's the little boy!" she said. "The one you saved!" Cayaba Gossip Cable was clearly in full effect.

I steered the car one-handed onto the waterbus, found a place on the lower level where there was no view of the sea. Parked and pulled a flailing Agway into my arms. No way I could open the windows the whole way. "Baby boy, baby boy," I said, "you can't jump in the water. Not with this cast on your leg."

He kicked and shrieked. His hand got me a good one in the jaw. Then his elbow connected with the horn. It blatted, and he jumped. He went utterly still. He stared at the horn. He leaned over and hit it again. He chortled at the sound. The people in the cars around us glared at me. It was going to be a long ride home.

WHEN I FINALLY PULLED UP in front of Dadda's house, there was a small crowd outside the resurrected cashew grove. Lord, give me strength; what to tell all those people?

I turned off the ignition and thankfully opened the window. It had been blasted hot, having the windows up for the whole trip. Agway's first cheque was going to put air conditioning in my car. Keep both of us more comfortable.

Over by the orchard gate, Mr. Lessing asked Mrs. Lessing, "What kind of trees they are?" The Lessings were my closest neighbours, a good mile away.

"Like you don't have eyes?" she said. "Anybody could see arac apples growing on them."

Two teenaged boys were swinging on the low fence. "So climb over and go inside then, nuh?" one of them dared the other. His friend just kissed his teeth, trying to look cool.

"Those not no blasted arac apples," snapped Mr. Lessing.

"And besides, how a whole orchard just spring up like that overnight?"

The two young men started lobbing pebbles towards the cashew trees. Mrs. Lessing made them stop.

Maybe I could sneak past them all and get inside the house. I opened my door and pulled Agway towards me. I got him as far as the driver's seat when I heard: "Mummy, I could go and play in there?" My heart lurched. The little boy who'd asked the question was tugging at his mother's hem and pointing at the trees.

She stooped down till they were eye to eye. "You not going in there unless I give permission. You hear me?"

He pouted. "Yes, Mummy."

That's when Agway did his trick again. He leaned on the car horn, grinning. Shit. He giggled as I pulled him out of the car and up onto my hip. My left lower back twinged at the motion.

I turned to face the crowd. Everybody was staring at us. "You see what you did?" I muttered to Agway. He reached towards the beloved car horn, nearly overbalancing the two of us. I stepped away from Victoria, kicked her door shut.

"Calamity; you reach?" It was Mrs. Soledad, coming towards us out of the crowd. I took Agway to meet his new babysitter.

"So this is the boy?" she asked. Today the hat was a snappy purple fedora.

"I'm calling him Agway." Shy, Agway buried his face in my bosom.

Mrs. Soledad's topper kept drawing my eye. Attached to the hat band, a jungle of cloth flowers fought for space with plastic fruit whose real counterparts had no climate zones in common: bright red hibiscuses elbowed dewy purple grapes aside; bougainvilleas in every colour tickled the cheeks of plump maroon American cherries.

"Who let his hair get like that?"

"I guess his parents." There was even a snake lily in the hat band. And three loquats.

She kissed her teeth. "Have the child looking wild like that."

Wild. She didn't know the half of it.

"You going to want to get him some hats," she said. She pointed at the sky. "The cancers, you know."

Agway started to fuss. "He been cooped up in the car for too long," I said. "Come inside with me, nuh?"

The Lessings were heading our way, the rest of our neighbours not far behind. I groaned.

Mrs. Lessing asked her husband, "If it's not arac apples, then what?"

"Arac apples have their seed inside," he replied. "You don't see those have the seed on the outside? I don't know why you won't wear your glasses. Chastity; like you take up farming, or what?"

Mrs. Lessing added, "And who is this you have with you?"

"Don't tell me he and all spring up overnight," grumbled Mr. Lessing.

"He got lost at sea in the storm the other night," I answered.

Murmurs of pity came from the crowd. "I read about him in the papers," someone said. "It's Chastity who find him."

"He's staying with me for a little bit." Agway looked up at me, tried to reach for a nubbin of my hair.

"What's your name, baby?" Mrs. Soledad asked Agway. He ignored her.

"He's deaf?" asked Mrs. Lessing.

"Mannerless," her husband said. "All the youths mannerless nowadays." He glared at the two boys who'd been throwing stones.

"He just don't understand English," I told him.

"What then? French?" asked the woman whose son wanted to go and play in the cashew grove. I sometimes saw her riding the same waterbus with me on my way to work in the mornings. I'd never spoken to her before this.

I shook my head. "We don't know what he talks yet."

Agway, restless, started to fuss. "Look at that," said Mrs. Soledad. "Maybe he need to change his diaper. Big boy like this, and not potty-trained yet. Calamity, take him inside." She shooed me towards the house like any hen. Gratefully, I climbed the steps to the porch. To the crowd, she said, "Allyou must go away and leave the child to settle in. Calamity could explain about the cashew trees later."

Like hell I could. Inside, I put Agway on the couch and peeked through the jalousie windows at the front yard. With me no longer there to interrogate, the crowd began to thin. As the Lessings turned to leave, Mrs. Lessing said to her husband, "Cashew trees? Her father used to raise cashews once upon a time, nuh true?"

"So he tell me."

"I'm so glad you can do this, Mrs. Soledad. I can't thank you enough."

"Yeah, man." She was dandling Agway in her lap. She'd agreed to come and look after him every Tuesday through Thursday when I would be at work.

"Okay if I pay you every two weeks?"

"Ouch!" Her hat was on the floor, her head cranked towards

her shoulder. Agway had discovered her two long plaits and was yanking on one as hard as he could.

"Shit, I'm sorry!" I leapt up to help her. "It's just this thing he likes to do."

Between us, we got him to at least give her enough play so that she could hold her head upright. To distract him, I gave him Dumpy. Didn't work; he just took it in one hand.

"I should tell you, he don't seem to like sweet things." She nodded. Agway held Dumpy up in the air and inspected it.

"And I brought home some liquid painkiller. He might need to get it every four hours or so. Depend on if the leg's paining him or not."

"All right. Where he going to be sleeping?"

With a happy screech, Agway slung Dumpy across the room. Mrs. Soledad hissed as the motion pulled on her head. Dumpy hit the coffee table and knocked a vase down. I managed to catch it before it rolled off the table.

"You right, you know," said Mrs. Soledad.

"Pardon?"

"You can't thank me enough."

AT LUNCH Agway licked all the butter off his baked potato before eating the potato itself. Then I put him on Dadda's bed for a nap. I sat on the bed and watched him sleep. I would have to stay with him the first few nights to keep him from falling out of the bed, and to keep him company. But he would have to learn to sleep alone soon. After all, suppose I wanted to have an overnight guest? My body tingled with the memories of Gene's skin against mine; of Hector's eyes searching mine.

This room looked like an old man's, not a young boy's. I got a bucket from the kitchen and loaded it with Dadda's colognes and creams and medicines from the top of the dresser, leaving only the dust. I got a singlet out of the dresser drawer and used it as a dustcloth. Better. I was halfway to the living room when I remembered the bucket full of medicines I'd left in Dadda's room. I went back and got it. Threw them all out. Wasn't making that mistake twice in a lifetime.

I took Dumpy from the living room and put him on top of the dresser. More like it.

I pulled open Dadda's closet doors. A dry smell drifted out. I dove behind the hanging clothes, took out the suitcase Dadda kept in there. I piled all the clothes from the dresser into it and sat on it till I could get the zipper closed. "Beg pardon, Dadda," I whispered. "You see that it's in a good cause though, right?"

Out in the living room, the land line rang. So loud! It could wake Agway. I got to it on its third ring. "Hello?"

"Cal? That's you?"

"Michael?" My skin flushed hot. My fingers itched fiercely. Chastity's once favourite mug, her blue-and-white cocoa-tea mug to match the broken plate, rolled out from under the couch.

"Girl, you never answer your cell phone?"

"Uh, reception still not too good out here. How you got this number?"

"Well. Good to hear from you, too. I heard about your father. Ife called me. I'm so sorry."

"Beg pardon! I was going to phone you. Tomorrow. I just been so busy." I was going to kill Ifeoma.

"Cal, you don't have to pretend. I know how things stand between you and me."

I couldn't think of anything to say to that.

"Besides, it's hell organizing a funeral. When Orso's sister died last year, all the details simply overwhelmed us, you know. Phoning everyone, and the cards to be sent out, and the flowers. She had left Orso orders that she wanted a wreath made of pink orchids, and he couldn't find any anywhere in the city."

"Mm-hmm," I murmured. Orso. Michael's man. I would never get used to how affected Michael sounded now. It's so he used to sound when we were growing up? I couldn't remember.

"But listen to me rattling on," said Michael. "To tell the truth, I'm nervous. Didn't know if it would be okay to call you."

"It's good to hear your voice, Mikey." It was, too. That was a surprise.

"How are you?" he asked. "It must have been dreadful."

"I guess I'm all right. After all, I knew he was going. Was just a matter of when."

"And, girl, how did you manage out on that lonely little island for so long? You moving back to Cayaba now?"

"I don't have an apartment there any more. So I'm here in Dolorosse."

"My God. But you're selling that old house, aren't you? You're moving back into the city?"

Agway came crawling out of the bedroom, his face puffy with sleep. When he saw me, he rocked back onto his behind and sat rubbing his eyes.

"I'm probably going to stay here," I told Michael.

He was silent for a second. Then he said, "All right." Now he had on his brisk "here's what we'll do now" tone. "What kind of shape that house is in?"

"Truth? The outside steps falling down, and the porch feeling sort of rickety. And there's two broken windows that Dadda never fixed, just boarded up."

"That settles it, then. I'm coming out there."

"What?"

"Michael Jasper Construction is going to get your house back in shape. You home in the day tomorrow?"

"Yes, but—"

"Good. Eleven a.m. do you?"

"Michael, I can't just—"

"You will be there?"

". . . All right. Yes."

"We'll do a first inspection. Be good to see you again. Ciao, sweetie."

"But . . ."

I was talking to a dial tone. I hung up and went to check Agway's diaper.

The touch of chagrin I felt when I heard Michael's voice was still there. Three—no, nearly five years since I'd seen Ifeoma's father.

I slept beside Agway that night. About six next morning, I had a hot flash that half woke me up. Then I nearly died of fright when my old red tricycle landed with a crash right beside the bed. Scared the piss out of Agway. "It's okay," I said to him. "It's a tricycle. Can you say 'Trike'?"

He blinked sleepily at me. I got out of bed. My nightgown was soaked through with sweat. I had a look at the trike. It still had the slightly warped running board and rust spots in places. It still had the streamers coming out of the handlebars, raggedy where wind, sun, and a none-too-careful six-year-old me had torn them. My heart was stuttering from the scare, but I smiled. "I think you're going to like this one, Agway."

He kneed his way across the bed to me. I sat and pulled him into my lap. He got a fistful of my nightie in lieu of hair, and put his thumb in his mouth. He had dried tear-tracks on his face. The fright from the tricycle, or had he been crying in his sleep?

A CAR WAS PULLING UP in front of the house. I put *Hop on Pop* down on the couch beside me, scooped Agway up from my lap, and took him with me to the living room windows. "'Op," he said. "Pop."

"Good boy." It was Ife! And she'd brought Stanley. But on a weekday? We went out to meet them.

Stanley got out of the car and stared at the cashew grove. "Cool!" He slammed the door, catapulted himself toward the trees.

"Stanley Fernandez, come back here right now!" shouted Ifeoma.

"But, Mum . . . !" Stanley stopped on the gravel path outside the house, his shoulders slumped.

Ifeoma didn't remove her shocked gaze from the trees as she said, "This minute, Stanley. Come and stand by me. You are not going in there."

Good a time as any for me and Agway to make our entrance. I carried him down the porch steps to my family.

"Mummy," said Ifeoma, "how did that—?"

I gave Ife a kiss on the cheek. "Why you not at work?" I asked her. "Why Stanley not in school?"

"I just decided to give us a little holiday," she said. Then she bit her lip. Something she wanted to tell me, then.

I put Agway down on his feet in front of Stanley. "Stanley, meet Agway. Agway, Stanley."

Stanley stared doubtfully at him. Ife gave him a gentle push forward. "What do you say, Stanley?"

"Hello?" Stanley enquired.

Agway made a friendly warble. I'd heard it a few times now. I figured it was his equivalent of "'sup?"

"Agway's saying hello," I told him.

"You gave him a name?" Ife asked.

"I didn't hear him say hello," said Stanley.

"Of course I gave him a name. You want me to call him 'Hey, You'?"

"But his parents probably already gave him a name."

"They not around for me to ask them."

"Mum, can I get my hair like that?"

"Maybe, darling."

"*Maybe?* I'm cutting those horrible knots out of Agway's hair first chance I get. You can't be serious, Ife. Don't tease the poor boy."

Ife pulled Stanley to her side. "You mean, don't tell him I'm going to give him something when I have no intention of doing so?"

Here we go. That one was from chapter six, verse 212 of Ife's Epic Litany of The Wrongs of Calamity. "I got you Black Barbie," I told her.

"You said you were going to get me Pretty Changes Barbie."

"And you wanted your hair straightened to match hers, and you asked me how to make your skin 'nice and light' like hers. You wanted me to buy you self-hatred."

"Okay, you're right. Maybe I should let Stanley do something that would help him to love his blackness. Like . . ." She looked mock-thoughtful, then snapped her fingers. "I know! Locksing his hair!"

"Ife! Be serious!"

"As a heart attack."

God, Agway's hair. I'd managed to cut two or three locks off this morning, but he'd screamed bloody blue murder when he'd seen the pointy scissors. I'd had to stop. Couldn't take scissors to the head of a child who was squirming and fighting you the whole time.

Agway waddled a little way away, squatted down. Hugging his knees, he studied the ground all around him.

He best had learn to stand a proper haircut before he was old enough for school. Children were pack animals; let any one of them act different from the group, and the rest would bring him down.

"Why he walks so funny?" Stanley asked.

"It's those patches on his knees; see them? They stick together if his two legs touch."

Ifeoma looked at Agway's legs. Her face went smooth with pity. "My God," she whispered.

Agway picked up a pebble. He stood and came over to Stanley. Gravely, he handed Stanley the pebble. Stanley took it, stared aghast at his hand, then looked at me. "It's all dirty," he said. "Why he want to give me that for?"

Agway had been watching Stanley's reaction closely. He'd been doing this with me since we woke up this morning—giving me pebbles. I couldn't figure out what the blazes he wanted me to do with them. When I'd thanked him for one, he'd just looked disappointed. When I'd tried putting one in my purse, he'd burst into tears.

Stanley tossed the pebble away. "No!" I shouted, too late. But Agway shouted with laughter and clapped his hands. "To rass,"

I muttered. Ifeoma tisked at my language. "That's what he wants me to do with it."

Stanley picked up another stone and gave it to Agway. The child stared at it, turning it around in his fingers. Then he flung it away from himself as hard as he could. He made a little dancing motion with his feet, grinned and chirruped encouragingly at Stanley. He searched around in the dust at his feet, picked up and discarded two more pebbles before he found another that he liked. He handed it to Stanley.

Ifeoma and I watched them trade back and forth like that for a bit. "Children," I said to her. "For the first little while, they not exactly human, you don't find?"

She gave a little wry snort. "Yeah," she said. "Once I was in the shower, and I asked Stanley to look on my bed and bring me the bra that was on it. He brought me Clifton's jockstrap."

"No! Why?" This was more like it.

"That's the only thing he could find that looked to him like underwear. He say he thought it was a one-bubby brassiere."

I laughed. "You want to come inside for something cold to drink?"

"Okay."

The boys were still doing their pebble toss. "Stanley, you want to go inside and watch tv with Agway?"

"Yes, Grandma." Stanley wasn't looking at us. He was looking for a stone for Agway.

"Well, don't wait for us. Just go on in."

"All right. Come, Agway." Stanley reached for Agway's hand.

The child gazed up at him, his face open and innocent. He put his hand into Stanley's. They toddled up the stairs together.

When they were inside, I said to Ife, "You want to tell me what's wrong?"

She replied, "I pined for that Pretty Changes Barbie for weeks, you know."

"I'll take that as a 'no,' then."

"I didn't sleep all night Christmas Eve. I kept imagining opening the box and seeing her inside."

"Okay. I going to break this down for you. What happened to the Raggedy Ann I got you for your birthday that time?"

"That not fair! You can't—"

"What happened to her?"

Small voice: "I tried to put her through the meat grinder."

"What happened to the whatchacallit there—the Turnip Patch doll?"

"*Cabbage* Patch."

"And?"

Smaller voice: "Left it outside in the rain."

"For three days. Don't forget that part. It was slimy with mildew when I found it."

"Well, all right. Dolls kind of bored me. They looked so nice on tv, but when I got them, they were just plastic."

"You see? So how I was to know you could tell one from another?"

"Because it was the one I *asked* for."

I sighed, took her arm. "I have lime wash with brown sugar. Just the way you like it."

"With ice?"

"Plenty ice. Come."

IN THE KITCHEN, I got the ice and the bottle of drink out of the fridge, and poured lime wash for all four of us. I put Agway's into a child's sippy cup, the kind with the lid and the teat. He understood teats.

"Soon come, Ife." I took the drinks out to the boys. Stanley was introducing Agway to the joys of science fiction tv.

Ife came out of the kitchen with our glasses. She handed one to me. Sotto voce, she said to me, "Clifton didn't come home last night."

"I see. You want to go out on the porch and talk?"

She nodded.

We sat on the porch steps. Ife said, "How that cashew farm come to be there, again?"

"I came home one night and it was just there." I didn't mention the little detail of my magical power surges. Sometimes a half-truth is better than a whole one. "You know strange things always happening in Cayaba."

"But that don't make no sense!"

"True that." I swirled my lime wash around in my glass. The ice cubes clinked in the translucent pale green. "Plenty in this world don't make sense."

"Not like this!" She took a big gulp of her drink. Thought a bit. "Two, three weeks since I last been here? Maybe in that time—"

"In that time what, Ife? A whole cashew grove sprout and grow in two weeks?"

"Well, the trees not so tall . . ." she said lamely.

"Don't."

"Don't what?"

"Don't do like everybody around me doing. Don't try to come up with a story to explain it, then talk yourself into believing the story. That thing out there don't have no explanation. Until or unless it choose to go away back again, I have to live with that knowledge every morning I wake up and see it. Don't let me have to live with that alone."

"But—"

"Please, Ife."

Ife stared into her glass.

"Now, tell me about Clifton. What's wrong? Something happen to him?"

She shook her head. "No. He texted me this morning. He's okay."

"Then why he didn't come back? Don't tell me he's seeing somebody."

"Nah. We were fighting. Again."

"What about?"

Her smile was sad. "Better you ask what we *don't* fight about. We war about whether Stanley going to take cricket or band. Whose turn it is to wash the dishes. Whether hotels should be able to have a lockdown on beachfront property or not."

"And last night? What the fight was about then? It's you who started it? I know your mouth hot."

"I had a good teacher."

"You know, I have this book you should read: *Anger Management for Women*."

"Oh, yes? You read it yet?"

"Don't be fresh. I'm your mother."

She laughed bitterly. "Not 'Calamity'?"

I closed my eyes. "Bravo. Hat-trick."

The silence stretched between us like chewed-out gum.

"You been inside the cashew grove?" she asked me finally.

"A little way in; not far." Thank you, daughter mine, for the change of subject.

She drained her glass, put it down. "You want you and me to go explore it?"

I gulped. Casually, I said, "Nah, it's all right. Could always do that another day."

Ife grinned. "You frightened!"

"No, that's not it—"

"Big old hard-back woman like you, frightened of a few little trees."

"Oh, yes? You think so, enh?" I knocked back the rest of my lime wash, clunked the glass down. "All right, I dare you. You and me, right now. In the cashews."

She stood. "Right this minute. I double dog dare you!"

"What?"

She shrugged. "Don't ask me. I hear Stanley say it."

We let Stanley and Agway know where we were going. Stanley didn't even look up from the television. He just grunted. As we went through the front door, I heard him say to Agway, "Those are Cylons. They're the bad guys."

WE PUSHED OPEN THE OLD GATE. The twisted trees huddled together shoulder to shoulder, blocking our view of what was inside. All we could see beyond the first row of trees was darkness.

Ife got a puzzled look. "But wait," she said. "I *remember* this. How come I remember it? The pattern of the chicken wire on the gate, and this little picky path, how it jog to the left up ahead. Dadda brought me cashew-picking in here one time."

My heart climbing up my throat, I shrugged *I don't know*. Let Ife judge for herself.

"Mummy, this is Dadda's cashew grove?"

I could breathe again. "It seem so."

"But it can't be the same one. How it could be the same one?"

"I don't exactly know."

"I remember that tree there"—she pointed—"how it look like a man holding his arms up in the air, with big long fingers, waving for us to stay out."

"Oh, fuck. Why you had to go and say that?" It *did* look like an angry man with grasping claws.

"Beg pardon. Here. Make the sign of the cross and stamp your right foot two times. Then turn around in a circle— clockwise only!—and say, 'The Devil can't touch me, Santa Maria.'"

She demonstrated. I goggled. "Ifeoma Fernandez, where you learn that piece of nonsense?"

"You not going to do it?"

"No."

"Then don't tell me nothing when the Devil grab you and not me." She smiled her pointy, impish smile, showing all her teeth. That meant she was scared, too.

I kissed my teeth. "Just hold my hand."

We advanced into the trees. It was hot and close in there. The ground was dappled with sunlight. A breeze ssu-ssued in the trees, and the heat baked the sweetness from the fruits both fresh and fallen.

"I started working for Caroline Sookdeo-Grant's campaign," said Ife. "That's why Clifton's mad at me."

"Another project? So the thing where you read people's minds by watching which direction they look in not working out?" I scraped my hand against my jeans.

"NLP? It's working fine. Caroline says it could come in handy. She wants me to come with her when she goes to talk to that foreign aid agency. She's been working with the fishermen. They want to have a permanent shop in the market, but they need start-up capital, so Caroline's going to try to help them to get a loan from the FFWD."

"Mm-hmm. You know I don't pay too much attention to politics. But all that sound pretty harmless to me."

"Clifton don't want me working for her. He say I shouldn't be helping her party get into power, because she want to kick the big hotels out of Cayaba. He's trying to work a deal with the Grand Tamany to host an annual music festival here, and he say he will look bad if his wife is working for Sookdeo-Grant. He say if the hotels go, then he and me going to be broke even worse than now."

"Not you alone. Half of Cayaba." My two fused fingers were prickling. Hot flash coming. Shit. I let go of Ife's hand to scratch mine.

"But she don't want to get rid of the hotels! She just think Cayabans should own them."

"Whoever own them, I bet you a rum-and-water still going to cost ten American dollars at the Tamany." I rubbed the itchy hand. What was going to appear out of thin air this time? My first training bra with its pointy, itchy cups of white cotton? That Beatles eight-track I used to have, that would change tracks with a clunk in the middle of "Blue Jay Way?" Some things need to stay lost. "Ife, I don't know what to tell you about Clifton. I never lived with a man more than a few months. If I ever get so lucky, you going to have to teach me."

That got a rueful laugh. "That would be a first."

I chuckled. "Your backside." We tromped on a bit more. "Remember that summer I took you to see Dadda? I think you were seven."

"You took me a few times. They kind of mixed up in my head."

"Well, that summer, your grandfather told me that I was a fool for dating the guy I was seeing at the time."

"Doug," said Ife.

"Dadda said I was never going to amount to anything if I didn't finish school and go university. I told him I was making more than he, so he could just kiss my black ass. He invited me to leave. So I took you home. The following Monday, Doug phoned me. Told me had married a girl from Copra Corners on the weekend. Said him and me had only ever been casual anyway, and he hope I didn't mind."

Ifeoma kissed her teeth. "I remember Doug. He used to call that girl from your phone when you weren't around."

"He did?"

"I heard him. Plenty times. I didn't like Doug. But he made you laugh."

"True that. I met the girl afterwards. She seemed like a nice girl."

"Not like you, enh?"

I grinned into the dark. "Never like me. Nice girls don't have fun."

Something rustled from deeper inside the grove. Ifeoma gasped. "What's that noise?"

"Don't squeeze my hand so hard!" I said.

"You squeezing mine!"

"You want us to turn back?"

"No."

We took a few more steps. I stumbled on a rock. Ife held me up. Then she walked face-first into a tree. My breathless giggle had an edge of hysteria to it. She cut her eyes at me. She looked over my shoulder, and frowned.

"What?" I asked. The skin on my back was crawling. But I wasn't going to look behind me. "You trying to psych me out, nuh true?"

Ife shook her head. "I know a way to see if this is really Dadda's grove."

"How?" I was beginning to get warm.

"Come over here." She led me off to the left, then through two trees standing in each other's arms. She stopped again. "I trying to remember . . . I think we go this way now."

The core of me flared like a wick. "No, it's this way." I pointed.

"How you know?"

"Let's just say it's like playing hot and cold. You coming?"

"You even know what it is I'm looking for?"

"Not a clue."

But she followed.

I took us right, then left. Less sunlight here. My eyes were taking their sweet time adjusting. "Damn it, I can't see a fucking thing."

"Mind your mouth."

"I'm fifty-three years old. I will swear if I want to swear."

Something bonked me on the head. I nearly peed myself with fright. A cashew apple.

My left hand started to burn like I'd stuck it into a nest of fire ants. Then the other hand began burning, too. "All right," I groused at them. "Jesus." I backtracked us a bit and took a different turn. The itching eased.

"You still talk to yourself," Ife said.

"Yeah, man. If I want intelligent conversation."

"You are so weird."

"Then I guess Cayaba is right where I belong. Go left here."

Ife gasped. "Look it there."

"What?"

"Just come, nuh?"

A few more feet, and we stood in front of yet another cashew tree. It was gnarled and half its branches were dead. Ife reached out and touched its bark. "Don't touch it!" I said.

"Lord have mercy," she said in a whisper.

I screwed my myopic eyes up and stared at the tree as hard as I could. The bark was studded with the heads of iron nails. "What kind of obeah this?" I asked Ife.

"Dadda did it."

She put her palms flush against the nail heads. "It's Dadda's wish tree, come out of the sea." Her voice was reverent.

"What you mean, 'wish tree'?" He must have done this after I left. Chastity knew the cashew orchard like the back of her hand, and she'd never bucked up something like this in there.

Ife leaned her cheek gently against the nail heads. "He said to me, 'Iron is magic, Ife. And living wood is magic.' And then he gave me a nail and a hammer. He showed me how to put the point of the nail against the bark. 'Hold it good,' he said. 'Don't make the hammer mash your hand.'"

"And all of that was in aid of what?"

"He told me to think about something I wanted real bad, to wish for it as I was driving the nail into the tree."

"Dadda was like you that way." I kicked through the undergrowth at the foot of the wish tree. Nothing. "Always some little ritual, some superstition." I scrubbed my hands against the thighs of my jeans. "Jesus fuck, if my hands don't stop itching me soon, I'm going to scratch them right off!"

"You allergic to something?"

"Menopause."

"For true? Yes, I guess you about the right age."

"No age could be the right age for this kind of botheration." If Ife could be brave, I could be brave, too. I touched the tree.

The itching faded to a tickle. I took my hands off the tree. The sensation ramped back up to burning. "Awoah. I get you now." I started feeling up the tree itself.

"Mummy, what you doing?"

"When I figure that out, you will be the first to know."

My hands found a hole. "Ah, look at that. Your wish tree is hollow."

The burning was telling me to stick my hand down into the hole. "You must be mad," I muttered. "You know what could be waiting in there to bite me?"

But apparently the burning did know its own mind, for it sped like bush fire up my two arms and blossomed into a power surge. "All right! Crap." I looked around the ground until I found a good, long stick. I stood as far away from the hole in the tree as the stick would let me, and poked the tip of it down inside.

"Jeez, Mummy; be careful!"

"Doing my best." The burning in my hands had faded to a faint pins-and-needles. I poked about inside the hole. Nothing, nothing. Then the tip of the stick jammed up against something soft and yielding. I dropped it and jumped away.

"What happen?" said Ifeoma. She was at my side in a second.

"It's all right. I just jumpy." I picked up the stick, poked around in the hole in the tree some more. The thing in there yielded when I prodded. "Feel like a pillow, or something."

"Not a dead animal?" asked Ife.

"Jeezam. Could be." The skin on my arms went into goose-bumps. I drew the stick out. A loop of heavy cord was snagged around it. "Huh. If it's a dead animal, it have its own leash."

"Euw."

I untangled the cord from the stick and pulled on it. After a little resistance, a dingy canvas duffel bag came out. It was knotted tight shut. Something had been stuffed inside. The bag wasn't as heavy as I would have expected.

"What is that?" asked Ife.

"No idea." My hands felt normal again. "I know about the bag, at least. Was Dadda's." It had probably been white once. But even when I was little, it had had this same stained cement colour. "He used to take it when he went fishing."

The hot flash faded. Chills not too bad this time. I rested the bag on the ground and worked at the knot. Ife felt the bag. "Whatever's in there is soft. Feel like cloth, or something."

"Pity. I was hoping it was my inheritance." I was joking, but my mind was running riot. Mumma's clothes in there, maybe. The ones she'd worn on that last night, soaked in her own blood.

I finally got the knot undone. I pulled the mouth of the bag open, but in the twilight under the trees, I couldn't make it out.

"Empty it out," suggested Ife.

So I upended the bag. Something furry fell out and landed silently on the ground. I gave a little squeak and stepped back. I put the stick to work again. I unrolled the balled-up thing. "It's some kind of animal hide," I told Ife.

Stretched out, it looked to be at least six feet long. I couldn't smell any decay. I threw down the stick and laid a hand on the pelt. It was supple. Good tanning job. I crouched down to see what I had caught. "I think it's a fur coat," I said. "Why, though?"

I picked it up. It was lighter than it looked. I shook it out. "Ife, you ever see a fur coat where they leave the head on?"

"I never see a fur coat, full stop. Not in real life, anyway. No, I lie. Sometimes hotel guests have them." She came and looked at it. "Oh, God." Her voice was sad. "This is a crime. Who would do something like this?"

I could make out the flippers now. I dropped it back onto the ground and wiped my hands against my shirt. "It's not a fur coat yet, is it."

"No. Monk seal pelt."

"Why you figure Mumma and Dadda had a sealskin?"

"These fetch a *lot* of money. One time, police came to the Tamany and broke down a guest's door. Took her right out of there in handcuffs. Confiscated two seal pelts she'd bought on the black market here. She was going to take them back to foreign and sell them."

I had a sudden, sickening thought. "Oh, milord. Cashew bark."

"Come again?"

"You use it to tan leather."

"Euw."

"Maybe they fell out over this, Ife! Mumma and Dadda. One of them wanted to tan seal hides to sell, and one didn't."

"Or they were arguing over the money."

"My parents," I whispered. "You think you know who people are."

"Christ. Let's just bury it," said Ife.

"I will go you one better," I told her. A bilious anger was bubbling up in me. "I'm going to burn the damned thing."

I snatched up the pelt and wadded it into a bundle. I stuffed it back into the duffel bag and slung it over my shoulder. "Let's go."

Ife was staring at the wish tree.

"Dadda said I didn't have to tell him my wish. So I only whispered it. Dadda never heard what I said."

I thought she wouldn't tell me, either. But then she said, "I wished for you and him to stop fighting. I wished we could go and live with him, not with Doug or Carlyle or—who was the boyfriend before that?"

"Nathan."

The tears just sprung, no warning. I put my arms around Ife. She hugged me back and held me till I was quieter. "I have a hair clip in my pocket," she said.

"I don't follow you."

"It's made of steel, but steel is iron and something else, right?"

"Yeah. Nickel, chromium, or tungsten."

"I hate it when you do that."

"Go 'weh. You just jealous because my memory better than yours."

"You making this wish or not?"

The clip was short and wide, its two halves hinged at one end. It was sturdy enough to drive into the wood without bending. Ifeoma pulled out the pin that held the hinge together. She handed me half of the clip. "One wish for you, one for me."

"You go first."

We searched around until we found a rock to use as a hammer. When we lifted it, earthworms writhed away from the open air. Ife squealed.

"Don't fret," I said to her. "We going to leave soon."

She found a clear place on the bark of the cashew tree and positioned her "nail."

"What you going to wish?" I asked her.

That brave, pointy smile again. "Not telling you this time."

She drove the rock against the head of the clip. The tree shook and came alive. Pink things flapped and fluttered against our faces, grunting. Ife screamed. We ran, and didn't stop until we were through the grove and into the sunshine. Ife was batting at her hair, screaming, "Get them out! Get them out!" Beyond the gate, Stanley was showing off his glider to Agway. Agway was looking up into the sky. His eyes and mouth went round with wonder. He pointed into the air above the cashew grove.

"Buuds!" he said. He was already picking up a word or two. He had trouble with his *r*'s.

I looked where Agway was pointing. I shook Ifeoma's shoulder and pointed there, too.

Agway was right. Birds. Spoonbills. We'd disturbed them by hammering on the tree. They onked their curses at us and headed off in a diagonal line, their pink bodies glowing in the sunlight. Stanley struggled to get the glider to follow them.

Ife laughed. "That's all it was? Birds?"

I couldn't find my half of the hair clip. I'd dropped it when we ran. Wasn't sure what I would have wished for, anyway. The past to stop haunting me, maybe.

A car pulled up on the road; a bright yellow Beamer convertible. "Who's this now?" I said. Somebody had plenty money to spend on a fancy ride.

Two men got out. One of them waved at us. Ife waved back. "Daddy!" she shouted.

Michael. And he'd brought Orso with him.

I strode out to meet them. "You said you would call first! I thought you were coming later."

"You going to give me a hug, or what?" He opened his arms. I stayed where I was. He stepped back from me. "You know Orso," he said.

I tried to smile back at Orso. It felt fake on my face. Probably showed.

Ife'd come running to greet them. Michael hugged her instead. He asked me, "This is a bad time? We called. About a billion times. No answer on either phone."

Right. Hadn't turned my cell on for the day. As to the land line phone, I'd unplugged it and hidden it away last night after Agway had assaulted it once too often.

"I called Ife, though. She said it was all right."

"She did, enh?"

"Ifeoma tells me you have a new dependent now?" asked Michael. "You still full of surprises. Where he came from? You hiding a paramour here you not telling me about?"

I scowled. "He's a little boy, maybe three years old. His parents got killed at sea in that bad storm."

"Christ."

"I found him washed up on the beach the next morning. They're letting me foster him till they know what to do with him. He don't speak English."

"Wow. You want to keep him, then?"

"I don't know." *I don't need you*, I thought. *I got a baby without you this time.*

Michael eyeballed the house. "Not bad," he said. "Good bones."

Orso said, "I'd like to figure out the facing direction, though. Maybe the entrance should be somewhere else."

"Why?" I asked him. "I like it where it is. You know; right off the driveway?"

Ife was glaring at me. Now what?

"It's a matter of balance," Orso replied. "The line the eye follows as you enter the property. What parts of it get the morning sun first, where you plant your decorative shrubs, that kind of thing. You see? The built environment should complement the natural environment."

"I get it!" said Ife. "The chi of the land needs to be in harmony."

Orso lit up like a Christmas tree. "Exactly! I didn't know you were into feng shui?"

"Just a little. I took a course last year."

Someone else was tromping up the gravel road. I squinted. Blocky body. Grapefruit pink t-shirt. Black walking shorts. Oh, shit. Hector, just dropping by, like I'd told him he could. Yes, the universe was unfolding the way it always did: in chaos.

Hector waved when he saw us. "Good afternoon," he said when he was in earshot. Ife pursed her lips when she saw him. I was pretty bemused myself. First time I'd seen him in something that wasn't neon and skin tight. His colour sense hadn't changed, though.

"I'm interrupting something?" Hector asked. "I could come back another time."

"No; stay." Be good to have at least one adult in the party that I wasn't vexed with.

"I brought beer."

"Then definitely stay! This is my daughter Ifeoma, and that's Michael, and that's his friend Orso."

Orso and Michael exchanged glances. Hector smiled a greeting. Then he spied the tricycle where I'd stashed it beside the house. "Yours that?" he asked me. "I used to have one like it. In green."

"I figure maybe Agway could use it," I told him. "But it going to need fixing up."

He went over and inspected the trike. "It only need some screws tightened and a new seat. New wheels. Maybe a fresh paint job. You want me to do it for you?"

"All right," I told him. Be a good way to get to know him.

Michael said, "We could go in and look around now?"

"I guess so." To Hector I said, "Michael wants to renovate the house for me."

Orso told Ife, "You know, I even make up a bagua first for each property we design? Mikey, you coming?" Orso and Ife headed up the porch steps together, chattering happily about whatever a bagua was.

Blast you. I was calling him "Mikey" long before you even knew him. Chuh. I picked up the duffel bag. Hector and I followed.

"Saturday a good time to come and fix up the tricycle?"

"Yeah, man."

"YOUR LIVING ROOM WINDOWS TOO SMALL and dark," said Michael. He and Orso were sitting on my couch, poring over a lined notebook they had put on the coffee table. "What you think about one big picture window?" He reached for his beer bottle and had a drink.

"Maybe. You went grey since I saw you last."

"Salt and pepper, thank you, please."

"You look good." He did, damn him. If anything, more beautiful than he'd been at seventeen. He used to be lean like a whip snake. He had filled out. He was sporting a sexy goatee. And he looked relaxed.

"And that pantry is a disaster; you saw it, Orso? Narrow and dark with a naked lightbulb and a pull string."

"I saw," said Orso.

Over by the television, Agway, enraptured, was watching a fashion makeover programme. Stanley had wandered over to us to see what the adults were up to. He patted my arm.

"Grandma-I-mean-Calamity; you could help me pick a science fair project?"

"We'll talk about it later."

"But I need to tell my teacher my project next week!"

"Of course, darling. I'm back to work next week. Come to the library then, and we'll find you a good project."

"What kind of science you like, Stanley?" asked Hector. I'd brought the chairs from the kitchen and put them around the coffee table.

"I don't know," Stanley answered shyly.

"You can give Hector a more informative answer than that, Stanley," said Ife.

Stanley looked at the floor. "The cool stuff, I guess."

Hector laughed. "So, you think biology is cool?"

Stanley screwed up his face.

"Okay, guess not. Not even boa constrictors?"

Stanley shook his head.

"Not even sharks?"

Stanley's eyes lit up. "Yeah! Sharks kick ass!"

"Stanley!" said Michael. "Sorry, Ife. Beat you to it."

Michael reached for Orso's hand. I wished they wouldn't do that in public.

Hector said, "I once spent a summer catching sharks and sticking cameras to them."

"You did?" Hector had made a new friend.

"I did. Maybe your gran can bring you by my boat one day, and I'll show you what the sea looks like from shark's-eye view. I even have a few shots of a shark making a kill."

"Cool!" said Stanley. "Calamity, we can really go to Hector's boat?"

I nodded.

Hector glanced Orso and Michael. They were still holding hands. "The two of you live here on Dolorosse?" Hector asked them.

"No," Orso replied. "We have a beautiful house on the big island. Up by the hill at the foot of Grandcastle Street. Michael's construction company built it." And he patted Michael's hand. They beamed at each other.

Time to nip that line of conversation in the bud. I leapt to my feet. "Anyone like a drink? Coffee? Tea? Cashew wine? Hector, come and help me throw together some snacks."

"Nothing for me, thanks," said Orso.

"Me neither, Cal," said Michael. He turned back to Hector. "And it's Dolores."

"You mean, like Mary? Pleased to meet you, Dolores."

Michael laughed. "No, I mean that's how we pronounce the name of the island. Like the woman's name."

Orso leaned back in the settee. "You were on the right track, though." He pointed to himself. "Mary." Then at me, with a sly smirk. "Not Mary."

Ife and Hector cracked up laughing. What the ass? Then Michael must have gotten the foolishness devil in him too, for he pointed to himself. "Mary."

Ife tapped her own chest. "Not Mary. Not last I checked, anyway."

Quizzically, Michael pointed at Hector. Hector flicked a glance at me. "Mary," he said.

Orso snapped his fingers. "Yes!"

". . . and Joseph."

"Oh," said Orso. He didn't look any too pleased.

"Really?" Ife asked.

I shook my head and stood up. "Well, since I'm clearly not

part of this conversation, why don't I just get us some snacks? Sound good?"

Michael said, "You know, it's kinda isolated all the way out here. You should come and visit us, Hector. Meet some of the gang."

"I could fry up some plantain."

"I would love that," Hector replied.

"Good," I said, pretending I'd misunderstood. "So you can come to the kitchen and give me a hand, then."

"Mummy, I'll help you. Looks like the guys are getting to know one another."

Hector smiled his thanks at her. "Really?" she asked him again. He laughed.

I picked Agway up from in front of the television. "Come, babby," I said through my teeth. "Time for your lunch."

As Ife followed me and Agway into the kitchen, I heard Hector say, "So, you live together, then?"

"Oh, yes, my dear. Number thirteen Grandcastle; a good luck number."

I waited till I was out of earshot, in the kitchen. "*Oh, yes, my dear, a good luck number,*" I mimicked under my breath. I sucked my teeth.

"Please don't start that," said Ife. She sounded exasperated.

I put Agway in the highchair. Sally from over the way had lent it to me. I got a broad mango from the fridge; put it on a plastic plate and set it down on the table in front of Agway. I fetched two ripe plantains from the pantry. "Put the frying pan on to heat for me, nuh?" I asked Ife.

But she wasn't going to let it drop. "Why you get on so bad around Daddy all the time?"

I got a sharp knife, started peeling the plantains. "Because he

don't have manners. Why he and Orso have to be always flaunting themselves like that?"

"Flaunting how?"

Agway had peeled his mango with his teeth. He put it down
on the table beside the plate and started happily devouring the
skin.

"Holding hands like two nanas, telling people they living in
the same house, calling other men 'my dear.'"

"And when you do that, what you call it?"

"When I do what?"

"Hold hands with some guy. Call him 'my dear.'"

I sucked my teeth. "Oh, don't be dense. You know that's different." Sometimes I couldn't understand what went on in the
child's crystal-gazing mind.

"Buuds!" said Agway, showing me the seagull design on his
plate. "Buuds, Mamma!"

"Oh, isn't he sweet, Ife? He's learning so fast!"

"You make him call you Mamma?"

That pulled me up short. "I didn't make him do anything."

"How come you want that little boy? You never wanted me."
Ife's voice was tight.

"What? Ife, that's nonsense."

"It is not! You make him call you Mamma when you don't
even want me to call you Mummy. You never used to want people to know you had a daughter. So how come he's calling you
his mother?"

"Ife!"

"You didn't want me then, and you still don't want me."

"Stop the stupidness. Just put some oil in the frying pan for
me, please."

"No." She went and sat beside Agway. He was drawing sticky

circles on the table with the peeled mango. "Nobody want fried plantain, not even you. You just trying to distract the three of them from talking to each other." She held her hand out to Agway for his unwanted mango. He put it in her palm. She started eating it.

"More sweet things again? Last thing you need, you know." When the silence had gone on a little too long, I looked up from my chopping to see her hurt, wet eyes. My heart clenched. I sighed. "Oh, sweetheart," I said. "I didn't mean it like tha—"

"Ifeoma is fine the way she is," came a voice from the doorway. Michael was standing there. "She's all curves, just like you. She have your eyes, the shape of your face. It's just your sharp tongue she don't have."

"How long you been eavesdropping on me and my daughter?"

"She's my daughter too. At least her *father* wanted her."

"Mummy, Daddy, don't fight," moaned Ifeoma. Agway's eyes were taking it all in.

"And how come you call him 'Daddy'? That man was never a father to you!"

"And whose fault was that?" Michael demanded.

Orso and Hector had joined Michael in the doorway, and Stanley was peeking around the jamb. "What going on?" asked Orso. He put a protective arm around Michael's waist.

I stamped my foot. "Don't *touch* him like that! Not in my house!"

"Calamity," came Hector's voice. "Please put down the knife."

I'd been pointing with the sharp kitchen knife in my hand. They were all staring at me, even Agway. I put the knife down on the stove. "I don't like it," I said slowly and carefully to Michael and Orso, "when you carry on with your sodomite ways in front of children. This is the house my father died in, and I'll thank you to respect his memory."

"Clearly that respect don't cut two ways," Orso said.

"I think I'm going back to the boat now," Hector told us.

I glared at Orso, my mouth working. My blood was boiling. I could feel the sweat popping out on my forehead. I rushed at him. "You. Shut. Up. You just shut up right now!"

Something materialized out of the air and landed on the ground between us. It shattered when it hit.

"Now she's throwing things at us!" hissed Orso. Agway started to cry. "Michael, we leaving this house this minute! I refuse to do any work for that woman."

From the shards mixed in with a few coins, it looked like the piggybank that used to sit on my little vanity table in the house on Blessée.

Michael cut his eyes at me. "Later, Ife," he said, his voice low and controlled. "Same time Sunday?" She nodded.

Michael and Orso left the kitchen. As they headed through the living room, Orso said loudly: "I told you that woman don't have no kind feelings in her heart for you! Never did, never will."

My ass. "What you know about it?" I yelled after him.

Hector's eyes were big as limes. He cleared his throat. "Maybe they could give me a lift into town. To buy the things for the tricycle." And he fled too.

I rounded on Ife. "What he mean by 'same time Sunday'?"

"Sunday is when we go and see Grandpa," Stanley piped up, mischief on his face.

"I told you not to tell her!" Ife said to him. "I told you it would only cause trouble."

Stanley pouted. "Grandpa told her first."

"And so everything Grandpa do, you going to do?"

The hot flash passed, leaving me shocky and shivering. "You go to Michael's house every Sunday?" I asked them. "When it's like pulling teeth to get you to come and see me?"

Ife looked down at her hands. "I finally realised you couldn't stop me," she said. "I found his number one day and called him. It's been good for Stanley to have more men in his life."

"*Men?*" I squeaked. "Michael and Orso?"

"Orso's teaching me how to play cricket!" Stanley told me. I just stared from one to the other, lost.

Ife stood up. "You happy now?" she asked me. "Now that you've tried to make everybody as miserable as you?" She wiped Agway's hands clean with a corner of her sackcloth dress. "I pity this child," she said. "Come, Stanley."

"Okay. Ka odi," he said to Agway, waving.

"Ka odi," Agway replied.

"What, like even the two of you talking so I can't understand?"

"Who have ears to hear, will hear," Ife told me. She stepped over the ceramic shards, out into the living room. Stanley followed.

I yelled, "You best watch Orso with that child! You hear what I'm telling you, Ifeoma?"

The front door closed very quietly. A few seconds later I heard Ife start up her car and drive away.

"Shit. I really gone and done it now, Agway."

He climbed backwards off the chair, toddled over to the tv and plumped himself down to watch the cartoons.

I got the broom, started cleaning the mess up. I knelt with the dustpan to sweep up the piggybank pieces. As I did, a stab of pain went through my trick knee. I used one hand on the floor to steady myself, then began brushing the shards into the dustpan.

My hands. When age spots started coming out on my hands? I put down the dustpan, sat back on my haunches. My palms still looked more or less like I remembered them, but the backs of my hands were a roadmap of the tiniest wrinkles. "Next thing you know," I whispered, "my bubbies going to be neighbours with my navel, and I going to be wearing a diaper."

Who tell me to set my cap for Hector, anyway? What a forty-year-old man could want with a matriarch? I watched the wet tears plop into the dustpan amongst the pieces of broken crockery.

Uncle Time is a spider-man, cunnin' an' cool,
him tell yu: watch de hill an yu se mi.
Huhn! Fe yu yi no quick enough fe si
how 'im move like mongoose; man, yu tink 'im fool?
                              —*Dennis Scott, "Uncle Time"*

Someone knocked at the door. It was about the time when Mr. Mckinley came by every Saturday with the morning's catch. I put my hand over the receiver. "One minute!"

"You have to go?" asked Gene. He'd called to see how Agway was doing.

The knock came again. "Soon come!" I yelled at the door. "Yeah, I have to go."

"You busy Thursday evening?"

"No. Why?"

"You want to go and catch a bite?"

"Yes! I mean, that would be nice. Listen, talk to you later, all right?"

"Later."

I swear I sprouted wings and flew all the way to the door. Mr. Mckinley and his two strapping sons had given up on me and were walking away. "Morning, Mr. Mckinley," I called out. "Morning, Gerald, Leonard."

They came back.

"What allyou have for me today?"

"Nothing," answered Mr. Mckinley.

"Nothing?"

"Me and the boys didn't catch nothing but few little shrimps today. Other than that, not a stinking thing in the nets, pardon my language."

"But how—?"

"It's Gilmor. Years now the fishermen been saying that Gilmor killing the fish."

"You want any of the shrimps?" asked Leonard, a beefy man in his twenties with arm muscles like cable from hauling nets.

"Yeah, give me about two pounds, nuh? Let me get a bowl from the kitchen."

They ladled fresh shrimp into my bowl. I counted out the money from my purse and handed it to Gerald. "So what allyou going to do about this state of affairs?" I said lightly. "Can't make us have to import snapper from Trinidad." My mind was really on seeing Gene next Thursday.

"We going to do something," said Mr. Mckinley. "That's for sure. That's what we come to tell you. A week Monday."

"What happening then?"

"Johnson having the ceremony to open the new Gilmor plant."

"Here on Dolorosse."

He nodded. "The fishermen and the salt farmers; Gilmor being doing us wrong ever since they opened shop in Cayaba. Now they going to bankrupt the few salt farmers left on Dolorosse and Tingle. I don't know yet what we going to do, but we going to do something." He handed his tackle box to Gerald, shook my hand between two of his. His palms were hard like horn. "Hope you going to come out and support us, Miz Lambkin."

"I . . . well . . . I'm working that day."

"Ah. Be with us in spirit then, yes? I know how you like your snapper. Walk good."

I watched them go on towards the next house to spread the word.

I took the shrimps into the kitchen, to find that Agway had abandoned the sheets of foolscap I'd given him and was drawing on the wall with a purple crayon. "No, Agway! Bad!"

I put the bowl down on the table and went to get him away from the wall.

Thursday evening, me and Gene! I tried to weigh who I liked better, Gene or Hector. I picked a surprised Agway up and took him on a waltz around the kitchen. "I'm going on a *date*, babbins!"

Agway eyed the shrimps on the table.

5

I DROVE MY CAR DOWN THE FERRY'S OFF-RAMP, following the cars in front of me. Traffic moved slowly this morning, with much blaring of horns. February was the height of tourist season, and the hotels at the Cayaba harbour would be cluttered with visitors until early May. Sure enough, there was one of their massive cruise ships, just docked. Bloody thing was the size of a mountain, gleaming white as the mounds of the salt stacks in the distance, from the original Gilmor Saline plant.

By the time I was able to edge my car out of the harbour zone, I'd had to back up twice to find streets that weren't clogged, and I'd witnessed three near-accidents as vehicles came close to rear-ending each other. The smell of exhaust and diesel turned my stomach. The noise was abominable. I drove past a big billboard that read, WELCOME TO CAYABA; HOME OF THE RARE MONK SEAL. The picture showed three seals frolicking in the surf—two adults and a child—as though seals hooked up in nuclear family units. At each corner of the image was a mermaid, exotically brown but not too dark. No obvious negroes in Cayaba Tourist Board publicity, unless they were dressed as smiling servers. The fish women sported the kind of long, flowing hair that most black women had to buy in a bottle of straightening solution. They had shells covering their teacup breasts. I would love to see the shell big enough to hide one of my bubbies. My first day going back to work, and already I was in a mood. Agway was prob- ably eating Mrs. Soledad's green banana porridge right now. Then she was going to take him for a walk, introduce him to the neighbours.

I turned onto St. Christopher Street, right into a traffic jam that went as far as I could see. Backside. St. Christopher Street was long, one-way, and lined with expensive "boo-teeks" selling all kinds of nonsense: lamps made of old rum bottles covered in glued-on shells (the shells were imported in bulk from China); neon bikinis no bigger than a farthing; a zillion zillion t-shirts, coasters, baseball caps, mugs, and canvas shopping bags, all im- printed with images of monk seals and mermaids and the Cay- aba Tourist Board logo ("Cayaba; Our Doors Are Open"). This was the heart of what Cayabans called the Tourist Entrapment Zone. There was no turnoff for a while.

Traffic crawled. I tried to ignore the tourists clogging the sidewalks, the bright sarongs and Hawaiian shirts embossed with those fucking mermaids, the reggae music already blaring at 8:45 in the blessèd morning from every restaurant I passed. Why we had to import reggae? What the blast was wrong with tumpa?

Maybe Mrs. Soledad would take Agway to my almond tree. They could collect ripe almonds from under the tree. Eat them down to the bitter, fibrous part. Find rockstones and crack the almond shells open for the nuts inside. Would Agway like almonds? Maybe he knew them already; plenty of them fell into the water. Would he miss me? Mrs. Soledad had better remember that she wasn't to take him near the water. Didn't want him trying to jump in with that cast on his leg.

I hit the brakes; it was either that or hit the young white man who'd stepped into the road without looking. He was wearing only muddy surf jammers and rubber sandals. His shoulders and back were red as boiled shrimp. The colour offset the scrappy blond dreads hanging down his back. He gave me a lopsided grin and made the peace sign with his fingers. "No prahblem, mon; no prahblem," he drawled in his best Hollywood Jamaican. "Cool runnings." He staggered across the street.

"You not in Jamaica!" I yelled at him. Damned fool. Probably high. I was practically growling by the time I was able to turn off St. Christopher and continue to work.

When I got home, I would read *The Cat in the Hat* to Agway.

I parked in the staff parking, went in the back door, through Deliveries. Colin and, what was his name? Yes, Riddell. They were both loading up the bookmobile. Riddell looked up from the low, wheeled booktruck loaded down with that day's bookmobile reserve requests. "Miz Lambkin!" He put down the box he was carrying and came over to me. Shyness froze my face. I cracked the ice into a smile. To my surprise, Riddell gravely took my hand and shook it. "I'm glad to see you back," he said, "real glad."

"Uh, thank you." The true warmth of his smile was a balm. Made me shamed; I had barely remembered his name.

Colin had come up behind Riddell. He nodded to me. "Sorry for your loss, Miz Lambkin."

"Thank you." I released Riddell's hand. The three of us stood there for a second in uncomfortable silence. "Well," I said to them, "I talk to you later, okay?"

"Okay." They returned to their work, and I scurried away. *I'll talk to you later.* People say that all the time. Half the time it's an untruth. We promise to come back so people won't carry on bad when we leave.

You know how it is when you go back to your old school as an adult? How everything looks the same, but different? Children in the hallways and the classrooms, but not the faces you expect to see? The staff workroom was like someplace that I used to know. That clack-clack sound: Myrtle in her ever-present high heels. She wore them even more than me. David Stowar waved at me as he rushed for the elevator. He mouthed the word *late*. As usual. And he was sneaking a coffee up to the information desk, as always. I checked the schedule tacked up on the bulletin board. I had a workroom period for the first part of the morning. On the checkout desk after break. Good; I could ease into being back at work.

Mrs. Winter sat at her desk, her chair angled away from it. She had her foot up on one of the library's wheeled stepstools, with a cushion from the Children's Department under her ankle. She was pencilling names into a blank schedule grid. She gave me a look as frosty as her name.

My desk was a mess. Piled high with computer printouts of reserves that hadn't been filled. I threw the strap of my purse over the back of my chair and got to work sorting.

"You still looking after that little boy?" asked Mrs. Winter.

"Last I checked, yes."

"You didn't leave him alone for the day?"

"He can't be more than three, Mrs. Winter. You think I would leave a toddler home alone?" I started in on the other pile on my desk: damaged books and CDs that couldn't be given to the patrons who'd reserved them.

"Beg pardon. It's just that your mothering days gone so long now. Easy to forget how to do it."

"Nope. Like riding a bicycle." One CD case looked like somebody had dropped it into a mug of Ovaltine. "Or falling out of a tree." I hoped Mrs. Soledad had remembered not to sugar Agway's breakfast.

"Too besides," said Mrs. Winter, "you had Ifeoma so young!"

"Mm." I was sixteen when I brought Ife to Auntie Pearl and Uncle Edward's house from the hospital. The first time I had to change her diaper by myself, I cried for my mother. In those days, I had cried as much as baby Ife.

Now I was at the pile of sticky notes fringing my inbox. Most of them were reserves questions that staff members had taken from patrons.

Mrs. Winter scowled at her schedule, turned her pencil over, and erased something she'd written there. "It's like the two of you raised each other," she said.

"Mm." Mr. Bailey wanted to know why his book on World War One heroes hadn't come in. He was a war vet. He read only nonfiction books about soldiers. He'd been through every book we had on every war going, and was on his second go-round. I looked up his card number on my terminal, reserved that new biography on Desert Storm for him. He wouldn't have read it yet. Millie Marshall wanted to know when we'd be getting the new Laurelle Silver novel. Laurelle Silver had died five years ago and there was now a team of six writers churning out breathless novels of sex and scandal amongst the rich and infamous under her name, yet they still couldn't produce new titles quickly enough for Millie. I reserved a Kelly Sheldon and that new Carrie Jason novel for her; that'd hold her until Ms. Silver posthumously committed bad prose again.

Mrs. Winter held the completed schedule sheet out to me. "Chastity, pin this up on the board for me, nuh?"

"Calamity." I stood and took it from her.

That chilly smile again. "You know how my head small, my dear. Can't get my mind around everything you young people get up to nowadays. Changing your God-given names."

The phone at my desk rang. It was David Stowar, calling from the information desk. "We need you up here, please." There was a smile in his voice.

"Why?" Only librarians worked at the info desk.

"Just come, nuh? And make sure you don't have any crumbs from breakfast on your shirt."

"I had cocoa-tea for breakfast."

"Well, no cocoa stains, then. Those don't wash out for nothing. And come up here. Now."

Mystified, I took the elevator up to the main floor. As I stepped out, I just had time to hear David say, "That's her," before I was surrounded by reporters. Camera flashes started to go off. I tried to put my hand up in front of my face. Someone took the hand and shook it.

"Sister Lambkin," said the woman, "I'm so pleased to meet you. Such a selfless act on your part." The woman looked a little younger than me. Probably dougla, with that flowing black hair and those full African lips. Speaky-spokey, too. Come from money. And wasn't that a Chanel suit? In this heat?

Oh, shit. It was Caroline Sookdeo-Grant. Shaking my hand. "What selfless act?" I asked.

"You plucked that little boy from the waves in the middle of a storm—"

"Agway? But the storm was over by then. And he had already washed up onto—"

"You kept him alive until the ambulance arrived—"

"When I got to him, he wasn't in any danger of being anything but alive."

"And now that his family has perished in that tragic accident, you've taken him into your home. Such generosity, Sister."

"How you even come to hear about me?" I asked her.

"Mrs. Sookdeo-Grant, Mrs. Lambkin, look this way, please."

We looked that way. Sookdeo-Grant grabbed my hand again in one of those disturbingly firm handshakes. We smiled. "Your daughter told me," she said. "Wonderful person. You must be very proud of her."

The flash went off. By the time my dazzled eyes could see again, Sookdeo-Grant was being escorted out of the library. Passers-by were calling out her name. She stopped, shook a few hands, smiled a lot. Then she stepped into the back of a nondescript beige car and was driven away.

More flashes popped, and someone stuck a microphone that had the CNT logo on it in front of my face. "Just look at me, not the camera," said the camera man. So of course, after that, I couldn't see anything *but* the camera. It was a very big camera.

"Look this way, please," said the reporter. She had that glamour that people get on them when they live their lives on television. "That's good, Mizziz Lambkin. Now, tell the audience; how does Mr. Lambkin feel about you bringing an orphan into your home?"

"Mr. Lambkin's dead," I replied. "The funeral was last Saturday." My cell phone rang. I pulled it out of my skirt pocket. "Hello?"

"Grandma?"

"Stanley?"

"Well, there you have it, folks," said the reporter into her microphone. The big camera was pointed at her now. "Not only did this brave woman throw herself into a raging sea to save a child she didn't know—"

"Grandma, you really think a kite would work?"

"—she did so on the way home from burying her husband, who had tragically passed away that same day."

"The day before," I said. "Only he wasn't my—"

"For my science fair project, I mean? Remember?"

"Just a minute, Stanley."

"For Cayaba National Television, this is Jane Goodright, reporting live from the main branch of the Cayaba Public Library."

"But he wasn't my husba—"

"Maybe I could tie a camera to a kite?"

"Don't be silly," I said, eyeing the very large camera in front of me. "A camera's much too big."

"Thank you so much, Mizziz Lambkin. Please sign this release. It just says that you're okay with us putting this little interview on the air."

I took the pen she handed me, and struggled to sign the release and juggle the cell phone at the same time.

"A small camera, Grandma. A disposable. Only I don't know how to make it take the pictures from up in the air. . . . Grandma?"

"Stanley, I call you back later, okay?" I handed the reporter back the piece of paper.

"But I need to decide now! I have to tell my teacher by next period what my project is!"

"All right, all right. I think a kite would work fine. Wonderful idea. Call me tonight and we'll figure out how to do it. Okay?"

"I can come to the library tomorrow?"

"Yes. I'll be here. I have to go, Stanley."

I snapped the phone shut and turned to tell the reporter the real story. She and the camera man were gone.

"I'm going to kill my daughter," I said to David.

He looked like he'd had a vision. "That was Jane Goodright," he whispered. "Standing not two yards from me."

The info desk phone rang. David answered it. "It's for you," he said. I took the receiver from him.

"Calamity?"

"It just might be a calamity. For my wretched girl child, anyway."

"Pardon?" It was Gene's voice.

"Long story. Look, I not supposed to take personal calls at work. You could make this quick?"

"Okay. You know that rusty cutlass I had the other day?"

"Yes?"

"Well, I told you a little untruth."

"Gene, I need to get off the phone."

"I found it in the cashew grove. It has Mr. Lambkin's name on the handle."

Ah, shit. How to explain that? No, it was okay. I had Gene half-convinced the cashews had always been there. "And?"

David said, "You think I should have asked Jane Goodright out? I hear she not seeing anybody."

"I'm really sorry," said Gene. "The lab found traces of blood and tissue on the blade."

I dropped the receiver.

*   *   *

And what a piece of business trying to find someone to watch Agway for me for a few hours on Thursday so I could spend time with Gene! Three days a week was all Mrs. Soledad could spare. Ifeoma was going to a meditation class, or something like that; Clifton and Stanley were going to Stanley's weekly karate practice. When I had lived in the little apartment building on Lucy Street, and Ifeoma had wanted watching, my neighbour Maxine was more than willing to do it, especially if I kept her up to date on my adventures with my latest boyfriend. What had happened to Maxine? I had lost touch with her when I got the library job and moved into a bigger apartment.

I knew Ev wasn't free. Wasn't going to ask Hector. I didn't know him well enough. And besides, I kind of had my eye on both him and Gene, so it didn't seem right to ask him to babysit for me so I could go and pitch woo with the other guy. Oh, so lovely to have prospects again!

But I had to eat dirt to get Agway a babysitter, and I knew it. I dialled the phone.

"Hello?"

"Michael?"

"Yes, Calamity."

Uh-oh. I knew that flat tone. He was going to milk my blow-up for every drop of juice he could wring out of it. "How you doing, Michael? Things good?"

"You have a reason to call me?"

Fuck. He was going to make this hard. I swallowed. "Well, yes." Shit, this was like spitting out nails. "I'm sorry."

"That's interesting."

"Michael, cut me some slack, nuh? I'm sorry I said those things to you, okay?"

"You said them to Orso, too."

"Okay. My apologies to him, too. Michael, I need your help."

"Ah. So you're sorry because you need my help."

"Yes, I . . . No! I just need someone to babysit Agway for a few hours." Damn. That didn't sound too good, either.

"Calamity, you can't try to make it up to us just because you need a babysitter!"

I expected him to sound angry. I hadn't expected him to sound hurt.

"I didn't mean it," I mumbled. "You know how my temper stay."

"True that. And I have to tell you; five years without having to deal with your temper was five peaceful years."

Now he was exasperating me. "You're really so sensitive, Michael?"

"Of course. Don't you know, that's what we faggots are like?" he said bitterly.

I heard someone speaking to him. "Wait," he said to me. "Hold on."

I could hear the conversation, but I couldn't make out the words. I could only sit there and feel bad.

Michael came back on the line. "When you need the sitter?"

I brightened up. "Six p.m.," I replied. "I'll probably be back home around eleven."

More conversation with the other voice.

"Okay," said Michael. "You'll have a sitter."

"Thank you, sweetheart. You always come through for me."

"I'm not coming."

"But, Michael, you just said—"

"*I'm* not coming. Orso says he can babysit for you."

Michael's fancy man? Alone with Agway? "But I don't—"

"Don't start with me, Calamity. You should thank your lucky stars he's willing to help you after how you treated us."

I had to ask. "Orso . . . he's okay with children?"

"I don't even want to think about what you getting at with that little piece of veiled contempt. So I going to pretend I don't understand you. If you had ever made the time to get to know him, you would know that Orso is the eldest of six brothers and sisters. When his parents were working, it's he looked after them."

"He did?"

"Orso know about feeding times and reading bed-time stories and wiping runny noses. He know all that that I didn't have no chance to learn."

Ifeoma had never spent a single night in her father's care. I wouldn't allow it. Who knew what kinda carousing he was getting up to? I wasn't going to put my baby into the middle of that.

"Orso say he will see you five-thirty sharp. And now I'm hanging up this phone. Good day, Calamity."

The phone went dead. I put the receiver into its cradle. Back in the day, Michael and me could never stay on the outs for long. He would probably get over being upset. Probably.

GENE WAS COMING AT SIX. At five-fifteen, I still wasn't ready. I had showered and bathed both me and Agway. I was powdered and perfumed, and I had tried on one outfit after the other, and none of them worked. The green blouse made my belly look too fat. The lavender dress with the roses on it was too dressy, plus I had to wear panty hose with it or my legs would chafe, and

I wasn't wearing no blasted panty hose in this heat. My arms looked too flabby in the striped t-shirt. And the black slacks just made me look old, old, old.

Agway was out in the living room, singing along with the theme song to his favourite television cartoon. When he didn't know the words—which was often—he made them up. Shoulda been funny, but I was in no mood. Actually, I was in quite a mood. The four or five outfits spread out on the bed all looked like crap on me. I was getting sweatier and sweatier and more and more miserable.

Someone knocked on the front door. I reached for my bathrobe, but Agway was way ahead of me. I could hear his feet pattering as he ran to the door.

"Agway!" I yelled. "Careful! You going to trip! And don't open that door without me!" Damned child had no native caution when it came to other people. Don't know what his parents had been teaching him.

Sure enough, by the time I had the bathrobe on and had made it to the front door, Agway had opened it and was burbling happily at Orso. Orso was squatted down, talking back. "What is that you say? Yes, I'm very pleased to see you, too."

Orso grinned as Agway threw himself into his arms. He stood, swirled Agway around in the air. Man and boy chortled. Then Orso saw me. "Excuse me, Agway." He set the child down on his feet. "Good evening," he said to me. He stood with his arms crossed, waiting.

He was wearing perfectly faded jeans, a stylin' pair of leather sandals polished to a fare-thee-well, and an impeccably ironed navy blue cotton shirt that made his dark skin gleam. It just wasn't right for a man to be so well turned out. Made me feel frumpy. And he was waiting for me to say what I knew I had to say. "Well, thank you for babysitting Agway for me. That's really generous of you."

"Mm-hm . . ."

Man, I hated backing down! I nerved myself up for my apology, but Agway was having none of this boring big people palaver. He kept chattering at Orso, tugged at his hand to try to pull him into the living room.

Orso smiled at him and picked him up. "Looks like he's happy with you," he said.

"I'm trying. It's good having him here."

"And you looked like you were about to say something to me just now."

I closed my eyes, clenched my teeth. Twelve hundred pounds of pressure per square inch. "I'm. Sorry." I opened my eyes. He still had that expectant look. So I said, "I behaved badly the other day."

"True that."

"I should have minded my manners," I told him in a rush. "You and Michael were guests in my house."

Orso had more hair to pull than I did. Agway was yanking on it now and pointing into the living room, urging him to come and see some wonderful thing or other. Orso laughed and disentangled his hand. "You not going to let me squeeze every last little drop of remorse from her, that it?" He put Agway to stand and took his hand. "Apology accepted," he said to me. "For now. I tell you true, though; you on sufferance with me. Michael loves you so much he'll put up with any nonsense from you, but I won't let anybody speak to me like that twice." Then he toddled off with Agway into the living room. I followed, speechless. Michael loved me?

In the living room, Agway dropped Orso's hand and grabbed

his latest toy—an old briefcase of Dadda's—off the coffee table, and proceeded to demonstrate to Orso how he had learned to undo the clasp, and how well chunky Dumpy (didn't) fit inside the slim briefcase.

Orso sat on the floor and got into the game with him, loading Agway's toys into the briefcase and struggling to close it. That quickly became a game of tummy tickle, with Agway wriggling and laughing. Orso looked up and saw my expression. He stood up.

"Calamity, we need to get one more thing out of the way right now."

"What's that?"

"Men get me hot. Not children."

My face warmed up, and it wasn't no blasted hot flash, neither. "Okay," I whispered, shame-facedly.

"Okay for true?" he asked.

My face never did hide anything very well. He sighed. "You know, you have the perfect good reference for me if you want one."

"Who?"

"Stanley. He been at our house almost every Sunday for the past five years."

Jealousy knotted up my belly. "So I hear." I checked my watch. "Gene's late."

"That's a girl's prerogative."

"If a narrow, dark-skinned man about our age knock on the door, that's probably Gene. You could just tell him I'm dressing?"

"Cool breeze."

I settled on the jeans and the green shirt. Sucked my tummy in and checked myself out in the bedroom mirror.

Not too bad, if I kept the gut in. I got Agway's snack from the fridge and took it for him. He plumped himself down on the floor to eat it.

Orso was watching a reality show. It looked like the one where bosses switched lives with their employees for a month.

I sat on the arm of the couch. "We just going to Mrs. Smalley's; you know, the chicken place? You will call me if anything happen to Agway?"

"Yes, ma'am. And if I can't get through to you on your cell, I will ring for the ambulance, the Fire Department, the Coast Guard, and hail any cute passing fishermen and beg them all to come find you."

I couldn't help it. I giggled.

"What time Agway goes to bed?"

"Seven, seven-thirty. I find if you turn the lights down around then, he will start to get sleepy." Yay for diurnal rhythms. "I have some maami apple sliced up in the fridge. If he looking peckish, you could give him some for a snack. You help yourself, too, all right? Anything you want to eat. I curried some channa and beef, and there's rice boiled, and ground provisions. And I'm babbling."

"Nervous?" He'd stood and was looking through the bookshelves.

"Yeah." I checked my watch again.

"About me, or about your date?"

I snorted. "You not easy, you know?"

Small, wary smile. "Take one to know one." He slid two or three picture books off the shelf and brought them back to the couch.

"Probably about both of you. More about him, though." I pointed at one of the books. "*Cendrillon* missing page five. Not that Agway can tell."

That small smile again. "When you like this, I can see why you and Mikey used to be tight. He like us hot-mouth people."

"You want the hot-mouth truth, then? I hate it when you call him 'Mikey.' That's what I call him."

"That's all the bite you got? That was only ginger hot, not scotch bonnet pepper hot."

I sighed. "You right. Losing strength in my waning years, I suppose."

"Don't fool yourself. Pepper sauce get hotter the longer you keep it. Agway, you want me to read you a story? Oh, I see you understand the word 'story.'"

I went and got myself a shawl from the bedroom, checked my makeup for the umpteenth time. When I came back out, Orso and Agway were deep into a copy of *Horton Hears a Who.* Orso stopped reading when he saw me.

"You going to wear that blouse like that?"

"Like what?" I tried to look down over my bosom.

"Pull it out of the waist band lemme see?"

I did. He nodded. "That suit you better."

"Thank you."

Someone knocked at the door. Agway scampered for it, Orso after him. Agway got there first and opened the door. It was Gene. He'd just come from work, was still wearing his uniform. Hot. My nipples got pointy just looking at him.

He smiled at us. "Good evening," he said. I introduced him to Orso, re-introduced him to Agway, who ducked behind my leg. Gene held out a new beach ball, uninflated. It was red and white. "For Agway. I could give it to him?"

Which made him Agway's new best friend, even though Agway didn't have a clue what the ball was.

"I won't stay late," I told him and Orso.

"Have a good time."

*　　*　　*

At eighty-seven years old, Mrs. Smalley of Mrs. Smalley's Chicken Boutique had passed away gently in her sleep one night. Her grandson Kevin ran the place now, and he knew better than to change the name of the restaurant that had been a Cayaba tradition for so long.

Gene put the cafeteria tray with our fried chicken on it down on the table between us. "They didn't have Pear Solo," he said. "Shampa suit you?"

I nodded. I had to strain to hear him over the loud tumpa rhythms blaring from Mrs. Smalley's speakers, the cash register staff yelling orders at the cooks in the back, the customers yelling orders at the cash register staff. The place smelled of hot grease, fried chicken, and pepper sauce. I loved it here.

Gene sat down and contemplated the plate on his tray: four pieces of chicken, about three potatoes' worth of french fries, a tub of coleslaw, and two bottles of sorrel. "How you manage to eat all that?" I asked him.

"You should see me if I don't. You think I'm skinny now?"

"Lean, not skinny." But it's lie I was telling. He was skinny.

A hot flash came and went. I scarcely noticed it in the heat from the restaurant stoves. But I did notice the balsa wood glider plane that appeared in the air near the ceiling of the restaurant and began spiralling down. "Excuse me," I said to Gene. I stood, pushed my chair back, caught the plane by its body. Only a small boy sitting at a table beside his mummy seemed to have noticed. His mouth was hanging open. I winked at him.

Nine years old when I got the Pigeon glider. Not as fancy as Stanley's; no motor or remote control. As I remembered, the wings and tail fins slipped neatly out of the body so it could all lie flat. I tucked the pieces into my handbag and sat back down.

"Everything all right?" asked Gene, busy shovelling coleslaw into his mouth.

"Totally fine. I just needed to stretch my legs out a bit."

The small boy was tugging on his mother's sleeve and pointing at me, but she was watching the latest Roger Dodger music video on the television, rocking her head in time to the music.

I bit into one of my chicken legs. The skin was crispy, and the meat was hot, peppery, and tender. The juice burst from it into my mouth. "Damn, I was hungry. I wonder what they put in the chicken to make it taste like this?"

"Ground allspice," he said through a mouthful of coleslaw. "In the breading."

"How you know?"

He grinned. "I'm an officer of the nation, ma'am. People have to tell me things."

"Oh, yes? Well, I'm a citizen of the nation and it's people like me you're protecting, right? So tell me this, Officer; why you took the cutlass from the house without my permission?"

His look was sharp. "Not from the house. We were outside."

"From my *premises*, then. Don't try to twist words on me. Why you looking into my dead parents' private business?"

His head came up. His eyes were narrowed. "Come again? I don't exactly need your permission to do my job."

"Uh-huh. You mean somebody re-opened the case? And your superiors put you on it?" I leaned across the table and hissed, "And was fucking me on my father's funeral day part of your investigation?"

He flinched. "No, no, and no," he said, shame-faced. "Besides, if they re-opened it, would be the police handling it, not the Coast Guard. Tell you the truth, I just got a mind to look into your mother's disappearance. On the side, you know? In private."

"Why? Anybody ask you?"

"You know how sad Mr. Lambkin remained, long after your mother left? Some evenings I would go there after school for lessons, and he would still be in the pyjamas he slept in all night. Sink full up of dirty dishes. Eating peanut butter right from the jar, with his fingers if he couldn't find a clean spoon. Couple-three times I did the dishes for him and got him some cooked food."

The old guilt. "Crap. I figured he was having a hard time. But in those days he wasn't talking to me."

"I not giving you static over it. After I lost touch with him for so many years? I'm just saying, it's because of Mr. Lambkin's coaching that I made it into college at all. It's he why I have this job. So if I can use the tools the job give me to clear his name, well, maybe I owe it to him to try. But I will stop right now if you want me to."

Christ. The food didn't taste so good any more. "Not much hope of clearing his name now, though. Not with blood on the cutlass blade."

He saw my face, and held out his hand for mine. I couldn't find my serviettes. Oh, those awkward social moments; lick the chicken grease off and *then* put my hand in his? Put my greasy hand in his and hope he didn't notice?

He quirked a smile at me and gave me a couple of his serviettes.

"Thanks." I cleaned my hand. He took it.

"All right," he said. "Look me in my face, now. You mustn't fret."

"But . . . on the cutlass—"

"I don't even really know what it is yet. Might not be human."

"How you mean?"

"The sample is old, and there was only little bit of it. It might have been contaminated with other things that were on the blade. They not sure whether it's human or animal."

It was like I could breathe again. "You think it might be animal?" His eyes were hazel. I hadn't noticed that before.

"He used that cutlass for all kinds of things, right?"

"True that. Even to chop up the chicken for dinner. Mumma was always after him to wash it." I almost told him about the sealskin. I hadn't found the time or privacy to burn it after all. I decided not to borrow trouble. If the stuff on the blade turned out to be seal, I would cross that bridge when I reached it.

"Well, that's most likely what it is." He let my hand go, got back to his supper. "Nobody ever found a body—sorry—that might have been your mother's. So maybe she just ups and left allyou that night."

"Maybe," I said bitterly. With my fork, I paddled around in my coleslaw.

"So, if you give me permission, I would try to find out where she used to go, who she used to hang out with. See if I can turn up anything the Police missed." He smiled. "Be kinda nice to rub their faces in it. Up to you, though. I not going to do anything unless you say."

He was on his third piece of chicken. Most of the fries were gone.

"Christ. Watching you eat is like watching a Hoover vacuum."

He grinned and kept chewing. I opened my tangerine Shampa. In the years before the company specified that it was supposed to be tangerine, me and Michael used to try to guess what fruit the "real fruit flavour" on the label was meant to be. Lime? June plum? Shaddock? I took a sip of the yellow-green drink. No. Still didn't taste a bit like tangerine.

"They were fighting," I said. "Mumma and Dadda. That night."

Gene didn't seem to change his steady, focussed attack on the food at all, but something about him came fully alert to what I was saying. "Fighting? What about?"

"I don't know, some big-people something. They used to fight every now and again."

"He ever hit her?"

"No. He would strap me if I crossed him. West Indian tough love. But he never touched Mumma. He wasn't that kind of man." I laughed. "Though I think he would have lost if he had been foolish enough to take Mumma on. She was taller than him, and wider. She used to joke she could pick him up and carry him out of a burning building if she had to. But I don't think it was completely joke."

"They used to fight plenty?"

"No. Just every so often."

"And what would happen then?"

"Mumma would threaten to leave. Dadda would tell her to feel free. Sometimes she would go out for a few hours."

"To where?"

"I don't know. For a walk, probably. To cool down. Little more, she would come back. They would talk. By next morning, they would be laughing and joking with each other again."

Gene studiously poured ketchup on his fries in a spiral pattern. "Kiss and make up?"

I nodded. "I guess. But sometimes she would stay out overnight instead."

He put the ketchup bottle down and looked at me. "A whole night?"

On the television, the music programme ended. Time for the news. Good. Now I would be able to hear myself think.

"Yeah," I said, "a whole night. She would row over to the big island, stay with relatives. Sometimes two nights, till her anger blow over. Gene, what if you find out that he killed her in truth?"

His face crumpled. "I don't even want to think about that. I want him to be the hero in my mind, you know? The man who made the world make sense for me." He was silent for a bit. "But the truth is, if we find out he was guilty, nobody know but you and me."

I sputtered on my Shampa. He said it so calmly.

"But we couldn't do that!" I said. "We would have to let the authorities know!"

Some of the spark came back. "Sweetheart, I *am* the authorities."

"Not you one! Not all by yourself!" My heart was thumping at that "sweetheart," but this was more important.

Gene gave me a long, measuring look. "You something else, you know that?" He sounded bemused. "You cuss like a sailor, you have a temper like a crocodile, but you more honest than any judge I know."

My face was heating up. "That not any virtue to speak of. The honesty, I mean. Only backtracking. I do it because my first impulse is to lie."

"How you mean?"

"You ever try being a nineteen-year-old single mother in this country?"

"Nah, man. Maybe when I retire."

I threw a serviette at him. He laughed.

"Serious, though," I said. "A teenager on her own with a three-year-old on her hip, and no baby father in sight. Try renting an apartment. Getting a fucking bank account."

He shrugged. "All legal. Nothing to prevent you."

"Man, you know better than that. Or is what kind of officer of the law you are?" I was waving my Shampa bottle around in the air to make my point. I kissed my teeth, put down my bottle. "Nineteen is in between. You can't drink booze yet, but you old enough to have a child walking and talking. Try to get a driver's licence, they either want to know where your husband or where your parents. And when you can't produce either, you going to wait till you drop while they check every friggin piece of i.d. you have, and call your job, and verify your signature. You ever try waiting in a bank line-up with a three-year-old?"

He laughed. "Yeah. I can match you there."

I realised I didn't know plenty about him. Cool breeze; he would get his grilling later. "People have a way to judge you. That's all I'm saying." Remembering those times was making me grumpy.

"True that. But what it have to do with being honest?"

For a second, I didn't know what he was talking about. Then I remembered. "Oh. That. Sorry. Forgetful nowadays. I just mean that I got good at lying. I would tell people my husband working in foreign. Or that Auntie Pearl was my mother. Sometimes I even pretended that Ifeoma was my little sister."

Sometimes I would pretend I wasn't Ifeoma's mother.

I managed to keep talking. "But then my conscience would start pronging me," I told him. "And I would take back the lie, but sometimes people will get on so bad when they find out you tricked them that it would have been better to just leave them ignorant. So now I try to tell the truth right off the bat. Stand tall, look people in the eye, and tell them about me. If they going to make trouble for me because of it, best I find out one time, so I don't have nothing more to do with them." But my little girl had heard me telling people that she wasn't mine.

"And how you figure that's not a virtue?"

I gave an embarrassed laugh. "Because sometimes I still tell a lie, and have to take it back afterwards."

He wasn't paying attention. He was looking at the television. I turned to see what was so absorbing. The announcer was saying:

"*. . . race heated up this morning, when prime minister Garth Johnson and minister of Foreign Trade and Economic Affairs Guinevere Poon announced the date of the ribbon-cutting ceremony to officially open the new Gilmor Saline, Incorporated, plant that has recently been completed on the island of Dolorosse.*

"*Last year, reduced restrictions on foreign investment in Cayaba made it possible for the Johnson government to lease the small island of Dolorosse to Gilmor Saline. The U.S.-based company, which has operated a salt production factory on the main island of Cayaba since 1955, has created artificial salt ponds and constructed a second factory on the southwest coast of Dolorosse.*"

The shot cut to Johnson at his press conference. He was saying:

"*Cayaba citizens deserve a high-quality standard of living—*"

"Damn right!" a woman from another table burst out. The woman with her shushed her.

"*—to provide well for their families. That has been and will always be my priority for this country. For more than five decades, Gilmor Saline has been a key partner with the government of Cayaba, providing employment for a significant proportion of the Cayaba population. This new venture* *between us is a tangible demonstration of the exemplary cooperation that exists between Cayaba and Gilmor Saline."*

"As part of the agreement between Gilmor Saline and the Cayaba government," said the announcer, *"the corporation will provide three new, state-of-the-art waterbuses to increase service on the ferry route, and is currently building towers and installing antennae on Dolorosse to boost cell phone reception for Dolorosse residents."*

"That's the part I like," I told Gene.

"Opposition leader Caroline Sookdeo-Grant was on hand for comment. She applauded the increased employment that the second plant has brought and congratulated the prime minister in that regard. She also joked about the apparently strategic timing of the ceremony, which will take place just three days before the upcoming election. But speaking on a more serious note, Mrs. Sookdeo-Grant also had a caution for the prime minister."

Now we were seeing Sookdeo-Grant at the press conference, with the noise and bustle of people milling around her. She said: *"Cayaba should be moving very carefully in any dealings we make with foreign multinationals or accepting more foreign aid. The FFWD demands that we reduce trade restrictions as a condition of lending us money. This allows foreign multinationals such as Gilmor Saline to grow unchecked in our country, forcing small farmers out of business. What will happen to the independent small salt farms on Dolorosse and the other islands? Will they be priced out of business? Forced to seek work in the Gilmor Saline factory for minimum wage?"*

"Tell them!" shouted an old East Indian man sitting alone with the paper and a Banks beer.

"Mr. Ramlal, hush, nuh?" said Kevin Smalley's wife from over by the cash register. She pointed at the television. "Listen."

The announcer was saying, *"Mrs. Sookdeo-Grant says that should her party win the upcoming elections, it intends to implement programmes to foster small business growth."*

The din in the restaurant got worse as people began to argue.

"And in other news . . ."

Gene still watching the blasted television. "Like that tv have you hypnotized," I said. He just pointed at it with his chin.

"Opposition party leader Mrs. Caroline Sookdeo-Grant paid a visit today to a remarkable woman."

Crap. It was me on the television, looking stunned and shaking Sookdeo-Grant's hand.

Gene said, "You know, I just had a feeling you were a remarkable woman."

". . . leapt into the rough seas off Dolorosse on Sunday, to save the life of a little boy in the water."

In the restaurant, a woman called out, "Look her there!" She was pointing at me.

The announcer said, *"Mrs. Lambkin, a recent widow, had buried her husband only the day before . . ."*

I put my head in my hands. From inside my handbag, my cell phone started ringing.

ONE, TWO, THREE, FOUR, FIVE. Six. Today Alexander Tremaine counted six monk seals in the Zooquarium where five were supposed to be. But Crab Cake was not one of them. She was missing. Alexander closed his eyes. She would be back in a few days. They always were.

And the hell with the incident report. Management had never responded to a single one of them.

Alexander made a note to get in extra seal chow. Heaven only knew how many seals would be in the enclosure tomorrow.

* * *

"Wоɪ." Hector threw down the sandpaper and wiped his brow with the back of his hand. He was sitting on an upturned bucket in the back yard, fixing up the tricycle like he'd promised. "I just need to tighten up that back wheel now, and put on a coat of paint." He was sweating in the hot sun.

"I really appreciate your doing this, you know?" I poured him a glass of pineapple juice from the frosty jug I'd brought out, with plenty ice cubes. He pushed the container of fried ripe plantain that he'd brought with him closer to me.

"Don't mention it. It's a good thing for Agway to have."

Hector was being friendly enough, but a little cool. Hadn't been smart of me, going off on Michael and Orso like that with Hector to witness it. I was working hard to regain lost ground.

Agway brought his sippy cup back for more. Without the sea to cool him off, the heat was making him weary and fractious. I'd put a blanket down for him just inside the kitchen door where he'd be in the shade but I could still keep an eye on him. I tried again to offer him some plantain, but he pushed my hand away. He had his own snack.

Hector sucked down about half his glass one time and helped himself to some fried plantain. He opened up the paint can and got back to work.

I munched on some of the plantain slices myself. A flock of spoonbills flew over us. Hector watched them. "They kinda pale," he said.

"Those must be the ones from the lagoon. No shrimp there to make them pink."

Hector shook his head. "You impress me."

"What? Why?"

"Plenty people wouldn't know that it's shrimp that gives the roseate spoonbill its colour."

"Stanley knows."

"I not surprised. They say the fruit don't fall far from the tree. Ifeoma has a mind like yours, too."

"Ife? Yes, she's pretty smart. And curious. Just flighty-flighty."

"Very smart. And pretty. Cayaba is something else, you know? Everywhere you turn, something else precious and rare." Not looking at me, he smiled. Lawdamercy. This time, the heat I was feeling wasn't from no hot flash.

He glanced inside the kitchen, and his face took on an expression somewhere between horror and disgust. "Calamity, what is that child eating?"

"His afternoon snack. Shrimps." Tailor-sat on the kitchen floor with his bowl, Agway was happily tearing each shrimp out of its cuticle shell with his teeth, chewing it down, and swallowing the yellow matter out of the head. He had a growing pile of empty shrimp shells on the floor beside him.

"He eating them *raw*?"

"Apparently he likes them like that."

"Well, best he eat his fill now," he said. "The day might come soon that you have to watch how much fish you eat from Cayaba waters."

"Why?"

He pursed his lips like he was trying to make up his mind about something. "You could keep a secret?" he asked.

"Man, you asking a Yaban if they know how to be close-mouthed? This whole country would collapse if people didn't mind whose business they talk."

Ruefully, he said, "So I coming to find out. All right. You

know I'm trying to figure out how Mediterranean monk seals come to be here."

"Yeah."

"It's not the only thing I'm doing. You shouldn't tell anyone, you understand? There might not even be a problem. Don't want to frighten people before we know for sure."

"Yeah, yeah. Just blasted well tell me, nuh?"

"I'm spying on Gilmor Saline."

"You kidding!"

"No lie."

"Why?"

"They might be dumping their bittern illegally."

"Their what?"

"Bittern. That's what get leave behind when you manufacture salt. Every pound of salt give you a pound of bittern. And bittern in high levels is toxic. Gilmor Saline supposed to dilute it three hundred to one with water and pipe it way out to sea. We think they releasing it strong just so into the waters around Cayaba."

"Oh, shit." The water the sea people lived in. I took Agway's bowl from him, though he'd already finished the shrimps and had curled up on his blanket to nap. "I should make him vomit them up?" I remembered the sound little Ife had made when I put my finger down her throat.

"Nah, man. Would take plenty plenty bittern to make him sick. It's edible in reasonable amounts. It's what they use to make tofu."

"Thank heaven for that." I put the shells into a plastic bag and threw them in the garbage.

"Mightn't be anything to worry about," Hector said. "In fact, the salt plant is good for wading birds; they eat the brine shrimp and so on you find in some of the evaporation ponds. But Gilmor can't pump toxic levels of bittern too close to shore. You know the fishermen been complaining from since that the fish getting scarce? Your Fisheries Department been checking it out, and it's true. Thirty percent reduction in some stocks."

"Shit. You find out whether they dumping it for true?"

He shook his head, frowning. "Composition of the water around Cayaba is normal one day, and too high in bittern the next. The outlet pipes from both processing plants lead to deep water like they supposed to. But still the fish stocks going down. I been trying to find out if it's affecting the seals. And I can't get a good count on the blasted things to save my life! Different numbers every three days. Making me crazy! Nothing wrong with my instruments. I using the same procedure I use every time. Worked in Turkey, worked in Hawai'i. It's just a simple census! Should be easy!"

He took off his t-shirt and mopped his brow with it. He had the kind of tubby barrel-body I liked in a man. And skin that made you want to lick it. I poured him some more pine drink. "I don't know much about you," I told him. "You have a poor, long-suffering wife waiting on dry land for you while you spend your nights out on the water watching the seals?"

He glanced at me, kept painting. "No wife," he said.

"Oh."

"Or girlfriend either."

"Oh."

"My ex-wife remarried last year. I guess she got over me faster than I got over her."

"Oh!" Nothing to worry about, then. I poured myself some drink, shifted over a little closer to him. Was I even his type?

Was I coming on like some of them old women trying to pose as twenty-one? Damn; this used to be so much easier.

He looked into my eyes. Hah. Bet you I knew what that sultry gaze meant. We were playing on my court now. He said, "You not easy to figure out, you know."

"Lady has to keep some mystery about herself."

"I see the side of you that's smart, and generous, and funny. The side that could sing 'Jane and Louisa' together with a stranger, just to keep a scared little boy from being more scared."

I sketched a mock bow from the waist up. "Thank you, sir. I do my best."

"Well, don't dig nothin', but you have kind of an ugly side too, you know."

But wait. "How you mean?"

"Well, the way you talked to Michael and Orso."

Play it light, Calamity. "Oh, that!" I said with a guilty giggle. "I really went overboard, nuh true?"

"Yeah."

"Hormones," I said. "You know how it is with women some-times." Let him think I meant my period.

He didn't look up from his painting. "Those were some rahtid hormones."

Chuh. Man barely out of little boy short pants, and he scold-ing me? Second wrong note he had hit. Three strikes and you out, Mister. All right; for that behind, I'd give him four strikes. "Hector, I can't tell you how sorry I am I subjected you to such a scene."

"Not just me. All of us."

Watch it, son. You easing towards number four. "Yeah. And now I'm just embarrassed, you know?" Coy it up, warm him up. "Sometimes I'm not so very smart after all."

He nodded! The bastard man nodded! "You been really nice to me, Calamity. Inviting me to visit, introducing me to your family. I would like for you and me to be friends."

"Mm-hmm . . ."

He looked unhappy. "So I need to speak plain," he said.

I had an uncomfortable feeling in the pit of my stomach. "Go on."

"You see," he said, "this thing not joke in the Caribbean. I learned the hard way to keep my distance from people who have a problem with me being bisexual."

It's like somebody threw cold water on me. I froze right where I sat. "What?"

He gave a regretful shrug. "When I heard how you talked to Orso and Michael the other day—"

"You're gay? Just like Michael?"

He looked perplexed. "You really didn't understand the joke the rest of us were making the other day? I like men and women. Mary *and* Joseph. True a little bit more Mary than Joseph nowadays, though that have a way to change."

Stupid, stupid, Calamity. Shame. I blurted out, "And I just ate from the same dish as you?"

And for the first time, I saw Hector Goonan get angry. He jammed the lid back onto the paint, hammered it on with the handle of the brush. He slammed the lid back onto the container that the fried plantain had been in. "Let me just take this back with me then, since my contaminated lips touched it."

I stood up. "I don't know why you getting on so bad," I said, my voice trembling with fury. "It's not you who got lied to."

His hands were shaking as he put away his tools. "I never lied to you. Who have ears to hear will hear. I said it right in front of you only a few days ago."

"And how I was supposed to understand that two-faced chat the four of you were doing?" I hated the tears running down my face, hated the weakness they showed.

He stood up. "You know, you don't make it so easy for a person to speak plain." He headed round the side of the house towards the front yard. I followed him.

"You're sick!" I snarled at him. "Can't even make up your mind. Going back and forth from women to men, spreading diseases!"

He stopped so suddenly I almost ran into him. He turned to face me. "Actually," he said in a low, dangerous voice, "*I* know I'm not sick. Get tested every year, use barrier protection. I bet you money *you* don't do the same."

The memory of Gene's naked cock sliding into me betrayed me. Words stuck in my throat.

Hector saw my face fall. He kissed his teeth. "I thought so," he said. "So it seem to me that you're the one who stand a chance of putting your lovers at risk, not me. It's people like you why I make sure to use latex. You tell you last lover yet that he should get tested?"

And he slung his bag over his shoulder, turned on his heel, and walked away.

I found my voice. "Faggot!" I cried. He kept on walking. I followed. "Anti-man! Dirty, stinking, lying *hen!*" My voice cracked on the last word. I was crying so hard that I had trouble getting my breath. Everywhere I turn, another one of those nasty men, thiefing away any joy in my life. It's like somebody curse me.

What right he had to be angry? I was the injured party! Me!

On the big ship one of the sailors who brought them the thin pap that was their only food was an Igbo man. He joked that the whites were cannibals who were going to eat them. It could be true. Why else truss people up like chickens for the market?

Every few days the sailors would open the hatch, cursing and holding their noses against the smell. It was the only time when the people got a glimpse of sky, a sip of fresh air. The sailors would remove the dead and dying. The more that died, the more space for those remaining. The dada-hair lady was heartsick at the relief she felt when another body was removed. The Igbo sailor described how they threw the dead bodies over the side, how large fish with sharp teeth were following the ship now, waiting for their next meal.

After a lifetime of a misery she could never have imagined before this, the sailors came down one day and took them out of the hold, those who could stand. So long the dada-hair lady's eyes had been yearning for the sight of the sky, but now the light pierced them like knives. Fresh, cool air to breathe made the dada-hair lady feel almost drunk.

The men had been brought out of their section of the hold, too. So thin they were, and weak-looking! The dada-hair looked at her own arm. Yes, the flesh had wasted.

The sailors sluiced them down with buckets of salted water. The water made her shiver. The salt stung the chafed skin on her wrists and ankles where the shackles rubbed.

There was a child near her, maybe eight years old. She hadn't seen him before. It'd been too dark in the hold. He dragged two empty shackles where his fellows should have been. He shook and blubbered with his fear, and wailed softly in his language. The dada-hair lady didn't know what he

said, but "Mamma" would be a likely bet. She knelt. Her
two shackle-mates had to kneel with her. She took the boy in
her arms. He came, wriggling his way in among the chains
binding her wrists, hungry for loving touch, his tiny body like
chicken bones wrapped in skin. He had weeping yaws on his
legs.

The sailors doused everyone with oil, signalled for them to
rub themselves down. The dada-hair lady rubbed oil into her
skin, and into the little boy's. It made them gleam, as though
they were healthy. "Maybe they'll throw perfume on us next?"
joked Belite, who had lain beside her in the hold. She was
a young Arada woman. They were Igbos and Ewes and
Aradas in that place. Different languages, different ways, but
they had been learning each other's speech in the long dark
misery of their days.

The scrawny boy fell asleep in the dada-hair lady's arms.

There were tree branches floating in the water, birds
perched on the sails. There was a shadow on the horizon.
The white man who looked like the boss man was conferring
with another, looking at a sheet of paper. They pointed at the
shadow and babbled their nonsense talk. They frowned, and
the sailors near them looked nervous. Was that land? She
had to do something soon.

Truth was, she hadn't reckoned what she was going to do.
All she could think was poison. For them all to take poison to
shunt them into the world beneath the waters.

If she were at home, and free, she could easily have found
the ingredients to make a strong dose. But she had nothing
here, only the chancy power of the blood in her, and starving
on the ship, she hadn't been bleeding. But some few days
ago, their rations had been increased. Now she was only

constantly a little hungry, not half-fainting her days through from starvation.

A flurry in the water beside the ship caught the dada-hair lady's eye. Efiok—the Efiok whose place in the hold was two souls over from hers—she saw it, too. She looked to the dada-hair lady, jerked her chin in the direction of the disturbance in the water. The dada-hair lady moved a little closer to the edge.

At first the dada-hair lady could see nothing. Then her soul leapt in her breast; a head, grey-brown with curious black eyes, staring after the ship! Had one of their band jumped, then?

Then the person dove down into the water. The dada-hair lady had only a brief glimpse of its body slipping bent as a sickle forward into the sea. It was cylindrical, curved, and fat with good food. Sea cow? Seal? At home, the older people sometimes talked about sea cows who lived in the coastal waters, how you shouldn't look directly at them, lest they drag you down to the depths with them for your presumption. The dada-hair lady had never seen one up close, but the fishermen described them: they stole fish from their nets. Momi Wata, thought the dada-hair lady respectfully to the thing she'd seen, beg you please take a message to Uhamiri for me. Tell her we need her help here. Tell her I am hers. I pledge to always faithfully be hers, but please would she help us now, before we land and the white people eat us. The dada-hair lady peered at the water, but she couldn't see any sign of the sea cow, or whatever it had been. Her heart ached for what she'd promised: the women who were called to serve Uhamiri remained barren.

But she'd made her plea, and her pledge. The dada-hair

*lady held the boy's small shivering body and whispered in his
shell of an ear, "Soon. Something will happen." It must.*

∽

Agway tried to go on tippy toes to reach for the kitchen sink, but
the cast was cramping his style.

"I know what you want," I told him. "Let's set you up first,
all right?"

I carried him into the bathroom and got the fancy neoprene
cast protector out of the cupboard under the sink. The hospital
had given it to me, and it was a wonderful thing. Back in the
kitchen, I sat him on the floor. He watched gravely as I covered his cast with the cast protector, attached the air bulb, and
pumped all the air out.

"Now you ready to go." I took all the breakable dishes out of
the sink and lifted him up onto the counter so he could sit with
his feet in the sink. "Here." I gave him the soap and a cloth. With
a serious look, he turned on the tap, dabbled his feet in the water,
and set about washing the dishes. He loved doing it. He'd make
some woman a wonderful husband.

Not like certain men, playing Mr. Sensitive but all the time
having it both ways.

I peeled and grated raw Irish potato into a small pot for porridge for Agway's breakfast. I tossed in a cinnamon stick, filled
the pot with water and put it to boil.

Stringing people along until they make fools of themselves.

I put two eggs on to boil for me, and started frying up bacon
for me and Agway. It was the one kind of meat he would tolerate
cooked.

Getting vexed at people when they go off on you. I turned the bacon over and over in the pan, trying to scrub the image out of my mind of me sweet-talking Hector when all the while . . . but it kept popping up to shame me.

Foul-smelling smoke was rising from the frying pan. I was turning burnt bacon with my spatula. "Shit!" I twisted the heat dial to off. It came away in my hand. I screamed and threw it out the open window. "He can just go and take a flying fuck at a rolling doughnut!" I sobbed.

"Flying fuck," repeated Agway with perfect diction as he poured water from a bowl over his lower legs. He even got the L right. He'd been having trouble with the letter L.

"Oh, great. Just don't say that in front of Evelyn tonight, all right?"

Screw the bacon. I boiled another egg. I could persuade Agway to eat an egg if I mashed it and put enough butter in it. I puréed the porridge in the blender, added milk and a dab of butter. Threw my eggs onto a plate with a mound of salt and black pepper beside them, and buttered couple-three slices of harddough bread for the two of us.

I was scraping his mashed egg into his bowl when I heard a rustle behind me. Agway had climbed down off the counter. Even with the cast, the damned boy was agile as a mongoose. He had fished the eggshells out of the garbage and was holding them wadded in his fist, except for the one he was chewing.

"Agway! Bad!" I flicked the broken eggshell out of his mouth. "You mustn't do that! You understand me? No playing in the garbage!"

He already knew when I was telling him he had done wrong, but I could see that the poor soul couldn't understand what I was scolding him for. I sighed. "I can't wait for you to learn more than seven words of English." I washed his mouth out and found a way to close the garbage can that he couldn't figure out; not yet, anyway. I sat him at the table and persuaded him to eat his egg, spoonful by spoonful, out of the *spoon*, not with his hands. That battle came to a draw.

What did Hector looked like when he . . . ? I got a mental flash of Hector and another man (who looked a bit like Michael) touching, hugging, their lips meeting. I shut the image down quickly. It mocked me. It looked too much like my secret, voyeur fantasies.

I needed some distraction from this black mood. I took us out into the living room and put on an old DVD: *A Shark's Tale*. As each movie finished, I fed another one into the player: *Sukey and the Mermaid, Lilo & Stitch VII, In the Time of the Drums*.

Eventually I got up and began tucking books away. I cleaned up a bit. Place needed to look good for Evelyn's visit this evening.

While Agway was preoccupied with a movie and his toys, I set up a card table on the porch with one of the stacks of Dadda's papers on it. He had more documents stashed everywhere in the house. Sorting his life was going to be a job and a half.

Then I hauled Agway out to the front yard and showed him how to use the tricycle. He got the trick of it, and pretty soon he was zooming around the yard, hunting down the tiny green lizards and yelling as he did. I just prayed he wouldn't actually catch any of the lizards; with his love of raw food, I didn't want to see what he would do with it. I flipped through Dadda's papers. Old water bill receipts: toss. Credit card information: keep, so I could cancel them.

"Child, come away from my tomato plants!" Blasted boy hadn't learned yet that the green ones gave him a bellyache. His nappy needed changing, too. I plucked him off the tricycle he'd just deliberately crashed into my tomato plants. I took him up onto the porch and stood him on his feet in front of me. He had a saggy diaper, dirt on his hands and knees, more smeared across his face, and little tomato seeds drying around his mouth. "What I going to do with you, enh?"

He tried to go back down the porch stairs. "Wait, hang on!" I grabbed him up by his middle and took him, kicking, into the bathroom.

Using the toilet as a bench, I sat with him in my lap, stripped off his diaper and wiped him clean. He was beginning to get the hang of toilet-training. He didn't like having a dirty nappy.

I tossed the soiled toilet paper into the bowl. "You want to flush?" I asked him.

He grabbed the handle on the toilet and yanked on it with all his weight. Then he leaned over the bowl to watch the magic. He was fascinated by the toilet, where you could make water run on command. Twice now I'd caught him trying to climb into the bowl. When he wasn't doing that, he was flushing it, over and over.

Good thing I'd been too lazy to take the cast protector off. One less step to do. I changed into my bath suit, grabbed two towels, and ran after Agway, who had scampered out of the bathroom, *clonk-slap* on his one bare foot and the one with the cast on. I caught up with him in the living room. "Tuck!" he protested as I took him back out to the yard.

"You can play with your truck later. I have something else for you right now." I set the sprinkler on Dadda's miserable excuse for a lawn, and made sure I could see it from the porch. I turned it on to "oscillate." Agway's eyes got round as the moon when he saw the water come out. Soon he was dashing back and forth through the water, naked as any egg, screeching with glee. He used his all-fours wolf lope. That leg must be healing, if he could do that. I played catch with him in the sprinkler for a while, then I left him sitting under the sprinkler shower, trying to pull up lawn grass by its roots. I was exhausted. Not even lunch time, and a whole day ahead of me of Agway being rambunctious. I returned to the porch, dried off, and kept going through Dadda's things.

Mortgage papers for the house on Blessée: keep, for nostalgia's sake; the insurance money done spend long time ago. Card Chastity had given Dadda for his thirtieth birthday: toss; and stop sniffling. Then a legal-size document. The paper had aged to yellow.

I leafed through the dog-eared sheets. There was a section that described a business plan. Apparently, Dadda had wanted to grow cashews and sell and distribute cashew products. Train local workers, expand the production to other islands. Big ideas. Clearly didn't go nowhere, though.

I turned to the final page. Lender's line signed on behalf of the FFWD by Messrs. Gray and Gray. The borrowers' line was signed by Dadda and someone else. I peered at the signature. To rass. Mr. Kite! So they had known each other from before, then. Maybe that's why he'd been so ready to take Dadda in? Best I call Gene and tell him, nuh true? Could be important.

Chuh. I wasn't fooling myself. I just wanted an excuse to call him. I reached for my phone and dialled his cell.

He answered the phone with a gruff "Yeah?"

My heart gave a little leap when I heard his voice. "It's Calamity. I'm not interrupting anything?" I asked, straining to figure out what the noises in the background were.

"Hold on; too much static." After a few seconds, I heard generic street noises. "Okay," he said. "I'm outside. Who's this?"

"Calamity."

"Wow. *You* calling *me*. Usually I have to do the calling."

I flushed. "I just found something."

"What?"

"Dadda and Mr. Kite knew each other from before I was born. I just found papers for a loan they took out to start cashew farming and processing in Cayaba."

"Awoah."

"I thought they only met when he rescued Dadda from the docks here right after the hurricane. I wonder what happened to the business?"

"Businesses fail."

"I'm going through all Dadda's papers now. Maybe I'll find something that will tell me."

"Maybe." He sounded preoccupied.

"You busy? I can call another time."

"Nah, man, no need for that! Okay. You have my full attention now."

But he still didn't volunteer any information. I recognised what he was doing; had done it myself sometimes. Keep somebody at a distance by telling them as little about yourself as you could get away with. Paper over it by being friendly, but play your cards close to your chest. "Gene, what you and I really doing any at all?"

"How you mean?"

"We seeing each other? We not seeing each other? We friends, we booty-calling, what?"

His laugh was relaxed and open. "That's all? Well, tell me what you want us to be doing here."

"And you will go along with whatever I want, is that it?"

"No, you not getting off that easy. Because after you tell me what you want, you have to ask me what I want."

"You strike a hard bargain, Mr. Meeks."

"You gotta play to play."

"Okay," I replied. I was all nerves. Suppose I was misreading him same way I'd misread Hector? "I not sure what I want," I told him. "I been thinking maybe I should keep things simple for a while. We were supposed to be doing anonymous funeral sex, remember?"

"That? We did that already. I crossed it off my list long time. You still keeping it on yours?"

I laughed. "Maybe. It had a certain appeal."

"You can't be anonymous twice in a row, you know."

"Not with the same person, anyway."

"Oh."

"Sorry," I said. "I just like to tease. Truth is, I not sure I have any business dating anybody right now. The heart kind of tender, you know?" I pushed Hector out of my mind.

"Good," he said, and my spirits sank down even deeper into the crab barrel. "Because I learned long ago not to get involved with anybody who in a big life transition. You have grieving to do, and your life to start over."

Relief made me giggly. "And a new child to look after. Don't forget that."

"You can handle that one," he said. "I have every confidence."

"And once I'm done . . . transitioning, then what?"

"Then we'll have to see, nuh true? You going to be a whole different person. Maybe you won't find me interesting any more."

"And we can still keep company till then?"

"If you want to."

"I want to." I was smiling so broadly it was hard to talk.

"Tell me," he said, "why you call me about Mr. Lambkin and Mr. Kite? I thought you didn't want any poking around in your parents' past?"

"It's your fault, you know. You got me interested, and now it look like I can't leave it alone."

"You free Monday night?"

My heart made a little leap. "Pretty sure, yes. Why?"

"Maybe I could come and see you?"

"Yeah, man." I smiled. The day was looking bright all of a sudden.

Mr. Lessing was coming down my gravel road with a kicking and wailing Agway under one arm, and carrying the tricycle in the other hand. Shit. When the backside the boy had left the yard? "I have to go," I told Gene. I hung up the phone and went to greet Mr. Lessing. He put Agway and the tricycle down. Agway ran into my arms, complaining. I picked him up. He grabbed my ear.

"I find him down by the Corrolyons'," said Mr. Lessing, "pedalling that tricycle like jumbie was on his tail."

"All the way over there?" The Corrolyons lived about half a mile away.

"You going to have to watch him, you know? That's the sea road he was on."

"I *was* watching him."

Mr. Lessing only nodded. I gave him a grudging thank you and took Agway inside. I locked the front door and the back. Suppose a car had hit him? Suppose he'd reached the water? My heart sank as quickly as Agway would if he fell into the sea with a cast dragging him down. "Poor baby," I said to him. "Your home is here now. And I going to do my best to make it a good place for you to live."

I would have to put a fence around the yard, with a strong lock on the gate.

* * *

EVELYN SHOWED UP right on time that evening. She was wearing a cotton skirt in beige, A-line, with a tasteful lace trim at its hem. A matching t-shirt. A crocheted cotton shawl, cream colour, as were the espadrilles on her feet. She'd pulled her greying black hair back into a loose bun, let some tendrils of it escape artfully to frame her face. Damned woman was as bad as Orso; always made me feel like I had yampie in my eye corners and stains on the knees of my jeans. "Come in, nuh?"

She slipped off the espadrilles, left them on the mat outside the door. I showed her into the kitchen. "I running late," I told her. "Still haven't shelled the peas."

"Don't worry. I not in a hurry." We were still bashful and awkward with each other. Probably would be for a while.

Then she spied Agway. She tossed her wrap onto a chair and squatted down under the table beside him.

"Hello, precious," she said. "You remember me?"

Agway handed her one of the plastic mugs he was playing with.

"Thank you, my darling. What you want me to do with this?"

And for the next five minutes, the two of them built towers of plastic mugs, laughing when they collapsed. When she clambered out from under the table, her skirt was wrinkled and most of her hair had come loose from its bun. She was still chuckling. "Well, he looks happy," she said. She gathered her hair, knotted it, stuck the clip back through it.

"Yeah, man. He's doing good here."

"Seem he's in good hands. You got me convinced, anyway."

I let out a relieved breath. "Then I rest my case."

She smiled. "Same thing you used to say back in school."

"True that." She had laughter lines at the corners of her eyes and mouth. So strange to be seeing Evelyn's face, but on a middle-aged woman.

"And you were such a tomboy," she said.

"I know. Always getting into trouble."

She sat on a chair at the table and started shelling the congo peas I had in a bowl there. I gave Agway a handful of the peas in their pods and joined her in shelling the rest.

She said, "Remember the time you went up on the roof of the school?"

The black tar that had melted in the noon-day heat, sticking to the soles of my shoes. I smiled. "Dadda used to call me 'Calamity Jane.'"

"That's where you took your new name from, then?"

"I guess so. I never really thought about it before."

"And is what made you go up onto the school roof?"

"I just wanted to see what I would see."

Sitting on the floor, Agway was cracking open the peas pods and eating the hulls. Raw green peas were scattered all around him.

I hadn't had a chance to see much up on the school roof. A loose gable came away in my hands and nearly sent me tumbling three storeys to the ground. "Almost killed myself that day. Good thing that little ledge was there, just below the overhang. Got my feet on it in time, held on to the edge of the roof, and started screaming for help."

"Ulric said his heart nearly jumped right out his mouth and died flopping at his feet when he looked up and saw you hanging there."

The school janitor. So many years I hadn't thought about him. Grumpy old black man, or he had seemed grumpy to me then. But the strangest things could make him smile; a little lizard cupped gently in a curious child's hands, for instance.

"Ulric was giving me instructions the whole time he was putting the ladder up to come and get me. 'I want you to breathe slow and even, Chastity, you hear me? Breathe strong. And use them muscles that you got. You good as any boy when it come to climbing. Hold on, girl, hold on; I coming.' "

Mumma had come to the principal's office when he had sent for her. She saw me with my skinned-up hands and my school uniform fouled with tar. With her mouth, she'd scolded me, but with her body, she was holding me tightly to her, checking every limb to make sure I was all right, patting my face, arms, and legs and looking at me love, love.

And I'd looked back at her wearing her cafeteria staff uniform—a hideous dark grey polyester dress—with her hair in a net and a smear of flour on her face, and I'd been ashamed. I'd pushed myself out of her arms and snapped, "I'm all *right*! You have to come outside in your work clothes and make everybody see you?"

Her face had closed up tight. She stood, swiped some of the flour off her face with the heel of her hand. "Thank you for calling me," she said to Principal Cramer. Then she left the office without saying another word to me.

That had been on a Friday. On the Saturday, she was gone for good.

I shook the memories off. "You want some wine?" I asked Ev. "I have red."

"That sound good. It in the pantry? I could get it."

"All right." I took up the bowl of shelled peas and put them to cook in the pot with rice and creamed coconut. Agway was nodding off, rubbing his eyes.

I opened the wine Evelyn handed me and poured her a big glass.

"You not having any?"

"Soon. I just putting Agway to bed first."

* * *

"You never liked the name Chastity, nuh true?" asked Evelyn. She prepared to tuck into a plate of peas and rice, and dry-fried fish with seviche sauce.

"No. Maybe my parents thought giving me that name would make me meek and biddable. It didn't go so."

Evelyn tasted the fish. "God, this is good. Janet never cooks anything like this for us."

"Janet?"

"We have a helper who comes in during the days. She makes dinner and leaves it for us for when we get home. Maybe your parents just wanted to give you a name that would keep you safe."

"*Chastity?*" I rolled my eyes at her.

"So that when the boys started sniffing around you, you would try to live up to your name," she teased.

I snorted. "And you see how well that worked. Fifteen years old, and me and Michael un-chastitied me one afternoon after school."

"Michael? Your good friend Michael?"

"He same one."

"He's your baby father?"

"Mm-hmm."

"But the two of you didn't stay together?"

"It didn't work out. I don't like to talk about it."

"Imagine that. You and Michael. Fifteen years old."

"I guess I was precocious."

"No, my dear. I beat you to it. Thirteen and a half."

I goggled at her. "You?"

She chuckled. "Me. Whose parents never let her out of their sight."

"Who? When?"

"Steven Baldwin. In the girls' bathroom after school one day, before Mummy and Daddy picked me up."

I sat back down and looked good at her. "Steve? The one with the big mole on his forehead?"

Evelyn frowned. "I thought that mole was kind of sweet. Made him look intellectual."

"And you did it in the *bathroom*?"

"In one of the stalls. Standing up, girl! We could hear Ulric moving around in the hallway the whole time, vacuuming. Knew he was going to come in soon to clean the bathroom. When Steven was about to, you know—"

I poured us more wine. "Evelyn, you're a doctor. You don't get to say, 'You know.'"

She giggled. "I do when it's me having sex I'm talking about. Old training dies hard. When it's other people, I get to use words like 'engorgement' and 'ejaculation.'"

"So that's what you're trying to tell me? That when Steven was about to come . . . what then?"

She was actually blushing. "He pulled out," she said softly. "It ran all down his leg, leaving this sticky, drippy trail on his school uniform pants."

I laughed.

"As he was, um, coming, he was trying so hard not to make any noise that he roared into the side of my neck."

She was smiling, stroking the place on her neck as though she was touching a lover's skin. "In the hollow," she said, "right here so. I still remember how his voice felt, vibrating through my collar bone."

When Michael came, he'd thrown his arm over his eyes. I guess that way, he didn't have to see me. I could really pick 'em.

"Steven had to shinny out the window when we heard Ulric opening the door. He didn't even have time to zip his pants back up."

"Christ on a cracker. And you thought *I* was brave."

"Hormones, man, hormones. Make you do madness."

Only they had thought to at least try not to get her pregnant. Pulling out was a risky method, but at least it was a method. I cleared the empty dishes off the table. "I thought you wanted to talk to me about Agway being a sea child?"

She looked embarrassed and waved it away. "No need, man. We could do that any time." She stood. "Listen, I don't like to eat and run, but Samuel going to be here soon."

"I know. I was late with dinner." I frowned. One mention of sea people and she was hurrying out the door?

"I could visit your facilities?"

"Sure. Just down the hall, first door on your right."

"I could peek in and see Agway, too?"

"Of course."

She was gone for so long that eventually I went looking for her. Door to the bathroom was open, nobody inside. Puzzled, I went to Dadda's bedroom. Quietly, I pushed the door open a crack. Agway was splayed carelessly on the bed, sleeping the sleep of someone with a clear conscience. Evelyn was bent over him, her ear close to his face. What the hell? I opened the door and stepped inside. Evelyn put a finger to her lips when she saw me. She indicated that we should go outside.

Agway exhaled a long, shuddery breath. He stirred, but didn't wake. I checked that he was sleeping comfortably. I planted a kiss on my fingertips—the two webbed ones, for luck—and transferred it to his forehead. Then I went with Evelyn into the living room.

"Do you know his breathing is interrupted while he's sleeping?" Her face was really serious.

"Yeah. But he always starts again. I'm getting used to it."

"Calamity, just now he stopped breathing for nearly two minutes. I was about to start rescue breathing when his own kicked in again. I'm scheduling a sleep clinic appointment for him *tomorrow*."

She was frightening me. "What's wrong with him?"

"I don't know until I check. But that pattern looks a lot like sleep apnea."

"And what that does?"

"Causes sleep deprivation, can contribute to stroke. If it isn't treated, the patient is at risk of cardiac arrest while he sleeps."

"Heart attack?!"

"It mightn't be anything. Just bring him in tomorrow night, about eight o'clock. He'll have to sleep in the clinic so they can test him. You can stay the night with him. That way, he won't be frightened. But keep an eye on him tonight, you hear?"

"Shit." I sat heavily on the settee.

We heard the popcorn sound of gravel under car tyres. Samuel had come to pick Evelyn up. At the door, we hesitated for a split second, then hugged each other goodnight. "Don't fret," she said. "Whatever it is, we will handle it."

The second they had driven away, I went back to Agway's room. I watched his chest rise and fall, rise, then stop. My heart hitching in my throat, I counted off the seconds. At one minute, I was about to shake him awake when he coughed and started breathing on his own again.

I got myself a t-shirt of Dadda's. I would sleep in that. Or rather, I would stay awake in that. I climbed into bed and lay beside Agway. Even in his sleep, he tried to reach for my hair. I had already started growing it for him. I pillowed my head on my other arm and prepared myself for the alert half sleep of a mother with a sick child.

"In this morning's news: it appears that the current government of Cayaba is moving to institute nationwide austerity measures as part of an agreement being negotiated with the FFWD. The general terms of the agreement with the American corporation of the Fiscal Foundation for Worldwide Development were contained in a secret 'progress advisory' drafted in Washington last week by Samuel Tanner, economic advisor to prime minister Garth Johnson, and Angelica Gray, the CEO of the FFWD. The advisory report, leaked to opposition leader Caroline Sookdeo-Grant by an anonymous source, was published in this morning's edition of the Cayaba Informer. *The agreement was apparently solidified in advance of the deadline for the Cayaba government to reach an accord on an economic management strategy with the FFWD. Under the terms of the agreement, China and a group of other creditor banks are slated to help Cayaba to repay past-due interest exceeding $750 million on loans from the FFWD.*

"Mrs. Sookdeo-Grant has called on prime minister Johnson to confirm or deny the existence of the agreement. In a press conference called today, Mrs. Sookdeo-Grant said, 'A few days from now, the citizens of our country will be casting their votes to decide the leadership of this nation. It is therefore incumbent upon the prime minister to come clean about his party's plans for our future so that Cayabans have full information in order to decide how to vote.'

"At this time, there has been no response from the office of the prime minister."

Stanley came running over to the library checkout desk where I was working. "I found one!" he said. "Come! Come and look!"

Myrtle of the sky-high heels was working the desk with me. She smiled when she saw him. "Go on," she said. "Not busy here right now."

"Thanks."

I took Stanley's hand and let him pull me towards the computer terminal he'd been using. He pointed at the screen. "I could make a kite! And attach a camera to it, and take pictures of Cayaba from the air!" He took me through a Web site about home-made aerial cameras.

"All right, so what you need to make this wonder?" I clicked on the link that said "equipment."

Stanley's face fell when he saw the list. "It's too hard." His shoulders slumped. "I think I'm just going to help Hector make a seal cam. He said I could."

My hackles rose at the sound of that name. "No. I don't want you having anything to do with Hector. You're not to talk to him any more."

"But why?"

"He's not a nice man. You don't need to be messing around with him and his seals. I'll help you do this project. Look like a breeze." Man, what a lie. What the hell was "Picavet suspension"? And where would I find an anemometer? I grabbed some scrap paper from the box of it beside the computer terminal and started making notes. "We going to need a digital camera," I told Stanley. Maybe we could make the anemometer.

Someone touched my shoulder. Gavin. "Next shift," he said. "I'm relieving you."

"Already?" My eye fell on the clock in the corner of the computer screen. Just past five p.m. I leapt to my feet. "Shit. Stanley, I have to run!"

"But—"

"I have to get home on time so Mrs. Soledad can leave. I can't be late."

He pouted. "All right."

"Good boy." I kissed him on the cheek. "Call me tonight, all right?"

His face had gone sad. I squatted down so I could look him in the eye. "This is going to be the best science project in the whole parish. You hear me, Stanley?"

He glanced at me, looked back down at the floor. "Yes."

"You're going to blow everybody else right out of the water."

Again a glance, a little more hopeful now. "Even Godfrey Mordecai?"

"Why? What Godfrey Mordecai doing for his project?"

"A robot."

"That's all? Stanley, I used to make robots for fun. Out of shoeboxes and silver paint."

He brightened. "For true? And yours were voice-activated, too?"

"Voice-activated?"

"Yes. Godfrey Mordecai's robot is going to have wheels, and it'll be able to go backwards and forwards, but it's only going to go when he tells it to."

I gulped. "Yes, my love. Your project is going to make Godfrey Mordecai's look like dog doo-doo."

That got me a big grin. "Okay!"

I kissed him goodbye, waved at Myrtle, went downstairs for my purse, and fled out the delivery exit. Wasn't till I got home that I remembered that Agway and I were going to sleep at the sleep clinic tonight. And Gene was coming over. Looked like this menopause thing could make you forget your own blasted name.

I called Stanley and talked to him a bit about his project while I tried to prepare supper for Agway. I kept eyeing the clock. When I heard the knock at the front door, I swear my heart started a drum roll. I told Stanley I'd talk to him the next day.

Not only was Gene still in his uniform, he was a little bit sweaty, too. Loved that smell.

Agway and I didn't have to be at the sleep clinic until eight p.m. If I put him to sleep at the regular time, maybe he would doze through the waterbus ride and I wouldn't have the drama from him that I'd had the first time. So when he started looking sleepy around six-thirty, I put him to bed.

Then I took Gene and a blanket out to the back yard. After a few minutes, I realised that Cecil had been right about the dryness. I would have to buy some lubricant tomorrow.

I'd expected an argument about the rubbers, but Gene never said a thing. When I pulled it out of my jeans pocket, he just put it on and then pulled me on top of him. Like Cayaba men had modernised while I wasn't paying attention.

We lay on the blanket and humped each other silly by the light of the stars and the fireflies. If my little boy turned out to be sick, that would be another challenge to take on. But right then, lying naked in the outdoors with my head on a man's chest and my nipples crinkling in the breeze, life was good.

And busy. Only a few minutes later, I waved Gene goodbye, then put myself, Agway, and our overnight bags into the car. My plan worked like a charm; Agway didn't really wake up until I took him into the bright lights of the clinic waiting room.

"Okay. I have the results," said Evelyn. I was sitting in her office. Agway was on the floor, playing with the bead maze she kept in there.

I had fretted all night on the hard hospital bed, watching Agway sleep with electrodes attached to his scalp. "What's wrong with him?"

She frowned. "We couldn't find any malformations in his sinuses or anything that would cause obstructive sleep apnea."

"So he's all right?" I crossed the two joined fingers.

"I don't know."

"How you mean?"

"Obstructive sleep apnea is the most common kind. Would have been fairly easy to treat. So now we are looking at whether it might be central sleep apnea."

"Which is what?"

"Obstructive sleep apnea is mechanical. Something physical literally obstructs the normal pattern of breathing, causing the patient's muscles to relax before he or she can inhale properly. The obstruction could be in the sinuses. Being overweight can cause it too. Agway doesn't have any of that. He's plump, but not exceedingly so."

"The body fat keeps him warm in the ocean."

She looked uncomfortable.

I shrugged. "So, what about the other kind of apnea?"

"The central kind? It's neurological. The right message isn't getting from the brain to the muscles that make breathing work. The patient inhales all right, but has trouble exhaling. Once Agway began to dream, he would stop breathing from time to time, for up to 110 seconds. He would inhale, but he wouldn't exhale."

"So, central sleep apnea, then." I was frightened.

"You would think so, yes. But he has some anomalies."

Worse and worse. "How you mean?"

She leaned forward. "His heart rate should have been going up when he stopped breathing. Instead, it went down. He displayed vasoconstriction in his extremities. The blood flow to the core of his body increased. None of those things is consistent with either kind of sleep apnea."

Oh, God. Agway was really sick. "What's wrong with him?"

Now Evelyn looked very upset. "I only know of one phenomenon which produces that reaction in humans."

I sat up straight, squared my shoulders. "Tell me."

For a few long seconds, she didn't. Then she said: "Bradycardia, peripheral vasoconstriction, blood shift; facial cooling triggers it. Now, Calamity, I don't want you to make too much of this, okay?"

"Just tell me!"

"It's how mammals respond to being submerged in water. It's called mammalian diving reflex," she said unhappily. "You see it in seals, dolphins, whales, otters. But human beings can do it too."

I was on my feet before I knew it. I barely heard the chair crashing to the floor. Agway, startled, looked up to see what I was doing. "You see, you see!" I crowed. "I'm right! He *is* a sea child!"

Evelyn shook her head firmly. "You have to stop saying that! I have to walk careful right now, Calamity. Samuel's coming under fire for signing that agreement with the FFWD. I can't be associated with anything or anyone irregular."

"Irregular. I see."

"Besides, you ever think there might be another explanation? You found that child half-drowned. You ever stop to think what a nightmare that was for him?"

"Well, yes, but I—"

"You told me he cries when he sleeps! You ever think he might be having nightmares? Enh? Nightmares about drowning?"

Oh, lord. I hadn't thought that. He'd been snagged in seaweed, at the mercy of the waves. Even a sea child can drown.

"He dreams he's drowning again, and mammalian diving reflex kicks in, just like it kicked in when he fell into the water during the storm. It doesn't need cold water, you know. Experienced divers can initiate it with the right kind of breathing."

Agway had been looking from one to the other of us as we argued. He had no idea what all this palaver was about; he just knew that the adults were fighting. "We're scaring him," I told Evelyn.

"I'm sorry."

"No, it's not just you."

"The thing is, it's a lovely idea that he's some kind of marine human, but if the wrong people hear you going on about it, all of us stand to lose. You, me, Samuel. I could be forbidden from practising medicine. You could lose Agway. And Samuel—well, he might lose his job anyway." Worry had made her features haggard.

I nodded. "All right. I'll act normal."

"Thank you." She glanced at the clock on her wall and stood up. "I have to go on rounds now."

"Agway and I can go?"

"Yes. Near as I can tell, he's healthy. Physically, anyway. Emotionally, I'm not so sure. I'm going to set up an appointment here at the hospital, for a child psychologist to assess him."

"I can look after him!"

"*I* don't doubt that. But I should have done this from the start. I'm ashamed of myself that I waited so long." She gave me a little smile. "Don't worry. This is what's best for Agway."

In the doorway, she stopped and turned back. "And since we're talking about what's best for Agway, I want to do something about those skin patches. Should be an easy day surgery. Quick laser treatment, then he's back home to you. I've scheduled it for this Thursday."

6

"CAMITY!" PIPED AGWAY. WE WERE INSIDE THE cashew grove. "Look!" He held up his little bucket to show me. It was full of fat, grey cashew seeds. And a rockstone or two, and his shorts and wee-wee damp diaper that he'd discarded. He still couldn't be convinced to keep much clothing on. His little boy's totie, brown and perfect as a mushroom, was all exposed. Well, we had a little time before I had to civilise him enough to enter the real world. Let him enjoy it. I smiled.

"What you bring for me, baby?"

"Ka-soos," he said proudly. The bandages at his knees were coming loose again. I'd have to replace the dressings soon. But he seemed to be healing fine from the surgery.

"That's right, baby; cashews. Thank you." Me, I wasn't doing as well as Agway. Kept asking myself if I should have let Evelyn order the surgery, superficial as it was. But I couldn't have stopped her. I wasn't Agway's legal guardian yet.

He was good at tearing the grey nut free of the fruit, but he wasn't tidy at it. From fingertips to elbows, he was smeared in red and yellow flecks of cashew fruit. He must have been eating them, too; fruit mush was all around his mouth, which was gritty with dirt where he'd wiped his hands against it. At least his hair was finally neat and trim. He'd given me such a fight when I tried to chop off that rats' nest! Eventually I had just done it in his sleep. He'd been furious when he woke up. But I had given him one of the chopped-off locks; the one that had the shell tied into it that he most liked to rub between his fingers. He kept it in his dresser drawer now; whenever he needed comforting, he got it and held it and worried away at the shell between his fingers.

I took his bucket and emptied it into my bigger one. I pulled out the rockstones and tossed his shorts and diaper into the wheelbarrow. I handed him his bucket back. "You going to get some more for Mamma?"

"No." He squatted and began trying to jam the mouth of the bucket into the gravelly soil.

"What you going to do, then?" I rolled the wheelbarrow to the foot of the next nearest tree. Plenty of freshly fallen nuts there. I bent, began twisting the grey pericarps free from the red, pear-shaped flesh of the fruit, tossing the nuts into the wheelbarrow and the fruit onto the growing pile of red-yellow mush that oozed happily in the clearing. The flies had already gathered for the banquet. The smell of fermented cashew juice and the buzzing blue-bottle flashes of blue from the flies made the warm morning air sleepy.

Agway stood, bowlegged, the battered red bucket at his feet. He frowned gravely at me. He still stood a little too wide-legged. But partly that was the cast on his leg. Once it was off, he'd be able to walk normally. He'd fit in just fine. "Want to play with the . . . ," he told me, making a liquid noise that I couldn't follow.

"Play with what, baby?"

He pointed with a chubby finger. I looked. Sir Grandad was in the tree above me, staring curiously down at us. "That's a mongoose," I told Agway. "What you called it?"

He said the word again. I wondered what it was the word for; what in his old watery home looked like a mongoose. I tried to imitate him.

"No" He chuckled, holding his little round belly.

I laughed and said it again.

"No! No!" He looked irritated this time. "Stop! Stop talking like me!"

The buzz of flies around the clotted remains of the fruit suddenly seemed less pleasant. I held my hand out for Agway's. "Come. We have to change your dressings." It was almost time for Ifeoma to come by, anyway. I hoped she'd found St. Julian mangoes in the market. Was the season for them.

Agway toddled over to me, put his hand in mine. I grabbed up his discarded clothes on the way out. I left the wheelbarrow for now.

He stumbled. I was walking too quickly for him. The child had just had surgery to his legs. I slowed down. "You want a Popsicle when we get to the house?"

He frowned up at me, confused. "Popsicle," I told him. "Remember? It's cold and sweet and you eat it?"

"No. Want stimps," he informed me.

"What a way you own-way today! Mr. Mckinley didn't come yet. How about some breadfruit? With butter?"

He nodded. "Beddfooot." Child after my own heart.

A wash of heat soaked me. "Hold on a minute, Agway." I stood to let the hot flash pass. No itching fingers this time. Nothing popped out of the air. More and more, I was having just the regular hot flashes. The after-chill came on, but in the heat of the day, it was almost a pleasant thing. If the manifestations had stopped, I could handle this menopause business. I took Agway's hand again. "Come. Almost time for *Dora the Explorer*."

"Mummy! You home?"

Uh-oh. In only three words from her, I could name that tone. Ifeoma was on the warpath.

She shoved the front door open before I could get to it. Right in the entranceway, she put down the plastic shopping bags she was carrying. What the hell was her problem?

"Thank you," I said prettily, picking up the bags. "And don't worry if you couldn't find any smoked herring. I'm sure that everything you brought is fine." First step: try harmless disarmament.

She glared and walked past me into the living room. She pulled Agway away from the bookcase he'd started climbing in the few seconds I hadn't had my eye on him. She put him on her hip. "What's your problem with Hector? Eh? Why you told Stanley not to do his science fair project with him?"

I put down the bags and took Agway away from her. "*I* will

help Stanley with his project! You don't let me spend enough time with him as it is." If step one fails: self-defense.

Then I couldn't resist saying: "Besides, Hector's not a nice person."

She sucked her teeth. "Bullshit, he's not nice."

I blinked. She hardly ever swore. She picked up the bags. I turned the television on for Agway and followed Ife into the kitchen.

As she unpacked the produce onto the kitchen counter, she said, "I have plenty of opportunity to see what Hector is like. I'm the one who hired him for Caroline."

"*You* hired him? For that politician woman? She trust you with a job like that?"

She took a dozen eggs out of a bag and very carefully set the box down. She growled, "You even know what it is I do?"

"How you mean? You work the front desk at the Tamany."

She sighed. "Not any more. I told you that a couple weeks ago."

"You didn't tell me you left! I thought you were doing the other thing in the evenings, or something! That little piece of work is enough to support you and Stanley? Especially now that Clifton gone?" Step three: destabilize.

"You right, I didn't tell you. Didn't want to give you more ammunition against me. And what it is I do in Caroline's office?"

I shrugged. "I don't know. Answering phones and so."

"I am the junior research assistant for the leader of this country's opposition party. They made me full-time last week."

"What?"

"You even have any idea why I want to work for Caroline Sookdeo-Grant? Enh? When I joined the 4-H club in high school, you laughed at me. When I organized that letter campaign in '02 to protest the death penalty, you told me I was wasting my time. Nothing I do is good enough for you. I don't think you ever had a word of praise for me yet."

I think I actually rocked back on my heels with the shock of that one. Who had taught her step three?

She started unpacking one of the bags. "This nonsense about Hector is really because he not interested in you, nuh true? It don't have anything to do with Stanley's project."

Shame heated up my face. I covered quickly: "Chuh. I wouldn't want Hector if he was the last man on earth. Next thing I know, he go and leave me for some man."

She grimaced. "God, that attitude is so backward."

"You need to watch yourself with me, Ife. I not in a mood to hear no stupidness today."

"You know what your problem is? You jealous."

I guffawed. She wanted to play rough, I would unleash step four on her ass: berserker rage. "Me, jealous? Of what? Tell me, nuh? Your flour sack dresses and your bad diet? Your marriage that dying on you? Maybe I jealous that the two-three men in your life more interested in each other than you? Or that your own mother could thief a man right out from under your twenty-one-year-old nose? What I have to be jealous of, Ife? Enh?"

To my astonishment she surged right over me with: "You give yourself as a gift to your best friend one day, and you still can't forgive him for saying 'no thank you.'"

She dare to talk to me that way? Meek little Ife? She went on, "Nearly forty years now you chewing on that grudge like a wad of old gum that have all the taste suck out of it."

"And who it is still whining about how her mother didn't buy her the right colour dolly when she was nine?"

No reaction from her. Ife was as cool as running water, and as impossible to make a mark in. I'd never seen her like this before. I didn't have a step five. Stammering, I improvised: "I still don't hear what I have to be so jealous of."

"Anybody Daddy have in his life, Mummy! You ever watch at yourself? The way you carry on? You look at Orso like you starving and he hoarding all the food."

I gaped at her, completely off my stride.

"Tell me," she said, "when exactly it is you got stuck? 'Cause it seem like you reached a certain place in your life, and you never managed to move on from there."

I was trembling. The roaring in my ears was too loud to let me think up a comeback.

"You know what the sad thing is?" she said. "You could have been part of Daddy's life any time you wanted. But if you couldn't have him all to yourself, you didn't want nobody else to have him, neither. Wouldn't even let his own daughter get to know him."

I found my voice. "I did that to protect you!"

"The same way so you protecting Agway? By shutting him away from everyone?"

"The child is an *orphan*! He need somebody to look out for him. You didn't need Michael. You had me."

She kissed her teeth. "If you looking out for Agway so good, why you not finding out what language he speak? Enh? You quick to go and research what steel make of, but you can't trace down one language? Why you not trying to learn what Agway saying to you? Stanley spend couple-three hours with the boy, and already he could talk a few words to Agway. Like you frighten?"

"Your rass. Frighten of what? What a three-year-old boy could say to frighten me?"

"He could tell you something about himself and where he came from. He could tell you what really happened to him. He could tell you his *name*, Mummy."

I was breathing in little gasps. "He *have* a name! I give him a perfectly good name!"

"Make me wonder it's who really wanted a black dolly to dress up and parade around and keep in a box."

My hand actually twitched towards her face to give it a good slap. I killed the impulse, but Ife still saw. She didn't even flinch, and she didn't back down. She just drew herself up tall and looked me in my face.

I swallowed. "Leave my house," I whispered.

"Not until I tell you this." Gently, she set down the tin of salmon she'd been about to put in the pantry. "I am ashamed of you. You hear me good? *Ashamed*."

As she was leaving, she stopped in the kitchen doorway and looked back at me. I couldn't meet her eyes. "Every good deed you do have a price attached," she said.

AGWAY WAS FRACTIOUS ALL EVENING. I had hell to pay trying to keep his hands from his dressings. Looked like he'd reached that itchy stage they'd warned me about at the hospital. Nothing to do but put on the ointment they'd given me and give him some painkiller. That seemed to help the discomfort a little, but Christ, he was irritable! Eventually I just picked him up and paced back and forth across the living room with him, like I had done when Ife was teething. I kept the tv on just to distract him. I think it was more to distract me. The memories of Ife's words to me before she left were churning and sour in my gut. Well, if life give you lemons, suck them, I suppose. People had said worse to me before, when I was a teenage mother. I'd survived.

Slowly, Agway quieted in my arms and fell asleep. I lowered myself onto the settee; the few steps into the bedroom seemed like a marathon.

I must have dropped off to sleep. A clunk woke me. I was drenched in sweat. Damn. So tired, I had slept through a hot flash. That one had brought me something, too; I'd heard it land. What was it? Couldn't see anything, and I didn't want to move and maybe wake Agway. Tomorrow. I laid my head back. If I slept right here so, I would wake up so cricked I wouldn't be able to crack. But fatigue was like waves washing over me.

"Are there mermaids swimming in Cayaba's waters?" chirped the television.

Oh, bite me. The eleven o'clock "news" with the same old filler crap.

"Finally," said the announcer, *"we may have proof."*

I raised my head. On the tv screen was a blurry, green-tinged photograph of two naked brown women floating in the sea. One had a baby lolling on her breast. The other one was doing a frog-swim. Her long, ratty hair rayed out from the top of her head. A second baby floated in the water, clinging to her hair. The two women were looking up, presumably at a plane or helicopter above them, where someone with a camera was taking their picture.

"Shit," I said. "This is bad."

The photo shrank and tucked itself to a corner of the screen so that we could see the announcer. *"This nighttime photograph was taken by an ingenious young man whose name is Stanley Fernandez."*

Oh, God. He did his project already? Without me?

The announcer continued, *"It is only one in a series of photographs of Cayaba taken by Stanley's airborne glider-cam."*

Blurry photo stills, very close-up, started flashing by on the television: two men in police force uniforms sitting on a sea wall—one was in the act of handing a forty-ouncer of something to the other; what looked to be a very startled fishing bat, clutching the silver flash of a minnow; a thin-faced, big-eyed young man with hands like shovels, sitting behind the wheel of a car with a look of bliss on his face, holding—a huge pair of panties?—to his nose; a totally mystifying shot of two young men and a woman, all quite fat, climbing out of the seal enclosure at the Zooquarium. They were naked.

How the hell he had gotten those pictures? For a moment, pride for my grandson quieted my guilt for not having helped him.

The announcer came back on screen, smiling a little and shuffling her notes. *"Stanley put the mini digital camera on his remote controlled glider with the help of a family friend, Mr. Hector Goonan."*

Oh, Ife. You came here knowing this had all happened.

"Stanley only meant to take daytime photographs for a science fair project, but one night he took the glider for a spin, just for a lark. Only a handful of the photos were good images, but a few of those were very good indeed. When Stanley realised what he had on his hands, he wisely sought the advice of another adult, his grandfather, Michael Jasper."

"Oh, God. Michael's mixed up into this, too?"

"Mr. Jasper sent copies of the images to us." And there he was on the screen. *"I'm very proud of my grandson,"* Michael said. *"He's showed a lot of initiative in putting this project together."*

Agway stirred and woke.

"Clearly," said the announcer, *"the citizens of Cayaba have a very active night life indeed! The police will be investigating some of the instances*

of apparent mischief revealed by the photos. One question remains: is this photograph of the women swimming nude finally proof of the existence of fish people? Or is it just an example of the types of hijinks performed by some of the more boisterous visitors to Cayaba? We may never know. And perhaps, to keep Cayaba the beautiful mystery that she is, it's best not to look too closely."

Agway looked muzzily at the screen, just as they blew up the photo of the sea women to full size again. He gasped and reached a hand towards the screen. "Mamma," he said quite clearly. He was not looking at me when he said it. Then he burst into tears.

It was like somebody had splashed cold water on me.

The photo had gone from the screen. The news continued. I got Agway's attention. "Pet, is that your mother? Your mamma?"

"Jes!" he sobbed. "Mamma!" He said a long, mournful sentence in his language. I didn't understand a word. Might be his mother, or a relative. Or it might only be that he'd seen home, and people who looked like sea people. He was tired, and probably in a bit of pain from the surgery. Maybe I could put him to sleep, and he would be fine in the morning. "You sure that was your mamma?"

He shrieked, "Mamma!" and arched his back like toddlers will do when they're agitated. He kicked, too. Got me a good one in the thigh with the heel of his cast. I managed to hold on to him and get him upright again. Agway's mother was alive?

"Who really wanted a black dolly to dress up and parade around and keep in a box?"

I went to the phone. Fumbling, I dialled Ife's number. But I hung up on the first ring. Couldn't face her. She wouldn't understand about Agway, anyway.

I took a child from his family!

Gene's cell went straight to voice mail. He was probably working tonight. "Gene, you have to help me," I whimpered into the phone. "Agway's mother not dead, I just saw her on the news in Stanley's picture. We should find her. The sea woman. Give her back her boy. God, call me as soon as you get this, please?" I hung up the phone.

Agway had subsided into a low, bubbly sobbing. The woe on his face made me feel sick with guilt. "Pet, I'm so sorry. I can't tell you how sorry I am." Three weeks since I'd found him. And he still cried himself to sleep nearly every night. Because of me. And what had his mother been going through, and the rest of his family, if he had any? All this time, they would have been thinking they'd lost him.

Lost.

He wasn't lost! I'd *found* him; Maybe I could find his family, too. I had to do it. Had to bring his mother to him. Goddamned hot flashes could materialise a whole cashew grove, they could help me call one woman.

Couldn't wait for Gene. I had to do this myself. I had made it wrong: I could make it right.

I hitched Agway up a little more comfortably on my hip. "We're going to find your mother. Hear me? Going to get your mamma."

He sniffled.

Mrs. Lessing had brought me a toddler life jacket that her great-grandson had outgrown. I picked it up and left the house with Agway. I had to jog through a light rain to get to the car. I drove us both towards the private slip where Dolorosse people kept their boats.

Agway was sitting in the passenger seat. I glanced at his bandaged knees. And all the way to the slip with the wailing child, I kept hearing Ife's voice in my head:

"Every good deed you do have a price attached."

Maybe so, but this boy shouldn't be the one paying it.

EVEN GRIEF HAS TO GIVE WAY to sleep. Agway's eyes were closed when I took him in his life jacket out of the car. Wrapped in his blanket, he was just conscious enough to put his thumb in his mouth and rest his head on my shoulder. The drizzle seemed to be easing up.

He didn't even stir when I took him into the boat. I put him under a tarp to keep him dry, and laid him down far enough from me to balance the boat a little better. It made me nervous to have him even that little distance out of reach. But even if he fell in, the life jacket would keep the weight of the cast from dragging him down.

I was so upset and shaky that it took me two tries to start the engine. Agway startled at the noise. He stirred, but his exhausted little body hung on to sleep. I headed us out further along the archipelago, towards the tiniest islands.

"I am ashamed of you."

Find the sea people. Find Agway's mother. Just fix your mind on that. Give Agway back. I had to have a hot flash. I had to.

But all I willed it to happen, my fingers wouldn't itch, and the heat wouldn't rise. Old Slave Joe the finder had been able to use his power at will. "I can't even tell which muscles to flex," I grumbled.

"If you couldn't have him all to yourself, you didn't want nobody else to have him, neither."

Tiny Dutchie Island was somewhere here-bout, nuh true? Didn't think to bring the fucking compass. Shit, shit, shit. Okay.

Just keep looking for the whiteheads of its reefs, and wait. Bloody hot flashes were like buses; there was always another one coming.

I had cut Agway's hair. I had let the hospital cut his legs. What the sea people would do when they saw all that? I blinked the warm drizzle out of my eyes.

The skimming boat hit a swell especially hard, and sea water splashed us. That woke Agway. He sat up. Saw that we were in the sea. I cut the engine so I could hold him. Probably best to just let her drift, anyway. The noise of the engine might frighten them away. For good measure, I turned off the green starboard light. The port light was dead. I hadn't used the boat in a while.

Silence and dark blanketed us, and the percussion of rain-drops. I hated the sea at night. If it wasn't for the reflective patches on his life jacket, I'd have had a hard time seeing Agway.

I sat him beside me, rewrapped him in the tarp, and put an arm around him. "We going to find her," I told him. "Somehow."

He asked me a question.

"I don't understand you, Pet. Ife was right. I didn't even try to learn."

What a three-year-old boy could say to frighten me?

Fingers itching any at all? No, not a rass. No sensation like ants crawling on my skin. "I don't know how to do this!" I said, frustrated.

The darkness was getting to me. Every slap of sea water against the boat made me jump. Except where there were stars, and the light cloud that Dolorosse cast above itself, I couldn't dis-tinguish sea different from sky. "I don't know how allyou manage out here come nighttime," I told Agway. The rain was making me shivery.

I decided to keep looking for Dutchie Island. Go slow. Keeping the engine revving low. When I opened up the throttle again, the prow of the boat began slapping the water, too hard. We were overbalanced. But now that Agway was awake, I needed to keep him within reach. I slowed us down even more, and sat him on the floor at my feet.

He pointed out into the water. "Mamma!"

"Smart boy. Yes, we going to find Mamma. You just sit right here, you understand? Don't stand up, you will fall out. You will sit, Agway?"

"Ehe."

We crawled along. I kept trying to will the magic to happen. I didn't know how far out we were. Could have reached the shipping lanes, for all I knew. And still the feeling of being weightless in an infinity of ink. I kept looking all around us, trying to get oriented in space, trying to spot any trouble before it got to us.

What the rass I was doing, really? This was ridiculous. It was dangerous for the child, and I was cold. Take us both back. Get a good night's sleep, and tomorrow, ask Gene's advice.

I was concentrating on turning us around: that's how I came to have my eyes off Agway. Only a splash slightly louder than the rain told me that he had gone overboard.

"Agway!" I screamed. I slipped my alpagats off. "Agway, I coming!"

I jumped. The blood-warm water took me in. When I surfaced, the life jacket was floating beside me, empty, on a pockmarked sea like black glass.

"Agway!" I couldn't *see* him! I screamed for help, but the open expanse of water swallowed my voice.

*. . . So the devil woman of the sea wait until the ship was
approaching the archipelago. Then she swim close to the
porthole of the cabin where the young woman was sitting in
chains, and she sing,*

> *Young girl, young girl,*
> *Drop your hat in the water.*

Agway's empty life jacket was a small orange blur, bobbing away
from me quickly, disappearing into darkness. Without it, the cast
would have dragged him down. I tried to dive, but the groaning
black of the sea entombed me immediately. There was no way to
see, no air to breathe. Mindless with terror, I surfaced, choking.
I felt at my waist for my cell phone. I hadn't been in the water
long; it just might work.

It wasn't there. Must have fallen off when I jumped in. I had
to go for help. Fast. I slewed around in the water; tried to peer
through the rain.

I couldn't see the boat any more. The sea was obsidian. I
stopped, bobbed in the water and tried to listen for the slap of
the waves against the hull of the boat. But my panicked heart was
beating too hard, my breath coming too quickly; they and the rain
were all I could hear. Weeping, I struck out again, heading for
where I thought the boat might be. Didn't even know what direction I was facing any more. The sea was vast; it went on around
and beneath me in blackness forever. My boy was drowning, and
the nighttime ocean was monstrous. There was no way to know
what could be rising from the depths this very moment, its maw

stretched wide around dagger teeth the length of my arm. My lizard back-brain screamed at me to get *out! Out!* A cold water current ran just below the surface. Every time I dipped a hand or foot into the ribbon of cold, I knew it was taking my scent, carrying it to the invisible horror rising up from way down deep. I swam harder, going nowhere. My side began to ache. I was gasping, my strokes getting weaker, my head dipping occasionally below the water. No boat. "Agway!" It came out a hoarse whisper. I coughed and sputtered on brine. I was scarcely paddling at all now, too tired to move my arms. The pain in my gut made my belly feel distended. Salt syrup burned my throat.

I panicked completely, struck out in one direction, then the next, never finding the safety of the boat. I whimpered and spat out water.

Exhaustion had set in. My arms felt so heavy. All of me, heavy as rockstones. Rain water filled my eyes, and sea water kept getting into my nose. In the back of my brain, I knew I should go horizontal, try to float, but terror and despair kept me thrashing. Please, please let Agway still be alive. Let me get help.

But it was too late, for both of us. I couldn't make my legs scissor any more. They sank into the chilly current, and the rest of me began to follow. My head sank into the water.

Something hard touched my ankle. I screamed, sucked in the sea.

Something held me, bore me up. My head surfaced. I coughed out the water. It was hands I was feeling on me, many hands, not the grip of a massive jaw. In the dark I could just make out the heads of people bobbing in the sea with me.

"Thank you," I shouted hoarsely, over the increasing storm.

One of them gurgled a reply, a liquid sound. So did another. Sea people. Agway's people. Holding me fast. "You found him?" I heard myself ask, my teeth chattering. "You found Agway?" *Just this once, let my name not hold true.*

A little voice warbled, "Camity!"

I twisted about to try to see where it was coming from. I saw him. Agway! A sea man was towing him through the water. I held on weakly to the shoulder of one of the people holding me up, and sobbed for joy. Agway held tight to the man's long hair. So that was why he grabbed hair like that.

"Nna," he informed me merrily. He tugged at the hair of the man towing him. The man grinned.

"Pleased to meet you," I said. My body was shaking with cold and after-reaction. Through the water blurring my eyes, I peered at the man. Did he and Agway have the same nose, the same shape mouth? The man sank quietly beneath the water, taking Agway down with him. I gasped. But seconds later they surfaced again. Agway was laughing. He spat a stream of water from his mouth. "Camity," he chirruped. He swatted his father on the head. "Nna."

"Yes, baby, I think I understand you now. So stop beating up your daddy, all right?"

Agway pointed at another man and then a third, called them both "Nna." So it meant something like "uncle," then? No matter. Family.

"I'm sorry," I said to them. "I should have brought him back earlier."

Another creature broke surface not two feet from me. I yelped. It snorted, as though in surprise, and sank again. "What the fuck is that?" I asked. Some of the people holding me laughed and joked. Fuckers. I grabbed the shoulders of one of them, and pulled my feet up as close to my body as I could. So hard to see in the dark with water stinging my eyes! A dog? A seal? I thought I'd seen large, liquid eyes. An intelligent face. The sea people didn't seem worried at it being there. They kept pets?

Another head broke the water, this time beside Agway. A person. "Mamma!" squealed Agway, and tried to throw himself into her arms.

"Chiabuotu," she said, with a catch in her voice. She gave the man towing Agway something large and floppy to hold. A blanket? I could use one of those right now. Then she took Agway into her arms. "Chichi," she murmured. She was definitely weeping. I felt heartsick at what I'd put her through. She bobbed upright in the water like a bottle, holding Agway tightly to her, laughing through her tears and chatting back with him as he tried to catch her up on everything he'd seen and done. And the whole time, she kept inspecting his shorn hair, touching his arms, patting his face, stroking his back. Every touch said love, love, and Agway echoed it back at her. He curled his fist tightly in her hair.

Damn. One thing to see a dead one, or a little boy who might or might not be one. Something else again to be right here in their own environment with them. Sea people were real!

We were moving. Where were they taking me? Not deeper out to sea! "No, no, I can't." I tried to pull free from the ones holding me. "I'm not made like you. I have to go back to land." They ignored me. I pushed against the bodies moving me. I was too weak, there were too many of them, and they were in their element. Didn't stop me trying to break free. I fought and fought until I heard a hollow "thunk." I shook water out of my eyes and peered. One of the sea people had just slapped his hand against the side of my boat.

"Oh," I said. "My mistake. So sorry."

The next five minutes or so were pure joke as the sea people tried to help me into my boat. Every last one of them naked, wet, and slippery. Me shaking so much I couldn't control my muscles. I would get a foot up on a helpful shoulder, but it would slide off one time, and *braps!* I'd go into the water again. It would have been funny, but I was so tired. And so cold! My arthritic knee was giving off a bright, gonging pain. "Should have climbed that blasted almond tree a few more times for practice," I gasped at them.

Finally a sea man leapt agilely into the boat. He was fat. Right now, I envied him that. But that hair, milord, just hanging off his head like seaweed in the surf! So much for the legends of mermaids combing their hair out while sitting on the rocks. Whatever they were doing on those rocks, it wasn't grooming. Getting warm, maybe. Or playing dangerous jumping games with little land girls.

The man got to his knees, held out his hand to me through the pelting rain. I reached for it with both of mine. He began to pull, but I couldn't hold on. I wasn't light like little Chastity used to be. I wasn't nimble any longer like she had been. And I couldn't make my fingers grasp. The man grabbed my wrists. The boat dipped sideways. If it shipped too much water, it would sink.

In the water, a pair of hands brushed my behind. I jumped. The hands held me firmly, long fingers wrapped around my ample thighs. "Leave me alone!" I croaked, no voice left to yell. Agway chuckled and shouted something out. He thought it was a game. I was in deep shit; half-drowned, and now about to be sexually assaulted by a sea creature. I kicked out at him. The water dragged at my leg and slowed it down.

The man in the boat was crooning something in a soft, encouraging tone. Then I felt a head between my thighs. "Get the fuck away from me!" I tried to push off, away from the person feeling me up so.

I was rising higher in the water. Oh. A piggyback, then, not freshness. The man in the boat made an approving sound. When the one below had got me high enough, the man in the boat leaned forward and wrapped his thick, strong arms around me, just under my armpits. He crushed my breasts to his naked chest. His breath smelled like raw fish, and under that, like human breath. "Up little more," I said, panting. There . . . almost . . .

Just a few more inches and I was able to get one knee against the inside of the boat. The man in the boat called out something. The others in the water echoed it. Fuck me; they were cheering me on! That gave me little more strength. I dug my knee into the side of the boat. Of course it was the bad knee. The man below heaved, and the one above pulled, his face right up against mine. Suddenly I was up on the boat's rim. My weight overbalanced the man pulling on me, and we both fell inside. The boat rocked beneath us.

I was in the boat. I lay there, pulling in air and wiping rain out of my eyes. "Oh, migod." The rain felt chilly. My arms were all goosebumps. I was woozy.

The man under me was making funny heaving noises.

"Sorry," I panted, but I had no energy left for moving. He had to roll my dead weight off him.

He was laughing! Blasted fish man was laughing at me!

And then I was laughing too, though I was dizzy and it hurt my chest. The two of us lay there, trying to catch our breath, laughing with each other. I could hear others in the water chatting, and Agway's cheerful, high voice amongst them.

I managed to lift my head to look over the side. I ate Agway up with my eyes. Little brute. Clasps on the life jacket were just like the one on the old briefcase I'd given him to play with.

The man sat up. His knees and ankles pulled apart with a wet Velcro sound, and he tailor-sat. Christ. That's what the patches were for. To streamline the legs so they could swim better. And I had let Evelyn take Agway's away. I had fucked everything up so badly, I didn't know how to unfuck it.

The boat was moving. They were towing it. Good, 'cause I didn't feel in any shape to steer it myself. I didn't even have the strength to bail. I lay and looked up at the stars. I was going to get up. Soon. For real. "I just hope it's back to shore you taking me," I said to the man. I barely understood myself, my teeth were chattering so hard.

"Yes," he replied.

Holy shit. "You talk," I gasped.

"I talk like you talk," he said.

Nice accent. "All of you speak English?"

"No. Only some. We hear when land people speak." He said something over the side.

"Where the fuck's the rum?" a voice called out from the water, in a fair, though somewhat bubbly, imitation of an American accent.

"My God," said another, *"this is some shit-kicking weed. Trust the natives to grow the good stuff."*

From the other side of the boat came *"Steven! Steven! Drop the anchor! Plenty fish here-bout!"* That one was pure Cayaba.

And, *"So I put twenty thou into the bank they have here. Offshore investment fucking rocks, man."*

From behind the boat, *"Daddydaddydaddy! Look at me! Look at me, Daddy!"*

When one of them launched into the sound of the Coast

Guard siren Dopplering across the water, I wept, too far gone to laugh.

"The problem is heat," I creaked at my new friend. "Water will chill your body down twenty times faster than air. Can't remember where I put my fucking glasses, but I can quote back a fact somebody said to me weeks ago."

A shriek from the water nearly stopped my already stuttering heart. A woman's voice, swelled with outrage and fury. Something heavy slapped against the boat. A hand grabbed the side of the boat and bodily tilted it towards the water. I nearly rolled out. The man in the boat held on to me.

A head followed the hand from the water. Agway's mother. She was big and strong enough to tilt the boat, and even to my blurry vision, she looked ready to kill. She cradled a scared Agway along one arm. She turned one of his thighs outwards to show me. The bandages had long washed off. I whispered, "The doctors did it." Couldn't hear whether I was speaking aloud. I was shuddering with cold. Hypothermia could kill, even in the tropics sometimes.

My friend in the boat translated for me. Mamma made it clear that she didn't give two shits for that lame-ass answer, and she was going to reach into my mouth and tear my liver out with her bare hands. I said, "He couldn't manage on land with those things, waddling around like that."

The man translated. Still no go. I was shaking like a leaf from the cold, the shock, the confrontation. The woman shoved herself off from the boat and lunged towards one of Agway's nnas. She pushed Agway into his arms and demanded her wrap back, or whatever it was. The man refused, though it looked like she outweighed him. She got into a tug of war with him, raging the whole time. Agway kept trying to get a word in edgewise. Finally she dragged the thing out of the man's arms. She put it around her shoulders. Agway shouted something as loudly as his little body could manage, launched himself towards her, and yanked on her hair.

She stopped. He said it again. I made out "Camity," and "nne." So I was his uncle, too? So difficult to hear over the driving rain.

My mind was wandering. Concentrate, Calamity. "I fucked up!" I shouted. Barely a squeak came out. I tried to raise my hands towards her, but I couldn't feel my arms any more. Just a thump as my head hit the floor of the boat, and everything went black. My last sight, strangely clear, was of the sea woman with her sealskin fur coat clutched around her. *What is this fashion for leaving the heads on?* I wondered. Then I didn't think anything at all.

The ship began to creak more, and to shudder. The dada-hair lady could hear the thundering of the surf. The boss man was shouting orders, the sailors running back and forth. Some of the sailors began pushing the people back towards the stinking, cramped holds. Some of the men tried to resist, but they were beaten for their trouble. And no sign from Uhamiri.

The ship slowed down, then tacked. The turning motion brought the dada-hair lady's nausea back. Some of the others retched, too. The ship proceeded a little way further, then lurched, throwing them all to the deck. There was a thump and a massive cracking sound. The child was thrown from the dada-hair lady's arms when she fell, dragging the two chained to her along with her. Boards snapped. People were screaming and calling on their Gods. Not the dada-hair lady. She had already begged help, but none had come.

As she lay tumbled on the deck, the dada-hair lady felt wetness between her thighs, and a cramping of her womb. Her monthly blood had returned. She grinned fiercely. "She heard me," she said to her shipmates, who were too terrified to pay her mind. Holding on to whatever she could, the dada-hair lady dragged herself upright. She looked around wildly for the little boy she had held. There! He had seen her. He was so small that the sailors couldn't really see him in the throng. He was pushing his way through adult bodies to get to her. And the determined little child made it; squeezed between the last two people separating him from the dada-hair lady, and ran to her. She swept him up, laughing even through her own terror. She readied herself. It was time. The lost ones would go home.

The ship was tilted perilously to one side, and breaking up as they watched. The noises of cracking timbers, sliding cannon, and screaming people were astonishing.

The dada-hair lady bade her gift come down.

And for the first time in months, it did.

☞

Me Uncle Time smile black as sorrow;
'im voice is sof' as bamboo leaf
But Lawd, me Uncle cruel.
When 'im play in de street
wid yu woman—watch 'im! By tomorrow
she dry as cane-fire, bitter as cassava.
An' when 'im teach yu son, long after
yu walk wid stranger, an' yu bread is grief.
Watch how 'im spin web roun' yu house, an' creep
inside; an' when 'im touch yu, weep . . .

—Dennis Scott, "Uncle Time"

7

T URQUOISE. LAPIS. VIRIDIAN. I SHIFTED MY BOTTOM
to a more comfortable position on the almond tree branch and
tried to name all the blues and greens of the sea this afternoon.
Cerulean. Teal. Indigo. I filled up my head with sea colours, and
wondered what Agway's words for them were.

"Look her there!" shouted a child's voice, a boy's. My heart
hammered in my chest before I realised it could not be Agway.
Stanley ran to the foot of the almond tree and peered up at me.
He had to look into the sun to do so. No flicker of a second eyelid, though.

"Calamity, what you doing way up there?"

"Watching the sea."

Ife appeared over the rise. Michael was with her. They joined Stanley, and the three of them stared up at me gape-mouthed.

"Everybody's here now," said Michael. "You going to come down and eat something?"

"Just one second." I went back to my watching. The police and the Coast Guard had declared Agway missing, presumed dead. While in my care. Hector surprised me by telling them we had been coming to pay him a visit. Jade. Royal. Mint. "She takes people, you know?" I told them. "The sea does. And she never gives them back."

I had had flash after flash, but no Agway came to me. Why would he? From the time he had jumped into that water, he wasn't lost any more.

"I found the dump truck that Agway used to play with," said Stanley. "Your old dump truck." Stanley was crying. For Agway. Agway was alive and happy, but I couldn't tell them that. Only Gene knew. I had to watch my grandson wrestle with the pain of a grief I couldn't relieve.

I got off my branch and started climbing down.

"Careful," Ife cautioned. Michael tried to help me the rest of the way down.

"Last man who tried to hold me up nearly sprain his back," I said. I got down by myself and took Stanley's hand.

"Come and show me where you found the truck," I told him. After we'd walked for a bit, I said to him, "I meant to help you with your project. I never wanted to let you down like that. But I did. It wasn't right, and I'm very sorry." He looked at me, perplexed. "Maybe one day you'll give me another chance." A few more steps, and I said, "And your science fair project was brilliant."

He smiled a little. "The bat was the best," he said. "It was right down low, close to the water. But I didn't sink the glider."

"I'm very proud of you."

We had to walk past the orchard on the way to the house. It was rioting out of control. Branches had extended themselves, looping into sideways knots and tangles that defied gravity. Every morning I found that new shoots had thrown themselves skywards overnight, to fight with their predecessors for light and air. The trees were clotted with blossoms and with fruit in all stages of development; in the early afternoon heat, the perfumed stench of both was cloying. Even the tiny saplings were bearing before their time. Overripe fruit fell constantly as we watched, to smash against others already on the ground. The unharvested cashew apples rotted within a day; the air below the trees buzzed thick with blue-bottle flies, drunk on fermenting cashew ichor. The trees bore and bore and bore. In the space of a week, some of them were already dying. The prodigious growth had started when Agway went from me.

Ife took Stanley's other hand as we sidled past the mad orchard.

Men's voices rumbled from the kitchen. Good smells, too: coffee brewing, fish, spices. I peeked in. Orso and Hector, cooking up a storm. I couldn't face Hector just yet. "Where you found the truck?" I asked Stanley.

"In here." He led me into the bedroom that had been Agway's, and Dadda's. The Aqua Man sheet I'd bought was still on the bed. Dumpy lay on the pillow. Stanley ran and picked it up, brought it, held out, towards me.

"It was under the bed," he said. His face was crumpling into sadness again. I reached for the truck, but he cried out and threw it at me. He missed. It smashed through the window glass. I heard exclamations from the kitchen; chairs being pushed back; feet running in our direction. "Why you had to take him out on the water like that!" sobbed Stanley. "It's your fault!"

"Stanley!" said Ife.

"No, let him say it. It's the same thing all of allyou thinking, anyway."

Stanley hugged himself and cried. I bent and picked up the truck, over the protests of my back and both knees. "Agway used to throw it like that," I told Stanley. "Will you let me hold you?"

He threw his arms around my legs.

That wake nearly killed me. Then they could have just waked for two. Mrs. Soledad accepted many refills of white rum, and told stories about the cute things Agway had done that I had missed because I was at work. Stanley taught us Agway's words for man, and boy, and goodbye, and told us that his name was— had been—Chichi. Silence fell when he said that. Three chi-chi men of a different kind right here in the room. I looked at the floor. That writer guy was right; God *is* an irony. When Hector, a catch in his voice, launched into the story about Agway eating raw shrimps, I excused myself and went out onto the porch. If I'd stayed in there any longer, I'd have broken and written my-self a ticket straight to the madhouse by informing them all that Agway was a mermaid who had gone back to his home in the sea. So I sat and breathed, and watched the cashews ripen and fall, fall, fall.

Ife came outside and sat beside me. She said, "Don't watch the news for the next little while, okay?"

"I can just imagine what they're saying about me."

Her dress was shapeless as usual, but this time it was a *stylish* shapeless, in a nubbly indigo silk that brought out her colouring. Even her sandals were pretty. "You looking good," I said. She raised her eyebrows. I ignored it. "Like breaking up with Clifton is suiting you?"

She looked down at her hands. "It has its advantages." She wasn't wearing her wedding rings. "But I still miss him. Half of me wants to work things out with him, and half of me wants to leave."

"Something I never told you."

"What?" she asked, her tone wary.

Push on, Calamity. "You right; I didn't want to have you."

Ife pressed her lips together and made to stand up. I was doing it all wrong. I took her hand. "Please wait, Ife. Just hear me out."

She sat back down, her face unhappy.

"Over the months of carrying you," I said, "I got used to having you right next to my heart. Could put my arms around you any time I wanted. Then time came I had to push you out. Finally got to meet the prettiest baby in the world."

She gave me a sad, surprised smile.

"And looking after you was the hardest thing I ever did in my life. Plenty of times I hated it. Plenty of times I wanted to stop. Give you up for adoption. Something.

"But then I got to know *you*. A mischievous little girl with a curious mind. A dreamy, impatient young woman who was always looking for magic. Fuck. I'm not saying this right."

"I think I'm kind of liking it," she replied. "Keep trying."

"I didn't start out loving you. I had to learn to love you. It was like an arranged marriage, you know? Only not."

She was half-laughing now. "You say the strangest things, Mummy."

"Calamity. And I not finished."

"What else?"

"I had to learn to love you for who you are. About half the time I screw it up."

Obsidian glint to those eyes. "Go on."

"So from now on, I want you to tell me right away when I get it wrong. Don't save it up for thirty-eight years."

She took that in, and nodded. "Sound good," she said. My spirits started to lift. "But one pretty speech not going to fix it."

I bit back the ready barb and waited for her to finish. "You have to walk the talk for a while before I'm going to trust you," she told me. "You on sufferance."

"Christ. You and Orso been comparing notes, or something?"

She nodded. "Something like that." We watched the cashews fall. Ife said, "You know, I never told you the wish Dadda made at the wishing tree."

"Not sure I want to know."

"He wished for Mumma to forgive him and come back. He said even if not for him, that you had suffered enough."

Then she hugged me and went back inside. She still wasn't wearing a bra.

So now Granny decide to get rid of the devil baby. She yank it off her shoulders and she throw it hard as she could. She pitch that devil baby into the sea. And the minute it land up in the water, the devil baby start to laugh, and to swell: big as a pumpkin; big as a grouper fish; big as a whale, and then bigger. That devil baby turn into the devil woman

of the sea with her blue skin, and her sharp teeth, and her long, long arms for dragging ships down. "THANK YOU, GRANNY, DO," the devil woman say. "FOR YOU JUST GIVE ME EXACTLY WHAT I WANT." Her voice make Granny's ears ache.

Then the devil woman fling a handful of gold pieces at Granny. One land on her face; till her dying day, you could still see the mark. "FOR YOUR TROUBLE," the devil woman say. And she dive down to go and wait for a ship for her dinner. Granny hear her laughing all the way down to the bottom.

I crashed gratefully down onto the lounge chair out on the porch. "I'm so glad everybody gone home, I can't tell you!"

"Sound like it wasn't fun." Gene gestured at the plate in his lap. "What is this I eating?"

"Ackee and saltfish. Some Jamaican thing Hector make."

"It's strange. Like if scrambled eggs was a vegetable."

"He still vexed with me. Hector."

"Yeah, I could see that. I wouldn't brook nobody speaking to me like that neither."

"Duly noted, Mr. Meeks."

He put the half-finished plate of food down on the floor. "I have to run. Working tonight."

"You want a lift down to the dock?"

"Sure."

I got an idea. "All right. Just hang on a second."

Dumpy was still on the floor in Dadda's room. I fished it out of the broken glass.

In the night air, the rankness of the cashews was less. But you could still hear the gentle *plop* of fruit after fruit throwing itself from the branch. The sickle moon looked fresh and clean, wearing one coy wisp of cloud.

I let Gene into the car. We headed for the dock.

"Mrs. Winter gave me bereavement leave."

"Ouch."

"Who knew she had a heart?" I pulled up at the dock. "You have a few minutes? You could take me out a little way in your boat and then back?"

"You mean I get to spend a few more minutes with you?"

"Sweet-talker."

"My middle name. Come." He opened the car door, but before he got out, he took a shaky breath and said, "You know that night, when I found you?"

"Yeah. What about it?"

Gene had gotten my half-hysterical phone message about Agway's mother being alive. He came rushing over right after work to find us both gone, and me not answering my phone. He dashed back to the dock, thinking he'd go out on the water and search for us. He'd found me lying on the dock in the rain, half-dead from hypothermia.

"As I laid eyes on you on the dock the other night, I hear a big splash, like something went into the water."

"I know. I told you what happened. And if you tell me I was hallucinating, I swear—"

He shook his head. "I think I saw shapes swimming away under the water."

"Fuck me! A part of me been wondering if I didn't just make

it all up. So I wouldn't feel guilty about letting Agway fall over the side."

"But I saw them too. Never seen them alive before." His smile was soft and wondering. "What a miraculous world, nuh true?"

We went out in his launch. When we were out of sight of Dolorosse, I yelled, "Right here!" over the sound of the engine. Gene cut the power and we rocked in silence on the sea. I held Dumpy in my hands one final time. Then I dropped it over the side. *Drop your scarf in the water.* I blew a kiss after it.

She couldn't say how she did it; for her safety, she'd never tried to describe it to anyone. She liked to think it was a bit like how it might feel when a baby pulled at your breast with its hungry mouth to make the milk come. But she didn't know that sensation. To her, it was like letting go finally when you'd long been wanting to piss, and feeling the hot wetness splash out of you and keep coming like it would never stop. It was like that, and yet it was nothing at all like that. Bring us home, *she begged, of Uhamiri, of her gift; as she tried to keep her balance it was all getting confused in her mind. She was a sluice, and power surged through her. She tried to guide it as it flowed. It was like holding back the seas with a winnowing basket, but the dada-hair lady shaped her power as best she might.*

It was the strongest flow she'd ever felt, frightening in its force.

The boss man was yelling orders in the shouting and the

screaming and the running about, but few were listening. His two desperate eyes made four with the dada-hair lady's own. If she were a Momi Wata, he'd be foolish to stare at her like that. She stood tall and looked right back at him.

The first thing that happened was that any of her people still standing fell to the decks. Not her; she remained upright. She nodded and smiled. "We are leaving now!" she shouted in Igbo, for those who could understand. Some of those raised up a cheer, which became a high piping. The people were changing! That startled her. But the ocean strength of blood would not be held back. The dada-hair lady accepted it. That is how it would be. Then let it be.

The people's arms flattened out into flexible flippers. The shackles slipped off their wrists. The two women who had been chained to her flopped away, free, but the dada-hair lady remained unchanged and shackled. The little boy in her arms was transforming, though. He lifted one hand and spread his fingers to investigate the webbing that now extended between them. Some of the people who had been forced back into the holds were making their way out, now that their shackles had slid off. The ship was so far tilted that they didn't have to climb; just clamber up the shallow incline that led to the hatch.

The people's bodies grew thick and fat. Legs melted together. The little boy chuckled, a sound she'd not heard from him before this. The chuckle became a high-pitched call.

The people's faces swelled and transformed: round heads with snouts. Big, liquid eyes. Would she not change, too? Was this Uhamiri's price?

The sailors had been dodging them, too terrified to pay attention to what was happening. Many sailors had *already leapt over the side. A mast snapped and crashed down, killing sailors and destroying more of the ship. The weight of the mast pulled the ship over even further on its side. The captain rushed to the cracked stump and yelled, likely for an axe to cut the mast free. He was ignored. The ship began to go down. The captain glared at the dada-hair lady as though she were responsible. He braced himself against the stump of the mast, pulled out his pistol, and shot at her. The jerking of the ship threw his shot wide. He started picking off her people, one by one, even as they grew thick, protective coatings of fat and fur sprouted on their bodies. "Over the side!" the dada-hair lady yelled at them. "Go into the water!" The sound became a deep, urgent bubbling noise. The dada-hair lady was changing too. Uhamiri would not abandon her!*

The gift roared through her. She threw the boy from her, into the sea, just before her arms became flippers. She swelled large as an ox. She flopped to the deck, landing heavily beside one of the white sailors. He went even whiter as he saw her alter. He backed away, pulling at his pistol as he tried to get it free of his belt.

The dada-hair lady started working her body clumsily to the ship's railing. Others of the people were already there, levering themselves up and over, into the sea. The splashing, the shouting, the strange animal calls; all was confusion, and the gift was burning through her so hard she could barely see.

The captain roared at her and took aim again. The dada-hair lady lumped her heavy body against the ship's side. She reared up against the railing, which creaked with her weight. The changed people who had made it into the water

were swimming clumsily away from the ship, learning the use
of their new limbs as they worked them.

A shot winged by her ear. The dada-hair lady looked
back. A few of the people lay broken on the deck, shot midway
through the change. The dada-hair lady's heart broke to see
that Belite was one of the dead, but she had no time to stop;
the captain was taking aim again. She tumbled herself over
the side. As she fell towards the welcoming sea, a bright pain
exploded in her foot. With a belching roar, she splashed into
the water, and down. She looked. A thread of blood followed
her down, trailing from her flipper. The captain had shot a
hole clean through it. The frightening wound and the salty
sting of the sea searing it made the dada-hair lady gasp. She
took in water, coughed it out again, flailed with her new front
limbs. Blood. She had to be giving blood to the earth in order
to find a thing lost. But now she gave her blood to the sea.
She had asked Uhamiri to bring them home. The gods almost
never gave you exactly what you'd asked for.

Where was her boy? There! He must be that one, that
little one, who swam so vigorously towards her, pushing
his way through the other sleek, fat bodies. He came. She
nuzzled him, urged him with her flipper to swim on ahead of
her. Driven by the sound of the ship cracking apart and the
danger of falling debris, she followed, learning her limbs as
she went, trying not to faint away from the pain of the injured
one. The sea was blue and held them on its breast. They were
no longer lost.

And with that, the dada-hair lady felt the gift leave her.
Not stop, as it had every time before; leave. She had used all
her blood power to bring the people home. They were bahari
now. The sea was where they would live.

By the time I pulled the car up to the house, fingers of fog were stretching through the air. Jumbie weather. Mischief weather, swirling all around me. I couldn't see more than a few feet ahead. I got out of the car, locked the door.

From out in the fog over by the road, someone called, "Calamity? It's you that?"

"Mrs. Soledad?"

"You all right, child?" She sounded suspicious. I could see her a little more clearly now. She had someone with her. As they came closer, I saw who it was. Mr. Mckinley.

"I'm fine," I said to them. Began to say, "Never better," but with Agway gone only a few days ago, that would sound wrong. I bit it back.

Mrs. Soledad was wearing a pretty flowered dress. Her greying hair hung down in front in two long, girlish braids that went nearly to her waist. On her head, she was sporting a leather peaked cap; purple to match the flowers on her dress. She had it turned backwards. And was that lipstick on her lips?

Mr. Mckinley's khaki pants were pressed. He had one button open at the neck of his plaid shirt, to show just a little bit of chest hair.

"How come allyou out on a night like this?" I asked them.

"Little bit of fog not going to hurt us," replied Mr. Mckinley.

Mrs. Soledad reached out and pinched my arm.

"Ow!" I yelped, pulling it away from her.

"You're real," she said.

"Yes! What you do that for?"

Mr. Mckinley chuckled. "Jumbie weather. She not taking any chances."

"Too right," said Mrs. Soledad. "Thaddeus and I just taking the night air." She reached for Mr. Mckinley's hand. He took hers gently, like a gift, and shot her a shy glance.

My brain was looping, on input overload. Mrs. Soledad and Mr. Mckinley were having a hot affair. And on top of all that, Mr. Mckinley's first name was Thaddeus. Who got named Thaddeus nowadays?

Under his arm, Mr. Mckinley had his battered yellow tackle box. How could the two of them be seeing each other? He was probably a good fifteen years younger than she. And how he could take his fishing hooks out on a date?

"Heavy rain this afternoon," I said, making small talk.

Mr. Mckinley nodded. "True that. Glad I wasn't out in the boat."

"Good thing, too," said Mrs. Soledad. "Otherwise, who woulda bring me another blanket to wrap my feet in?"

He smiled at her. "Best way to spend a rainy afternoon. Warm in bed, with one blanket sharing between the two of we, and the rain going *prangalang* on your tinning roof."

"Was like young married days all over again," she said softly.

Mr. Mckinley coughed. They both looked at the ground, but that didn't hide the big grins on their faces. They had been in bed together, in her house, listening to the rain. I didn't know them at all.

"You coming to the protest tomorrow?" asked Mrs. Soledad. "Going to be a lime and a half."

"I going to try," I said guiltily. I intended to sleep in tomorrow.

I shooed them off to continue their walk. Even when the fog

started to make them difficult to see, I could still hear the companionable rise and fall of their conversation and their laughter. Seem like everybody had somebody for company. I thought about calling Gene, but I stopped myself. Never went good when I tried to force-ripe a relationship. Same thing with Evelyn. I sat on the warm hood of the car and breathed in the milky night. When the fog had me wreathed in cloud, I went inside to bed.

ALEXANDER LET HIMSELF INTO THE SEAL PEN, just to be sure. He looked in the water, in the caves. He picked up the sodden piece of paper he found in one of the caves and inspected it. Then, calmly, he let himself back out, locked the high gate—not that it seemed to make any difference—and walked the grounds of the Zooquarium until he found Dennis. "Come and see something with me, nuh?"

Dennis looked baffled, but he followed Alexander back to the seal pen.

"How many seals?" said Alexander.

"No seals in there, sir."

"Not a one?"

"No."

"It's not just me imagining it?"

"No, sir."

"That's what I thought."

He handed Dennis the yellow foolscap sheet. It was one of the flyers that had been pinned up everywhere for a few days now. The workers' co-op people were staging a protest at the new Gilmor plant this morning.

Dennis flattened out the soggy sheet as best as he could. "What this is?" he asked, pointing to some marks on the paper. You might get marks like that if you dampened a nugget of seal chow and scraped it on the paper. "Look like writing," said Dennis.

"You think so?" Alexander replied in a weary tone.

"Yeah, but half of it wash out."

"True that." They both stared at the flyer. If you used your imagination, the smudged marks could look like "BACK SOON."

"I considering becoming a drinking man," said Alexander.

IT WAS THE SCENT that woke me up next morning. Right in my bedroom with me, the strong smell of the sea.

I sat up and looked around. Something on the floor. My eyes were still blurry with sleep. I reached for my specs and put them on. Between me and the bedroom door was a pile of bladder-wrack as high as my shin, and so fresh it was still wet. On top of that was a slit, L-shaped tube of white plaster, half-dissolved, but recognizable as Agway's cast. Lying on sea grape leaves beside that was a pile of fresh raw shrimp, a good five pounds of it. The heads were still on.

I picked up my cell phone and went to check the rest of the house. Out in the hallway, I nearly tripped on Dadda's old duffel bag. I'd put it in my closet until I could get around to burning the sealskin inside it.

But the bag was empty. I combed the whole house looking for the skin. I ended up in Dadda's room. There was the window

Stanley had broken when he threw Dumpy. I'd swept all the broken glass out of it, taped plastic over it.

The plastic was torn.

The empty pane was plenty big enough to let a person through.

I let out a whoop. "You see why I live in Cayaba?" I asked myself. "Never a dull moment."

Ife was in charge of arranging Sookdeo-Grant's appearance at the protest with a group of opposition party supporters. She had been fretting about all the details for days now.

I double dog dare you, Mummy.

I called Ifeoma's house. "Hector, it's you that? Awoah." I let that sink in, then said, "Put Ife on the phone for me, please?"

Ife came on the line. "Mummy? Something wrong?"

"Not a thing. I'm as right as rain. So, where exactly this protest is? Yes, I know it's on Dolorosse, but *where*? You have enough water for everybody you looking after? Bottled water? Good. You have ice? No, don't worry. You doing good. I will stop off at Mr. Robinson's on the way and get some bags of ice. How you mean, how come? I can't come and show my daughter some support? You could use a extra cooler? And you have food? Only patties? That not enough. I going to make a big pot of curry shrimp. See you at ten, then? Okay."

I hung up the phone and went to the kitchen for a bowl big enough to hold five pounds of shrimp. "If allyou ever find any snapper," I announced to the empty house, "I would be very grateful."